DOUBLE PLAY

DAYTONA FURY SERIES
BOOK 3

C.L. ROSE

————

Cover Illustrations: Breanne at Breezy Book Art

Chapter Breaks: Maggie Marrero

Edits and Proofreading: Breanne at Breezy Book Edits

To Clair, Jaime, and Maggie.

CONTENT INFO

Double Play tells the story of a polyamorous relationship in which two men fall in love with the same woman and agree to share her, but do not have romantic feelings toward each other.

AUTHOR'S NOTE

This book contains sexual scenes that are rough in nature. They include heavy degradation, orgasm denial, light slapping, spitting, stretching, and similar acts that may be triggering to some readers. Everything that happens between the characters is agreed upon and consented to. It also includes talk of a character's experience with an alcoholic parent, as well as an on-page panic attack. Please use caution when moving forward if you have sensitivities to this type of content.

As always, please research thoroughly before engaging in any type of kink with an experienced partner.

xoxo,

Candice

PLAYLIST

1. ocean eyes - Billie Eilish
2. MIDDLE OF THE NIGHT - Elley Duhé
3. Dancing On My Own - Calum Scott
4. Come Back…Be Here (Taylor's Version) - Taylor Swift
5. Panic Attacks in Paradise - Ashnikko
6. Everything Has Changed (ft. Ed Sheeran) - Taylor Swift
7. Into Your Arms - The Maine
8. Cold Water - Major Lazer, Justin Bieber, MØ
9. Skinny Love - Bon Iver
10. Jealous - Labrinth
11. Pretty Ugly - TIMMS
12. 11 Minutes (ft. Halsey, Travis Barker) - YUNGBLUD
13. Pretty Scars - Jiinzo
14. Make Me Feel - Elvis Drew
15. Shameless - Camila Cabello

16. Save Me (ft. Lainey Wilson) - Jelly Roll
17. Haunted (ft. Jelly Roll) - Kane Brown
18. Only Girl (In The World) - Rihanna
19. Raw Raw - K.Flay
20. Make You Mine - Madison Beer
21. War of Hearts - Ruelle
22. The Heart Wants What It Wants - Selena Gomez
23. Dangerous Hands - Austin Giorgio
24. Hell is a Dance Floor - Vincent Mason
25. Bad Things - Nation Haven
26. Fuck Away the Pain - Divide The Day
27. LOVE LOOKS PRETTY ON YOU - Nessa Barrett
28. Lady, Touch Yourself - Nikki Idol
29. Ride - SoMo
30. One Man Band - Old Dominion
31. Renegade - Big Red Machine, Taylor Swift
32. She Knows It - Steven Rodriguez
33. Sin So Sweet - Warren Zeiders
34. Into It - Chase Atlantic
35. Play with Fire (ft. Yacht Money) - Sam Tinnesz
36. P*RNSTAR. - Nessa Barrett
37. Damage (ft. Halsey) - PARTYNEXTDOOR
38. Peaches - Jack Black

PROLOGUE

ARDEN

"WITH THE THIRTY-SIXTH pick of the inaugural Pro Volleyball Federation draft, the Florida Flare select Arden Levine, setter, Penn State."

As soon as the words are out of the commissioner's mouth, my whole body freezes. Cheers from my dad, stepmom, and best friend Stella fill the air around me, but they're drowned out by the sound of my own heart pounding in my chest.

When I got the call about a new professional volleyball league that was taking over North America, a fire that I thought had burned out within me stoked back to life. I never dreamed that I'd get another shot at playing again—especially not on this big of a stage. But here I am, a member of Florida's first major league women's team.

"Go!" Stella says, practically pulling me up from where I'm sitting like a statue in my chair. "Get up there!"

I shake my head rapidly, clearing the fog before

standing to my feet and smoothing down the front of my black body-con dress. My legs shake with every step, so I focus on not tripping in my six-inch stilettos as I make my way to the stage. At five foot seven, I'm well under the average height for my position, so I chose the tallest shoes in my closet for tonight. The last thing I need is for everyone watching ESPN to wonder who let an actual child onto a team full of Amazons.

Carefully taking the stairs one at a time, I walk to the podium, where the league commissioner stands next to Dahlia Owens, my new head coach. She's only a few years older than me and a former college team-mate, so it'll be a strange dynamic at first. But I'm deter-mined to show her that she made the right choice by drafting me to the Flare.

"Congratulations," the commissioner says, shaking my hand before offering the purple and blue jersey that's clutched in his fist. I take it, holding it up in front of me as a wide smile blooms across my face.

Holy fucking shit. I'm a professional volleyball player.

The rest of the ceremony is a blur as my mind begins to strategize. We ended up with two powerhouse outside hitters and a rookie libero who shows so much potential that I can't help but get excited. All ten teams in the league came into today with clean slates, so only time will tell how the upcoming season will pan out.

"I'm so proud of you, baby," my dad says, pulling me into his arms for a hug as soon as they find me in the crowd. "You're the real deal now." He steps back, allowing Stella room to wrap me in a tight embrace.

"It's true. My bestie is about to be famous. I can't

wait to see your spandex-covered ass on my big screen every weekend."

I roll my eyes. "You guys said that last year." When I signed with a semi-pro team in Argentina last March, I was ecstatic to get back on the court. Unfortunately, volleyball players make next to nothing there, and it was impossible to juggle practice and work full-time in order to pay my monthly bills. I have a college degree, but my Spanish is subpar at best, so job options were limited and *very* low-paying. I ended up having no choice but to step away and return to Pennsylvania before we even had our first game. It broke my heart, and I've felt like a piece of me has been missing ever since.

"Well, I mean it this time," my dad replies with a wink. I can't help the smile that breaks free at the sight of the proud look that's painted across his face. My father has always been my biggest fan. From the first time I touched a volleyball, he's been by my side, making sure I had every opportunity to go as far as the game could take me. He spent countless hours working overtime just so I could attend private lessons and play for the most prestigious—and expensive—club teams. He'd sleep in his car outside the arena between matches, never missing a single set, no matter how exhausted he was. I owe him everything, and I just want to continue to make him proud.

"I agree," my stepmom Gina says, nudging my shoulder with hers. "I have a great feeling about this one. I've done a lot of research on the PVF, and it looks like they've got a pretty good plan. They already have a contract with ESPN to broadcast games, some pretty big sponsors have signed on, and their league minimum is almost double what you were making in Argentina. I'm sure we'll be able to negotiate for more after the first season is in the books."

"I hope so," I reply. When Gina and my dad got married right before my senior year of high school, I was excited to have a strong female presence in my life, which I never really got from my own mother. After my parents divorced, she accepted a job overseas and was all too happy to let me stay behind with my dad. We were great on our own, but Gina was a welcome addition as I attempted to navigate teenage girlhood. She immediately stepped in to help me with college preparations, since she played for Penn State too, and I was grateful to have someone in my corner who had already been through the experience. Her career ended with an unfortunate ankle injury, but as soon as I knew I'd need an agent that I could trust to get me started in the pros, it wasn't even a question that I'd pick her. I'm her only client, but her son plays in the MLB, so she has connections and has been working around the clock to learn everything she can about contracts and branding. With her very low fee of absolutely nothing, she's about the only person within my budget at the moment—not that I'd pick anyone else even if I had millions. Nobody has my best interest at heart more than she does.

"I still don't know how I'm going to afford to move to Florida until I sign my contract," I say, my teeth digging into my lower lip. Being in Argentina while still paying bills in America left me with almost nothing in my savings, and I've been playing catch-up ever since.

She looks at me, and I can tell by her expression that she's been plotting. "I think I have an idea, but I don't know if you're going to like it." My brows pull in, but she stops me before I can fire any questions her way. "The Flare practice facility is only thirty minutes outside of Daytona. Jackson and Hawk just bought a five-bedroom, six-bathroom condo on the beach, and I'm sure they wouldn't mind having you stay with them until you can get into a place of your own."

My eyes widen, and I shake my head, anxiety flowing through my veins. "I don't know, Gina," I reply on an exhale. "I wouldn't want to intrude."

She waves a dismissive hand. "Nonsense. You and Jacks have known each other since elementary school, and Hawk is practically family. It's not like you'd be a stranger."

I shrug. "I barely know Hawk. He's spoken like, ten words to me over the last five years. For all I know, he hates me."

"Who could ever hate you?" Stella pipes in. "You're a goddamn delight."

"Let me call Jacks," Gina says. "I'll bring it up to him and see what he thinks. I'm sure it'll be fine."

Fine.

Living with my stepbrother and his grumpy, yet undeniably hot-as-fuck best friend is going to be anything but *fine.*

ONE
JACKSON

I PULL up to the curb, throwing Hawk's truck that I borrowed for the day into park. Traffic at the airport is usually a mess, but thankfully, I think I can get away with hanging in the white zone until Arden comes out. I got a notification that her flight landed on time, so she should be walking out of the doors as soon as she has her bags.

Blowing out a breath, I tap my thumbs on the steering wheel, fidgeting nervously. When I agreed to let my stepsister stay in one of the extra rooms of the condo I share with my best friend, I'll admit I was reluctant. Our history is complicated, even if I'm the only one who really knows the full extent of it, while she's stayed completely oblivious. And now that we'll be living under the same roof again, I don't know how I feel about it.

My friendship with Arden began in the fourth grade. Her mom had just been relocated to France for work, and she moved to our small town of Tinsville,

Pennsylvania with her dad. From the moment my teacher asked me to show her around the school, we were inseparable. I immediately took on the role of her protector, and that's how it was for years. It wasn't until eleventh grade that I realized my feelings for her had begun to morph into something else.

I had a few girlfriends in high school, but baseball was my main priority. Rumors were already swirling that I would be one of the top second base prospects during my senior year, and I was focused on perfecting my craft. When it wasn't school or travel ball season, I spent multiple nights a week doing private lessons, which put a damper on my social life.

Arden was the exact opposite. She played volleyball but always made the time to go out with friends. It wasn't that she wasn't dedicated to the game—she just didn't have to work as hard to be great. She was a natural talent from the moment she touched the court, giving her a little more freedom to enjoy her teenage years. While I was holed up in batting cages, working on my swing night after night, she was going on dates and having fun. It wasn't until I saw her kissing one of my teammates outside the biology lab one day that I realized how I really felt about her.

"Cooper Peterson?" I asked, making her jump from where she was standing, watching as he walked away. "When did that happen?"

She whipped around, laying a hand over her heart. "Jesus, Jacks! You scared the shit out of me!" Her shock melted into a silly smile, her cheeks pinkening the way they always did when she was embarrassed. "Last night," she replied. "He took me to play miniature golf and kissed me when he dropped me back off at my house."

I could feel the rage bubbling up inside me as I took in her love-struck expression, jealousy coursing through me as I did my best to keep it from rearing its ugly head. We had been friends for years and I never even considered making a move on her, so why all of a sudden, was I pissed at the thought of anyone else kissing her?

"So now you're a thing?" I asked, scrunching my eyebrows together. I was trying to stay calm, but I fucking hated every bit of the situation.

She shrugged. "Not really. He said he didn't want to put a label on things, but that we could see where it goes."

Of fucking course, he did.

"He's an idiot," I replied, shaking my head. I knew he was leading her on, but if I said that out loud, it would've made me sound like a dick. So, I chose to cut myself off, but the newly unveiled emotions inside me continued battling one another as I stood there, well and truly confused by every one of them.

She shrugged. "I've been single for a long time, Jacks. Our junior prom is in like, two months and I don't even have a date. I don't want to go alone. Maybe Cooper will ask me if things go well."

I swallowed hard, my fists clenching at my sides as the thought of the two of them at the prom together hit me. Or worse, after it. *I had been listening to my teammates talk in the locker room for weeks about their post-prom plans of getting fake IDs and renting hotel rooms to bring their dates to. It didn't bother me before—but now? I couldn't let it happen. Cooper Peterson had already broken too many hearts in our grade, and I wasn't about to let him add Arden's to his list.*

Fuck that. I had to do something.

"Hello?" a muffled voice says, ripping me from my memory as a fist raps against the truck window rapidly. I whip my head up, eyes locking onto Arden's while she stands there with about six duffel bags hanging from her small frame. Her dark brown hair is piled into a messy bun on top of her head, and her brows are pulled in as though she's wondering why it took me so long to notice her there. "Unlock the door, jackass."

"Fuck," I mutter, pressing the button to disengage the locks before throwing my door open and hurrying around the hood. By the time I get to her side, she's already beginning to lower the bags from her shoulders, loading them into the back seat.

"I got it," I say, reaching out to take over. She rolls her eyes, handing them to me one by one as I make room on the seat. I can hear the toes of her shoes tapping against the pavement as she exhales, and I already know it's probably the first full breath she's taken all day. Arden hates traveling. It ramps up her anxiety, which is something she's struggled with since I've known her. Whenever she's in high-stress situations, she turns into a ball of nerves, doing everything she can to hide it because she insists it makes her look weak.

I shove the last of her luggage into the back seat, turning to her with my arms open. "Come here," I say, and she steps into me. Wrapping her in a tight embrace, I feel the tension in her body melt away, a tiny whine of frustration slipping from her lips. I can't help but chuckle. After all these years, you'd think she'd give herself a little grace when her anxiety gets the best of her, but she never does.

"Rough flight?" I ask, resting my chin on the top of her head. She smells the same as she has since I've known her—strawberries and cream, mixed with *her*. Even though there was a split second in high school where the scent affected me in other ways, it's always given me a familiar comfort. And although we've drifted apart over the last six or seven years, it still does.

"So much turbulence," she replies as I rub my hand up and down her back to soothe her. "And newborn twins. Of course, my AirPods died after the first hour."

I suck a breath through my teeth. "Yikes. Let's get you home so you can relax."

TWO
JACKSON

FORTY MINUTES LATER, we pull into the parking garage of my building, and I look over to find Arden out cold in the passenger seat. It took her a few minutes to calm down once we loaded up her things, but after a long hug and a trip to Starbucks for some lavender tea, she was as good as new. I just hate that I have to wake her now.

"Hey, Princess," I say, using the nickname I gave her after our fourth-grade Halloween party, where she made me dress up as Mario so she could be Princess Peach. I begged her to let me be Bowser because I thought the shell and spikes were cool, but she insisted, so I gave in. To this day, a photo of us in those costumes hangs on the wall in our parents' living room. It seems like a lifetime ago.

"Noooo…" she whines, her brows knitting together in annoyance before she turns away. "Five more minutes."

I chuckle, playfully flicking her neck with my

middle finger. "No. Get up, or I'll leave you in here alone. I heard they once had a panther on the loose in this garage."

She rolls her head against the headrest to face me again, peeking with one eye. "You're lying."

I shrug. "Am I?" Opening the door, I slide out of the truck, hearing her huff an exhale as she does the same. I round the back, bumping her out of the way with my hip and earning a much more lighthearted eye roll now that her nerves are calmer. Making quick work of loading her bags onto my shoulders, I lead the way to the elevator, ushering Arden inside and pressing the button for the thirty-fifth floor. It worked out that today is one of the team's rare days off since she couldn't find a moving company to transport her car from Pennsylvania to Florida before she left. I didn't want her taking an Uber from the airport and being dropped off in a strange place all by herself with no way of getting around. Although playoffs are coming up, and I should be getting in some extra reps at the batting cages today, I'd much rather be here making sure she's settling in okay.

The metal doors slide open, and I step out, adjusting the bags on my shoulder before starting down the hall toward my condo. Arden yawns behind me, telling me that her tea did its job and the nap she took on the ride over wasn't nearly enough. It's another effect of her anxiety. She tries so hard to keep it at bay sometimes that it physically drains her. It's not even dark outside, and I can already tell she'll be hitting the hay as soon as she can.

"Home, sweet home," I say, stepping through the door and moving aside for her to pass. I watch as her exhausted eyes widen, ping-ponging around the expansive living area as if she doesn't know what to look at first. Hawk and I only bought this place a few months ago, so none of my family has gotten a chance to see it. Arden saw the old place once, but it was a shack compared to the almost six thousand square feet we have now.

"This isn't a home," she replies, her jaw practically on the floor. "It's a fucking castle." I chuckle as she steps further into the room, taking in the luxurious custom carpet and plush white furniture as she passes. Tinsville is full of modest, middle-class homes like the ones we were raised in. Neither of us could've even dreamt something like this up when we were kids. It's still surreal to me that I own it, and I'm here every day. It almost felt like overkill when the realtor gave us the tour. Did we really *need* five bedrooms, six bathrooms, and a media room with a wall-to-wall bed? No. Not even a little bit. But we bought it anyway.

Arden is the first family member to set foot in here since my mom and her dad haven't made it out yet. And Hawk's family may as well be non-existent. If any of them ever showed up here, they'd play hell getting to him when they'd have to make it through me first.

"Oh my God," Arden says, stepping up to the wall of windows that gives a panoramic view of the Daytona skyline. The other side of the building, where my teammate Riggs Valentine lives with his girlfriend Monroe, looks over a topless beach. As tempting as it was to purchase a unit over there, you can't beat the twinkling city lights at night. Turning back toward me, a smile blooms across her face. "Are you kidding me, Jacks? This is insane."

I shrug, gripping the back of my neck because I don't know what to say. Between my best friend and me, we could've bought ten of these condos, but I know she's struggled to make ends meet since college. She took a chance to play the sport she loves in Argentina, but all it did was put her further into debt. It's unfair how volleyball players don't get the respect they deserve. While Arden makes it look effortless, the amount of strength, coordination, and knowledge it takes to play are skills not many people can master. That's why I'm hoping this new league can turn things around.

"Oh, are you modest now?" she mocks. "How many women have you brought here as a flex to get them to sleep with you?" She's goading me, as usual—trying to get a reaction. I've always been weak to it. Joking around and bantering with one another is what we do, and it's how our friendship lasted as long as it did. At least before my mind got all muddied. Add in our parents getting married and us being thrust into a house together—things were bound to change at least a little bit.

I scoff playfully. "I don't bring women to my house. What do you think I am? An amateur? I'd like to live peacefully, sans stalkers, thank you very much."

She raises a dubious brow. "Better not. I'd rather live

in a crowded alley than deal with the cleat chasers you spend your time with."

"First of all," I reply, grinning, "they're lovely girls. Secondly, how do you know who I'm spending my time with? I haven't seen you since last Christmas." She's not wrong. I do enjoy the company of some of the women I meet while I'm on the road. I do less of it here in Daytona because, believe it or not, I'm a homebody. When I have the chance to relax in my own space, I take it. I'll go out on occasion during the offseason, but even that's a rare occurrence.

She walks toward me, smoothing her hand over the luxe upholstery of the gray sectional in the middle of the room as she passes. "You realize you're all over the tabloids, right? A new girl on your arm every night of the week? Never the same one twice?"

My eyes go wide with faux shock. "Princess, are you *slut shaming me*? Because that's what it sounds like."

"No," she says, popping her hip in a spectacular show of attitude. "Just wanted to know what I signed myself up for. Get your dick wet, Jacks. I'd just rather not run into your flavors of the week on my way to the kitchen in the middle of the night, so I'll make sure to stay in my room if you have someone here."

Said dick twitches behind my zipper as if he's being summoned, and I have to warn him to stand down. It's Arden, and we can't react to her that way. No matter how old we were when it happened, she's my stepsister, and I have to treat her as such. I'd give anything to go back and slap the fuck out of my seventeen-year-old self for even entertaining the idea that he should like her as more than a friend, because even though most of the time I can keep my thoughts under control, one slips through every now and then.

I swallow thickly at the reminder, a mask of seriousness falling over my expression. Thankfully, she doesn't notice the change in my demeanor as her jaw goes slack in a deep yawn. "Let me show you your room," I say, jutting my chin at the staircase behind her. She nods, following me as I walk up the stairs, turning to the right and leading her into the biggest guest room we have. My room is across from it, and Hawk's is practically on the other side of the house, which worked well when it was just the two of us. I figured keeping her and me on the same part of the floor would be less of an inconvenience for him, since he keeps to himself. He said he was fine with having her here, but I don't want him to be uncomfortable. He knows Arden, but the few times they've been around each other, he seemed to clam up even more than usual, which is crazy since he's already pretty reserved around anyone but me. We became fast friends seven years ago when we were drafted, both ending up on the Fury's Triple-A team in Sarasota. Our contracts were being negotiated, and we weren't sure what our futures held, so we decided to live together to save money. We both signed multi-million dollar deals with the Fury, but when it came time to upgrade our tiny apartment, the idea of going our separate ways never even came up. And here we are.

"This is perfect," she says on a relieved exhale, walking over and faceplanting onto the queen-sized mattress. I laugh, pulling open the door to the large walk-in closet and carefully setting her bags down one by one so she can unpack them when she's ready.

"You have your own bathroom and—" I cut myself off when I step out, finding her curled up in a ball against the mattress. Tiny snores come from her body as she peacefully sleeps, a rogue piece of chocolate-brown hair hanging over one eye. I huff a quiet laugh, not surprised that she barely made it onto the pillow before she knocked out. Quietly padding her way, I take the thick throw blanket that's draped across the end of the bed, pull it open, and cover her as carefully as I can. It's not as heavy as the weighted blanket she used to use after a particularly stressful day, but it'll have to suffice. Because judging by the lightness of the bags I brought in here, that will be coming with the rest of her belongings from the moving company tomorrow.

I back away, looking down at the girl who used to be a constant in my life, but may as well be a stranger now with the distance that's separated us over the last handful of years. Even though it's normal for that to happen after high school, it doesn't mean I don't wish it was different.

It's going to take some effort to keep things from getting awkward on my part now that she's living here. I need to focus on all of our years of friendship rather than the sliver of time when I thought I wanted more. That ship sailed the moment I knocked on her door that day.

I smoothed the non-existent wrinkles from my Tinsville High Baseball hoodie, gripping the steering wheel of my car and exhaling a slow breath. When I overheard Cooper in the locker room talking about how he wasn't sure which of the three girls he was dating he'd ask to prom, I knew I had to act fast. Because I didn't think I could live with myself if he chose Arden, and I hadn't at least tried. I knew she was a virgin, and I also knew what the guys were expecting to happen at the hotel afterward. She was old enough to make her own choices and understand the consequences if that's what she ultimately decided, but the thought of him using and hurting her made me see red. Cooper had no intention of being her boyfriend, and that was clear from the way he seemed to be playing the field. Why Arden still thought she could change that was a mystery to me.

"Just go up there, knock on the door, and ask," I mumbled to myself. I had been friends with her for seven years and couldn't remember a time I had ever been nervous to talk to her. But now that I was seeing her in a different light—as something more*—I was terrified. What if she rejected me? I worried about what that could've meant for us, and if it would ruin the strong friendship we had built. But I wasn't willing to risk her ending up with Cooper and not knowing how I felt.*

I grabbed the flowers from my passenger seat and stepped out into the cool Pennsylvania air. It nipped at the heated skin of my cheeks as I made my way from the car-lined street down the walkway toward Arden's house. Inhaling one last big breath before I reached the door, I found the courage to reach out and ring the bell. I waited, hoping like hell that she was home, because I didn't know if I had the balls to come back and try again if she wasn't.

Moments later, a very familiar laugh seeped through the thick wood, making my brows knit tightly together. It was feminine and soft, one I had heard a million times before—but it didn't belong to the girl I came here for.

The door swung open, and my shock turned to horror when my speculations were confirmed.

"Mom?" I croaked, taking in the way she was tightening the long, white robe around her body. It was the middle of the day. And this wasn't *our house.*

"Oh my God, Jackson," she said, her stunned expression mirroring my own. "Honey, what are you doing here? I thought you had practice."

"I-I—" I stuttered, still completely aghast. "Coach had to cancel. I…what's going on?"

Just as she opened her mouth to speak, a male voice rang out behind her. "Who is it, baby?" Slade asked, coming into view over her shoulder. I'd just seen him that morning when I picked Arden up for school. He was dressed then…a stark contrast from the way he looked as I stared at him now, my jaw practically on the floor as he adjusted the towel around his waist.

"What the fuck?" I said quietly, wishing I could erase the sight from my brain. "Were you two…?" I couldn't even finish the question, for fear that every bit of my shitty school lunch would end up all over the porch in front of me.

I knew my mom had started dating. And I was happy for her. When my dad decided to leave, it took her a long time to put herself back out there. There were times when she was so sad and lonely, I practically begged her to sign up for a dating app so she could see that her best years were still ahead of her. But Slade Levine, *Arden's fucking dad, was not who I had in mind.*

My mom blew out a long breath, opening the door further

and stepping out of the way so I could come inside. I hesitated, unsure if I even wanted to. My entire system was still in shock, and I was afraid of what would happen if I let them tell me what was going on. My purpose for coming here felt like a distant memory, even though I was still clutching the dozen pink roses in my hand.

"Come in, Jacks," she coaxed, and my feet carried me through the opening, where Slade returned at her side, now covered by a t-shirt and sweatpants. I was so busy staring blankly at my mother that I hadn't even noticed he slipped away to get dressed.

A full-body shiver rolled through me at the thought of them both being naked before I knocked on the door.

So fucking gross.

"Honey," my mother began, shutting the door quietly. "We didn't want you to find out this way, but we have something to tell you."

They were married three months later. It threw my whole world off its axis, and I had to shove my newly found attraction for Arden into a box and lock that bitch up tight. We were officially stepsiblings, and we could never be more.

I can't say it wasn't hard at first. My mom and I moved into their house before the wedding because it was bigger. Our bedrooms shared an adjoining bathroom, so she was constantly in my space, completely unaware of how close I was to asking her to prom, and maybe even for more beyond that. Thankfully, it only lasted a year before she went off to Penn State, and I became a rookie in the minors. I finally felt like I could breathe again.

The years that followed made it easier to stop thinking of her that way with the distance—and the revolving door of women that were vying for my attention while I worked my way up to the major leagues. I became acquainted with the idea of one-night stands and *no-strings-attached* sex pretty quickly, and I learned to embrace it since it's impossible to nurture a budding relationship while I'm on the road for half the year. One day, I'll meet a girl who will make me want to put in the work, but for now, I'm good with the way things are.

Even though having Arden here will take some adjusting on all our parts, I'm excited about it. I miss her friendship. It was my fault for putting too much space between us and pulling away, but I was young, and it was the only way I knew how to cope with all the changes in my life at the time. Hopefully, we can make up for the time we lost and get to know each other again.

THREE
ARDEN

"WHAT FUCKING TIME IS IT?" I mumble, sitting up in the bed and digging into the pocket of my hoodie for my phone. It's dark out, the dim light of the moon filtering through the sheer curtains hanging from the sliding glass door in my room. Unlocking the device, my eyes focus on the clock, which tells me it's after midnight. I can't believe I passed out before Jackson even left the room. As proud of myself as I am for managing my panic attack once the plane landed, it took a lot out of me, and now I'm paying the price. My head is pounding, my bladder is screaming, and if I don't get some food in me, we're going to have even bigger problems. I was too nervous to eat before my flight, and I barely stayed awake for five minutes after my head hit the pillow. I'm on the verge of a hangry meltdown, and I need to find the kitchen, stat.

I make my way to the en suite bathroom, doing my business and washing my hands before quietly opening the bedroom door and padding into the hallway. This place is huge, and Jackson didn't get a chance to give me the tour, so I'm just going to retrace my steps from earlier and wander around until I find the refrigerator. It's not the soundest plan, but it's better than waking him up when he likely has to be at the stadium in the morning.

Tiptoeing across the plush carpet, I try my best to stay quiet. But as soon as I round the corner that leads to the staircase, I crash into a hard, warm wall of muscle. I suck in a gasp when two large hands wrap around my waist to steady me, going into survival mode as I throw a hard right hook.

"Jesus fucking Christ, Arden! It's just me!" Hawk's deep voice hisses as he lets go, cupping his hand over his cheek. I squint, waiting for my eyes to adjust enough to make out his features in the nearly pitch-black space. He's hunched forward, groaning in discomfort, gently rubbing the skin of his face with his fingertips.

"Oh my God!" I gasp, my hands shooting up over my mouth. "Hawk, I'm so sorry. I thought you were a murderer! Are you okay?" Without even waiting for an answer, I grab his hand and yank him quickly through the door of my room. I bypass the bed, hauling him into the bathroom as I flip the light switch and immediately bring my hands to his face. A big, red welt mars the skin under his eye, and I push to my tiptoes to see better. I'm five foot seven, but he's got to be at least eight inches taller than me, with firm, bulging muscles and a wide frame.

It's just dawning on me that this is the closest I've ever gotten to him. He's fucking beautiful with his tan skin, full lips, and deep, Caribbean-blue eyes. His black hair falls over his forehead as he angles down, allowing me to inspect the damage my fist did to his cheek and eye. I run my fingertips over the red mark, sucking a quiet breath through my teeth as he winces. He bites his lip to stifle a pained groan, and I can't stop my gaze from homing in on the motion. All of a sudden, I'm frozen. I can't move, I can't blink, and it feels like all the oxygen has been sucked from the room as flashes of his mouth running along my heated skin play on a loop in my head. I stand there for what feels like a lifetime, struggling to break out of the fantasy as if it's holding me hostage. Finally escaping its clutches, I shift my eyes upward, locking onto his endless cerulean pools as he studies me.

What's happening? What are words? I'm pretty sure I know some, but—wait, no. I don't.

"Arden?" he rasps, snapping me out of whatever the hell that was, and I shake my head rapidly, clearing my throat. "Are you alright?"

Oh my God.

"Yeah," I say on a breathy laugh. "I just woke up and I haven't eaten all day. I guess it's making me loopy. Are you okay? I'm really sor—"

"What do you mean, you haven't eaten?" he cuts me off, his expression growing even more serious than usual. I open my mouth to reply but close it again when his glare hardens.

Fidgeting, I wring my hands together in front of me

like a child who's getting scolded, speaking quietly. "I was nervous before my flight, then I got really anxious with the noise and turbulence. Jacks took me to Starbucks for a tea to calm me down on the way here, but my stomach was still in knots. It's just—this stupid thing that happens to me sometimes."

He gives me a sharp nod, his scowl relaxing slightly. "I understand. Come on." He reaches down, takes my hand, and pulls me back through my room the way we came. I follow, staring perplexed at where we're joined because, not only is this the most he's ever spoken to me, but he's *never* touched me. And now here we are, him encasing my small hand in his and leading me through the dark house as I try to ignore the sparks of electricity that prick up my arm at the contact.

I've always thought Hawk was hot as fuck, but it was never more than that. He's like a random celebrity you see on TV, drool over, then move on with your life because he's unattainable. Even now, I know that's true, but I can't stop my traitorous body from reacting to the innocent gesture. He's just helping me because it's the middle of the night and I don't know my way around. I'm in his house, and he's being a decent human being because I'm Jackson's stepsister. Nothing more.

We make our way down the stairs, him slowing so I can carefully take them one by one. He never breaks our connection, reaching to the wall at the bottom of the landing and sliding the dimmer up so a soft glow casts across the open living area. Continuing through the condo, he stops and finally drops my hand when we reach the kitchen. Flipping on the light, he strides across the room while I take in my surroundings.

Just like the rest of the place, it's clean and modern. How two grown-ass bachelors live here is a mystery to me, because everything from the white marble counter-tops to the stainless-steel appliances looks completely untouched. It's all state-of-the-art technology with touch-screen displays, which is a hell of a lot nicer than anything I've ever lived in—especially since graduating from college. I'm used to ramen noodle cups and microwaves that you have to smack every now and then to make the plate spin. You know…*non-millionaire stuff*.

"You never answered me," I say as he dips down, grabbing a frying pan from under the cupboard and placing it on the stove. "Are you okay? Your cheek and eye look a little swollen."

"I'm fine," he grunts, opening the refrigerator and pulling out the tub of butter and a bag of deli cheese before returning to the counter. I stand there awkwardly, wanting to fill the uncomfortable silence with words, but I honestly don't know what to say. In the last fifteen minutes, I've punched him in the face, made the weirdest extended eye contact in the history of the world, and now he seems kind of mad. So maybe I should just zip it and see what happens.

I quietly step up to the island in the middle of the kitchen, slide onto one of the white leather barstools, rest my elbows against the smooth marble, and drop my chin into my open palms. I can't help but admire the way the ink-covered muscles in his arms strain against the fabric of his black t-shirt every time he moves, even though I probably shouldn't. Not only is he Jackson's best friend, but he's also my new roommate. Getting caught ogling his body would make our interactions even more awkward than they already are.

He butters two pieces of bread, setting one into the pan before adding two slices of cheese and topping it with the other. The butter sizzles and pops, filling the room with the most mouthwatering scent. I don't know what I'm drooling over more. The grilled cheese that's browning to perfection across the room, or the strong, silent beast of a man holding the spatula in front of it.

Both? *Both.*

He plates the sandwich, turning to me just as I avert my gaze to the refrigerator, pretending to read the shopping list glowing on the LED screen of the freezer door. "Eat," he demands, catching me off guard with the firm bite to his tone. My head rears back for a moment, but he stops me before I can protest. "You can't go all day without eating, especially when your anxiety is bothering you. It's dangerous. So, eat. *Please.*" His voice is much softer, making me stand down and obey his order. As hard as it is to admit, he's right. I need to take better care of my body, especially now that I'm a legit pro athlete. I won't do my team or myself any favors if I'm not at my best, starting with eating right and facing my anxiety instead of acting like it hasn't gotten worse since I left Argentina.

I swallow, nodding my head as I pick up the grilled cheese and take a bite. It melts on my tongue and an obscene moan falls from my lips as my eyes roll back. "Holy mother of balls, I've never tasted anything this good in my life," I say on a contented sigh, looking up to find him staring at me like I have an arm growing out of the top of my head. His brows are bunched, and his Adam's apple bobs in his throat while his deep blue eyes stare at me like I'm some kind of science experiment. I realize that I voiced that thought *out loud*, and suddenly, I'm mortified. I literally just sounded like I was having the best orgasm of my life, then uttered the phrase *Holy mother of balls* in front of Hawk Mason.

Smooth, Arden.

I clear my throat awkwardly. "Sorry. I guess I was hungrier than I thought. Where did this bread come from? It's really good." I'm just trying to make small talk so that maybe he'll forget about the carb-induced climax he just witnessed, so I'm surprised by his answer.

"I made it," he mutters flatly, returning to the stove and placing the dirty pan in the sink. I look down at the sandwich, then back up at him as he takes a glass from the cupboard, fills it with water from the tap, and walks over to set it in front of me.

"You made this bread? Where'd you learn to do that?" He freezes at the question, the mask of indifference that had melted the smallest amount slipping right back over his face. Obviously, I struck some kind of sore spot because before I can say another word, he disappears from the kitchen, stomping toward the stairs. For the tiniest second, I almost felt like he was showing me a side of him I'd never seen before…a side nobody but

Jacks gets to experience. But I guess I was misreading the situation, because here I am, alone with my grilled cheese, wondering what the hell just happened with Hawk—and how awkward as fuck it's going to be living under the same roof until I have enough money to find a place of my own.

FOUR
HAWK

"FUCK," I growl quietly, leaning my back against the closed door of my room before sliding down to my ass. I drop my head into my hands, gripping my thick black hair in my fists and pulling until the sharp bite of pain grounds me, slowing my heart rate as I take a deep breath through my nose and let it out slowly.

Knowing Arden was moving in today, I purposely stayed away. I wasn't ready to be near her, not with the thoughts that always seem to plague my mind when she's close. I've only met her a handful of times, but each one had me more confused than the last, even though we've barely spoken. I wish I could explain any of it, but I just can't. And the worst part of it all is that I can't even talk to Jackson about it.

Because he's in love with her.

He has no idea I know, which is good because I'd hate to tell him that I'm fully aware, yet still have an overwhelming need to possess every part of her body and soul. That can never happen. If he's not willing to put his feelings for her into the universe, neither am I. It's going to kill me being in such close proximity to her, but I need to get my shit under control. I can't continue to snap at her every time she touches a raw nerve. She's the purest fucking soul, and she doesn't deserve my indifference. Especially when she's one of the two people in this world who look at me like I'm not broken.

But the truth is—I am. No matter how much I try to forget my fucked-up past or how many hours of therapy I sit through, it always has a way of resurfacing and reminding me of who I really am. Tonight, it was Arden asking me where I learned to make bread. As much as baking is an outlet for my anxiety, some memories have the opposite effect.

"Hawk, I'm hungry," my five-year-old brother Hayden said, his arms hugged around his stomach that I knew was empty. It was Sunday morning, which meant he likely hadn't eaten anything of substance since his school lunch on Friday. Mom had been on a drunken bender for a week straight, only coming home last night after midnight and passing out on the couch. I'd tried waking her to tell her we needed groceries, but she just groaned, rolled over, and left me to figure out what to feed the boys. Hayden was the easier of the two because he could eat anything, but Henry had allergies, so we had to be careful with him.

"I'm working on it," I replied, pulling open the cupboards that were nearly bare. Mom couldn't work, so we got food stamps, but she often traded them for liquor, so the end of every month was tough. I'd learned how to make some easy meals with cheap ingredients, but those were all gone. And it

wasn't like I could drive to the store even if I did have money. I was still two years away from getting my license, so I'd have to figure it out.

I walked over to the computer, hoping like hell that I could find something. I'd been using a website where you typed in what you had lying around, and it gave you recipes that would work. It had saved me more times than I could count, but today would be a long shot.

Entering every single thing we had in our cupboards and refrigerator, I crossed my fingers as I hit the enter button. The machine froze for several moments, which was nothing new for the old piece of junk, before a single recipe finally popped up on the screen. Reading it, I breathed a sigh of relief, knowing my brothers wouldn't have to go to bed hungry again.

I hopped up, walking into the kitchen with Hayden following me like a shadow, as always. Thankfully, Henry was entranced in the Elmo DVD he watched on a loop all day, every day, so I didn't have to worry about making sure he wasn't messing with things.

"Should we call an ambulance for Mommy?" he asked as I preheated the oven. "She keeps making those noises like she's hurt."

I shook my head. "No, she's okay. She just needs a nap." The truth was, I never knew if she was okay. I'd called our dad on multiple occasions, but he had married a wealthy woman on the other side of the country and started a new family with her, so he wasn't much help. My grandparents kicked my mom out when she was pregnant with me, and we rarely saw them. She was all we had, and more importantly, calling the police or paramedics to help her meant they'd see *the shit we lived in. Our one-bedroom apartment was falling apart, and there was rarely food. I did my best to keep my brothers clean and fed, but if any other adults knew what it was really like, they'd separate us. And I couldn't bear the thought.*

"Can you get me the big red bowl, Hay?" I asked, trying to divert his attention. He loved to help me, so I used it to my advantage, giving him random jobs to do as I worked. Keeping the two of them safe and happy was always my number one concern, as difficult as it was at times.

"This one?" he shouted, holding it up above his head triumphantly, his little feet slapping against the floor as he ran my way and hoisted it onto the counter.

"Yep," I replied, ruffling his hair. "Now go check on Henry so I can make us some bread. There are two pieces of cheese left over from last month that are probably still good. You guys can have sandwiches."

"Ok," he said, heading toward the living room but turning back to me as he reached the archway. "Hawk?"

"What's up?" I asked, looking up from where I was pouring flour into the measuring cup.

"You're the best big brother ever."

His words play over and over in my head as I wipe away the tears that have spilled down my cheeks, standing and walking to the bed and climbing under the thick, heavy comforter. Thinking about Hayden and Henry still hurts, even though it's been over seven years since I've seen either of them. Last I knew, they were living in Arizona with our dad and calling his new wife *Mom*. They became a family, and I was left behind.

When he showed up at our doorstep with a police officer during my senior year of high school, I was surprised, to say the least. He walked out on us when Henry was an infant, and we hardly ever heard from him until he rode in on his white horse, acting like he gave a fuck. Apparently, a friend of his who had a son in Henry's class had made him aware of how we were living, and he hopped on the first plane to Walton, Virginia with custody papers for the two of them in tow. At first, I wanted to slam the door in his face, cops be damned—but I knew my brothers' well-being was at risk every day in our old, dilapidated apartment. So I did the one thing I never thought I'd do. I didn't put up a fight when he said he wanted to take them home with him. He told me he'd raise them with his new wife since they were never able to conceive, giving them a real home with a loving extended family, away from Mom and her addiction. She had already done enough damage to their childhoods.

I didn't really question why he didn't want me too, since leaving her wasn't an option anyway. I was technically an adult and had a promising future playing baseball, despite my shitty situation. I thought I'd be able to find a way to get her into rehab so she could get better without worrying about who was taking care of the boys. Then I could enter the MLB draft without feeling the guilt of leaving her alone while she drank herself to death. I even had hopes that she'd someday work to get them back, or that once I'd made my way to the big leagues and had the means to provide for them, they'd come live with me. What I didn't expect was for our dad to brainwash them into thinking I didn't love them anymore.

I've tried calling him and messaging him on social media several times, but he's made it clear that they don't want to talk to me. Since he has full custody and they're still minors, I can't contact them to plead my case. Instead, I have to live every day knowing that they're across the country thinking I chose our alcoholic mother over them. Which, I can't say is completely inaccurate. But what choice did I have when she wasn't going to help herself?

Things didn't get much better after the boys left. Mom kept up with her old habits, disappearing without a word for days at a time while I drove around looking for her before dragging my ass to school and practice on no sleep. I begged her to get help before I graduated, but she refused every time. Until she was forced into rehab by a judge after multiple DUIs. To this day, she remains in a halfway house she'll likely never get out of. While she's sober, we all know it isn't by choice. I eventually had to step away from our relationship because it was causing more harm than good with me worrying about her relapsing twenty-four-seven. It wasn't any easier than losing my brothers, and I think a lot about what could've been if she had just chosen us over her addiction. That shit still plagues me when it comes to trusting others or believing I'll ever be good enough to be a priority to anyone.

Except for Jackson. From the moment we became roommates in the minors, I latched onto him. I can't explain why, but I just felt it—he was the real deal when it came to friendship. In the last seven years, I've shown him the parts of me that I've kept hidden from everyone else, and he's never judged. He's always accepted me with all my hang-ups and flaws, never expecting me to water myself down to fit in with him. He made room for me, and I love the fuck out of him for that. He's the closest thing I have to a brother right now—at least until my own turn eighteen and decide whether or not they still want me out of their lives. Which is exactly why I need to stay in my lane when it comes to Arden. As beautiful and kind as she is, I can't act on my urges to be near her. It wouldn't be right, and I refuse to put my friendship with Jacks in jeopardy.

Because absolutely nothing is more important to me than that.

FIVE

JACKSON

"YOU'VE GOT THIS, VAL!" I yell from my spot at the edge of the infield near second base. We're playing a home game against San Francisco, and we're struggling. It's the bottom of the seventh; we're trailing by three runs with one out, and our defense is racking up errors like it's our job. We're coming off back-to-back series without a single day off, and it's showing. We're fucking exhausted. Riggs winds up, pitching a low fastball right into Ace's mitt as the batter lets it go by.

"Strike!" the umpire yells, causing the crowd to clap and cheer in response. I watch as the batter gets in his stance again, trying my best to keep an eye on the runner at first while he takes a few lead-off steps.

The next pitch is thrown, and the bat makes contact, sending a grounder between first and second base. My body moves before I even have time to think, leaping to the left and catching the ball in my glove, landing on my stomach after it takes a lucky bounce. Despite the wind being knocked out of me, I know we have a runner advancing to second, and if I move quick enough, we can try for the double play. I shoot up to one knee, firing the ball as fast as I can to our shortstop, Dante Cole, who's already on the bag. He stretches, catching it easily and getting the out. Like lightning, he sends it to first, and it lands in Kaflin's glove just as the batter's foot slaps against the base.

"You're out!" the ump yells, balling his hand into a fist above his head and throwing it forward animatedly as the crowd goes wild. I jump to my feet, a sharp pain radiating up the inside of my thigh and making me rethink my celebration. It's not awful, but I can tell I must've tweaked my hamstring when I made the play. I'm certainly no stranger to injuries on the field, but the last thing I want is for our manager, Clyde, to pull me because I'm hurt. So I steel my expression, doing my best to look perfectly fine as we head to the dugout for our turn at bat.

"You okay?" Hawk mumbles as I take a seat on the bench, tossing my glove aside. Lowering myself onto the hard pine makes me wince, so I quickly look around to make sure nobody saw. I take my injuries seriously, but I can't tell if this one is bad enough to make a fuss about—at least not until I try to walk it off a little.

"I'm fine," I reply quietly. I don't know why I'm even trying to lie to him. He always knows. Right now isn't the time to discuss it out loud, though. It's likely just a pulled muscle, but I'll swing by the trainer's office on my way out of here today and get it checked. I'm sure a little rest and ice will fix me up. We have the next couple of days off, and I'll take it easy. It's looking like we're going to secure a spot in the postseason, so I have to be in top shape in order to make a push for the World Series with my team.

"Right," he grunts, pulling on his batting gloves and securing them around his wrists. I roll my eyes, leaning back against the brick wall behind me as I bring my hands up to the gold chain hanging around my neck and grip it tightly in my fists. The warm metal rope bites into my palms, grounding and calming me as Hawk steps up to bat.

The first ball is high and outside, so he waits, letting it by. He may look like a wild card with his black hair and tattoo-covered body, but Hawk Mason is one of the most intuitive and patient baseball players I've ever met. I swear, he can see the pitch before it's thrown half the time. It rattles the fuck out of even the most self-assured pitchers, making them second guess their own plans. Between him and Ace, we have two of the best power hitters in the league on the Fury.

The next one is sent his way, and he's locked in, waiting until the perfect time to bring his bat around. It connects loudly, and he takes off like a bullet, already knowing it doesn't have quite enough distance to go over the wall. The placement is fucking perfect, landing just short of where the center fielder stands and bouncing off the grass as Hawk rounds first base. He hits the ground, sliding into the bag with seconds to spare before he's tagged, standing and dusting himself off like hitting a double is easy work. Because it is for him. He has a top-five batting average in the entire league, and if he's standing on first base, there's a very high chance that it's because he was intentionally walked.

Ace is up next, finding that same gap in the outfield and sending Hawk home. Those two are a lethal pair, and I'm definitely happy they're on my team. I'd hate to have to defend either of them.

We end up winning the game by two runs, my final at-bat resulting in a strikeout, which sucks, but also—no running. Hitting the showers, I wash and dry myself quickly, tossing on a white t-shirt and black basketball shorts before making my way to see the trainer. Thankfully, I wasn't set to do any post-game interviews, so I step through the door to the sterile-smelling room, hoping the wait is short. I rode here with Hawk but told him I'd call for a car so he didn't have to stick around. They almost never arrange for him to speak with the media since he doesn't give them much to work with. At home, he's not as quiet, although he *has* been making himself a little more scarce now that Arden is living with us. I'm sure he'll warm up to her eventually. At least, I hope so.

"Hey, Jacks!" the assistant trainer, Reese, says when she notices me, a bright smile blooming across her face. She's cute, probably in her late twenties, with golden blonde hair and sparkling green eyes. Her curves go on for days, and she's exactly the kind of girl I'd go nuts over. All the single guys on the team do, even though we have a very strict No Fraternization policy here— not that anyone follows it. I'm about ninety-eight percent sure our Public Relations manager, Taylor, is fucking our mascot, Friggle. Well, the guy who wears the costume. His real name is Brent, and up until earlier this year, he was just some tall, lanky kid who did his job and went home. But lately, I've been noticing the way he's putting more effort into looking good, even spending some time in the team gym, which I have no idea how he gets access to. Pair that with the eyebrow-raising amount of times I've seen the two of them come in and out of the equipment closet together, and I'd bet money they're banging.

I wonder if he keeps the costume on.

I cringe internally, looking up to see Reese staring at me with a confused look on her face. I shake my head rapidly, trying to rid it of the mascot porn that's now flashing through my mind before I reply.

"Hey." I step closer, trying to mask my slight limp. If I don't, she may call the team physician, and I'd prefer not to get him involved yet. "So, I think I tweaked my right hamstring or something. It isn't awful, and I'll rest it while we're off, but I wanted to get your opinion on what else I could do to make sure I'm feeling one hundred percent as fast as possible."

"Want to hop up and let me take a look?" she asks, patting the padded exam table before turning to the sink and washing her hands. I lie down, the cold pleather making me shiver as it seeps through the thin material of my shirt. Reese rubs her hands together, creating enough friction to warm them before she reaches out and runs them up my thigh. I tense at first, waiting for her to press into the muscle, but when she kneads it with her thumbs gently, it doesn't hurt nearly as much as I expected it to. Relief washes over me, and I let out a steady breath as she gently massages the area before pulling away.

"It's a little swollen and tender, but I think you'll be okay. Take it easy at home for the next two days, keep it elevated, ice it for twenty to thirty minutes every four hours, and you can take some Tylenol for the pain if you need it. I'd like to see you before you leave for Milwaukee, so how about you swing by that morning so I can make sure you're good?"

I sit up, turning myself so my legs are hanging off the side of the table and adjusting my shorts before finding the floor. I'm thankful that she validated my thoughts about it not being too serious. It probably could be if we were playing again tomorrow, but the time off will help me heal. I'll do everything she said to get ready for the Lynx this weekend. They beat us the last time we played, so the stakes are even higher for me to be at my best.

"Thanks, Reese," I say with a wave, heading toward the door. She returns the gesture, and I slip into the hall-way, expecting it to be nearly cleared out. So, I'm shocked when I see Hawk leaning up against the wall in front of me.

"Why didn't you leave?" I ask, my brows knitting tightly. "I told you I'd be a while."

He shrugs, and we walk down the corridor that leads to the elevators. There's a special parking lot for players and staff, but it's a bit of a trek since it's on the opposite side of the stadium. Our steps fall in sync with one another, and he shoves his hands into his pockets like he's trying to decide if he wants to talk or not. He's normally like this around other people, but not when we're alone, so it's raising some red flags.

"What?" I ask. "Why are you being weird?"

"I'm not," he grunts, pausing for a moment. "It's just that Arden is probably home, and I didn't want it to be awkward if we were the only two in the house."

I stop, throwing my head back in annoyance. "She's been here for three weeks, and I haven't seen you speak to her once. If it's awkward, it's because you're making it that way. She has an outgoing personality, but she's holding it back because she's afraid she's disrupting our lives."

"Did she say that?" he says, concern blanketing his expression.

"No, but I know her, and she isn't being herself. She's quieter and more reserved." I blow out a breath, looking down at my feet. "I'm guilty of it too. She was practically my best friend growing up, and when our parents got married, our whole dynamic changed. It was easy to grow apart when we had states or countries separating us, but now that she's here, I miss being able to hang out and joke around with her.

"Here she is in a brand-new city with no friends, other than her teammates, and the two people she lives with don't even ask about her day or how practice has been going. The last thing she needs right now is to feel cut off from the world when she's making such big changes. Let's at least *try* to make her feel welcome. She's a really good girl, Hawk. You can trust her."

He swallows, nodding, but I can see the trepidation in his eyes. I get it. He's been abandoned by his dad, his mom didn't give enough of a shit to get sober for him, and he hasn't spoken to his brothers since the day they were ripped away from him. He never keeps women around for more than one night, our teammates hardly know a single thing about him, and other than me, he doesn't trust anyone not to hurt and leave him. But I know if he gave her a chance, Arden would be the kind of friend to him that she was to me before I pushed her away. Someone he can count on and maybe even get him to open up a little.

"Okay," he says quietly. "You're right. I'll try harder."

SIX
ARDEN

"YOU'RE HOME LATE," Jackson says over the back of the couch as I trudge through the door, my feet screaming at me from the longest practice I've ever endured. It wasn't long time-wise, but Dahlia made the entire team run wind sprints for over thirty minutes. Then, when we were nice and exhausted, she had us do hitting lines against our defense. We've only been practicing as a team for two and a half weeks, so I'm still learning my passers' techniques and my hitters' strengths and weaknesses to set to them properly. Everyone is different and I have to memorize all of it, including the backup players, in case someone gets injured. It's a lot of pressure, but I live and breathe for volleyball, and my spot on the Flare can be given to someone else at any time—so I need to give it my all.

"Sorry," I reply, dropping my duffle bag and kicking my slides off before putting them in the closet. "I stayed after with one of my hitters to make sure we were on the same page." Zara Ellis is fresh out of college and has surprised us all with her dedication these past couple of weeks, so I have a feeling she'll be named starting right outside hitter before our first game. I hope she does, because she's the only one who's shown me grace while I'm learning what they all need from me. We work well together, and I'd hate to be on the receiving end of one of her hits. She's an absolute powerhouse. I can't wait to dominate the court with her, as well as the rest of the girls.

"Don't be. We just wanted to eat dinner with you."

"We?" I ask, entering the room to see Hawk sitting on the opposite end of the couch, breaking his connection from the action movie that's playing on the TV to look at me. I've hardly seen him since the first night I got here, and even when I have, it's only been while passing each other in the hallway or kitchen. I obviously said something wrong and upset him, and he hasn't forgotten. It's been uncomfortable, to say the least.

"Yeah," Jacks says with a smile. "We were going to order from somewhere but wanted to see if maybe you were down to hang out. We have a couple of days off, and I know your practices are always in the afternoon, so how about some roommate bonding time?" I look between the two of them as they stare, shock obviously very evident in my expression because Jackson rolls his eyes, laughing. "I know it's weird, but we realized today that we haven't really given you much attention since you got here. And everybody knows how you need it to survive."

My jaw drops, and I huff an incredulous laugh. "I do

not need it to survive. I'm perfectly fine on my own, thank you very much. The two of you can take your pity attention and shove it up your asses. I don't want it," I reply, crossing my arms over my chest. I'm mostly joking. I know they're busy, and when they're home, which hasn't been often, they're tired. By the time they're up and around on their days off, I'm already gone to practice or the gym. Our schedules haven't really matched up, even if we did want to spend time together.

He laughs harder. "Princess, I'm injured, so if you don't come over here willingly, I'm going to have to make my grumpy friend carry you to the couch. Make a choice."

I scoff, rolling my eyes. "Yeah, okay." Like Hawk is going to touch me when he's barely even looked at me in the last three weeks. "Goodnight." I turn, heading toward the stairs, but only get about five steps before a strong, thick arm wraps around my waist tightly. Electricity snakes its way throughout my body as a quiet voice speaks into my ear.

"He warned you, Hellcat," Hawk says, his minty breath puffing against my cheek. The nickname sounds sinful coming from his mouth, and I have to actively stop myself from moaning out loud at the sound. I'm frozen in place, knowing I should pull away, but when he splays his hand over my lower stomach, I do the exact opposite and press myself into him. His muscular chest is warm against my back, and I let out a shaky exhale, closing my eyes and trying to stop the dizziness that's threatening to pull me under just from being held by him, even though my brain is telling me he's only doing it because Jacks told him to. But when he drags his nose from my neck to the sensitive spot under my ear, I'm light years away from any semblance of a rational thought.

My knees buckle just as he scoops me up from the ground. I instinctively wrap my arms around his neck, yet I'm unable to make a sound as he carries me bridal style across the room and deposits me next to Jackson on the couch before dropping down on my other side. The scent of their cologne, Hawk's spicy and Jackson's sweet, mix with the oxygen that slowly refills my lungs, and the fuzziness in my brain dissipates now that I'm no longer being held so tightly.

What the fuck was that? The last thing I need is to be affected by my stepbrother's best friend and roommate. This is the second time his hands on me have made me feel something, and I really need to get it together before I embarrass myself. At this point, the simple thought of friendship with this guy seems impossible. Other than this very moment, he's been so quiet and closed off—even more so than I remember. So why am I wishing he'd wrap around me again?

"Anyway," Jackson says, snapping me back to reality. I swallow loudly, looking straight at the TV because if I look at either of them, they'll know what I'm thinking. So, I stay quiet as he continues. "I need comfort food. Pizza sound okay? There's a place right down the street that has the best sauce, and they do low-carb crust."

I nod my head way too fast to look sane, but whatever. It's better than the alternative, which is sitting there like a rock while he asks me a question. "Mhmm," I force out.

"You okay?" I snap my head in his direction, and suddenly I can breathe again. I don't know why, but since I've known him, Jackson has always made me feel calm when my anxiety starts to pull me under. Even now, when the most confusing thoughts about Hawk are running rampant in my mind, his presence slows them so I can recenter myself.

"Yes," I reply, smiling warmly. "It's been a long day. My brain and body both hurt."

His expression softens. "Let me order our food, then we can relax. Mushrooms and sausage for you, and supreme for us, right?" he says, pulling up the app to order on his phone. I nod, biting the inside of my cheek to hide my smile, because he still remembers my pizza order. Memories from the past resurface, and I realize exactly how much I miss his friendship. Things got a little weird after our parents got married, but it was probably a culmination of Jackson and Gina moving into a space they had to share with other people, and nerves for the upcoming MLB draft. He spent so much time perfecting his craft that year, that he was hardly around. I had already been offered a partial athletic scholarship from Penn State by the time the wedding rolled around, so I was all about having fun and going out during our senior year. But he spent his free time at the batting cages and updating his highlight reels so scouts would notice him. It paid off in a big way, because now he's in the big leagues, but I definitely missed him. I still do. I hope that, eventually, we can get back to what we used to be.

He taps the screen a few times before setting the device on the large ottoman in front of the couch and pressing a button on the remote controller next to it. The lights in the room dim to almost nothing and the TV switches to the opening credits of a movie. I relax into the cushions, but before I can get comfortable, Jacks nudges my shoulder.

"Turn," he orders softly. I look at him, confused, before he puts a finger in the air and motions in a circle, as if to mimic the word. Slowly, I angle myself so my back is to him, but immediately regret it when I realize that it puts me directly facing Hawk. My whole body heats, and I'm sure that if I weren't wearing a cropped t-shirt, he'd see the visible flush across my chest as he looks at me while I pretend not to notice.

I jump when Jackson's strong hands slide over my shoulders and he begins massaging the tight muscles. It's a nice gesture—one that wouldn't have phased me when we were seventeen. But being touched by him after all this time, paired with the way Hawk hasn't taken his eyes off me since I turned toward him, is making me squirm in my seat.

"Is this okay?" Jacks asks. "You seem even more tense now. Should I stop?"

I shake my head, blowing out a forced exhale. This is ridiculous—he's just being his normal self, trying to help because he knows I need it. So what if it happens to put me in Hawk's line of sight? We all live here, and we should be comfortable like this, right?

"No, don't stop," I reply. "My shoulders and neck are really tight." I turn more, giving him better access to work. The angle causes me to slide my knee onto the couch, brushing it along Hawk's thigh. I watch the pinky finger of his hand resting on top twitch, grazing the fabric of my leggings before he quickly pulls it away and stands up.

"I'll go wait for the food," he mutters, hauling ass toward the door and disappearing from the condo fast enough to make my head spin.

"I don't think he likes me. Just when I think maybe he does, he shows me the exact opposite. It makes me dizzy," I say as Jacks smooths his thumbs over the muscles in my shoulders. It feels amazing, and I drop my head forward, enjoying the relief.

"He likes you. He just doesn't really do emotions well. And it takes him a while to warm up to people."

I huff an incredulous laugh. "I've known him for years and he's barely spoken to me. I think I just need to keep my distance until I can get out of your hair and into a place of my own. I don't want to disturb your routine or make him feel like his privacy isn't respected."

"Arden, look at me," he says, dropping his hands. I twist myself so I'm sitting forward on the couch, turning my head to face him. "I'm telling you, we like having you here. Hawk has a lot going on in his head all the time, and he gets nervous letting people in. It's not you—shit, it's not even *him*. He wasn't given a very good start, and he's lost a lot, which is why he doesn't let anyone get too close." His eyes soften and his lips press together. "Just keep trying with him, okay? He deserves that."

My heart squeezes in my chest. Not only for Jackson and how much of a gift his friendship is to both of us, but also for Hawk and whatever happened that makes him feel like he can't open up to anyone. I'm glad he has Jacks, but that shouldn't be where his support system ends.

"Okay," I reply with an understanding nod. He nudges my shoulder with his and I return the gesture, barely able to move his six-foot-one, bulky frame. He smirks, the dimple on his cheek sinking in and making him look even more boyishly adorable. My mind floats back to the days when our friendship was easy and fun, and all I can think about is how I want that again. Being here is the perfect opportunity to close the distance that was created when we graduated and went our separate ways to achieve our dreams—which, coincidentally, are the same things that brought us back together here in Florida. It feels like a full-circle moment. Now that we're older and know where our lives are headed, we can focus on us.

"I'm glad you're here," he says, putting an arm around my shoulder and hugging me to his side. I bring my knees up, curling into a ball before leaning into him. The comfort is nice, especially after such a rough day at practice and the mini roller coaster ride my anxiety just took me on with Hawk.

"Me too," I reply with a yawn just as the door clicks

shut and the sound of Hawk's footsteps trail from the entryway to the kitchen behind us. My stomach clenches in hunger, and all I can think about is eating and falling asleep while I pretend to watch the movies they picked out. As much as I want to have roommate bonding time, I'm beat and can't imagine I'll make it very long before I pass out on the couch.

"Come on," Jackson says, standing and turning to extend his hand for me to take. I notice that he's babying his right leg just slightly, and I remember what he said earlier about being injured.

I grasp his hand, pushing myself off the cushions so he isn't bearing any of my weight. "You alright?"

He waves a dismissive hand. "I pulled my hamstring a little bit. I'll be fine. I'll rest it for a couple days, and I'll be good to go. But I bet it would make me feel better faster if you did all my laundry."

I scrunch my face in faux disgust, slapping his shoulder. "Not a fucking chance. I know how bad your gym clothes smelled in high school. I can only imagine how awful they are now that you're a grown-up."

His jaw drops before a devious grin stretches across his face, and he darts a hand out, wrapping it around my wrist and yanking me toward him before putting me in a headlock. I scream playfully as he laughs, trying my best to wiggle away, but it's futile. It's not so tight that I can't breathe, but I'm definitely not going anywhere on my own, instead moving beside him as he leads me to the kitchen.

"Still a smart ass," he says, ruffling my hair before

he loosens his hold and lets me go. Standing, I slap him again, and turn to see Hawk staring at us like he's utterly confused by what he's witnessing. I smile softly, and he shocks me by returning the gesture, reaching for a plate and setting a slice of mushroom and sausage pizza on it before handing it to me.

"Thank you," I say quietly, admiring his gorgeous features as I take it from his hand. His chiseled jawline ticks slightly under my gaze, but he keeps his blue eyes on me until I'm able to look away. Just like the last time we were in this kitchen together, I'm left wishing for more, but I know he has to give it willingly. And I'll be so grateful if he ever does.

"You're welcome," he replies, turning and getting his own food ready next to where Jacks is standing with a mountain of pizza on his plate. I roll my eyes play-fully, because apparently some things never change. He may be built and have an eight-pack of abs, but the man eats like shit. He always has, and it's obviously never going to catch up with him.

"Don't judge me, Princess," he says, pointing an accusing finger in my direction. "I'm injured and need greasy food to get better—and some cuddles probably wouldn't hurt. You two are just going to have to fight over who gets to do that."

"Your best friend or your stepsister," Hawk says, raising an eyebrow. "Either way, it's weird. You're on your own this time, right Hellcat?"

I suck a breath through my teeth. "Yeah, I'm all set on the brother cuddles. Thanks for the pizza, though."

"Fuck the both of you," he says sarcastically, limping out of the room with his plate in hand. I look over to Hawk, who I swear shoots me a wink before following suit, leaving me to wonder if maybe I *can* fit in with them after all.

SEVEN
HAWK

I LIE AWAKE, staring at the ceiling above my bed. I came upstairs as soon as I looked over and found that Jackson and Arden had fallen asleep on the couch, thinking I'd be more comfortable in here, but I've been tossing and turning the whole time.

After our talk at the stadium, I came home with an entirely different outlook on having Arden here. Jackson was right; neither of us has been putting forth enough effort to make her feel welcome—most of all, me. After I stormed out of the kitchen on her first night here, I didn't know how I should act. I was embarrassed by my reaction, but even with all the therapy I've received since I was a teenager, I'm still not the best at expressing my emotions. I guess I'll always be a work in progress when it comes to that.

My plan for the evening was to spend time with the two of them and try to stay out of my own head. It was going great until he suggested I carry her to the couch. As soon as I touched her, I felt a need like I'd never experienced before. It was like that first night when she brought me to her bathroom and traced her fingertips along my jaw, but much more intense. What should've been an innocent, playful moment turned into me pulling her close. Breathing her in. Saying the nickname I gave her in my head when I realized how fierce she is under that sweet exterior, out loud. As much as I tried to shake it off—to get used to this new normal of being okay with being near her—*fuck*. I wanted more. So much more that I had to leave the room to remind myself that no matter how strong of a pull there is, she can never be mine. It's something I've been fighting since the moment I met her.

"It's nice to meet you, Hawk," Slade said, clasping his hand around mine in a firm shake. "I'm a big fan."

"Thank you, sir," I replied awkwardly. It was my first time meeting Jackson's family, and although he told me how cool they were, I was always nervous around new people. Normally, I would've already retreated to the guest room in an effort to avoid answering the usual questions I expected in these situations, but these were my best friend's parents, and they'd opened their home to me for Thanksgiving dinner. I didn't want to be rude.

I couldn't remember the last time I'd celebrated the holiday, let alone with a home-cooked meal and people who truly enjoyed being around each other. Then again, it had been years since I'd had anything besides baseball to be thankful for. Contact with my brothers had been completely cut off, and my mother's intense rehab didn't allow for visitation yet, even if I was ready to forgive her for everything her addiction had done to me—which, I wasn't.

"Why don't you boys take your luggage upstairs and meet me back down here? Gina and Arden should be back from the grocery store any minute, then we can all catch up." I'd met Jackson's mom briefly via video chat, but his step-sister would be another first introduction. He'd told me a lot about her—how they were really close throughout their younger years but grew apart when he was drafted, and she'd gone off to play volleyball at Penn State. I swear, sometimes the look in his eyes when he talked about her was the same one I'd seen in my own reflection whenever thoughts of my brothers would enter my mind. It was almost as though he'd suffered a loss of his own, only she was still right here.

We made our way to the rooms we'd be staying in, and even though every instinct in my body was telling me to make up an excuse to stay put and be alone, I fought the urge. These people were important to Jacks, and I wanted to learn more about them. It was only a few days, and it's not like I'd be forced to tell them my depressing life story. I'd gotten pretty good at deflecting personal questions and was planning on using those tactics all weekend long. Just the thought of letting anyone see the parts of myself I tried so hard to hide made my stomach turn and my body tighten with anxiety.

Reluctantly, I stepped out of the room, padding down the staircase and following my best friend's voice as it led me to the kitchen. I rounded the corner, stopping in my tracks as I watched the scene in front of me unfold like it was happening on a movie screen.

"Oh my God, you're here!" a stunning brunette said, dropping the bags of groceries that had been hanging from her fingers and running across the room. A wide smile bloomed

across Jackson's face, and he opened his arms, catching her as she launched herself and wrapped him into the tightest hug I had ever seen.

"Hey, Princess," he sighed, tightening the embrace as his eyes fell shut. He inhaled deeply like he was trying to memorize her scent, and that's when all the puzzle pieces clicked into place. The way he spoke about her as if he had suffered a devastating loss. The constant subject changes when I asked why he didn't visit home more often. And the look of pure longing that was painted across his face as he held her in his arms, not realizing I had witnessed the entire thing.

He had feelings for her—ones that were stronger than it seemed he was ready to admit.

She pulled away, and their gazes found each other, lingering for just a moment too long before he quickly broke the connection, returning her to her feet and clearing his throat awkwardly. He looked around the room, relief flooding his entire body as he motioned for me to come closer. I swallowed nervously, doing my best to pretend I hadn't noticed the way he held her as I headed in their direction.

"Arden, this is Hawk Mason. Hawk, this is my…stepsister, Arden Levine." The title came out forced, like he hated the thought of it, and he stepped back so I could reach out to shake her hand. As soon as her palm slid into mine, her captivating brown eyes burning right through me, warmth traveled throughout my body. I wanted to look away—to deny the unexplainable way I felt as if I was being pulled to her like a magnet, but I was frozen. Her head tilted shyly, smiling as she broke the silence.

"Hello, Hawk. It's nice to meet you." My name sounded like a song falling from her lips, and I'd never wished for

temporary hearing and vision loss more than I had right then —because in that moment, I fully understood why he struggled with the fact that he couldn't have her. Not only was she beautiful, but the air around her was warm and inviting, making me wish I was the type of person who had something to offer to a conversation just so I could keep her talking. I wanted to know her, and for the first time in what felt like forever, I didn't want to run away. Instead, I had the most intense craving to let her know me, too. But that couldn't happen, especially now that I'd seen with my own two eyes what she meant to him, even if he refused to acknowledge it.

I had to keep my distance from her, no matter what.

"Hi," I grunted quietly, yanking my hand from her grip and shoving it into my pocket. Her face fell, and her eyes darted around the room, clearly uncomfortable by my short response. It felt wrong, and I wanted to apologize for being rude, but it was better this way. If I could keep her at a distance, I'd never have to face the feeling of wanting something I couldn't have.

"Damn it," I groan, dragging my hands down my face in an attempt to clear the fog from my brain. Sitting up, I swing my legs over the edge of the bed before slowly pushing to stand. I'm obviously not going to get any sleep with my mind racing a million miles a minute, so I may as well give up on that. I check my phone and see that it's after three in the morning, so I guess I can make myself a protein shake and head out for a run once I'm ready. It sure beats lying in bed thinking about how badly I want to touch my best friend's stepsister, who he's secretly in love with.

Padding toward the stairs, I approach the end of the

hallway that leads to both of their rooms, noticing that Jackson's door is closed while Arden's is wide open. They were both out cold when I left to go to my room, so I don't know if or when either of them made it upstairs. I quietly make my way down to the first floor, and I can tell immediately that the TV is still on by the soft glow that's blanketing the living area. From this angle, I can also see that the end of the large sectional where Jackson fell asleep is empty, a crumpled-up blanket draped over the back as though he tossed it there before leaving.

As light-footed as I can be, I move closer, peeking over the other end of the couch. Sure enough, Arden is sprawled out, looking all kinds of uncomfortable as she snores softly. She's on her back with one leg hanging over the edge, her foot dangling, but not reaching the carpet below. One hand is on her stomach, and the other is resting on the armrest above her head. Her neck is bent at an awkward angle, and the skin between her brows is scrunched as if she isn't sleeping peacefully. She said she was sore when she came home, and this will only make it worse. If I don't wake her and make sure she gets to bed, she'll have an even harder time tomorrow.

I quietly step in front of her, leaning down and placing a hand on her shoulder. "Arden," I whisper, hoping she's a light sleeper, but she doesn't stir. "Arden, wake up," I try again, and this time she moves, but then settles back in with her neck even more hunched than it was before. On instinct, I slide my hand under her cheek, tilting it so she's in a more comfortable position. She nuzzles into me, and I let out a pained exhale because I know what I need to do since she's not waking up on her own.

I gently grasp the wrist above her head, bringing it down to join the other on her belly before easing under and lifting her exhausted body into my arms. She sighs but never wakes up as I carry her toward the stairs, taking them as gracefully as possible so she stays asleep. Heat radiates from my chest, and she melts into me, making me suck in a shaky breath because I hate how good it feels. Just like earlier, I have her pulled close, but it's not enough. I want more.

I fight the baffling thought, making my way to the landing and through her door, stopping when my thighs hit the side of her bed. I steal a quick inhale of her sweet scent one last time before bending down and laying her on the soft mattress. She whimpers so quietly that I almost don't hear it, yet she doesn't rouse as I go to back away. Only I don't get far when I realize that both of her hands are clutching the fabric of my t-shirt.

"Fuck. Arden," I whisper, trying to pull away slowly, but this girl has to be the heaviest sleeper I've ever met, because even with a death grip on me, she's still out cold. With no other choice but to yank it out of her fists—which I'm not doing because I refuse to wake her when she's this tired—I lift her up, sit on the bed, and lean back against the pillow with her in my lap. She settles as my heart pounds so heavily in my chest that I can't believe she's still asleep with the way it's thudding against her ear. There are so many reasons I shouldn't be doing this, yet I can't seem to rip myself away. She's soft and warm, and her hair smells like heaven. The fact that she's oblivious to the way I'm soaking it all in makes it even worse, because if she were awake, would she *want* me touching her? Would she be okay with how close we are? Or would she push me away? I can't find a single fuck to give right now, though. Not with the way I feel calm—truly at peace—with her tucked into my body. It's been a long fucking time since I've experienced anything even close to this.

It isn't long before her grip loosens, and my shirt falls from her fingers. As much as I want to stay here with her for as long as I can, I know it's only a matter of time before she wakes up. I need to slip out of here unnoticed. Hopefully, she ends up thinking that Jackson brought her to her room, or that she got up here by herself and just doesn't remember. I'm sure the last thing on her mind will be that I was the one who carried her, especially given how I've been so cold for the past few weeks.

If I was smart, I'd keep that up. Holding her against me right now just solidifies what I already knew. I feel something for Arden. I have since the first time I met her, and although it was just an afterthought back then, having her in my arms is making me realize that the closer she is, the more I want to know what draws me to her.

I turn slowly, sliding her off of me and making sure her neck and head are comfortable before settling my feet on the floor and looking around for a blanket. I find a heavy throw draped across the bottom of the bed, pull it over her, and slowly back away, taking in her beautiful face for a few more moments. I wish I had the courage to really dig into my emotions and examine the feelings I have when I'm around her. But what good would that do, anyway? It's not like I can tell her and ask if she could ever see herself wanting to get to know each other on a deeper level. I'm far too broken for that. She'd take one look inside my dark soul and run the other way. She deserves someone like Jacks, who isn't afraid to be himself and show his heart to the people he cares about. Part of me almost wishes he'd just man up and tell her that he's been obsessed with her since they were kids, instead of this bullshit where he pretends like it never happened. She may be oblivious to it, but I see the way he looks at her when he thinks nobody's watching.

Either way, we're both feeling things we shouldn't, and I need to work on my own shit so I don't end up hurting anyone. I know I wouldn't survive losing Jackson…but the unexplainable connection I have to Arden is getting harder and harder to fight.

EIGHT
ARDEN

"SERVE'S UP!" I yell as one of our backup hitters sends the ball over the net. We're scrimmaging against our second-string players, although they're not playing like that's what they are. They won the first set, twenty-five to seventeen, and now we're struggling to keep up. You'd think that after almost two months of playing together, we'd be falling into a rhythm. However, with so many strong personalities from all over the world who've played at different levels, we're still working out the kinks. Most days are good, but today isn't one of them. The passing has been messy, there's been some minor miscommunication with my set signals, and hits are going out of bounds. Players are running into each other while switching positions—it's just been *rough*.

The serve goes to Zara, and she puts it up in the air, a loud smack echoing through the court as the ball bounces off her arms. It's right over my head and tight to the net, which makes it the perfect pass. My left outside hitter, Alaina Reeves, is ready and waiting, but I see a big opening in the middle of the floor that the other team has left unguarded, so I decide to change the plan to ensure we get the side-out.

I call for the four set, which is a high one to Alaina, but instead, I wait until the ball is almost at my finger-tips before launching myself up and using my right hand to tip it directly into the large, vacant space behind the blockers. Their back row catches on a little too late, diving for it but missing as it bounces off the floor.

"Yes!" I shout as my teammates run in to celebrate, returning high fives and smiles. Everyone is cheering loudly, a new fire lit under us to close the two-point deficit we're currently working with as the ball rolls under the net for us to serve.

"Levine!" Dahlia screams, blowing her whistle loudly as she storms onto the court. "Want to explain to me why you dumped the ball instead of setting Alaina while she's hot?" She's been on my ass all day, stopping the plays to point out what I'm doing wrong, when that's not the case at all. Just because I'm not doing things exactly her way doesn't mean they aren't working.

"There was a hole," I reply, trying not to show how fucking annoyed I am. I know she's my coach and I need to treat her with respect, but I swear she has it out for me. The team voted me captain last month because I'm a good leader and I know this game like the back of my hand. I just wish she'd let me run things the way I need to in the middle of a play. "I got the point. Why does it matter how it happened?"

Her eyes go wide and her nostrils flare as she steps closer, lowering her voice so the rest of the team, who've stopped cheering and are standing wordlessly while watching the exchange, can't hear. "Watch your fucking mouth, Arden. You may think you call the shots inside these lines, but you're wrong. Either you run the plays the way I tell you to, or your ass will be on a plane back to Pennsylvania." A devious smile curves her lips and she lowers her voice even more. "The owner and general manager may see something in you, but you aren't fooling me. You're expendable, and I have no problem benching you if you don't get your shit together. Understood?"

I swallow, nodding as I feel my cheeks heat. My heart is pounding out of my chest, and I can feel the anxiety as it snakes its way through my body, slowly beginning to wrap itself around my lungs. I need to stay calm, but it's hard when her threat hit as hard as it did. Volleyball is my life. It's where I feel the most at home. Playing at a professional level is something I've dreamed of since the first time I touched the court, and the pressure to be perfect so it doesn't get taken away from me is almost more than I can handle at times. I felt the same way in Argentina, but even though I did everything I could, I still failed. I *can't* lose this again.

"Good. Now show me that drafting you wasn't a fucking mistake." She flips her long dark hair over her shoulder and struts back to the sideline as I try to pull myself away from the edge of the panic attack that's threatening to suck me in. I can't do that here—not in front of my team. Not in front of *her*. I need to put on my mask and pretend I'm okay until I get home. Then I can break down and feel my emotions alone where nobody else can see, just like I always do.

The rest of practice goes by in a blur. I focus on not straying from the plays Dahlia wants, instead of reading the court and doing what I think is best. My heart feels like it's being squeezed in a vice grip every time the ball comes my way, but I somehow manage to avoid fucking up, even though my brain is trying to convince me that I don't have what it takes to be here— that it's only a matter of time before I'm cut from the team and living back in Tinsville, wishing I could've just been good enough.

As soon as my shoes are changed and all my gear is in my bag, I toss it over my shoulder and wordlessly walk out of the facility, not even bothering to shower or stick around while the others pack up. As the team captain, I make it a point to be the first one here and the last one to leave every day, but today…I just *can't.* I need to get out of here before anyone sees how fucking weak and unstable I really am, especially when I do everything I can to fool them into thinking the exact opposite.

I'm on autopilot as I make the long drive home, my mind going a million miles a minute with so many intrusive thoughts that I can barely register one before the next barrels toward me. My eyes are filled with unshed tears, and I hold them back for as long as I can until there's nowhere else for them to go but down my cheeks. But I refuse to break down until I'm locked in my room, where nobody can see me. Where I can let my anxiety consume me, take from me, and eventually leave me alone until the next time.

The elevator ride from the lobby seems to go on for hours, and I barely even take a breath because I'm still holding everything inside. My chest is unbearably tight, and if I hadn't been through this thousands of times over the years, I'd swear I was having a heart attack. The pit in my stomach is like a hundred-pound weight, the pressure inside me so intense that I feel like I can barely move as the suffocating metal box opens and I mindlessly make my way to the door of our condo. Placing my fingertip on the keypad, I watch as it blinks green before pushing the lever and entering the dark space.

The moment I know I'm inside and alone, with the guys still not back from their away trip, I break down. My bag falls from my shoulder, dropping to the floor with a thud as I take a few steps back, only stopping when the thick wood of the door presses against me. I lean on it as heavy tears spill over, running down my cheeks and soaking the fabric of my shirt. My legs wobble violently as I let go, dropping to my hands and knees because I can no longer bear the weight of my own body.

"No. No, no," I whisper over and over through sobs. I can't do this right here in the entryway. If Jackson and Hawk come home and find me like this, they'll know how bad things are, and I don't want them to see what a weak, pathetic girl I've become. So, I crawl. I do everything I can to move myself toward the stairs, knowing that if I can just get to my room and into the shower, I'll be able to ride this out by myself and act like nothing ever happened.

"You can do it. *Leg, arm, leg, arm,*" I say on broken breaths, willing my limbs to do what I want and get me out of the main area of the house. But they're heavy and I can't breathe—and the stairs are so far away, I don't think I can make it.

When it becomes too much, and I feel like every movement is depleting my oxygen supply, I give up, curling into the wall beside me, hugging my knees to my chest, and letting my anxiety pull me under…alone.

NINE
HAWK

I STEP out of the elevator, exhausted from a long game and an even longer flight. Jackson had to meet with the trainer to have his hamstring worked on, and normally I'd have hung around since we drove together, but I could barely keep my eyes open as I waited for our bags to be unloaded from the team plane. I tossed him the keys to my truck and got a car to bring me home, because God only knows how long his treatment will take. All I want is to sleep for an entire twenty-four hours, starting right now.

I drag my aching feet down the hallway to our door, placing my finger on the lock pad and listening for the telltale *click.* As soon as it disengages, I push my way inside. It's after nine at night, so I'm surprised when I don't at least see the glow from the TV, where Arden usually binges reality shows after practice. Maybe she's as tired as I am and already went to bed—or maybe she's out. The idea of her on a date with a random guy in Daytona immediately floods my mind, making my blood simmer in my veins. I think of all the bad shit that could happen to her, and I'm here, unable to help.

She may not belong to me, but I'll happily murder anyone who hurts her.

I slide the dimmer on the wall up, blanketing the living area in a low light as I head toward it. But a quiet, shaky gasp stops me in my tracks. I freeze, listening intently, stilling my own breaths until I hear it again. As soon as my eyes lock onto the source of the sound, I leap into action, dropping my bags where I stand and rushing over to where Arden is slumped in a heap against the wall of the entryway. She's visibly shaking, a blank expression covering her tear-stained face. Her knees are hugged to her chest with her arms wrapped tightly around them as she absent-mindedly rocks herself back and forth.

"Hey," I say, lowering myself to her level, cradling her cheeks in my hands, and tilting her head so she's looking at me. She stares right into my eyes, but it's like she's not there at all. "What happened? Who did this to you?" I'm trying to keep my voice calm because she's in the middle of one of the scariest panic attacks I've ever witnessed, but if I don't figure out what the fuck is going on, I'll burn this whole fucking city to the ground without asking a single question.

She sucks in a sharp breath. "I-I…" she struggles to push the words out, trailing off as they get caught in her throat. I wait, hoping she'll give me more, but she doesn't. She just continues looking through me with her eyes full of tears, tremors racking her fragile body while she falls deeper into the episode.

"I'm here, Hellcat," I whisper, rubbing my thumbs back and forth along her cheeks. I feel like I'm on the verge of spiraling myself, since I'm usually on the other end of these fucking things—but she needs me right now, and I have to focus on pulling her back to the present. "I need you to come back to me. Find me, Arden. Follow my voice."

"Hawk," she chokes out, attempting to gasp for air. Hearing her say my name is a relief, but we're not out of the woods yet—not by a long shot. If her anxiety is anything like mine, she's in another place right now, where she's in danger, and she either has to fight her way out or let it overtake her.

"Yeah. I'm with you. I'm not going anywhere. You're safe." With those words, her gaze focuses on mine, and although her expression is still blank, I swear she sees me. She's no longer looking *through* me; she's looking *inside* me. That's when I realize that her demons match mine. This beautiful, pure, sweet girl is battling something bigger than anyone knows, and the thought fucking kills me.

"It hurts," she whimpers weakly. "*Please.*"

As soon as the plea falls from her lips, I know there's no turning back. I'll deal with the consequences of my actions later. Right now, I have to get her out of the darkness. She doesn't belong there.

I tighten my grip on her face, leaning forward and pressing my mouth to hers. She's stiff at first, but when I part her lips with my tongue, plunging it inside, she lets out a sigh of relief. Her body relaxes as she returns the kiss, telling me that I made the right decision. I'm sure once it's over and I have time to replay the entire thing, my guilt will be all-consuming, but for now, I'm doing this for her.

I lick and suck gently—much gentler than I'm used to. A needy moan tumbles from her lips as she climbs to her knees and pushes me back onto my ass. I allow her to take what she needs as she straddles my lap, crashing her mouth to mine again and drawing every last molecule of air from my body. My head spins as her strawberry scent envelopes me, and I give in to my own desires for just a second. Instinctively, I wrap my arms around her waist, pulling her as close as I can—because if I'm going to betray my best friend and take this from the only girl he's ever loved, I might as well go all in.

Her fists ball over the fabric of my t-shirt, and her hips shift just enough to give me a taste of the hot friction I'd sell my soul for right now, but I restrain myself from doing what I really want—thrusting up into her so she can feel exactly what she's doing to me. Her moans and my growls fill the quiet room, and it makes me wonder what sounds she'd make when I sank inside her for the first time. Would she gasp? Scream? Cry? My cock weeps inside my boxer briefs, painfully hard and desperate to find out. My entire body is begging me to take her to my room and tie her up so I can feast on her the way I've been fantasizing about since the moment I met her, but I know I can't do that. I've already crossed enough lines just by kissing her. I can't lose Jackson. I wouldn't survive it.

Minutes go by as we make out, losing ourselves in one another until she eventually slows her movements.

I can tell the moment reality hits her because she goes rigid in my arms, an audible swallow working its way down her delicate throat as she backs away, until she climbs off me altogether, resting her ass on her feet as she fidgets with a hole in the knee of her leggings. I hate the distance immediately, although I'm used to it at this point. I wish we could just *exist* right now without having to worry about how it's going to hurt the one person we care about most in the world, but that's not our story. It never will be.

"I'm sorry," she says quietly, pushing a piece of chocolate-brown hair behind her ear. "I don't know what happened. I'm so tired and I didn't have a great practice. I think I jus—"

"You don't have to explain anything, Arden," I reply coldly. I shouldn't be hurt by the fact that she's lying about whatever triggered that episode, but I am. I know it's my own fault. I've done nothing but keep her at arm's length since she arrived. I can't expect her to trust me with something so vulnerable.

"Okay," she replies, pushing up to her feet. She stands there awkwardly for several beats, neither of us saying a word. My brain is screaming at me to tell her I see her—that I'm all too familiar with the things she just experienced—but my mouth won't say the words. I can't let her in like that, because I know if I do, I'll want to keep her. So instead, I say nothing, watching as she takes off up the stairs like her ass is on fire.

"Shit," I mutter, scrubbing my shaking hands down my face. Now that it's over and she's okay, I realize how everything that just went down affected me. Should I have kissed her? No, probably not. But I needed to shock her system. What better way to do that than to give her the last fucking thing she expected?

Fuck, she tasted good. And the way she gripped my shirt when she held me close had me wishing the situation was different so I could rid her head of the shit that's fucking with her—even if it were only for tonight.

I stay put for a few minutes longer, listening as the shower in Arden's room turns on and wondering if she's doing okay up there. Panic attacks can be extremely draining on your mind and body, and I hope she isn't in any pain now that it's over.

The door swings open, snapping me back to reality as Jackson hobbles through, clearly still struggling with his hamstring. His eyes land on me, still sitting with my elbows resting on my knees in the middle of the entryway. His brows knit in confusion as he drops his bag next to mine.

"What the hell are you doing on the floor?" he asks, and I don't know what to tell him. I know he's aware of Arden's anxiety, but I have no idea if he realizes the extent of it. I'd like to think she's opened up to him about it now that their friendship seems to be moving in the right direction, but maybe she hasn't. I know him, and if he was privy to what I walked into tonight, he'd be worried sick, hovering over her and overwhelming her when she needs rest. *So, I lie.*

For the first time ever, I fucking lie to my best friend.

"I dropped my phone, and it slid under the table." I reach into the pocket of my sweats, fishing out the device and holding it up like it hasn't been in there since I walked through the door. I'm a shit liar, so I'm assuming he'll see right through me, but I think he's too uncomfortable to care.

"Oh. Okay," he replies, limping past as I push to my feet. I dip under his arm, letting him lean his weight onto me while I lead him to the couch. "I'm fine, Hawk. I can walk. It's just sore."

"I know," I say. "I'm just helping you get settled. Then I'll fuck off and you can go back to being impossible."

He scoffs as I help him turn so he can lower himself onto the plush cushions. "Pot, meet kettle. You're the most combative person I know when you're injured. So is Arden. You two are a *match* made in heaven. Or hell."

My eyes go wide. "We're not a *match*," I rush out. "I barely even know her."

But I know what she tastes like.

"Whose fault is that? We agreed to do better, and you've barely given her anything," he scolds, pulling both legs up onto the couch. "She's trying, dude. But every time she gets close, you back away. She's a good person and an amazing friend. She's not going to hurt you."

I force an exhale, because would he even be saying this if he knew I just kissed her while she was in such a vulnerable state? He has no idea how aware I am of his feelings for her, but I know. He fucking loves her even though he can't have her, and I just took something that he'd give anything to experience.

Which makes me undeserving of them both.

TEN
ARDEN

"JUST GO TALK TO HIM," I mumble as I wear a path into the carpet at the foot of my bed. I've been pacing back and forth since I got out of the shower, feeling unsettled about what happened with Hawk. To be honest, I don't remember much before his lips met mine, but I can still feel them as I consider my next move.

As much as I know he only did it to snap me out of my panic attack, all I can think about is how I wish I could experience that kiss again, this time with full awareness. I'd give anything to feel his hot tongue pressed against mine for just a few more seconds, since I wasn't in the proper mental state to burn every detail of how he tasted into my memory. But it's not a possibility, and I need to accept that.

I have two choices right now. I can either pretend it never happened and make shit even more awkward than it's already been around here, or I can suck it up and address it. He just saw me at my absolute worst, and as embarrassed as I am, it'll only make me more anxious if I don't speak to him sooner, rather than later.

"You're fine," I say to my reflection in the full-length mirror that stands against the wall. "People have panic attacks every day. He helped you through it. Go thank him and get it over with. You'll feel so much better after." I smooth my oversized shirt down my thighs, making sure it's not too indecent to leave the room. After my shower, my body felt depleted of energy, and the best I could do was toss my hair up in a messy bun and throw on an old, comfy t-shirt with a pair of cotton panties. It's kind of my post-breakdown uniform, and definitely a go-to look when I'm feeling as exhausted as I am right now.

I give myself one last once-over before walking to the door and taking a deep, calming breath. As soon as I swing it open, I can hear the low hum of the TV coming from downstairs. I assume both guys are here since it's so late, so I peek over the banister as I pass, seeing Jackson's messy sandy-brown hair as he rests his head on the couch. His right leg is up on the ottoman, and I honestly can't tell if he's awake or asleep. But the lights are off and he looks to be alone down there, so I pad to the other end of the hall, stopping when I get to Hawk's room. I stand there for far too long, the familiar feeling of dread starting in the pit of my stomach and working its way up my throat until I feel like I'm choking on it.

What if he regrets kissing me? What if he thinks I'm some weak, fragile girl who can't handle a bad day without having a meltdown? It's bad enough that he found me curled up on the floor, but the fact that he had to guide me through it is so fucking humiliating.

Just as I'm about to turn and walk away because I simply can't bring myself to knock, the door swings open, revealing a nearly naked Hawk on the other side. My eyes lock onto his chest first, then roam to the tattoos that decorate both of his toned arms. It's too dark to make out what they are since the only light is coming from a small lamp next to his bed, but they're beautiful. *He's beautiful.* Each defined muscle is on display, a pair of short black boxer briefs the only thing stopping me from seeing his entire form. I fail miserably at not soaking in every inch of him, including the bulge that's straining against the tight fabric. I've never seen a human being so perfect in my entire life, and I'm in complete awe as he stands before me in all his sexy-as-sin glory. My braless nipples harden under the thin material of my t-shirt, and I let out a shuddered breath as my eyes slide up to his.

"Are you okay?" he asks, snapping me back to reality. My cheeks heat because there's no way he didn't notice me eye-fucking his gigantic dick for the last three minutes, but I'm grateful he isn't pointing it out. I hold his stare, taking note of the concern in his expression as he waits for me to answer.

"I'm—" I say, choking on the words as I nod my head rapidly. "Yeah. Thanks. Goodnight." I spin quickly, just wanting to get out of here before I humiliate myself further, but I don't get a single step before his large hand wraps around my wrist and he pulls me into his room, shutting the door behind us.

"Stop hiding from me, Arden," he says through clenched teeth. "What's going on?"

I swallow the lump in my throat. The last thing I want is to unload all the bullshit that happened today onto him when things are already so weird between us. I want to have a friendship with him, but he's not going to want that if he thinks I'm a basket case. I need to keep shit light so he'll stop acting like he can't stand being around me.

"Nothing," I lie quietly. "I just had a bad day at practice. It's really not a big deal. What happened downstairs…it wasn't wha—"

"Stop lying to me," he whisper-yells, taking a step closer. "I've never seen a panic attack that bad before. You were fucking *gone*. I wasn't sure if I'd be able to bring you back. So, tell me what the fuck happened."

Tears fill my eyes, but I blink them away, taking a deep breath and looking down at the floor before speaking. "There's just so much pressure. My whole team needs me to be perfect, and I'm failing them. I come home at night and replay every single thing I did wrong, racking my brain for ways to fix it, but maybe I'm just not enough." I look up at him, shaking my head. "I'm losing my mind, Hawk. And then all of that," I say, motioning toward the door. "You found me freaking out and kissed me, then I practically forced myself on you. I'm so fucking embarrassed. I'm sor—"

"You think you *forced yourself on me*?" he says, reaching out and collaring his hand around my throat. It catches me off guard and my eyes go wide as he steps closer, pushing me back until I'm wedged between him and the door. The hard wood cools the scorching skin under my shirt, and my head spins with every heaving exhale that puffs against my lips. "I was fucking terrified when I came inside and saw you on the floor. I'd have done anything to help you. But if you think I haven't spent every goddamn second since you moved in wondering what you'd taste like, or what sounds you'd make as you rubbed that warm, sweet cunt all over me, you're wrong. It's haunted my dreams, Arden."

My mouth falls open and I suck in a breath, surprised by his admission. He's been hot and cold toward me for months, so hearing him say he's wanted to kiss me is a shock, to say the least. My pulse beats wildly against his fingertips, and I lick my lips, watching as his eyes catch on the movement. He looks conflicted, lust crossing over his features as he presses his body to mine even tighter. I can feel his massive erection against my stomach, and I gasp loudly as he grinds it into me.

"Are you really surprised, Hellcat?" he drawls, dropping his lips to my ear. "The way you walk around here looking like *that*, with those hard nipples practically begging me to suck on them until you explode. Or those short fucking spandex you wear that show every goddamn curve and dip in your thighs—I'd give anything to mark them up with my teeth. I want to *wreck you*. It consumes every part of me."

"Then do it," I breathe. "Tear me apart. I don't want to feel anything but you."

He pulls back, his blue eyes burning into mine as

several emotions pass over his face in rapid succession. Each one is gone before I can really make it out, but I'm feeling more and more uncomfortable with each second that passes as he stares at me. Just as I blindly reach behind myself for the doorknob so I can get out of here before he tells me why we can't, he squeezes his fingers, pressing them firmly into the sides of my neck.

"He's going to fucking hate me," he says quietly. Before I can even ask what he means, he lunges forward, pressing his mouth to mine in a kiss so intense that I can feel my lips swelling from the force almost immediately. He parts them with his tongue, plunging it inside as I moan into his mouth. Hot sparks ignite throughout my body, swirling around and gathering between my legs. I bring one around his hip, hooking my ankle behind his thigh to draw him even closer, not that it's possible. We're practically fused together as we kiss and grind, quiet whimpers and growls being traded and swallowed as we devour each other like we need it to survive.

He reaches around, gripping my ass in both hands as he lifts me into his arms. I lock my ankles around his lower back, using them as leverage to rub my core against his rock-hard length. He helps by moving me up and down, and I imagine what it would be like if we didn't have any underwear between us. The way he's lifting me, I could slide right down on his cock, giving myself the fullness that my inner walls are currently clenching in search of. Would it be stupid to go further with Hawk right now with the way everything went down tonight? Yes. But I just want to let my mind go quiet, numbing myself from all the negative thoughts that plague me.

"You're killing me, Hellcat," he growls against my lips. "I want to bend you over my lap and spank this ass until you cry for tasting so good."

"Oh my God," I whimper, his dirty words like a lightning strike to my throbbing clit. As worked up as I am, it still feels as though my orgasm is miles away, so I squeeze my legs tighter, begging for more friction. He gives it, coasting his lips down my neck and licking from one side to the other before sinking his teeth into the sensitive skin under my ear. I moan out loud, my eyes rolling back with pleasure, but he stops abruptly when we hear a muffled *thud* coming from outside the door. In an instant, I'm standing on my feet and he's backing away like I'm on fire, adjusting himself before his hands shoot to his hair.

"It's Jacks," he rushes out, panic lacing his tone. "I have to go." I stumble out of the way just in time for him to rip the door open and run toward the stairs, my jaw hanging open and shame washing over me like hot lava. Tears well in my eyes again, this time because I can't shake the look of regret on his face as I awkwardly stand here by myself.

"I told you, I'm fine," I hear Jacks say from the other end of the hall "It's a goddamn muscle pull. I didn't break a hip. Go back to bed."

"You almost fell down the stairs, you fucking asshole," Hawk grunts, and I peek out, watching as he slides under Jackson's arm and helps him hobble to his room. Their backs are to me, so I wait until they're out of sight before quietly slipping into the hallway and back to my own bedroom, shutting and locking the door behind me.

Stupidly, I wait for him to come knock. But as the minutes tick by and I hear rustling in the distance, followed by silence, I slip under the covers, trying my best to fall asleep while I think about what just happened, and how truly fucked I am.

ELEVEN
JACKSON

"THIS SUCKS," I mumble to myself, quietly making my way to the kitchen to get breakfast started. Taking a few days off to rest my hamstring worked wonders, but it feels like I tweak it differently every game, so it's still bothering me. I talked to the team doctor this morning and he wants me to come in to get it checked out again this afternoon, so we can decide whether I'll need to be put on the disabled list for any amount of time. I hope not, since playoffs are right around the corner, but I also know the importance of taking injuries seriously to prevent them from becoming worse.

I walk gingerly to the cupboard, pull out a pan, and head to the refrigerator for some eggs. One by one, I crack them into a large bowl, assuming I won't be the only one eating this morning. Hawk and I don't have to be at the stadium until noon, but Arden will be out the door long before then for practice.

I busy myself, whisking and pouring the eggs into the pan, the low sizzle of them meeting the heat below filling the quiet room. I get lost in my thoughts, not realizing I'm no longer alone until I see Arden step up in front of the coffee maker out of the corner of my eye. She's barely awake, wearing only a t-shirt and panties—and as usual—I have to actively will myself not to look. I may have gotten my shit together with the way I used to want more with her, but the physical attraction has only gotten stronger over the years. I wish there was a way to make it stop, but there just *isn't*. She's drop-dead gorgeous, and her body is as close to perfection as it gets. A guy would have to be blind or crazy not to think so—and I'm neither.

"Morning, Princess," I say, startling her as she drops her empty mug onto the counter, taking a deep breath before looking at me with a tired smile. She looks like she was up all night, the dark circles under her eyes telling me I'm probably right in that assumption. I quickly make sure the eggs are cooked thoroughly before turning off the stove and walking over to take the cup, placing it under the spout of the machine just as hot liquid begins funneling out. She doesn't say a word as she huffs a defeated exhale, putting her elbows on the counter and dropping her head into her open palms.

"Hey," I mutter softly, pulling on her arm until she's standing straight, then yanking her into a tight embrace. Her body melts into mine like it always does when she's feeling anxious, and I revel in the fact that I can still be a source of comfort for her, even after all the years we had too much space between us. *Space that I put there, but whatever.* "What's wrong?"

"I'm just tired," she replies, wrapping her small arms around my waist. "Rough practice yesterday, and I didn't sleep well."

"You sure?" I ask, loosening my hold just enough to lean back and study her face for any signs that something else is going on. I want her to know she can talk to me, even if I do overreact sometimes. I try not to, but my protective instinct toward her has been at the same intensity since I was eight years old. I can't just turn it on and off, as much as I'm sure Arden wishes I could.

"Mhmm," she hums quietly, resting her cheek on my chest as I tighten my grip on her again. We stand there for a couple of minutes until Hawk rounds the corner, stepping into the kitchen. He stops abruptly, his normal blank expression morphing into one of bewilderment as he takes us in.

"Eggs are on the stove," I say, lifting my chin to where they're still sitting in the pan. At my words, Arden stiffens in my arms, pulling away and clearing her throat before she turns. She takes her full cup from the machine and walks over to the table, sitting down in one of the wooden chairs. I notice the way the vibe in the room changed when he came in, and I hope he hasn't said or done anything to upset her. He seemed more comfortable with her when we hung out last week, but that's Hawk. One minute he's fine, the next he's shutting you out. I know it's his upbringing that causes him to be so guarded around people, but I'm hoping eventually, he starts to trust her. They'd be good for each other. She'd open him up, and he'd provide another safe space for her here in Daytona. Someone who lives the pro athlete life and knows how full of ups and downs it can be.

"Thanks," he grunts, rounding the island and preparing a plate before setting it down beside her at the table. She looks up at him, her eyes full of puzzlement as he lowers himself into the seat next to hers. A small smile tugs at the corner of her mouth, and the fucker *returns it*, making my jaw practically bounce off the counter as it drops. It's not that he doesn't smile because, as much as our teammates would like to disagree, he does. He just has to be in a situation where he's comfortable enough to do it—which is why this is pretty big. Maybe he and Arden really are warming up to each other. Although I have a feeling he'd be more talkative if I weren't standing here watching them.

"I, uhh…" I stammer, trying to come up with an excuse for why I need to leave, even though I just made us food. They both turn as I pick up my phone from the counter in front of me, flailing it above my head wildly. "I got a text! I have to go!"

"I can help you," Hawk says, standing from his chair. But I cut him off, pushing my hand in his direction to stop him as I limp toward the door.

"No, no. I'm fine," I rush out. "You two stay here and eat up. I'll see you later…after the *thing* I have to do…from the text." They both stare at me like I'm crazy as I haul ass out of the room, cringing at my own awkward exit and hoping I didn't make things so weird that they don't stay here together after I'm gone.

Because, more than anything, I desperately want my best friends to be best friends, too.

HAWK

"That was weird, right?" I say to Arden as Jackson hustles out the front door, leaving us alone in the quiet condo.

She looks into her cup of coffee with a small smile, but it doesn't reach her eyes. "I've learned to never expect anything less from him. I'd think you'd know that by now too."

"Yeah," I reply. "You're right." She's avoiding eye contact, and I can feel the tension in the air as she fidgets with the handle of her mug, sliding the tip of her pointer finger up and down it while watching like it's the most interesting thing in the world.

I hate how awkward this all feels. I wanted to talk to her more last night, but when I returned to my room, she was already gone. I didn't want Jacks to hear me knocking on her door, so I went back to bed, tossing and turning for hours because it's all so fucking confusing.

I never should've kissed her. I was stupid to think I could convince myself it was a one-and-done thing to help her through the panic attack she was having. Because as soon as she walked away, I knew I wanted more. Her coming to my room to talk to me hours later only made things more complicated, since I couldn't restrain myself then, either. Kissing the way we were, with only a couple of thin layers of fabric separating us, had me ready to risk everything—because I wasn't even thinking about Jacks. All I cared about was that Arden was pressed against me, and I craved so much more than I could ever allow myself to have. I wanted to tie her up. Whip her. Spank her. Fuck every hole in her body until she was passed out, her exhausted limbs hanging from each one of my bedposts while spit and cum dripped from her skin. Instead, I pulled away like she had the plague when I heard him coming up the stairs, and that was the end.

I fucking hated leaving it like that, especially when she was vulnerable.

"About last night," I begin, but she cuts me off.

"It's fine. We don't have to talk about it. I don't know what got into me. I just had a really stressful practice. I need to learn how to handle stuff like that better. Let's just forget it ever happened. Please?" She looks my way with a pleading expression, and my heart cracks beneath the wall of ice that protects it. I hate that she's downplaying what she went through because she doesn't think she can talk to me about it. I get her apprehension because we don't truly know each other —but I don't want it to be like this. There's only one way to make her understand that I see her, and it's not going to be easy for me, since it's the one thing I normally avoid at all costs. I need to let her in.

I turn my body so I'm facing her, keeping my eyes trained on the mug in her hand because, as much as I know I have to say the words, I can't look at her while I do. "I get them too," I say quietly.

"You get what?" she asks, abandoning her coffee and turning toward me. Her bare knee brushes mine with the movement, and my eyes are drawn to the barely-there connection as warmth ghosts over my skin.

When I came into the kitchen and saw Jacks holding her, I'll admit I felt a pang of jealousy. Not because he was touching her—I like the bond they have and watching them strengthen it again after all the time they lost. I was jealous because he made it look so effortless. He provides her with the kind of familiar comfort that makes her feel safe and warm—and I hate knowing that no matter how hard I try, I'll never be able to do that. I'm too fucking broken. I have too many issues of my own for her to ever feel that security with me. None-theless, for reasons I can't explain, I wish she could.

I swallow hard as anxiety flows through my veins because, other than Jackson and my therapist, nobody knows this part of me. But I think telling her could help us both. "Panic attacks. Where you feel like you can't breathe, like you're going to die right where you stand —and there's no way to stop it from happening. I've been able to keep them at bay for the most part, but every now and then, they still hit me out of nowhere."

Her eyes soften and she pulls her bottom lip between her teeth, sinking them into the plump skin. I want to reach out and pull it free, but I don't, because I've already been selfish enough. I don't suspect that my cravings for Arden will go away any time soon, but I'm still conflicted about them, and I need to remember that my friendship with Jackson could be at stake if I'm not careful.

"How do you keep them under control?" she asks, barely a whisper. "I thought I was doing good until I came back from Argentina. Then, I started to feel more and more anxious when I thought about how badly I had failed. Now, it's on a whole other level. There's so much pressure to be perfect for my team—and for myself, so I don't get benched or cut. Sometimes I'm fine. Other times, I feel like the weight of the world is on my shoulders. It would be nice just to be able to let it all go, but I don't know how."

"It's a tightrope act," I reply. "I used to take meds for it, but there were too many side effects, so I had to find other ways to cope and get out of my own head. I still see the team therapist at least once a month to check in—sometimes more if I need to. There's no shame in asking for help, Arden."

She nods her head, shrugging. "Women's sports aren't exactly valued in our society, so we don't have all the perks you guys do. We have a team trainer, and there are doctors we can see if we get injured, but there aren't any mental health professionals on the Flare staff. My insurance covers it, but when I checked, the wait to see someone was weeks long. It seemed so daunting that I gave up. I thought if I just worked harder, I wouldn't be so stressed, and it would all go away."

On instinct, I reach out, placing my hand on her leg, just above the knee. It catches us both off guard because we simultaneously look down at the connection as though it's the most shocking thing we've ever seen.

Other than the occasional *We'll get 'em next time* to my teammates after a loss, I haven't attempted to comfort someone since my brothers were still around. But she needs it right now, and even though I may be shit at it, I want to try.

Rubbing my thumb over her warm, silky skin in slow circles, I meet her gaze with mine, conveying as much understanding as I'm capable of. "Jacks and I will do whatever we can, you know that, right? If you need help paying or finding somewhere to go, we'll take care of it. You shouldn't have to feel this way."

"Thank you," she whispers. "I'll make an appointment. But in the meantime, want to tell me about the other ways I could clear my head?"

Do I *want* to tell her? Fuck, yeah. I'd love to go into detail about the ways I could get her to let go for me. How I could turn her into an empty-headed little sub that I would bend and control at the snap of a finger. Flashes of Arden in a collar and leash, crawling behind me as I stroke her hair and tell her what a sweet little pet she is, play in my mind like a porno, and I hope she doesn't notice the way my cock twitches under the material of my shorts. I can't say any of that out loud. Hell, I shouldn't even be *thinking it*. But at this point, she's consuming my thoughts, so the best I can hope for is that she doesn't read me and realize what kind of filthy fucking fantasies I have about her.

"Maybe some other time, Hellcat," I reply, putting the subject to bed and turning back to my plate. I feel her gaze burn into me for a moment before she does the same, placing both hands on her mug and lifting it to her mouth. I try not to watch out of the corner of my eye as she swallows, licking the last drop from her plump lips and making me fight against the groan that's working its way up my throat.

This is fucking bad. Seeing how Jackson helps her and knowing that I might possibly have a way to bring her solace—albeit in a much different way—is killing me already. But would it be worth breaking his heart to give her what she needs?

I'm fighting it for now, but the tiny voice in the back of my head is telling me it's only a matter of time before I find out.

TWELVE
ARDEN

"IS this pity party open to the public, or do I need an invitation?" I ask, hovering over Jackson as he sits on the floor with his back resting against the couch. When he went to visit with the team doctor last week, they were concerned about him tearing his hamstring with the way he kept tweaking it, so they put him on the disabled list. He's almost a week in and has at least one more to go before they'll put him back in the lineup, pending a clean bill of health.

He scrunches his nose, looking up at me. "I told the bouncer to keep the riffraff out, but I guess they're just letting anybody in." He smirks and I playfully kick his arm, but he grabs my ankle, lifting it to his mouth and nipping at the skin of my lower calf. I bark a laugh, yanking out of his grip as his smile grows wider, the dimple in his cheek sinking in like it always does when he's truly happy. It's a welcome change from how sad he's been, having to watch his team play without him while he sits here unable to help. I've been trying to lighten the mood, but I get it. I wouldn't be very good company if I were in his shoes right now, either.

"How was practice?" he asks, patting the floor beside him in invitation. I sit, letting my head fall back onto the couch cushion behind me as I take a deep breath and exhale slowly.

"Better than it has been. I'm starting to fall into a rhythm with my hitters, which took a while, but we're really working well together. I swear, no matter how good of a day we have, Dahlia digs until she finds something wrong so she can yell at me in front of my teammates. Today, Zara tried to stick up for me and she ended up getting chewed out, too."

"Didn't you guys go to Penn State together?" he asks.

I nod my head. "Yep. And she was always kind of underhandedly mean, but I was younger than her, so I stayed in my lane and did my job. Then she randomly quit one day, and since I was her backup, that was my shot."

"Quit?" he questions. "Why?"

"No clue," I respond. "The team was really good, but they lost a lot of graduating seniors before I got there, so it was almost like a rebuild. Everyone said it was because she knew we wouldn't win a National Championship, although I can't imagine ending my final college season because of that."

"Don't take it personally. Some people are never happy." He picks up the remote, switching the TV to the Fury game. They're on a five-day road trip, playing their last one in Milwaukee tonight before heading to

Minneapolis for two in a row. It's weird how much I miss Hawk. The condo feels a little emptier without him, and I find myself counting the days until he's back home.

I wonder if he misses me too.

After our talk in the kitchen last week, I made an appointment to meet with a therapist about my anxiety. He was right. I shouldn't do this on my own. It'll be another ten days before I can see her, but it's better than pretending everything is fine when I know it's not. I need to work on my coping skills and unpack my thoughts every once in a while so they don't eat me up inside. I'm grateful that he opened up to me the way he did because it showed me that I'm not alone, and admitting that I struggle sometimes doesn't make me weak—in fact, now that I've taken the first step, I feel so much stronger.

"Here we go," Jackson says as the game broadcast fills the eighty-five-inch screen that's mounted on the wall in front of us. My eyes immediately find Hawk as the camera pans to third base, and butterflies take flight in my stomach at the sight of his perfectly symmetrical face. Black hair that's faded up the sides shows beneath his teal Daytona Fury ballcap as he catches the ball in his glove, licking his lips before leisurely sending a warm-up throw back to first. I'm instantly reminded of the way they felt as needy groans passed from his mouth to mine while he held me like he didn't want an inch of space between us. It's been a week since we kissed, but I swear sometimes I can still taste him.

It isn't long before my eyes grow heavy and I rest

my head on Jackson's shoulder, using my hand to cover the tired yawn I can't hold back. He chuckles, settling further against the couch so we're both more comfortable. Today kicked my ass, and the late start time for this game isn't helping matters, even if it means I can stare unabashedly at Hawk without anyone knowing. But I don't even make it through the first inning before exhaustion pulls me under and I fall asleep cuddled into Jackson's warm body.

The muffled sound of game highlights on the TV brings me back to consciousness, and the first thing I feel is how stiff my back is. The weight of a thick, muscular arm presses into my shoulder and my eyes flutter open to find Jacks fast asleep, holding me with his head leaned back onto the cushion behind it. I pull my knees up, shifting myself in his direction to ease the pressure from the hard floor against my ass. I'm uncomfortable, but entirely too wiped out to go to my room right now—not to mention the way it feels being held by him. I shouldn't like it this much, but I do. I always have. He may be my stepbrother, but there was a time when I saw the possibility of something completely different.

I carefully tilt my head so I can take in his face, his

expression soft and carefree as shallow breaths leave his open lips. I allow myself to study him freely, admiring the flawless features and chiseled jawline that I used to secretly drool over as a teen. I'm not sure how he's changed so much, yet still looks the same after all these years—but I'm grateful to have memories of the boy he was, and excited to make more with the man he's become.

Dragging my gaze across his tan skin, my eyes catch on the chain around his neck when the light from the TV glimmers off it. The gold rope looks oddly familiar, and I furrow my brows as I wonder if it could possibly be what I think it is. My rational brain tells me there's no way because it's been so long, but I can't help myself. I have to know.

I reach up, gently wrapping my fingers around the warm metal, doing my best not to wake him as I gingerly pull it from where it's tucked under the collar of his shirt. As soon as the pendant comes into view, memories from the past flood my mind as if they happened just yesterday.

"What are you doing out here?" I asked, closing the sliding door to our back patio before making my way to where Jackson sat on the steps. He turned slightly, looking up at me and scooting over to make room. The cold from the wood seeped through my sweatpants as soon as I lowered myself down, and I had to suppress the full-body shiver that threatened to flow through me. Christmas in Pennsylvania was always chilly, and that year was no exception.

"I just needed some peace and quiet," he said, looking up at the stars that twinkled above us. I huffed a laugh, because

while it wasn't the first time he'd experienced one of my dad's over-the-top holiday get-togethers, it was the first one he couldn't escape since he was living with us now.

The second half of the year had been a whirlwind for us, with our parents' lightning-fast engagement, the wedding, college applications, and the amount of time we spent playing our respective sports. Jacks and I had grown apart despite the fact that we spent our nights under the same roof. I hated it. I missed my friend, but our lives were already moving in different directions. Soon, we'd only see each other on holidays and special occasions.

"Well, I'm glad I found you," I began. "With all the commotion, I didn't have time to give you your gift."

His head snapped my way, his eyes going wide with surprise. "I didn't know we were exchanging presents. I didn—"

"It's fine," I replied, waving a dismissive hand between us as I pulled the slender velvet box from the pocket of my hoodie and extended it toward him. His gaze locked onto it for a moment, guilt blanketing his expression as I shook it in invitation. "Oh my God, take it. You can buy me two birthday presents when you sign your giant MLB contract. I wear a size Mercedes C-Class, for future reference."

"Noted," he said with a laugh, wrapping his fingers around the box and pulling it from my hand. Slowly, he lifted the lid, a grateful smile stretching across his face as the chain came into view.

"I know it's your high school jersey number," I warned, motioning to the #16 pendant hanging from the gold rope, "but I'll replace it if you end up with a new one after you're settled with a team."

He looked up at me, his emerald eyes sparkling in the moonlight. "Thank you, Princess. I love it." His voice was tight with emotion, and my throat went dry as he studied my face like he'd never seen it before. He leaned in just slightly, and every part of me wished he'd close the distance and kiss me. I knew it was wrong and that he was my stepbrother, but for years, I'd wondered if he'd ever seen me as anything more than a friend. It was risky and stupid, but it didn't stop me from wanting to feel it, if only for a second.

"You're welcome," I said, leaning in closer. I expected him to back away, but he didn't. Instead, he licked his lips and turned his body toward me as my heart pounded in my chest. My stomach flipped, and I closed my eyes, feeling his breath puff against my skin as he moved in. I couldn't believe what was about to happen. I was finally going to taste Jackson Blake.

"There you two are!" Gina's voice rang out behind us, causing us both to jump away from each other as she stepped outside. My cheeks burned despite the frigid temperatures, and I threw up a silent prayer that she hadn't seen us just inches away from kissing. We turned her way, and she looked at us confused for just a fraction of a moment before hitching a thumb over her shoulder. "Uncle Alex and Aunt Katie are heading out and wanted to say goodbye."

"Okay," Jackson rasped, standing and glancing down at me as I joined him. As much as I wanted to look at him — to see if there was any regret behind his eyes — I couldn't. Instead, we went back inside, leaving our almost-kiss as nothing but a memory that I'd never forget.

I stare at the pendant, my heart beating like a drum as I try to figure out why he still wears it. His jersey number has been twenty-six since he started playing for the Fury, so this one doesn't even make sense. Not to mention, he has enough money to buy an updated version that's bigger and better, yet he's choosing the fifty-dollar Christmas gift I gave him nearly a decade ago.

I still wonder where we'd be if our parents never got married. Would I have worked up the courage to ask him if he saw me as more? Or would we have continued to drift apart without a reason to bring us together a couple of times a year?

Pressing a gentle kiss to his cheek, I stand and quietly pad up the stairs toward my room. I do my best to push the racing thoughts of everything that could've been to the back of my mind, knowing that no matter how hard I try, I'll never be able to let them go for good.

THIRTEEN
HAWK

I PUSH my way into the dark condo, trying my best to be quiet so I don't wake Jacks and Arden. It's after midnight and the team just arrived home from our road trip. It was a long one, and I'm ready to relax for the next couple of days. Playoffs start in two weeks, so this will be the last break we have before things get crazy. Hopefully, by the end of October, the Daytona Fury will be World Series champs. This group of guys deserves it after everything they've sacrificed this year. The time away from their families, long hours at practice, and dedication to the team come at a price. Some feel it more than others. Guys like Riggs are away from their girls for days at a time, just to come home for a night before doing it all over again.

Baseball has always been an escape for me. A way to fill the emptiness in my life with something so I didn't dwell on everything I was missing. I never intended for it to be like that, but the longer I went without my brothers, the more I relied on the game to keep me from spiraling. I welcome the idea of going from city to city and spending nights in random hotel rooms because even my own home never truly felt full without Hayden and Henry in it.

At least not until recently.

As comfortable as I am with Jackson when we're here, I've struggled to feel like I really had a purpose in our roommate dynamic. Sure, I pay half the bills. I cook and clean. But at the end of the day, I have little to offer beyond that. When I'm grappling with my anxiety and abandonment issues, he's taking care of me—making sure I'm eating and getting to practice on time. I know he's lost sleep during my episodes, and I'll never be able to tell him how grateful I am. I'm terrible with words when it comes to my emotions, and he certainly doesn't need me to return any similar favors since he doesn't struggle with things the way I do. But with Arden here?

I make a difference.

The way I got her through her panic attack and then opened up a conversation that led to her decision to talk to someone made me feel like I truly helped. I mean, she took the big steps herself, but she might not have if I wasn't there to make her feel seen. That's all she really needed.

I remove my shoes, putting them in the entryway closet along with my suitcase and duffle bag. I'll need to sort through them tomorrow, but right now, I just want to go to bed. My whole body aches and my eyes burn with exhaustion. I don't know why, but I have trouble sleeping on the team plane, so I usually just stare out the window and crash in my own bed as soon as I get home.

As I make my way toward the living room, movement on the stairs catches my eye. I look up to find Arden, half asleep, walking toward me in nothing but an oversized t-shirt and panties. It's her normal bedtime attire, but every time I see those gorgeous, toned thighs on display, I feel like a fumbling virgin with the way my dick immediately swells. It's just the effect she's always had on me.

She doesn't notice me at first, rubbing her eyes as she descends. As soon as she does, a sleepy smile blooms across her face—one that I can't help but return because she's so goddamn cute.

"You're home," she says, finally reaching the floor and stopping just a few feet in front of me.

"Miss me?" I ask, raising a brow.

"Mhmm," she hums contentedly. At her admission, I can't stop myself from closing the distance and pulling her into a hug. Her fruity shampoo invades my senses, and I revel in her warmth as she wraps her small arms around my waist. It's completely out of character for me to be doing this since I'm not a hugger at all, but with her, continuing to fight it feels wrong. I know I'll have to talk with Jackson about it eventually, but we'll cross that bridge when we get there. For now, I just want to enjoy the time I have with her.

"What are you doing up so late?" I say, pulling back, but not letting her go. She tilts her head up, and I realize how small she is compared to me, despite playing a sport where she has to clear a seven-foot net to block. But I've seen her highlight reels online, and she has no issues with that.

"I'm hungry," she replies sheepishly. This girl is all about her midnight snacks, and I have to say, I kind of love them too.

"Oh yeah? How about some chocolate zucchini muffins?" I was planning on making them tomorrow, but if she's hungry now, there's no point in waiting.

"That's okay," she says, her smile fading. "I'll just have some cereal or something. You don't have to bake for me."

Memories of the first night she was here replay in my mind at her words. She asked me where I learned to bake, and like a dickhead, I stormed out of the room because the question made me think about my brothers. Although it wasn't that long ago, it feels like years have gone by since then. I've started to build a bond with Arden, and I'm already feeling differently about the parts of myself I was trying so hard to hide from her before.

"I *want* to bake for you," I reply, reaching up and pushing a rogue piece of hair behind her ear—another gentle gesture that's very unlike me, but I can't seem to stop myself from softening around this girl. I still want to rip her to shreds behind closed doors, but those fantasies are just for me—at least for now.

She nods. "Alright." I shoot her a satisfied grin, glad that she's agreeing after I dismissed her so badly last time before taking her hand in mine and leading her into the kitchen. I flip the light switch, illuminating the room, but immediately lower the dimmer so it's not as bright. With any luck, I can feed her, and she'll still be able to go back to sleep until it's time for her to get ready for practice.

She takes a seat at the table, and I make my way around the room, washing my hands and gathering the items to make muffins. This recipe is a quick one, so she won't have to wait long to eat. Setting the ingredients on the counter, I preheat the oven and get to work. She's pretty quiet at first, watching me prepare the batter, and when I catch her studying my face, I suddenly want to let her see even more of me.

"I used to bake for my younger brothers," I tell her. "I was a product of our mom and dad's early on-and-off relationship. She was always a drinker, but when it got really bad, my dad made her choose between him and the alcohol. It took her a while to get her shit together, but eventually, she got sober, and they reconciled.

"After Hayden and Henry were born, my mom relapsed, although I'm not entirely convinced she wasn't just really good at hiding shit the whole time. Our dad left again, and the responsibility of caring for my brothers was on my shoulders. Sometimes I had to get creative with the food we had, so we'd make a game of finding recipes that worked. Some were awful, but every now and then, I'd pull off a miracle and be able to give them dinner and dessert on the same night. Baking became our thing, and even now, it reminds me of them."

"Where are they now?" she asks, tilting her head in confusion. "You don't see them often?"

I look down into the bowl as zucchini shavings fall

through the grater in a heap. As much as I want to tell her everything, it's hard, because I know there's a chance this part of my life may never have a happy ending.

"Our dad came and took them right after I turned eighteen. I hadn't been drafted yet, so I didn't have the means to care for them. Right now, everything is fucked, but I'm hoping someday, they'll understand that I wanted them, and I've missed them every day since they left. The memories still take me to a scary place sometimes. It's not always easy to get out." Anxiety swirls and grips my heart like a vise, and I swallow the lump in my throat as I inhale deeply. Before it has a chance to drag me under, Arden is out of her chair and stepping up behind where I'm standing. Snaking her arms around my waist, she presses her head between my shoulder blades, holding me tightly.

"I've got you," she says, her fingers skating gently over the fabric of my t-shirt. I focus on the feeling, exhaling a shaky breath and dropping my head forward as I relax. This is a first for me. I've never been pulled away from the darkness so effortlessly before, but it's like she knew exactly what kind of light I needed. She really fucking *sees me*...the same way I see her.

I turn in her arms, bringing my hands to her face and falling into her deep brown eyes. They're full of emotion, and I feel like a million pounds have been lifted off my shoulders as she softly smiles up at me.

"I've got you, too," I say, leaning down and brushing my lips against hers. She sighs as though she's been waiting years for the kiss, and *fuck*, I feel the same.

She opens in invitation, allowing me to tangle my tongue with hers. Sparks of electricity skitter across my skin, and I deepen our connection, letting myself get lost in the way she tastes. Everything about this girl is an anomaly, starting with the way she makes me want to be gentle and rough all at once. I long to care for her and break her, then put her back together and do it all over again.

Pulling away reluctantly, I press another soft peck to her plump lips before this gets out of hand right in the middle of our kitchen. I'm prepared to tell Jacks how I feel about Arden, even though it's going to be hard, but I don't want him seeing us together before I get the chance. If I'm not careful, I could end up losing him, and that can't happen. No matter what, he's still the most important person in my life.

"Want to help me?" I ask, turning back to the bowls that sit on the counter. There honestly isn't much to this recipe, but if it means I can keep her close, I'll pretend it's the most complex thing I've ever baked.

She scrunches her nose. "Hawk, there's a reason I was coming in here for cereal. I can't cook. Like, at all. I promise, if you let me touch those muffins, I'll find a way to make them taste like ass."

A sly grin tugs at the corners of my mouth as I slide my eyes her way. "Lucky for you, I'm a big fan of eating ass." Her jaw falls open and she chokes out a gasp, making me chuckle in response. I hand her the whisk, emptying the measured ingredients into a bowl while she mixes them together. When it's ready, I pour it into the tins before dipping a finger into the thick batter and bringing it in front of her lips to taste. Her gaze burns into mine as she slowly leans forward, sucking it into her mouth and moaning as her tongue swirls around the tip. I stifle a groan as she takes it even deeper, her throat constricting around me when she swallows. I meant for it to be a playful gesture, but if I don't get her alone in about ten seconds, I'm going to take her right here on the counter.

"You're a bad fucking girl," I growl quietly, pulling my finger from her mouth and racing to get the muffins into the waiting oven. I check the clock, but don't bother setting a timer before yanking her through the pantry door and closing it behind us. It's dark, save for the small nightlights that line the shelves, but I can see everything I need to.

I waste no time pulling her into me and taking her lips in a searing kiss, this one much more demanding and desperate than the one we shared a few minutes ago. Her quiet whimpers intensify into needy whines as I turn us, pushing her against the door before shoving my hand inside her thin panties. She gasps loudly when my middle finger presses against her clit, and I cover her mouth with my free hand to muffle the sound.

"Shut the fuck up or I'll stop," I grit out, rubbing circles around the sensitive bundle of nerves. She nods frantically, her breathing becoming more labored as she widens her stance and invites me to slide between her slick lips. "You're soaked, baby," I say, pushing inside with two fingers. Her swollen flesh hugs me tightly, and I almost pass out just from the thought of how she'd grip my dick as I pounded into her.

"Mhmm," she mumbles beneath my hand, her eyes rolling back in pleasure as I pump in and out, coaxing her release to the surface.

"What a sweet little pussy you have," I coo, and her inner muscles flutter in response. "I'd split you right in half, Hellcat. And I'd love every minute of it."

She whines again, her legs beginning to shake as I press my body into hers for support. I'm shocked at how reactive she is to my touch, and how quickly I have her teetering on the precipice of an orgasm just from my fingers. I'd give anything to really play with her, bringing her to the edge and then ripping her away as she cried and begged for mercy. But right now…I just need to feel her explode.

Leaning in so my lips are ghosting against her ear, I test the theory I've had for a while but couldn't be sure of. "Come. Now," I demand, and just like that, she shatters. A scream works its way up her throat and her hands shoot to my wrist, holding me in place as she rides out her climax. Her hips mindlessly grind into my palm before her walls contract so intensely that I worry for a second that she might snap my fingers right off. I had a feeling she'd be the perfect sub, but I didn't know until just now how responsive she'd be to taking orders.

The waves slowly subside, and she relaxes against the door, her breaths steadying as I let my hand fall from her mouth. I press a gentle kiss to her cheek, smiling against the warm skin. "Such a good girl, coming when you're told." She hums contentedly, her eyes fluttering open to look at me like I just gave her everything she's ever wanted. "Did that feel good?"

She nods, a satiated smile pulling at the corners of her mouth. "I want to taste you. Can I?"

Fucking hell. She's flawless.

"I can't think of anything I want more, Hellcat. Are you sure you can be quiet, though? We wouldn't want to wake your brother when you're choking on my cock, would we?" I shouldn't bring Jacks into this, especially knowing how he feels about her, but I can't help it. Now that I've made her come, I want to defile her in the filthiest ways. Apparently, that isn't limited to involving him in what we're doing—or at least thinking about it.

"*Stepbrother*," she breathes, lowering to her knees as I chuckle darkly. I've always had a bit of a corruption kink, and I can't say the idea of him witnessing all the things I've fantasized about doing to her doesn't turn me on. Obviously, I wouldn't want that to happen before I got a chance to talk to him, so I'm going to have to take it easy on her for now.

Looking down, I focus on Arden as she slowly pulls at the waistband of my shorts and boxer briefs. I'm grateful that there's enough light for me to see her expression as my cock comes into view, because she *does not* disappoint. Her eyes go wide, and she trails her fingertip over the underside of my shaft, stopping to gently toy with the barbell that sits right beneath my head. I hiss a breath through my teeth as she continues to explore, finding the other piercing that decorates the top of the base, right over my pubic bone.

"Oh my God," she whispers, and my dick twitches when her tongue darts out to wet her lips. "You're pierced."

"You like them?" I ask, ghosting my hand along her cheek. She nods her head eagerly in approval, a shy smile forming on her gorgeous face. "Show me how much."

She doesn't need to be told twice, leaning forward and running her warm, wet tongue up my length with a satisfied moan. She stops, circling around the tip and playing with my piercing for a moment before wrapping her lips around me and sliding down until I'm touching the back of her throat. My cock grows harder as she grips onto my hips with both hands, slowly wiggling her head from side to side so she can work me in even further. Determined whimpers vibrate against me, and I look to the ceiling because, *goddamn*, this is the best head I've ever gotten in my life.

"Holy fuck, baby," I whisper into the quiet room. "You're making it impossible not to want to obliterate that tight little throat." I've been gentle with her in every sense of the word, but it's not what I'm used to. I rarely ever kiss the women I'm with, and the sex is always transactional. Our objective is to get what we need from one another and move on. But here, with Arden, it's not like that. She's the first person I've felt more for, and I don't know if I should show her how I really fuck. First, because I don't want her to feel disrespected, and second, because I'd never forgive myself if I hurt her in a way she didn't consent to.

She pulls back, using her hand to stroke me as her gaze finds mine. "Do it, Hawk. Fuck my face." Her eyes are pleading, and if I wasn't already hanging by a thread, looking at how full of need she is while she begs would definitely do the trick.

She waits, leisurely sliding her palm up and down my shaft as I consider what she's asking for. Her desirous expression never falters—not even for a second—until I finally give in to what we're both craving so badly.

Stepping closer, I cradle her cheeks in my hands and tilt her head so I have her undivided attention. "I'm not going to be easy on you," I say firmly. "If it's too much, I want you to tap my thigh twice. Do you understand?" She nods, but it's not enough for me. She has to say it. "Words, Arden. Give me words."

"I understand."

That's all I need to let go, taking my cock by the base and shoving it between her open lips. Her eyes go wide with surprise, both hands shooting up to my thighs and pushing against them as I hold her head and drive into her throat until I can't go any further. She gags in protest, so I pull back, allowing her to take a quick breath before pistoning forward again, this time setting a steady rhythm as I fuck her. She surrenders, letting me control the movements with my hands and hips while I slide her up and down my length.

"What a sweet little fleshlight you are, Hellcat. I had no idea you'd be so eager to choke on cock, but look at you. Taking it like you were made for it." Her eyes roll back at my words, and I watch with rapt attention as one hand leaves me and dives into her panties. The thought of her getting so turned on by how rough I'm being that she has to touch herself has me feeling like a caged animal, ready to chase down his prey and tear her apart.

A loud moan reverberates against the head of my dick, and I lightly slap my palm against her cheek. Her eyes shoot up as I continue brutalizing her throat, never slowing while I reprimand her. "Quiet down. You'll wake Jacks. Is that what you want?" To my surprise, she doesn't shake her head in disagreement, moaning louder as her entire body begins to shake.

Fuck. Me. She's going to come.

All of a sudden, I couldn't give less of a fuck how wrong it is. It seems the idea of him turns her on, and I'm dying to know how deep it runs.

"He could come in here right now and find you on your knees for me, Arden. What if he liked watching you suck this cock so much, he had to stroke his own? Would that make your pussy gush?" Her answer is a desperate whimper as her hand moves faster between her legs, her climax finally crashing into her like a tidal wave. Her eyes roll back as her body shudders, and I slow my thrusts so she can ride it out, watching in awe until she's wrung completely dry.

"Hands back on my thighs if you want me to fill your mouth," I tell her. She obeys immediately, and I don't miss how utterly soaked her fingers are when they press against my skin. I could tease her about squirting all over herself at the thought of me and Jackson using her at the same time, but I don't. It's definitely an interesting development, but not something we should be unpacking here in this pantry.

Gripping her hair in my hands, I pump my hips,

electricity shooting through my body and gathering deep inside my core. I grunt quietly as my balls draw tight, until I finally unload into her with one final thrust. Her throat constricts against my pulsing cock, prolonging my orgasm until I feel like I can't possibly give her another drop.

She slowly pulls back, sliding off me and using her finger to gather the cum that's rolling down her chin before sucking it between her red, swollen lips. She hums in satisfaction, smiling up at me innocently as if she didn't just suck me off like a goddamn pro. I choke out a surprised laugh as I reach under her arms and pull her to her feet, holding onto her waist while she attempts to regain her bearings.

"You okay? Did you like all of that?" I ask, hoping I didn't hurt her. I was rougher than I initially intended, but she seemed to be into it.

"Mhmm," she replies, leaning into my chest and nuzzling against it. I never skip out on aftercare, but cuddling isn't my go-to move. I don't normally like to be held after sex—or ever, really. Unsurprisingly, Arden is the exception to yet another rule as I wrap my arms around her and press my cheek to the top of her head.

We stand there holding one another in the quiet room until it hits me that I never set a timer. "Shit. I have to take the muffins out before they burn." As much as it pains me, I kiss her one last time before pulling away.

She giggles quietly, smoothing her hair and clothes as I open the door and peek into the kitchen to make sure we're still alone. Thankfully, we are, since we were definitely louder than we should've been. "My panties are wet. I need to go change into new ones before I eat."

"Not a chance," I reply, stepping out of the room with her following closely behind me. "Get that fine ass upstairs, get naked, and I'll be up in a few minutes with your snack. Then, I'm going to rub another orgasm out of you before I put you to bed." Her brows shoot up and an approving smile blooms across her face before she hurries out of the room, making me chuckle. When she's out of sight, I shake my head in wonder at what the fuck just happened, unable to ignore the unfamiliar feeling of contentment that's been rekindled deep inside me.

FOURTEEN
JACKSON

"LOOKS PRETTY GOOD," the doctor says as he turns back to his computer and types a note into my file. "I'm going to recommend that the team remove you from the DL, but I want you to let me know if anything changes. As long as there isn't pain between games, you can use a massage gun for recovery. Keep your diet the same and rest when you can, but you shouldn't have a problem making it through playoffs. Do you have any questions?"

I shake my head as relief washes over me. Coming in here, I was worried he was going to keep me out for another week. With our first official playoff game coming in just three days, we're cutting it pretty close. I worked my ass off rehabbing my hamstring so I'd be good to hit the field the moment they said I could. "I'm all set."

"Alright. Get out of my office," he replies with a playful smile. I laugh, standing and adjusting my shorts before thanking him for his help and heading out to the players' lot at the training facility. The first part of our next series is in Daytona, so we have tomorrow off to relax before we play two in a row at Fury Field. I'm excited to get home and celebrate with Arden and Hawk. He left here about an hour ago, and since she doesn't have practice on weekends, tonight and tomorrow will give the three of us some much-needed time off. With any luck, I'll be able to bribe them into staying up past our bedtimes with pizza, movies and video games.

The drive to our building doesn't take long, and I pull my car into my spot between Hawk's truck and Arden's sedan. She bought it used while she was in college, and it's kind of a shit box, but she wouldn't let me help her with money, so now it's down here sticking out like a sore thumb in a sea of luxury vehicles. Maybe someday she'll let me buy the Mercedes I promised her when we were teenagers, but I won't hold my breath. She's nothing if not stubborn when it comes to taking gifts.

The elevator is empty when I step in, press the button for our floor, and busy myself by scrolling through social media. The doors eventually slide open, and I mindlessly walk out, completely sucked into the algorithm I've worked hard to curate. It's mostly just a mixture of baseball stuff and videos of cats jumping off things and missing their targets, but it gets the job done when I need a distraction.

Stopping at our door, I unlock it, never looking up from my device as I step inside and kick off my shoes. I have a full plan to propose my idea of a lazy night to my roommates, but first, I need to shower and change into fresh clothes.

Pocketing my phone, I immediately notice that the living room is empty, causing me to furrow my brows in confusion because, at the very least, Arden should be on the couch watching TV. She usually lounges down here on her days off, so it's weird that there isn't a single blanket or bowl of snacks in sight.

Assuming she's napping or something, I make my way up the stairs, slowing as muffled laughs come from the direction of Hawk's bedroom. He rarely brings women here, and never without running it by me first —not that it matters because I'd know that excited squeal anywhere. My stomach drops when I hear it again, and my mouth goes dry as my feet carry me toward his door.

I reach the end of the hallway, listening in horror as her sweet voice utters his name, making him chuckle in response before the unmistakable sounds of them kissing bleed through the hard wood.

"Hawk, I have to go. Do you have an extra towel I can use or not?" she asks. He huffs a playful breath before moving across the floor, likely going into his en suite to give her what she went in there for. I panic, turning and rushing to my room before either of them can see me eavesdropping. As soon as I'm through the doorway, I close it as quietly as I can, pressing my back against it and dragging my hands down my face as my heart beats like a drum inside my ribcage.

Fuck.

Am I that stupid that I've been pushing them to be

friends, never expecting it to turn into more? I knew how perfect they'd be together deep down, but I honestly didn't think Hawk would ever allow himself to have anything good in this life. And that's exactly what she is—*good*. Just like he is.

So why the fuck am I ready to puke at the thought of them being together?

It took me a long time to come to grips with the fact that I'd never have anything more than friendship with Arden. Putting space between us after high school so I could move on from that was necessary, and it's why I jumped from woman to woman when I settled in Daytona. I thought if I did it enough, I'd be able to see her at family functions without blurting everything I've held in since the day I saw her kissing my teammate in the hallway. Now here I am, all these years later, right back where I started. Only this time, the teammate is my best friend, and we all live under the same roof. There's no way I won't eventually witness them together.

I can't be mad or blame either of them for any of this since I've kept everything to myself. It's not that I don't trust Hawk with the information, but what would saying it out loud do anyway? It doesn't change the situation. Arden is still my stepsister, which makes her completely off-limits.

My feet feel like two bricks weighing me down as I force myself into the bathroom, undress, and turn the shower up as hot as it'll go. When I step inside, the water feels like lava, making my outsides burn as badly as my insides do. Leaning my head against the wall, I envision the possibility of a future where they end up together. Coming home to find them stealing kisses in the spaces we share. Helping him pick out an engagement ring because I know exactly what she's wanted since she was a little girl. Doing my duty as his best man and delivering a sentimental gift to her on their wedding day. Being a godfather to their children. Watching him love her loudly and wishing it could be me. I know I'm moving fast, and maybe none of that will happen, but what if it does?

How the fuck am I going to do it?

I'm on autopilot as I shower and dry off, padding into my room and taking a t-shirt and shorts out of the dresser before robotically putting them on. My stomach is in knots, and my chest is tight with the anticipation of having to face them, pretending to be unbothered by the entire thing if and when they eventually tell me. I'm sure they will since I've never asked either of them to stay away from the other.

Stepping in front of the mirror, I take in my reflection, noticing how fucking broken I look already. I need to reel this shit in. The last thing I want is for the two people I care about most to feel like they're wrong for finding happiness, if that's even what this is. Maybe it's not, and I'm freaking out over nothing. I'll let myself sort through the emotions when I know for sure. But for now, I'm going to have to suck it up, go downstairs, and pretend like everything is fine and my heart isn't obliterated by something I can never change.

FIFTEEN
HAWK

"I'LL BE RIGHT BACK," Arden says as she slips on her shoes. When she said she had to run to the pharmacy to pick up a refill of one of her prescriptions, I was relieved. It's been over a week since our little tryst, and my feelings for her have only grown deeper. I can't continue to put off talking to Jackson about everything. Not fucking her is getting harder by the day, but I refuse to do it until he knows what's going on. I'm already riddled with guilt as it is from what we did in the pantry the other night and the few heated make-out sessions we've had since. I can't add to that.

"Okay," I reply lowly, wishing I could kiss her good-bye. But with him sitting in the next room, I know I can't. She leaves the condo, and I make my way to the couch, lowering down on the opposite end of where Jacks has been watching SportsCenter for the last hour. He's been uncharacteristically quiet, and I'm hoping his visit with the team doctor went well. He told me yesterday that he's feeling great, so I've had my fingers crossed that he'll be off the disabled list in time for our playoff series this week.

"How'd everything turn out with Dr. Wallace?" I ask, looking his way. His gaze stays locked onto the screen, taking several seconds before acknowledging my existence.

"Fine. I'm cleared to play."

I nod in approval. "That's good. We need you out there."

"Yeah." I can tell something is bothering him, and I hate throwing this whole thing on him when his mind is obviously elsewhere. But I don't have much time before Arden gets back, and I want to get it all out in case something goes awry.

I clear my throat, pushing the anxious feeling in my chest down as it threatens to rise to the surface. My fingers flex and release on their own, my body looking for ways to channel the nervous energy flowing through me. "I wanted to talk to you about something."

His eyes bounce to me before returning to the TV. "Okay."

Fuck. Just fucking say it, Hawk. Rip off the Band-Aid.

Swallowing thickly, I try my best to spit it out. "Arden and I...we," I pause, looking for the right words. "Some stuff happened between us, and I just want to make sure it's cool with you before we go any further."

"Why wouldn't it be?" he asks dryly, catching me off guard. I don't know what kind of reaction I was expecting, but an emotionless one wasn't it. He's obviously holding *something* back, and I just want to dig it all up so we don't leave anything unsaid. I'd hate for him to say he's okay with it when he really isn't. If not pursuing more with Arden is the only way to avoid irreparably damaging our friendship, then that's how it has to be. It'll kill me because I really fucking like her, but I refuse to lose him over this.

"You tell me," I reply, wishing he'd just say the words. The only thing that pisses me off more than the situation itself is the fact that he refuses to talk to me about it. And now he's shutting down completely. "Is there a reason I shouldn't?"

"Nope. Knock yourself out," he mutters, and that's the final fucking straw. He wants to act unbothered when his attitude is telling me something different? *Not happening.*

I reach forward, swiping the remote from the ottoman and powering the TV off. He whips his head my way, his brows pulled tight with anger before standing abruptly and turning to leave the room. He only makes it a few steps before I dart my hand out, grabbing him by the forearm and spinning him back around. "Don't fucking walk away from me," I seethe, stepping into his personal space. "Stop being a little bitch and talk."

He scoffs. "That's rich coming from you, *Mr. Haunted and Closed Off.* Getting you to discuss your feelings is like pulling teeth, but you expect me to just pour my heart out when you snap your fingers? What the fuck do you want from me, Hawk?" His entire body is heaving, and if looks could kill, I'd be bleeding to death in the middle of our living room floor. But it's sure as hell better than what he was giving me a minute ago. At least now, he's acting like he cares.

"I want you to stop lying to yourself and admit that you're in love with her!" I shout, shoving my finger into his chest. I take a breath, doing my best to calm myself before I go on. "You can act like you fucking don't, but I see the way you look at her. Tell me you want to give her everything she deserves, and I'll back off right now. I'd never fucking go after her if I knew you didn't want me to. But if you tell me to stay away and have no intentions of doing anything about the way you feel, everybody loses, Jacks. Most of all, her."

He stumbles backward, falling onto the couch and dropping his head into his hands. "Did you fuck her?" he chokes out. It isn't lost on me that he's not denying anything I said, but I understand why he'd want to know how far things have gone between me and Arden.

"No," I reply. I decide to spare him the details of our night in the kitchen because I doubt he wants to hear them. Maybe that makes me an asshole, but I really don't want to make this any harder on him than it very clearly is. I know I should feel regret—now that I'm seeing how badly it's hurting him—but I just can't find it in me to believe that anything that's happened with her was a mistake.

He looks up and my heart cracks in my chest. His

eyes are shining with emotion, and I can tell he's fucking crushed. I don't know the full extent of his history with her, but it's obvious that he's conflicted. He won't let himself have her, but it kills him to see her with anyone else.

I hang my head in defeat. This hurts a hell of a lot more than I expected, but I know what I need to do. "I'd fight anyone for her," I say quietly. "Anyone but you. I'll tell her we can't do this anymore. I'm sorry." Placing my hand on his shoulder as I pass, I walk toward the stairs, desperate to get out of here. This whole thing is fucked, and I need some time alone to sort it out. Arden will be back any minute, and I'm not the kind of guy who can just pretend things are fine when they're not. I'll go upstairs and let them spend some time together while I find a way to deal with this shitshow.

"Wait," he rasps as soon as my foot presses against the first step. I stop, turning toward him as he stands from the couch and comes my way. The tension in the air is thick, and for a second, I think he might knock my ass out. I don't really blame him, I guess. I'd probably want to hit me, too. But he doesn't. Instead, he shoves his hands into the pockets of his shorts, looking down at his feet. "If it can't be me, I want it to be you. You're good for her and I know you'll make each other happy." His gaze finds mine, hardening. "But if you ever hurt her, I'll kill you."

A half-smile tugs at one corner of my mouth. "I'd let you. But seriously, if this is going to be hard for you, I'll just tell her I'm not ready right now. You know, there's a strong possibility she feels the same way about you. Maybe you should talk to her about it."

He shakes his head. "I can't. Our parents would never be okay with it. You have to promise me you won't tell her about any of this. Just make her happy. Do it for me, *please*." His voice cracks on the last word as if he's struggling to push it out, and I'm torn between respectfully honoring his wishes and shaking his dumb ass until he realizes what he's about to lose.

I can't imagine how difficult this is for him right now, but I've thought about it a lot, and even if Arden and I decide to be in a relationship, I'd never deny them the chance to be together. If that means having to share her, I'd be okay with it. I won't push the issue with him now, but if it ever comes back up, I'll lay it all out for them both.

"Alright," I reply.

He nods, backing away. "I'm going to go drive around for a bit, then I'll probably stop by Ace's. It'll give the two of you time to talk or...whatever." I want to protest—tell him not to leave, and that she and I can be alone some other time—but I have a feeling he probably wants some time to himself. This isn't easy, and I need him to know I understand that.

"Okay. I'll see you later." I extend my hand, relief washing over me when he slaps his against it and pulls me into a hug. As much as I shy away from physical affection like this, the gesture brings me comfort, and I feel like once the dust settles, we're going to be alright. I'm still at war with myself over my feelings for Arden because I know they're causing him pain, but I can't just turn them off. The best I can do is treat her the way he'd want me to and hope that, someday, he'll find the nerve to tell her all the things he's never been able to say.

Because as much as I want her for myself, I want her for him too.

SIXTEEN
ARDEN

"IF YOU'RE NOT CALLING to tell me you fucked that tattooed sculpture of a man, I'm hanging up," Stella says, her not-so-warm greeting filling the cab of my car as soon as she answers the phone. I called her on my way home from the pharmacy because we haven't spoken since the day after Hawk pulled me into the pantry, and even then, our conversation wasn't long. We've texted—mainly her expecting details of my nonexistent sexcapades—but I haven't had much time to chat beyond that.

"I regret to inform you that he's still holding out, but hanging up on me wouldn't be fair. It's not my fault," I reply, flicking on my blinker and pulling out of the parking lot. It's about a fifteen-minute drive to our building, so I figured I'd try to catch her before she had to be at the hospital for her shift tonight. Stella is an emergency room nurse, and she's one of the hardest-working people I know. She's married to her job, so she lives vicariously through me when it comes to sex—which is pretty sad for us both, considering I haven't been laid since I was in Argentina. The other night with Hawk was the closest I've come in over a year. It's not that I haven't wanted to. The opportunity just hasn't presented itself in far too long. At this point, I'm ready to climb him like a fucking tree and let him do unspeakable things to me until I can't possibly take it anymore.

"That sounds suspicious. Why would he choose not to bang your brains out when you're super slutty and willing?" she asks.

I huff a frustrated breath. "He wants to talk to Jacks first. To get his blessing or whatever. Although I have no idea why he'd care. It's not like I'm his real sister, and prior to me coming to Daytona, he had all but cut me out of his life. It feels like we're finally getting back to normal now, but I can't imagine he'd give a shit if Hawk and I were sleeping together."

"Arden, are you really that blind?" she replies, and I can practically hear her eyes rolling as she says it. "Jackson has been obsessed with you for years. The fact that you can't see it is ridiculous. The way he used to stare at you almost made me spontaneously orgasm a few times, to be honest."

My brows bunch tightly in confusion. "Stell, I thought you got drug tested regularly for work. You're obviously on something strong if you think Jacks has ever seen me as anything more than a friend. If he had, he'd have said something by now."

"Whatever you want to tell yourself," she says with

a laugh. "I just got to the hospital and I'm about to be late, so I'll call you tomorrow. Love you."

"Love you too," I reply. We end the call just as I enter the parking garage, rounding the corner and pulling into my spot. I laugh as I think about her words because, as always, she went above and beyond with the dramatics. I've learned to take them with a grain of salt over the years, and this time is no different. My stepbrother isn't *obsessed with me.*

I look out my window, noticing that Jackson's car is gone, which is strange because I figured we'd hang out tonight like we normally do when we're all off at the same time. Maybe he just ran to get food or something. Technically, it would be his turn, but I'm sure I'll find out soon enough if that's the case.

I shove the pharmacy bag into my purse, get out, and lock up before I head up to our floor. My heart leaps in my chest at the idea of having a few minutes alone with Hawk, so I can kiss him out in the open. It's as far as we've gotten since the pantry, but it's fine because it's been building the most delicious tension between the two of us. I swear, just passing him in the hallways sends a jolt of electricity right between my legs, and I haven't felt this way in a long, long time.

Stepping into the condo, I make my way up the stairs toward my room, knowing that if I don't put my birth control pills next to the sink in the bathroom, I'll forget to take them. But I don't even make it to my doorway before a thick, muscular arm bands around my waist. "Took you long enough," Hawk says quietly, his minty breath fanning across my cheek. The dark mischief in his voice makes my core clench, and I let out a quiet moan when he nips at the sensitive spot below my ear. "We're all alone."

My eyes roll back as he continues teasing me with his teeth and tongue. "Oh yeah?" I ask. "And what does that mean?" I don't want to assume anything, but I'm hopeful he had the conversation with Jackson that he wanted to, so we can finally go further than the kissing we've been torturing each other with all week.

"Why don't you come to my room and find out, Hellcat?"

I turn, shooting him a devious grin over my shoulder as he walks us backward until we're in his room. The entire space is blanketed in grays and blacks, with red accents scattered throughout. The first time I came in here, other than thinking it was very *Hawk*, it gave me total *kink dungeon* vibes. Maybe it is—or it could just be because the man who sleeps here drips with a silent sexual energy. Either way, I can't help but wonder what he hides inside these four walls. Hope-fully, I'm about to find out.

He closes the door, spinning me around so we're face to face before dropping his lips to mine in a passionate kiss. He wastes no time pushing his tongue into my mouth, swallowing every needy whine that tumbles out of me while he does. His hands—that can't seem to settle on one part of my body at first—finally slide down to my ass, where he grips tightly, pulling my cheeks apart under the fabric of my cotton shorts and panties. He lifts me into his arms, urging me to wrap my legs around his waist as he carries me to the bed and breaks our connection by dropping me down onto the mattress.

"Look at you," he growls as I stare up at him, my lips swollen and tingling from his kisses. "You have no idea how many times I've wondered what you'd look like in my bed. How many times I've stroked my cock to the thought of you splayed out for me like you are right now. It's been *years,* Arden. I felt like such a fucking creep for fantasizing about you that way, but I couldn't help myself."

I try to hide my surprise at his admission, but it's not easy. I thought he hated me. Every time we were around each other prior to me moving here, he barely talked. I tried, but I never got more than a few words out of him before I took the hint and left. I would've never guessed he even gave me a second thought. But now that I know, I want to give him everything he's wanted.

"So have me," I whisper, squeezing my thighs together for relief because the intensity of his gaze as it roams over me is making me wetter by the second.

A cocky grin slowly spreads across his face. He's so fucking hot, I'm barely holding myself together with how desperate I am to feel him all over me. He pulls my shirt over my head, then reaches around and unfastens the clasp between my shoulder blades. I wiggle my bra down my arms, tossing it aside and watching his eyes burn as he takes in my bare tits. Without even blinking, he wraps his long, thick fingers around the fabric at my hips, yanking my shorts and panties down in one go. I squirm under his stare, his hungry eyes roving down my body at an agonizingly slow pace before locking onto my bare pussy.

"*Have* you?" he says, as if it's the most ridiculous thing he's ever heard. "Baby, I'm going to *destroy you.*" I whimper loudly when he steps between my legs, planting his hands behind my knees and shoving them toward my ears so I'm spread completely wide below him.

I look away, suddenly embarrassed by the fact that I'm literally dripping for him. I've never been this turned on in my entire life, and my body is reacting whether I want it to or not.

"Eyes on me, Arden," he demands, and I obey immediately, surprised at my willingness to do whatever he tells me to. Normally, I'd take pause at someone ordering me around, but with Hawk—I want it. I want to please him.

"There you go," he praises as he slides his thumb through my slit from bottom to top, gathering my arousal and pressing it to my clit. My body jolts at the contact, but relaxes again when he begins rubbing in teasing barely-there circles over the sensitive bundle of nerves. A shaky breath tumbles from my lips, and he chuckles darkly, adding even more pressure as he speeds up.

"What pretty, pathetic sounds you make," he says. "Does this desperate cunt need to come?" I nod my head frantically, shocked at how his words are bringing me to the edge so quickly. When I'm by myself, it takes a while—sometimes less if I'm using a toy—but it's barely been two minutes and I'm already nearing the summit. My orgasm barrels toward me as he expertly works my clit, using his free hand to hold me open so he can watch as he works me over. All the bashfulness I was feeling when we started is long gone, only to be replaced by my need to release.

"Do you want to unravel for me?" he taunts, pushing his bottom lip into a patronizing pout. It only makes me wetter as I submit, my eyes pleading for him to give me what I need. I don't care how pitiful I look. I just want him to get me there.

"Aww, I bet," he says darkly as I teeter on the edge. White light takes over my vision and my muscles wind tight. But before I can fully fall, he pulls away, landing a tight slap directly to my aching clit. I cry out, and he ghosts a finger around my pussy as I whimper and buck my hips in search of more contact.

"I have one rule, Hellcat," he says, never removing his gaze from where he's tracing my wet, swollen skin. I shake as my orgasm fades, squeezing my eyes shut tightly. "You do *nothing* without my permission. If I want you to come, I'll let you know when. And if you break this rule, I'll punish you. Do you understand?"

His gaze slides up to mine, and he must be able to see the worry written across my face, because he stops what he's doing and places a gentle hand on my cheek. "I want you to let go for me, Arden—to give up full control of your body and mind, and let me see how far I can get you out of your own head. I promise I'll take care of you, but you have to trust me, always. Can you do that?"

I exhale a shaky breath, letting his words fully register. I want this, but it isn't easy to submit in the way he's asking me to. He's already shown that he won't let anything bad happen to me, and I really do trust him. But can I be the girl he needs?

I know I want to try.

"Yes," I reply quietly. He leans down, pressing his lips to mine in a kiss that's much softer than a moment ago. But that's Hawk. Whatever you think you'll get, he'll surprise you.

"If you want me to stop at any time, say the word *muffins*, okay? I want to hurt you, but I want to bring you pleasure when I do it. You have to tell me if I'm crossing the line. Promise?"

I nod, this time more confidently than before. I understand what he's saying. It's just like when I went down on him in the pantry. It was rough, and the way he gripped my hair and fucked my throat was painful, but in the most erotic, mind-bending way. So much so that I had to rub myself just to case the ache it caused. I want to test the boundaries of that sort of thing, and knowing I can end it all with a single word makes me feel safe—like I can give him everything, and he'll take care of me.

"That's my good girl," he says proudly, pulling back before lowering his face between my legs and hovering right above where I'm throbbing for him. "I've been dying to lick this sweet pussy. You smell incredible." I suck in a breath as his tongue laps at my sensitive pearl, the pleasure from my stolen orgasm blooming back to life as he adds more pressure with each pass.

"Hawk," I moan as his lips wrap around me,

sucking gently at my desperate core. The feeling is inde-scribable, and it's mere seconds before I'm right back where I was before he pulled away the first time.

"You're mine," he growls, the vibration of his words intensifying the euphoria as he sinks a finger into me. As soon as he turns his palm upward, curling toward a spot deep inside that has me seeing stars, I know I won't be able to hold back for long.

"Please!" I beg, clenching involuntarily around him as he pumps in and out, his tongue expertly working in tandem to bring me dangerously close to the edge. "Hawk. I need to—*please*!"

"Come for me," he relents, the words barely out of his mouth before I detonate, surrendering to the plea-sure as it pulls me under. My vision goes blurry, and I scream into the empty room, not giving a fuck if anyone can hear me because I'm unable to control it anyway. I'm weightless as he continues licking and fucking me with his finger, only slowing when my body eventually begins to sink back into the mattress. I've never had an orgasm that intense before, and we've barely even started.

He wasn't lying. He *is* going to destroy me. And I'll fucking welcome it.

"I'm so hard just from tasting your cum, baby," he says, reaching behind himself and peeling his t-shirt over his head with one hand. He immediately follows the action by sliding down his shorts and briefs, his mouthwatering erection slapping against his stomach as soon as it's free from the material that was restraining it. I can't stop my eyes from bouncing around his naked body, because this is the first time I've seen his tattoos without feeling like I should look away. They cover the entirety of his arms, spreading from the backs of his hands and meeting behind him. I knew his back was fully covered in art, but I didn't realize until now that it was all one big scene. On his left, a silhouette stands in the middle of a serene river, the entire thing calm and peaceful. His right side is covered in darkness, starting with the demon on his hand ascending up a dark stone staircase. It leads into a cloud of thick smoke over his bicep, the entire piece the exact opposite of its lighter counterpart. I want to ask him what it all means, but I don't get a chance as he rubs his bare cock between my still-drenched pussy lips. I gasp when the piercing under his head grazes my overstimulated clit, clenching my hands into the sheets beside me as he repeats the motion. It's too much and not enough all at once, and I wonder for a second if I'll be able to handle whatever he's about to dish out. I know I can stop it if I want to, but the anticipation makes blood run through my veins like hot lava.

I've never wanted to be owned more than I do right now.

"Let me grab a condom," he says, leaning down for a quick kiss before he begins to back away. But I don't allow it, darting my hand out and grabbing his wrist to pull him back. I can't believe I'm about to say this, but I just can't stop the reckless words from bursting out of my mouth.

"I want you bare," I say. "I just picked up my birth control refill from the pharmacy. I've never missed one, and I've tested negative twice since the last time I had sex. If you're clean—and okay with it—we can go without a condom."

A sexy smirk lifts the corners of his lips, his eyes hooding with desire. "You want me to fuck you raw, Hellcat? Blow my thick, hot load into your begging cunt?"

"Oh my God," I say on a forced exhale. "Yes. I want you to fill me up." I have no idea where all of this is coming from. I'm normally not a dirty talker, but it's easy to match his energy when he's towering over me like this.

"Sit up on your elbows," he says, stepping in and yanking me closer to the edge of the bed. "Watch it go in." I oblige, pushing up so his gorgeous cock is in clear view as he thrusts forward, breaching my entrance. The stretch immediately makes me hiss a breath through my teeth, and he resumes rubbing my clit to help me relax.

"You're doing great, Arden," he praises, and I feel my muscles unclench, letting him sink in further. The barbell on the underside of his length rubs against my walls, and suddenly, I need it deeper. Wrapping my ankles around his ass, I pull him to me, gasping from the fullness when he's buried to the hilt. He leans forward so his hands are pressed to the mattress on either side of me and drops his lips to the heated skin of my neck. I lie back, reveling in the way he's making me feel worshiped and possessed at the same time.

"Fuck. You're tight," he grunts. His entire body is shaking, clearly holding back as he carefully withdraws and surges forward again. His heart pounds against mine in a fast but steady rhythm, every single part of him wound taut as he attempts to control himself. But I don't want that. I want him unleashed.

"Hawk, fuck me," I whine. "You're not giving me everything."

"Next time, baby. I promise," he replies, setting an even tempo as he moves his hips. It feels amazing, especially when he grinds his other piercing against my clit. "Just let me make you feel good. Come whenever you want. I've got you." He bands an arm around my waist, hoisting me up the bed and following until he's settled on top of me. The feel of his weight pressed tightly to my body has every nerve ending on high alert, and I know another orgasm is getting ready to take me away any second. He said I could, so I allow myself to succumb to the sensations, focusing on the metal bars as they work me to the edge.

"Come on, sweetheart," he coaxes. "Let me feel it on my cock." As if my pussy answers to him and him only, it clamps down, flooding his shaft as he steadily fucks me through it. I cry out, my clit pulsing against the metal barbell that's clearly prolonging my climax. It's complete euphoria, and I can't even imagine what it'll be like when he gives me everything.

"Holy fucking shit. I'm going to make you mine, Arden. Open your eyes." His words are a mix of demand and desperation, and I don't waste another second before following his order. As soon as the haze from my orgasm dissipates, I focus on his beautiful face just in time to watch it twist in pleasure. He stares into my soul, and I feel him throb inside me, thrusting one last time before filling me with rope after rope of cum.

He buries his face into my neck, groaning between heaving gulps of air while violent shivers rack his entire body. I've never had unprotected sex before, and the sensation of overflowing with this part of him is unlike anything I could've ever imagined. It's intense in the most primal way, and before he's even completely empty, I want more.

"Are you okay?" he asks, clearly exhausted and reeling from his release. Even though I had absolutely no physical control over anything we just did, I feel powerful knowing my body affected him this way.

"I'm perfect," I reply. "It's never been like that before."

He pushes up, lazily kissing me for a moment before dropping his forehead to mine. "I wanted it to just be about us tonight. I promise we'll try some new things and test your limits next time, if you're into it. I think it might help you let go in other aspects of your life, too. It does for me, at least."

"I'd like that," I say with a smile, wrapping my arms around his neck before he rolls to the side, bringing me with him so we're face to face. The motion separates us enough for his dick to slip out, and I feel warmth drip from my body, slowly running down my thigh. It's foreign, but knowing it's our cum mixed together makes me want to stay put for another minute or two before I clean up.

"You messy?" he says with a raised brow, and I laugh because, obviously, my face is telling him everything I'm feeling.

"A little, but I like it," I reply sheepishly, not sure if I should be embarrassed by the admission.

He chuckles darkly. "I bet you do, Hellcat. How about we hop in the shower? Get you nice and clean, just to dirty you up again later. I'll empty into you as many times as you want."

Sounds like the perfect evening to me.

SEVENTEEN
JACKSON

"WOW," Ace says, his eyes going wide as he leans back into the couch cushions. "So, your best friend and your stepsister are banging. And you're okay with it, but you're not."

My brows pull tight. "I *am* okay with it. I just told you that." I came over here because, to be honest, I didn't want to be alone, and I knew he wouldn't judge me if I told him the whole story. But the more I played it over in my head, the more I thought it would be a bad idea to give all the details—namely the one where Hawk called me out for being in love with Arden, and I didn't deny it.

I didn't deny it because that would make me a liar.

"Yeah, you did," he replies. "But the look on your face says otherwise. As your much wiser, engaged friend, I can tell when you're not being completely truthful."

My mouth presses into a flat line. "You've been engaged for five minutes. That hardly makes you wise."

We were all surprised when he popped the question to Lark a few months ago. Not because they aren't head over heels for one another, because they are. Sickeningly so, actually. It was mainly the fact that they hadn't known each other for very long that threw us off. But I knew from the first day I saw them together that they were endgame. It doesn't take a genius to figure that out, with the way they look at each other like nothing else matters. It's the same way I look at Arden.

And the way Hawk looks at her too.

This whole thing is a disaster. If I thought it was torture watching her kiss my teammate in high school when I knew the guy was completely wrong for her, it's going to be agony seeing her with Hawk. He's the best fucking person I know, and they're a perfect match. They understand each other in ways that even I can't comprehend, and pretty soon, there won't be room for me in either of their lives.

The words he said before I left have been playing over and over in my head for hours, and it's making me think about all the things I can't have.

You know, there's a strong possibility she feels the same way about you.

He suspects Arden has feelings for me, too. Even if that were the case, then what? We agree to date, live in our cozy little bubble here in Daytona, and then watch everything blow to bits when we arrive at this year's family Christmas party as a couple? We can't do that.

Even if we take our parents out of the equation, what about Hawk? Am I just going to steal her away and make him suffer yet *another* loss? I haven't seen him this happy since I met him. I know it's because of her. She gives him a reason to fight his demons—a reason to keep going when he's missing his brothers, and the darkness beckons him closer. Arden is a light. She's opened him up in ways nobody else ever could.

I'd love to say that there's a way for us both to have her, but that's not realistic. When he first told me stuff had gone down between the two of them, my initial instinct was to be jealous. But the more I sat with it, I realized it wasn't the type of jealousy I expected to feel. To be honest, I'm not even pissed when I think of the fact that they're probably fucking right now. I'm more upset that he gets to experience her in ways that I never will.

Ways I've dreamed of for years.

"Hey, space cowboy," Ace says, snapping his fingers in front of my face and breaking me from my cruel thoughts. "Where the fuck did you go?"

I shake my head, wanting to get the hell out of this conversation before I end up word-vomiting every detail to my twenty-one-year-old catcher who, until he met Lark, I suspect had never had a girlfriend in his life. Although maybe I *should* be taking his advice since he found the one and locked her down in less time than it takes to grow a Chia Pet. I just feel like I need some time to sort through my own emotions before I bring anyone else into this shit. "Nowhere. I'm just exhausted," I reply, thankful when he lets it go, focusing back on the football highlights that are playing on TV.

"Heard and felt that," he says, kicking his feet up on the coffee table. "I'm about to thoroughly enjoy the calm before the storm. Gotta recharge the batteries. The road to the World Series is long and bumpy, but we've got it in the bag."

I give him a tight nod, standing and stretching my arms above my head. "I'm gonna dip, man. Thanks for hanging out."

"Come around more often," he says. "We live on opposite sides of the same building, and I hardly ever see you unless it's work-related. Lark's been spending a lot of time with Monroe, so I'm just kicking back on the couch." He looks up at me, his blue eyes full of unspoken understanding. "And if you ever need to talk about anything, we're here."

I swallow thickly, wishing I knew I wouldn't be back here some night in the future doing just that. But the truth is, I don't. I'd like to think that Hawk fulfilling my request to treat her right for both of us will be enough to keep me from feeling so lost over the whole thing. If I were a good friend to both of them, it would be. Even if my own heart shatters in the process.

The walk to our door is short, and I throw up a silent prayer that they're both in bed when I get inside. Everything is still too raw to deal with tonight. Am I supposed to treat them differently? Will they treat *me* differently? Will we all just pretend it's not a thing at all? Will everything change? The questions plague my mind as I step into the living room, finding them on the couch, watching what looks to be a cheesy rom-com. Obviously, Arden has the remote, because Hawk would never willingly subject himself to this.

"Hey!" she says, looking over her shoulder to where

I'm standing like a fucking statue, unsure of how to act. My muscles ache as I tense up, ready to bolt because everything inside me feels off. *Did they fuck before they came down here? Was he good to her?* I know he has particular tastes when it comes to sex, and I don't want him to hurt her. She's too flawless to be marked up or treated like property. I'll kill him if he doesn't give her everything she wants and needs.

I push the thought from my mind, reminding myself that them being together is a good thing. What they do behind closed doors isn't my business. It never will be.

"Hi," I reply, waving awkwardly before shoving my hands into my pockets.

"Come on," she says, patting the free spot on the couch next to her. It's where I've been sitting when we all hang out, with him on the opposite side. "We just started this movie. I'd ask if you want me to go back to the beginning, but I already know the answer. Just come pretend you love it, like you always do. Then we can put on one of your stupid action movies and I'll fall asleep before the opening credits are done." She tosses me a smile and I return it, because *fuck. Everything still feels normal.* At the very least, I might not lose my best friends throughout this experience, which I need to remember is the most important thing.

I huff a laugh, the tension in my shoulders dissipating as I walk over and sit in my usual spot at her side. She pulls her knees to her chest, curling up before she leans over—into me. Her head rests on my shoulder, and she breathes a contented sigh, focusing her attention on the TV. I chance a quick glance at Hawk, wondering if he's reacting to her cuddled up against me instead of him. He's looking, but his expression isn't what I expect. Instead of annoyance that his girl is pressed into me, his mouth tugs into a satisfied smile before he pulls her feet into his lap.

She sighs as he begins massaging the muscles of her calves, and I instinctively wrap my arm around her shoulders as she relaxes, sliding further down the side of my body. She fits in the space perfectly, humming like she's never been happier when I mindlessly bring my hand up and smooth it through her hair. It's not abnormal for us to watch a movie like this, but having him on the other side with his hands on her too is definitely new. By the sounds she's making, and the way her shallow breaths are beginning to even out, I'd say she isn't uncomfortable with it one bit.

When the movie ends, Arden is out cold, snoring softly with her body still tucked under my arm.

"I'm going to bed," Hawk says, carefully removing her feet from where they sit in his lap and sliding out from under her. He stands, raising his arms above his head in a tired stretch. "You got her?" The question catches me off guard because, for all intents and purposes, Arden is his. They may not be official or anything, but I know that's where they're headed. So why would he want me to be the one to make sure she gets to bed tonight? He knows she's a sound sleeper, and that the likelihood of me carrying her to her room is pretty good, since we've both had to do it already.

I swallow the lump in my throat. "Yeah."

He nods tightly, reaching out and smoothing a hand

across Arden's cheek before putting his fist out for me to bump. I do, and then he's gone, making his way up to his room and shutting the door with a quiet *snick*.

I consider starting another movie because my mind is going a million miles a minute, but maybe taking some time to sort through everything I'm feeling is necessary—especially after the events of the last few hours.

Standing slowly, I scoop her into my arms and carry her up the stairs. I carefully twist my body through her bedroom doorway, walking straight to the bed. Reaching down, I pull the covers back before lowering her onto the soft mattress and tucking them around her. She snuggles in, getting comfortable on her side and sighing contentedly when she's settled. She's so fucking beautiful with her wild hair and bare face, that I can't stop myself from leaning down and pressing a soft kiss to her cheek.

"Jacks," she whispers, and although I should move away, I stay put, my breath fanning across her flawless skin as I reply.

"Yeah, Princess?"

"Stay." It's one word, but it's like a fucking jolt to my heart. Everything I thought would happen when I returned home from Ace's continues to fly out the window, and I'm both confused and relieved by it all. Would Hawk want me to sleep in her bed? Will he be pissed if he comes in here and finds me, even if it's innocent?

"I shouldn't," I argue half-heartedly. "Do you want me to go get Hawk so he can lie down with you?"

She shakes her head, and the motion makes the corner of her lips brush against mine. It's almost a kiss —maybe as close as I'll ever get to one with her—and I go lightheaded from the feel of it. "No. I want you."

I can't deny her what she's asking for. I've never been able to—let alone now when everything between us feels so raw.

So, I don't. Instead, I slide under the covers and pull her into me, falling asleep almost instantly as if it's right where I belong.

EIGHTEEN
HAWK

"LET'S FUCKING GO, ACEY BOY!" Riggs shouts from the dugout as our catcher steps up to the plate. I'm having a terrible game, going 0 for 2 so far and striking out on my last at-bat. None of us are immune to bad days, it just sucks that mine is coming when the Fury needs it the most.

It's game four of the Division Championship, and we're down by three runs at the bottom of the eighth. Coming into tonight, we were up two games to one, so all we needed to do was win. Then, we'd be on our way to the League Championship, which is the last stop on the road to the World Series. Unfortunately, unless we pull off some kind of miracle, we'll be headed back to Daytona tonight for a quick day off before playing the Boston Tide one last time.

The first pitch is thrown, a curveball that's high and outside, so Ace lets it go past. With two outs and a runner on second, we need both him and Jackson, who's on deck, to make a couple of big plays. That'll close the gap, and then hopefully we can pull ahead in the last inning.

The pitcher fires another one Ace's way, and he swings, getting a piece of it as it pops over his head, bounces off the netting behind him, and drops to the ground. "One and one," the umpire yells, crouching back down behind the catcher to await the next pitch. As soon as it's headed toward the plate, I know immediately that it's a beauty. Mathers is a sucker for a low ball, and he doesn't disappoint when he brings the bat around, connecting with a loud *crack*. He knows it's out of the park before any of us, flipping his bat like the cocky little shit he is and leisurely heading to first base as jeers from the Boston fans fill the stadium around us. Rounding toward second, he slows, making a heart with his hands so the cameras can catch the gesture for his fiancée Lark, who I'm sure is watching from their place. I huff a quiet laugh, because now that I understand what it's like to be falling for someone the way he did just a handful of months ago, his lovey-dovey bullshit is a lot less annoying. Or maybe I'm just going soft now that there's a beautiful woman waiting at home for me whether we win or lose.

Things with Arden have been great, but we haven't had much time together. After we had sex for the first time, we took a shower and went downstairs with every intention of sneaking back up for another round later. But when Jackson came home and sat down to watch a movie, there was no fucking way that was happening. Especially when she leaned into him and found a way to make us both feel needed at the same time. It all became crystal clear to me at that moment.

I want us to share her.

Jacks is my best friend. I love and trust him with every fiber of my being, and while I want Arden, I think there's room for both of us in her life. Their bond is something that brings me as much joy as it does them, and if I can just make them see how amazing it would be if they gave in to their true feelings, I know we could make it work.

"Alright, kid. You've got this," I say as Jackson steps up to the plate, bringing the bat over his shoulder and focusing in on the pitcher as he waits for the catcher's signal. He's notorious for letting the first one go by, even if it's perfect, so it's no surprise when he does exactly that. The second pitch, which looks way outside from where I'm sitting, is called strike two. Several boos —obviously from the fans we have in attendance—fill the air as arguments erupt from the dugout around me. It's not uncommon for bad calls to happen when the game is on the line, but it still stings nonetheless. And I can tell he's rattled from it.

"Calm down," I yell, loud enough for him to hear. He nods his head, letting me know he got the message, tapping the end of his bat against the rubber below him and returning to his stance. This pitcher definitely knows who he's throwing to, because the next one is exactly what Jackson likes, and he bites to protect the plate. Unfortunately, the pitch was a touch too high, causing a ground ball right to second base. He takes off as fast as he can, but the attempt is futile because, by the time his foot touches the bag, the first baseman has already made the catch, resulting in the final out of the inning. He hangs his head, and I can tell he's disappointed in himself as I grab his glove from the bench and meet him at the top of the steps.

"You're fine," I say quietly, doing my best to reassure him. "Let's just get out there and see if we can hold them off. If we can't, we'll do it on our own dirt."

He nods, giving me a small smile as we head to our bases. I'm glad I could bring him back to the present. There aren't many occasions where he needs me as much as I need him, but when we're down on the scoreboard, that's when I feel like I help him the most. He's hard on himself, and sometimes he needs to be reminded that it isn't the end of the world if he isn't playing his best.

Unfortunately, we don't make the comeback, so we'll have to fight through one more at home in two days. It sucks, but maybe having Arden in the stands cheering us on will be just what we need to get the job done—or at the very least, make us feel better if the season ends before we're ready.

NINETEEN
ARDEN

"ALRIGHT, ladies. Let's get the side out!" I shout, clapping before lowering my hand so my middle hitter, Izzy, can see the signal. The league isn't doing a formal pre-season for us, so instead, our coaches arranged for a joint practice with the Carolina Sparks so we can get some gameplay simulation before the real matches start. I've noticed that their back row has been dropping back for the entire set because Alaina has been hitting deep, so if I can trick them into thinking it's going to her again, we should have a nice open hole in the middle of the court.

"Alaina!" I say, grabbing her attention and giving a dummy signal before slyly switching to the real one quickly. She nods her head, pulling all the focus her way as the serve comes over. Zara passes it right to me, so I make a show of getting ready to shoot a high set to the outside where my hitter begins her approach. But as soon as the ball touches the tips of my fingers, I quickly pop it low and tight, just as Izzy comes flying through the air and hits it with exact precision, right into the giant empty space behind the middle blocker.

"Yes!" I cheer as we huddle up and congratulate each other. We're playing so well together now that we've had enough time to gel, and I'm ready to see what the season brings. I've played for a lot of different teams since high school, and I have to say, I've never been this excited about the prospect of a championship with any of them. But there's a strong possibility that come playoffs, I might experience the same thing the boys are feeling right now. Unfortunately, yesterday's game didn't pan out well for them, but I'm hoping tomorrow's will, and they'll be one step closer to the pennant they've been working so hard for.

My stomach flips when I remember that I'll get to see them as soon as I'm done with practice. The Fury caught a red-eye from Boston after their game last night, and Hawk and Jacks were both still asleep when I left for the practice facility. I almost woke Hawk because, even though it's only been a few days, it feels like an eternity since I felt his lips on mine—but I decided it could wait a little bit longer.

"Bring it in!" Dahlia yells through her cupped hands, beckoning us all to the sideline. This scrimmage isn't structured, and we aren't keeping score, so we abandon our spots on the court and head her way. "Nice hit, Izzy," she says, skimming right over me and looking at Alaina. "Great fake approach. Keep it up." I internally roll my eyes at how she's always quick to point out when I screw up but seems to be unable to give me credit when I make a good call.

I've been learning to let her actions and words roll off my back with the help of my new therapist. I can't believe that after just two visits, I'm already starting to focus more on the things I can control and less on the things I can't. Instead of panicking about being benched or cut, I've been doing my best to find a healthy balance of practicing, meditating, and giving myself the rest I need. That, paired with a low dose of anxiety medication, has made a huge difference, and I can already feel the pressure being lifted off my shoulders. I'm so grateful to Hawk for understanding what I needed—even when I didn't—and encouraging me to make the appointment. While I still get in my own head from time to time, at least now I'm learning some useful skills to cope with my anxiety in a much healthier way.

"I think that's good for the day," Dahlia says, getting a nod of affirmation from Carolina's coach. "Give me three laps to cool down, then you can get out of here." We all take off in a slow jog, Zara falling into step next to me as we run.

"Is she kidding me with that bullshit?" she mumbles. "You're the captain of this team, a great leader, and she can't bring herself to utter a single nice word after a solid set? Did you fuck her boyfriend in college or something?"

I purse my lips, pretending to think carefully. Her eyes go wide, and I bark out a laugh, shaking my head. "Definitely not. She was a senior when I was a freshman. I was so focused on being a starter that I don't even recall going on a single date that year. I can assure you that her apparent hatred toward me has nothing to do with anything I did to her personally."

She scoffs. "Well, she needs to get over whatever it is, because her inner mean girl is showing. Coach or not, people are going to have trouble respecting her when she isn't respecting her players."

"It is what it is," I reply. "I'm going to keep doing what I'm doing. If she wants to push me out of here, there's nothing I can do but show the other teams why I'm an asset." A month ago, I'd have never felt settled after saying those words, but I can honestly say I believe them with my whole heart. There's a reason my teammates chose me as their captain, and I've been giving one hundred percent to this game, day in and day out. It's taken a while to get here, but what I'm doing is good enough for me right now.

"Okay, fine," she says. "But if you want me to key her ugly brown Beemer, just say the word."

I laugh, shoving her in the shoulder as we finish our final lap and head to the locker room to shower. I race through the process of getting clean and dressed, refusing to waste precious minutes standing under the warm spray like I normally do. I just want to get home so I can spend as much time as possible with Hawk and Jackson before their game tomorrow night. It will be the first one I'm actually able to catch, and I'm beyond excited. I haven't watched them play in person in way too long. Hopefully, it'll be a fun night for us all.

I ride home with the windows down, the cool Daytona breeze blowing through my hair as I sing along to Bella Simon at full blast. After all the years I've been a fan of hers, she still hasn't made a song I don't like. She definitely makes a drive through rush hour traffic a little easier to handle, that's for sure.

I pull into the parking garage much later than I'd like, noticing that Jackson's car isn't where it was when I left. Although part of me is disappointed because I want to see him, I'm also kind of relieved that I won't have to be quiet if Hawk is as needy for me as I am for him right now.

I'm barely even through the door of our condo before he's rounding the corner, a mischievous smirk plastered across his handsome face. He looks as sexy as ever, wearing nothing but a pair of low-hanging gray shorts, with the waistband of his designer boxer briefs peeking from the top. My mouth waters as he stalks my way, wrapping his fingers around my delicate throat and pressing his lips to mine. I drop my bags where I stand, kicking off my shoes right before he slides his hands under my ass and lifts me from the floor.

"I fucking missed you," he rasps, urging me to wrap my legs around him as he heads straight for the stairs. We only get halfway up them before he pushes me against the wall, grinding his huge erection into my core.

"I missed you too," I moan, throwing my head back in pleasure as he makes a direct hit with the head of his cock to my aching bundle of nerves. "Where's Jacks?"

"Don't know, don't care," he growls, licking a hot line down my neck and nipping at the sensitive skin. I cry out, getting wetter by the minute as he works me into a desperate, horny mess in his arms. "I need to fuck you." The words are music to my ears, and suddenly, I no longer give a shit when or if Jackson will be home.

"Please," I beg, and he continues his ascent, carrying me down the hall to his room before tossing me onto the bed. I land with a bounce, air whooshing from my lungs. Before I can even react, he's lowering his wide body between my open thighs, thrusting forward and making me whimper with need.

"Yes, Hellcat. Let me hear those slutty fucking sounds. Show me how bad you want it." His hands and lips are everywhere, and if he doesn't get me naked soon, I'm fully prepared to tear everything off myself. I've had sex with this man one time, coming off the longest dry spell in the history of the world, and here I am ready to give him whatever he asks for just to feel him inside me.

"Hawk, I need you," I choke out, my pussy soaking the inside of my panties as he teases me relentlessly. He chuckles darkly in response, and just as I'm ready to shove my hand down my shorts for relief, he gives in, ridding me of all my clothes before moving to his own. I look down, watching as his impressive length comes into view, and my inner muscles clench when the metal of his piercings glints against the dim light of the room. My entire body is trembling with desire as he drags the head over my slit, stepping back the moment I begin bucking up to meet him.

"Bad girl," he scolds, landing a tight slap to my swollen clit that makes me cry out. I bunch the comforter in my fists so tightly, my knuckles ache as I do my best to focus on his stern voice. "I told you last time I'd give you everything, and that's what I'm going to do. But if you try to *take*, you'll be fucking sorry. Do you understand?"

I nod my head eagerly, fighting the instinct to argue. I want to be good for him. I want to see the raw, unleashed version of Hawk in every way he'll allow me to. "Yes."

"There's my obedient little whore," he replies. A shuddered exhale falls from my lips at his degrading words. I shouldn't love the way they make me feel, but I do. I want so much more. "What's your safe word?" he asks. It takes me a moment to clear the fog from my brain, recalling our last experience. I didn't use it, but I remember him making it very clear that I could put an end to everything with a single word.

"Muffins," I whisper.

"Beautiful," he replies, sliding his hand upward from my navel to my tits, stopping to collar my throat with gentle fingers. "I want to be rough with you. If you allow yourself to surrender to it, I promise I'll make you feel so good. If you don't like something, or my words are too much, tell me and we'll figure it out together. Can you do that, Arden? Can you let me own your pleasure and your pain?"

I swallow the lump in my throat, practically vibrating with excitement and fear at the same time. We haven't even started yet, and the rush he's giving me is already more intense than anything I've ever felt. "Yes." I slowly relax, truly wanting to give myself to him in every way. I'm unbearably wet, soaking the velvet skin of his cock when he leans in for a kiss. As soon as he feels it, he thrusts forward, sliding against me and making me suck in a gasp. The friction is amazing but doesn't last long before he walks away, his perfect ass and tattooed back on full display as he moves toward the dresser. I try to focus on the art that covers his skin, but my brain can't compute all the details through the desperation I'm feeling. I listen as he digs through a drawer, turning back to me with his hands full of various toys before dropping them onto the mattress.

"Before you ask, all of this is brand new. I bought it just for you, hoping like hell you'd let me use it someday." I definitely have questions about when and why he made these purchases, but they'll have to wait, because I'm currently more interested in the *how* part of everything. And there's only one way to find out.

He reaches down, picks up the first item, and holds it so I can see. It's a U-shaped vibrator, and I internally sigh in relief because I have a similar one in my room. This one has a clit sucker on the outer part, whereas mine doesn't. But otherwise, it's not much different. "I'm going to get you started with this. As long as you listen, I'll let you feel good. If you disobey"—he holds up a small, matching remote—"it all stops. I have no issues with jerking myself off into one of your holes and leaving you here unsatisfied if you're bad. You can test that theory if you want, but I don't recommend it."

"Okay," I say quietly, watching as he lowers the toy and swipes it through my wetness before sinking it inside me. Tapping the power button, he brings it to life, making me moan out loud as it vibrates against my walls. The pressure feels like heaven after being teased for what seems like forever. I relax into the mattress, letting my eyes flutter closed, and enjoy the sensations flowing through my body. Just as I feel my orgasm bloom to life, a sharp sting radiates throughout my thigh. I suck in a startled gasp, my gaze landing on Hawk as he towers over me with a heart-shaped crop in one hand.

He tilts his head to the side, a cocky grin stretching across his face. "Did that hurt?" he asks. I hesitate for a moment because, yes, it did—but it also felt good, and I don't know what to make of it. Apparently, I take too long, because he rears back, slapping the leather on the sensitive skin of my other thigh. "Answer me. *Did it hurt?*"

"No," I say, shaking my head rapidly as I blurt out what I really mean. "Yes."

A condescending laugh fills the air, making my orgasm build again. I never thought my body would react to being degraded in this way, but the more he does it, the closer I get to coming. "Which one is it?" he demands. "Or are you just conflicted because I'm slutting you out and you love the way it feels?"

"Yes," I moan, my legs shaking as my release barrels toward me. I spread wider, and my hips involuntary buck up, trying to chase the pleasure as warmth begins to flow through me.

"Arden," he warns. "You know you're not allowed to come unless I say so. Don't you fucking dare...unless you're ready to be punished."

Panic washes over me because I already know it's too late to stop myself. Between the vibrator, the way my skin is still stinging from the crop, and his dominant tone, it's happening whether I want it to or not.

I reach my hand down, attempting to pull the toy out, but he shoves me away, pushing it even tighter to my pussy as he climbs on top of me and holds my body down so I can't squirm away. The clit sucker hits dead-center, and my vision goes hazy as I pass the point of no return.

"Hawk!" I shout as electricity snakes throughout my limbs, gathering between my legs and exploding violently. My back bows off the mattress, and a string of unintelligible, guttural noises tumbles from my open lips as I attempt to endure the most intense climax I've ever experienced in my life. By the time I float back down to earth, I'm gasping for air, letting it out in harsh whines as the vibrator begins to cause painful overstim-ulation against my swollen, sensitive core.

He picks up the remote, cuts off the toy, and pulls it from my body before pressing a seemingly gentle kiss to my cheek, although I'm still numb and buzzing through the aftershocks of my orgasm. Exhaustion settles in, and I relax, humming contentedly. But before I can even form a coherent thought, his warm, comforting weight is gone, and I'm being flipped onto my stomach.

My eyes shoot open just as strong hands grip my hips, lifting me onto my knees seconds before an open palm cracks against my ass. I yelp, attempting to crawl away, but Hawk digs his free hand into my hair, halting me and bringing his mouth to my ear. "I told you I'd punish you if you didn't follow directions. You're going to learn that *I* control every part of you when we're in this room. By the time I have you fully trained, you'll come at the snap of my fingers, you'll kneel at my feet with a single look, and you'll let that sweet little head go empty as soon as my lips touch yours. Until then, there will be consequences for not listening. You're lucky I'm taking it easy on you because you're new. Next time, I won't be so understanding." Rearing his hand back, he spanks me again, but this time, a low moan bursts from my chest. He chuckles in response, and I feel the mattress dip under his weight right before the head of his cock presses through my opening. Even though I'm overstimulated, I push back, practically begging for him to sink all the way inside. But I stop in my tracks when he fists a thick chunk of my hair and squeezes tightly, making a delicious pain bite at the tender skin of my scalp. My eyes fill with tears, and an involuntary, very loud whimper escapes me.

"Shhh," he warns. "What if Jackson comes home and hears how needy his sweet sister is for his best friend's cock?" My inner muscles clench on their own accord, and Hawk goes still behind me for a moment as realization washes over us both. I swallow thickly, throwing up a silent prayer that he'll let it go, but of course, he doesn't. "Ooh. I think you like that idea," he chides. "Does that make you wet, Hellcat? Would you want him to come watch us? Or maybe you'd like it if he walked in and put his hands all over this hot little body while I made you come until you cried." I say nothing, because what the hell *can* I say when he's reading me like a fucking book? I do want that. I've fantasized about it more times than I'm proud to admit, but I certainly wasn't prepared for anyone to find out.

"Come on, baby," he mocks. "Answer the question. Or better yet"—he pauses, pulling my head up so I'm looking into the open doorway—"*tell him*."

I gasp, my eyes going wide in horror. "Jacks."

TWENTY
JACKSON

FUCK.

I should leave. I shouldn't have even walked down to this end of the hall. But when I heard Arden crying out in pain, I couldn't help myself. My feet carried me toward the sound of her voice, coming to a grinding stop when I saw them in Hawk's bed, both naked as he punished her from behind. My brain screamed at my body to move, but as soon as he asked her if she wanted me too, I might as well have been nailed to the floor, because like hell I was leaving without an answer. I need it more than my next breath.

Finding all the courage I have, I step forward, stopping when my thighs hit the side of the mattress. She looks up at me, her eyes filled with a million different emotions as I reach out and smooth my hand across her cheek. We stare at each other for several seconds before the words that are hanging on the tip of my tongue finally break free.

"Is that true?" I choke out. "Do you...want me

here?" My heart pounds inside my ribcage, and I wait with bated breath for her to put me out of my misery. Her attention flits back to Hawk, who I almost forgot was even here, and he nods in approval, rubbing a reassuring hand up her lower back as she returns her gaze to mine.

"Yes," she whispers, the word almost getting caught in her throat as she forces it out. But as soon as it passes her lips, she sighs in relief, like she's been holding it in for fucking *years*.

"Me too, Princess," I reply quietly, wishing I could tell her just how long I've been dying to hear her say it…and how badly I've craved the same thing. Sitting down on the bed next to where she's perched on all fours, I look up to my best friend and await his next move. He easily slips back into character, lowering his hand and palming her ass roughly. She winces, and I do my best to comfort her by ghosting the backs of my knuckles across her jaw.

"Our girl here was told that she wasn't allowed to come unless I gave her permission. She didn't follow my orders, so now she's being punished. Not that you'd know it with the way her cunt is dripping right now," Hawk says as he slowly drives into her. She gasps, her face twisting in discomfort when he surges forward, not stopping until the sound of his pelvis slapping against the supple flesh of her ass fills the room. Her slender back arches, and her full tits bounce as he bottoms out, sending a jolt of arousal straight to my dick. She's perfection in every sense of the word. Even my wildest fantasies don't hold a candle to the way she looks naked and flushed as he takes her from behind. A quiet whimper tumbles from her lips, and I lean forward, bringing my mouth to her ear.

"You're doing such a good job," I praise. "Are you okay?"

"Mhmm," she replies, focusing her attention on me as he pulls back, entering her again and making her moan. I back away just slightly, gripping her chin gently and watching her eyes as they begin to glaze over with lust. She bites her plump bottom lip, making me pull from the depths of my restraint so I don't dive forward and kiss her. As much as I want to, I can't...*yet*.

"What a perfect girl, taking his cock. Is he hitting all your little spots?" I ask, earning a frantic nod in response. She seems to love the way I'm talking her through it, so the harder his thrusts become, the softer I speak. "You're breathtaking when you're being fucked, Arden. So beautiful and sweet."

"She's a greedy whore," Hawk grits out. "You should feel the way she's choking me right now. It's fucking pathetic how she can barely take a simple instruction without acting like a slut in heat." He slaps her ass, making her cry out in a mix between pleasure and pain. "Arden, I swear to God if you come again, not even Jackson will be able to save you."

I weave my fingers into her hair, rubbing my thumb along her cheek as he pounds into her. "You can do it. Let him use your pussy." My dick is like stone, tenting the material of my basketball shorts, but I don't fucking care. This is the hottest experience of my life, praising her on one end as she gets brutally fucked on the other.

As much as I wondered if something like this could even work—or if either of us would get jealous—I can confidently say I have no problem watching him with her.

"I'm going to fill this tight hole," he grunts from behind her, pistoning his hips relentlessly. "Tell Jackson how you love being my cumslut."

Her eyes find mine, and I can tell she's struggling to hold back her own release. Her expression is pleading, and it's making me want to shove him away so I can make her feel better. But I don't. Instead, I wait for her to give him what he asked for.

"I-I love being his cumslut," she moans, her fists gripping the comforter tightly.

"I can't wait to see how well you take his load, Princess," I reply just as he thrusts one last time, finally emptying into her with a growl. I watch as he takes his pleasure, every muscle in his body contracting until he's completely spent before sinking down and curling his chest over her back. He presses gentle kisses to the side of her neck and face, moving his lips to her ear and speaking much softer than normal.

"You did so good," he praises. "I'm proud of you, baby."

"Mmm," she hums, her arms finally giving out so she's resting on her elbows with her forehead pressed against the mattress. Hawk looks up at me, and we exchange a knowing glance, him asking me without words if I can take it from here. I nod, and he backs off the bed, quietly disappearing into his en suite bathroom. I have a sneaking suspicion he was ready and willing to provide aftercare but wanted to give Arden and me some time alone. I'm grateful for that, because while I know we should hold off on talking about everything we just said and did, I'm far from finished with her. I've waited too long for this.

"Come here," I say, removing my shirt and lying on the mattress next to where she's slumped over. Reaching under her arms, I lift her so she's straddling my lap, the bare skin of our chests pressed together tightly as I rub soothing circles along her back. She hums contentedly, melting into me for several minutes until she's fully recovered.

She lifts her head, pulling away just enough so that we're able to look at each other. A million questions dance across her expression, all of which we'll have to sort through, but it can wait. Right now, I need to do something I should've done a long fucking time ago.

Sliding my hand around the back of her neck, I coax her toward me. She comes willingly, finally giving me everything I've wanted for what feels like a lifetime as her soft lips press against mine. Fireworks explode behind my eyes, and I can't stop the quiet whimper that leaves my body when she opens, plunging her tongue inside my waiting mouth as though she's needed me just as badly as I've needed her. If I didn't know it before, this definitely makes it all crystal clear—she's everything I've ever dreamed of. I never have, and never will, feel this way about another woman. It's always been her.

The kiss turns frantic, her hips moving along my erection as I swallow her desperate whines. I'm not surprised that she's so wound up, considering Hawk just fucked her brains out and refused to let her come. She was close—I could see it in her eyes—but she obeyed his order. He may be okay with leaving her to suffer, but I'm not. I hear him moving behind the bathroom door, followed by the quiet whistle of the shower being turned on, so I know we have at least ten minutes —maybe more.

Lowering my hand between us, I press the tip of my middle finger to her swollen, sensitive clit. She gasps in response, and I break our connection, bringing my mouth to her ear so she can hear me speak. "Shh," I warn. "He might hear you. Be a good girl and come quietly for me, okay?" She nods her head, and I slip back further, pushing two fingers into her wet heat. She's dripping with Hawk's release, and as surprised as I am by the revelation, it only turns me on more to feel how full she is. The urge to bury myself deep inside and give her a load of my own is almost overwhelming when she begins bouncing up and down, chasing her orgasm.

"That's it. Make that good girl pussy come." A shaky, flustered breath tumbles from her lips, and she changes tactics, grinding against my palm. Her inner muscles flutter around me as she works herself up, but I can tell she's needy for so much more.

"Jacks," she begs. "Please."

"Please *what*, Princess?" I'm almost positive I know what she's asking for, but I might die if I don't hear her say the words. Fuck pissing Hawk off or going against his wishes. This is about me and Arden.

"I want you inside me."

I exhale slowly. She has no idea how many times I've thought about that very thing, hating the fact that she could never be mine. Yet, here we are, and she's saying words I couldn't even fathom hearing before tonight.

"We don't have to right now," I whisper, pulling out of her warmth and ghosting my hands over her hips reassuringly. "I want you more than anything in this world, but I need to know we're on the same page. This isn't just sex for me."

She shakes her head, her fingers coming up to run along my cheek. "Jackson, you can't possibly think I haven't had feelings for you since we were kids. I've always hoped you felt the same, but that wasn't us."

I lean into her touch, relief flooding over me like a warm wave. "I felt the same. I was chicken shit. By the time I worked up the nerve, our parents were already together. There were so many times I wanted to blurt it out, but I was scared."

"I want this," she says with a soft smile. "But before we do, I need you to know that I really care about Hawk."

"Me too," I reply, and as if we had summoned him, the door opens, and he enters the bedroom with a white towel wrapped around his waist. He steps up to his dresser, gathers some clothes, and walks over to where we're lying on the bed before tipping Arden's chin up so she's looking at him.

"You're fucking incredible," he says, dropping a chaste kiss to her lips and standing to his full height.

"Just so you both know, I'm okay with whatever happens here. I'm going to go for a run so you can have some time to yourselves. Text me if you need anything." He winks at Arden before turning and leaving the room, and as fucking weird as all of this should be, it's not. The woman he just fucked, and has very deep feelings for, is naked on top of me, and he's leaving the condo so we can do the same, if that's what she wants. It's unconventional, for sure—but none of it feels wrong.

She turns my way, her eyes burning into mine. "Whatever this is…I want it all. It's not just sex for me, either."

I wrap my arms around her waist, turning us so I'm on top before leaning down and taking her lips in a passionate kiss. I'm caught somewhere between being desperate to get inside her and wanting to take my time. I finally decide that we can do *slow and exploratory* next round, because doing it now would only torture us both. She's needy because Hawk didn't let her come, and I want nothing more than to be the reason she does.

I reach down, shoving my shorts and boxer briefs over my thighs, never breaking our connection as I kick them off the side of the bed. The first slide of my erection through her cum-covered slit has me seeing stars, and I have to take a deep, slow breath just to stop myself from blowing before I even get a chance to feel her wrapped around me. I have no idea how I'll last, but hopefully, I can find a way to get her off before I finish.

"Fuck, Princess," I say on a harsh exhale. "How are you real?"

She giggles against my lips. "I've been right in front of you the whole time."

Pulling back, I smooth a hand through her hair, thankful that we're finally here. That we made it through all the bumps along our path, and now she's under me, saying everything I've only wished to hear. No matter what happens, I'll always remember this moment.

"Do you want me to use a condom?" I ask. I don't want to assume that just because she let Hawk come inside her, she'd want me to. I've certainly been with my fair share of women, where he's choosier because he doesn't like to let people get close to him in any capacity. But I've never fucked without protection, and I hope Arden knows I wouldn't put her at risk.

"I want you bare, if that's what you want," she replies. "I'm on birth control, and the only person I've been with in a long time just left the room, so it's up to you. I trust you completely."

"Me too," I whisper, dropping my lips to hers as I line myself up and slowly push inside. Her inner walls grip me as though they were made for my cock, and I sink in further, burying myself to the hilt, doing my best to burn everything about the way she feels into my brain. Not that I could ever forget.

"Fuck, you feel so good. Are you okay?" I leisurely drag my heavy length out, carefully driving forward again as she nods in response.

"So good. Oh my God. Please go faster, Jacks. I'm dying."

I chuckle, pulling her thigh over my hip and setting an even tempo so she's getting what she needs. It isn't long before her pussy is swelling and clenching, hugging my shaft so tightly, I can barely move.

"Such a sweet girl," I say, lowering my hand to her clit and rubbing in tight circles. "Let that aching cunt come all over my cock. You'll feel so much better once you do."

Her head thrashes back and forth as her nails dig into the skin of my shoulders, and I pick up speed, knowing that she's teetering on the edge of her orgasm. As good as it would feel to slow down and make this last, she's been through enough, so I fuck into her like a man possessed as she moans in pleasure.

The leg wrapped around my waist begins to shake uncontrollably, and her back bows off the bed. Before I can ask what else she needs, her pussy clamps down, pulsing against me. A string of almost unintelligible curses falls from her beautiful lips, and it takes every ounce of self-control I have not to follow her. I'm right there, but there's no way I'm coming if I don't have her full attention.

"Look at me, Arden," I plead. "I'm going to come inside you. Please fucking look at me." Hearing the desperation in my voice, she fights her instincts and her eyes flutter open. It takes a few seconds, but eventually, she comes back to the present, smiling as her hands begin to ghost along my sides.

"I'm here," she replies on a whisper. "Make me yours, Jackson."

Those words are all I need to detonate, shooting hot ropes of cum into her gorgeous body. I grunt loudly, succumbing to the feeling of sheer bliss, knowing I'm emptying myself inside the only girl I've ever loved. I want to blurt out the words as I fall, but I'm happy that at least some part of my brain is working, because the timing isn't right. Saying them now might diminish their meaning for her, and I need her to understand that it's so much more than I can articulate—especially in this moment.

I pump my hips one last time, making sure I've given her every last drop before leaning forward and gently coasting my lips against hers in a barely-there, yet epically monumental gesture.

"Hi," I say quietly, brushing a sweat-soaked strand of hair from her flushed cheek.

"Hi." Her exhausted giggle is like music to my ears, making me drop my head forward in relief that she's not immediately filled with regret. The last thing I want is for things to change or become awkward between us, so I'll do whatever I can to make sure that doesn't happen.

I lean back, slowly pulling my cock from her body and making her whimper in response. Looking down, I watch as a mixture of cum—mine, hers, and Hawk's—drips down the skin between her pussy and asshole, feeling a rush of possessiveness at the sight. We made her ours, and I fucking love it.

"That's...*different*," she says with an unsure expression painted across her face. I bark out a laugh, because she's filled to the brim and making a mess all over herself. I imagine it's probably not very comfortable.

"Come on." I slide off the mattress, extending my hand for her to take and pulling her to her feet. She wobbles, so I wrap an arm around her waist, giving her support as she regains her bearings. "Let's take a shower, then we can go downstairs and wait for Hawk to get back from his run."

She pushes to her tiptoes, tilting her head back and pursing her lips as if she's awaiting a kiss. She's fucking adorable with her eyes closed, trusting she'll get what she's asking for. *Of course, she will.* Taking her cheeks in my hands, I give her what she wants before landing a gentle slap to her ass and making her jaw drop in faux exasperation.

"Let's go, *cumslut*," I say with a cocky grin. "You're dripping on his floor."

TWENTY-ONE
HAWK

"WAKE UP, DICKHEAD," I grump, reaching over Arden and shaking Jackson's shoulder as he sleeps like he's dead. After I got home last night, I took another shower before joining the two of them where they had laid out several blankets and pillows on the living room floor. Historically, I'm not a cuddler, but both of us holding her as we drifted off to sleep is definitely something I can see myself getting used to.

My anxiety bubbled to the surface during my run, every bad scenario playing over and over in my head as I thought about what I'd find when I walked in the door. When I left them alone, hoping they'd finally give in to whatever feelings they'd been harboring since long before I came into the picture, I second-guessed whether or not it was the right choice. Would they have sex and realize they didn't want me around at all? Would they find out that they're better as friends? Would it make things weird between the two of them... or *all of us*? I couldn't bear the thought of any of that, so

I did my best to tune it out, focusing on the way my feet pressed into the sand along Daytona Beach and running until I was completely exhausted. But when I returned home to find them making out while a movie played as background noise on the TV, relief washed over me. And everything clicked into place when she reached out, beckoning me to join. We spent the rest of the night lounging as if it were the most normal thing in the world. Although Jacks and I agreed that we're both completely unwavering in our decision to share Arden, I know we still have to talk about what the future looks like for the three of us going forward. But for now, I'm happy just existing like this.

"Dude, wake the fuck up," I say again, slapping my open palm across his forehead. His face scrunches in annoyance and he groans, peeling his eyes open and immediately scowling in my direction.

"Leave me alone. I'm tired." He rolls to his side, nuzzling his face into Arden's tits as she snores softly between us. "Oh my God, I'm staying here all day." His words are muffled against her skin, and I roll my eyes, pressing a kiss to the top of her head before pushing up to my feet. My back aches from the hard floor I've been lying on for the last eight hours, but it was definitely worth it.

"No, you aren't," I deadpan. "We have to be at the stadium in two hours."

He looks up at me. "Tell Clyde I said thanks for the opportunity, but I quit."

"Get up," I reply, ignoring him. "I'll make breakfast." I stretch my back as I walk toward the kitchen and head to the refrigerator. Scanning the options, I reach inside for the turkey bacon, set it on the counter, and go back for a couple of avocados. I made two loaves of Arden's favorite bread before we left for our road trip, but she wasn't able to finish it, so I'll use the rest now.

Pulling a pan from the cupboard, I get to work, knowing we probably only have about an hour and fifteen minutes before we need to be out the door. Although the game isn't until much later, the media makes a bigger show of things during playoffs—especially since the series is tied and it's a win-or-go-home situation. I try pretty hard to stay away from the cameras, but even I'm not immune to doing numerous interviews on days like today. I understand the need for them, but it doesn't make me hate public speaking any less.

Just as I finish flipping the bacon, two small arms snake around my waist. I hum contentedly as Arden's fingertips ghost across my bare abs, enjoying the sensations while she explores every ridge and valley like she's studying a treasure map. It's as if she knew what I needed, her touch calming the nagging feeling in the pit of my stomach that began swirling around when I thought about what awaits me at the stadium.

I set the spatula down, turn so I'm facing her, and dip down for a kiss. My hands immediately find her ass, making her moan into my mouth as I knead her soft flesh. I swallow every sweet sound, reluctantly pulling back so I can look at her. A sleepy smile blooms across her face, and my heart skips a beat at how happy she is. The fact that Jackson and I had a hand in that is a gift she'll never even know she's given us.

"You hungry, Hellcat?" I ask.

"Mhmm," she replies, tilting her head up toward me. "I was kind of hoping for more muffins so we could sneak back into the pantry."

I raise a brow, a devious grin tugging at the corner of my mouth as she bites her lip. Before I can tell her what a dirty girl she is, Jacks interrupts, entering the room wearing only the black boxer briefs he slept in.

"What's in the pantry?" he questions, lazily pushing a hand through his messy brown hair. I chuckle darkly, focusing on the stove as Arden spins his way and pastes on her best innocent expression.

"Nothing," she rushes out. I toss a look over my shoulder, and he catches it, folding his arms over his chest. I can't help the laugh that bursts out of me as realization settles in. He stands there in shock, jaw practically on the floor as his eyes bounce rapidly between us.

"Please tell me you two didn't do dirty, disgusting things on or around my Doritos."

Arden's hand flies to her chest in the most unconvincing show of exasperation I've ever seen. Her mouth opens and closes several times, but no words come out while she tries to fabricate an explanation. As much as I'd love to watch her backpedal out of this, we need to get moving. I refuse to be late for one of the most important games of the season.

"I fingered her and fucked her face while the chocolate zucchini muffins you completely demolished were in the oven. Nobody touched your Doritos," I say dryly, setting a plate on the counter next to where he's gaping like a fish. "Hurry up and eat. We have to go."

His eyes grow even wider, sliding over to where Arden is looking everywhere but at him. "I'm not hungry anymore. And you," he scolds, pointing an accusing finger in her direction. She turns, her chin dipping to her chest as her cheeks pinken in the most adorable way. "I'm fucking your brains out in there later." He scoffs as though he's appalled before spinning on his heel and stomping out of the room like a petulant child. I laugh under my breath, because of course he wants to outdo me. Some things will never change, even if we *are* sharing the same girl.

And I wouldn't want it any other way.

TWENTY-TWO
ARDEN

"YOU MUST BE ARDEN!" a gorgeous blonde says as I arrive at my seat. It's the first Fury game I've been able to make it to since I moved here, and I'm definitely kicking things off with a bang because this place is already electric.

"Hi!" I reply. "Lark, right? Jackson told me I'd be sitting next to you!" She nods and I reach out, taking her extended hand in mine just as the most beautiful brunette I've ever seen pops out from behind her.

"Oh my God, we heard all about you at Ace's graduation! I'm Monroe!" I shake her hand as well, lowering myself into my seat as fans move around us. With more than thirty minutes until the first pitch, I'm guessing most people are still waiting in lines to get their food and memorabilia before they settle in. Jackson told me not to bother with any of that since his teammate, Ace, has his fiancée's snacks delivered down here anyway. I'll admit it's nice to be set up like one of the WAGs, even though I have no idea if I qualify. Hawk and I haven't defined our relationship yet, and I know Jacks and I have a lot to sort through before we can even begin to figure out what's going to happen with us. Our parents are obviously the main concern, since I doubt they'd accept us dating with open arms. But, at the end of the day, we're adults—and that decision is ours. As complicated as it all is, I know with absolute certainty that I want both Jackson and Hawk if they're okay with that. I can't imagine having to choose one over the other. I wouldn't be able to do it.

"So," Monroe says, leaning forward so she can see me, "you're a pro volleyball player. That's fucking badass!"

I smile in response. "It's crazy. We've only been practicing for a couple of months, but my teammates are all super talented. We're having a lot of fun." It's not a lie. Other than my coach giving me shit for absolutely no good reason, playing for the Flare is an amazing experience—one I'm extremely grateful for. I can't wait until the season starts so we can show the world that we're a force to be reckoned with.

"I told Ace that I wanted to catch a match," Lark says. "I hope that's not weird. I just feel like women's sports don't get the attention they deserve, and if we can help by shouting it from the rooftops, we should."

"Agreed," Monroe says, just as a giant, purple—well, I don't exactly know what it is—comes up behind her, catching my attention. It's like a train wreck I want to look away from, but somehow can't seem to even blink as I try to make sense of what I'm seeing. Big, googly eyes adorn its face, the center of which showcases a giant, teal nose. One arm hangs by its side, almost touching the ground, while the other holds a cup that looks to be full of gummy bears.

"Umm…" I trail off, pointing at it before both girls turn around.

"Hey, Friggle Baby!" Monroe exclaims, flicking one of the small horns that protrude from the top of the creature's head. "Been waiting for you to come say hi." It bounces up and down excitedly, reaching across and handing the cup to Lark.

"Thank you, Friggle," she sing-songs, turning back toward me. "He's the mascot. Creepy as fuck, but from what I can tell, completely harmless. Ace sends him down with candy every few innings. I'm not sure if it's to embarrass me, or just because he can't stand the thought of me not being completely sugared up at all times. Want some?" She tips it my way, and I oblige, plucking a red bear and popping it into my mouth.

"Thank you," I giggle, just as Fury players begin to funnel onto the field for warm-ups. Riggs Valentine runs out first, prompting Monroe to grab the purple monster by the furry hand.

"C'mon Frig," she says, tipping her chin toward the railing that runs along the third base line. "Let's go fuck with Val. We'll pretend to make out and see how long it takes him to chase us down." He resists, digging his giant feet into the concrete steps, but she wins, pulling him toward the field as he shakes his head in disagreement.

"That girl is a menace, and I love her for it," Lark says with a laugh right before her eyes light up and a wide smile stretches across her face. I follow her line of vision to see the Fury's catcher, Ace Mathers, waving up at her before making a heart with his hands. She sets her cup down, returning the gesture before mouthing *I love you*. I remember videos of their engagement going viral on social media not too long ago. They're the cutest couple I've ever seen, and I'm a tiny bit jealous of how open they are with their relationship.

I don't know what's going to happen with Hawk and Jackson, but if we decide to keep doing what we're doing, what'll it be like when we go public? Not only do Jacks and I have to worry about our parents—but how will people react when they find out their favorite baseball players are dating the same girl? Will I get shamed and disrespected for it? Is what we're building strong enough to withstand it, or will we break? The thought makes my stomach turn with anxiety. But before it has a chance to take hold, Hawk steps onto the field, eyes immediately finding mine. The smallest hint of a smile pulls at one corner of his mouth, and I'm instantly calm. It doesn't matter what people think about us, because this right here, is worth any number of hurtful words a bunch of strangers can hurl my way. Knowing I have someone—or *two* someones—to pull me out of the darkness when I need it, means everything to me.

We hold each other's gaze for a few beats longer until Jackson walks up behind him and slaps a hand on his shoulder. Like a magnet, he finds me, shooting a sexy wink my way. He's so hot with his messy chestnut-brown hair and chiseled features that it's hard not to drool knowing what he's hiding under that uniform. I look around nervously, checking to see if anyone is paying attention to the three of us sneakily flirting, but it seems we're going unnoticed as fans maneuver up and down the stairs around me.

"Umm, what am I watching right now?" Monroe says, snapping me from the trance the boys had me under. I didn't even see her come back, but by the confused look on her face, she's been standing here for more than a few seconds.

"What?" I reply, guilt written all over my face because I'm a terrible liar. My eyes bounce between her and Lark as they await my answer, but otherwise, I'm frozen. Sweat beads at the back of my neck and I swallow thickly, my heart practically jumping out of my chest. They both seem really nice, but I don't know them well enough to explain what they just witnessed.

Monroe leans in so only we can hear her. "Do you… *like them both*? Because, not to be gross, but I'm going to need some alone time after seeing the way they just looked at you like you were a whole damn meal."

My eyes go wide as Lark cuts in, also speaking quietly. "You don't have to tell us anything if you don't want to. It's none of our business. But if you need to talk"—she motions between the three of us—"this is a safe space."

I nod in understanding, relaxing slightly as I take in their soft expressions. Other than Stella—who's always supportive, but so far away—I don't have anyone I can confide in about this whole situation. I've started to build a good friendship with Zara, but as her teammate and captain, I've tried to keep my personal life separate for now. And as close as I am with my dad and Gina, there's no way I can talk to them about any of this. So maybe I should let Monroe and Lark in a little bit. Jackson told me how amazing they both are, and I trust him.

"It's…complicated," I whisper. "But I really like them." The word *like* is a bit of an understatement, and feels wrong as it rolls off my tongue, but I'm definitely not about to unpack any of that right now. The bond I have with Jackson grew into something much bigger the moment his lips touched mine, and Hawk knows me in ways nobody else does. It seems irreverent to diminish what I feel for either of them with such a simple word.

"Good for you," Monroe says with a sly grin, putting her fist out for me to bump. I roll my eyes, unable to hold back my laugh as I reach out and return the gesture.

"We're always here if you need us," Lark says sincerely. "Ace and I haven't been together long, but this team is one big family. We have your back, no matter what." My heart warms at her words, and I thank her with a grateful smile just as the National Anthem begins to play through the stadium speakers.

My eyes drift down to where the team is lined up, and I'm filled with a sense of pride as I look at my guys. Being in the MLB was Jackson's dream as a kid. He wasn't blessed with the kind of talent that made it easy —he really had to put in the work, day in and day out.

Seeing him down there doing what he loves makes me unbelievably happy.

And then there's Hawk. He had such a rough childhood with every card stacked against him. Losing his brothers could've broken him and made him give up on any type of a future for himself. He could've let his depression and anxiety consume him, but instead, he pushed forward. He got help, then encouraged me to do the same. I'll never be able to thank him enough for not giving up on either of us.

The Fury takes the field first, and almost immediately, it's a fight. For every player Riggs strikes out, another gets a big hit, and by the middle of the first, it's two to zero. As the players jog to the dugout, I can tell that Jacks is frustrated, but he reaches into his jersey, pulls out the chain I gave him, and wraps his fingers tightly around it. I have yet to ask him why he still wears it, but the sight of him holding onto the gold rope makes my heart beat wildly in my chest. It may just be a superstition, but part of me wonders if he kept it because it reminded him of me.

Dante Cole steps up to the plate, waiting for the first pitch to go by before he readies himself for the next. It's right down the middle of the strike zone, and he swings, sending a pop-fly directly into the left fielder's glove. The crowd claps in an attempt to keep the team in the game, but it continues to go downhill as the second batter strikes out in just three pitches.

Ace steps out of the dugout as Candy Girl by New Edition blares through the speakers. The fans, who had looked a bit deflated moments ago, stand from their seats, singing and dancing along. He puts on a show for the entire stadium, pointing directly at his fiancée as he does. Lark laughs loudly, catcalling her man until he blows her a kiss, takes his bat from the batboy, and heads to the plate as the song fades.

"That was the cutest thing I've ever seen," I say as she presses her hands to her heated cheeks, smiling sheepishly. You can tell how in love they are, despite what Jackson told me about their age difference and how they come from totally different worlds. They're going against what society says is normal, and that gives me hope that maybe someday, I can do the same.

The rest of the game is a knock-down, drag-out fight, but unfortunately, the Fury falls just short of the win. Although they only lose by a single run, I know the guys won't see it that way. A loss is a loss—one that ended a very promising season—and I'm sure it'll take a while for them to shake this one off. I don't blame them if that's the case since I know what it's like to get so close to achieving your dreams and missing by the smallest amount.

"Well, that sucks," Monroe says, turning toward us. "I doubt the guys will be going out tonight, so if you all want to swing by, our coolers are stocked with beer and wine. If anything, we can get them drunk, so they don't beat themselves up over this. Plus, we're all in the same building, which means everyone will be able to get home safely and not have to call for a ride."

"That's a great idea," Lark replies, looking at me. "Think you can talk your boys into it?"

My boys. I've said the words in my own head a few

times, even before everything went down with Jackson. But hearing them from someone else's mouth? I kind of love it.

I shrug. "Probably. I think we could all use a night of fun. I don't have practice until noon tomorrow, so I'm sure we'd be able to stop by for a bit."

We say our goodbyes—the girls heading to wait outside the locker rooms, while I drive myself back to our condo. Hawk and Jackson made sure my name was on the list to go down there, but I didn't think it was a good idea, especially after the way they lost. I'd want to hug and comfort them. Then I'd probably want to kiss them. We can't do that in public—at least not right now.

Just as I'm pulling into my parking spot, my phone vibrates. I take it out and swipe up to find a text from Jackson.

JACKS:

Where'd you go? We came out from our post-game interviews hoping to find you waiting for us.

ME:

I just thought I should let you guys process things alone. Are you okay?

JACKS:

It sucks, but there's always next year.

ME:

You gave it your all. Be proud of yourselves for that.

> Monroe asked if we wanted to go to their place for a bit. We don't have to if you're not feeling up to it, but I didn't want to be rude. Or I can go alone.

JACKS:

It's fine. Riggs mentioned it too. Should we just meet you there?

ME:

> Yeah. I'm about to go up now. I'll see you soon.

JACKS:

Sounds good, Princess.

My stomach flips with excitement, knowing they're on their way to me. As much as I want to spend more time getting to know the girls, I'll be counting down the minutes until I can be alone with them again...and fantasizing about all the filthy things I want them to do to me.

TWENTY-THREE
JACKSON

"OKAY, HEAR ME OUT," Ace says with a hiccup, downing what's left of his third beer. The dude is a total lightweight for his size. "What if the entire Tide team fails a PED test at the same time and gets disqualified? They'd have no choice but to send us to the division series, right? Or," he continues, waving his hand animatedly in the air, "what if the highway caves in and swallows their whole bus on the way to the airport? And they were just…*poof! Gone*." His eyes go wide as he considers his own ridiculous question.

Lark sets a gentle hand on his shoulder. He stumbles for a second but recovers, steadying himself before looking over at her with hearts in his eyes. "Baby, this is why we don't let you drink," she says sympathetically. "You can't handle your shit."

"You're pretty," he sighs, fluttering his lashes. She rolls her eyes, pretending to be annoyed before pushing to her tiptoes and pressing a chaste kiss to his lips. The whole situation would actually be hilarious if I wasn't so fucking frustrated.

We've been standing in Riggs and Monroe's kitchen for over an hour, and the entire time, Hawk has been touching Arden. Whether it's a hand on her lower back, an arm around her waist, or her leaning into him as she sips on her wine, it's pissing me off. Not because I'm envious that she's giving him attention, but because I feel like I can't do any of those things.

I trust everyone here. The guys are my brothers, and their girls are the most welcoming, non-judgmental people I've ever met. I don't give a fuck if they know about us, not that I think they'd care even if they did. But would Hawk and Arden feel the same if I walked over and touched her, too? I know that if we decide to move forward as a unit, my decisions affect more than just myself. I'm okay with that, but are they? It's been an emotional night, and while I enjoy the camaraderie of being around my teammates, I just want to hold my girl for a second.

"I have to pee," Arden says quietly, and Hawk nods in response as she slips out of the room. I look around, noticing all the others in deep conversation before trading a look with my best friend. He lifts his chin in understanding, and I sneak away, nonchalantly making my way down the hall until I reach the bathroom. I stand there like a fucking creep, listening carefully as she flushes the toilet and turns on the faucet to wash her hands. As soon as the lock disengages, I push my way in, making her gasp in surprise as I shut the door behind me.

"Jacks, what the f—"

I cut her off by taking her face in my hands and dropping my mouth to hers in a desperate kiss. She fists the cotton of my t-shirt as I drive my tongue past her lips, earning another hungry sound. I feel like I'm racing against the buzzer to get my fill of her before we have to go back out there and act like it isn't killing us to be so far away from each other.

"Fuck, I couldn't take it anymore. I needed to touch you," I say on a harsh exhale, delving back in for more as my hands slide down her body, unable to settle on one spot for long because it's just not enough.

"Touch me. Hurry," she whispers frantically, and it's like music to my fucking ears as I spin her in my arms, so her back is pressed tightly to my front. Our eyes lock onto one another in the mirror, and my heart swells in my chest as I take her in. Her cheeks are flushed, her lips are swollen, and she's so incredibly *mine*.

Gliding my hands down her stomach, I bring my mouth to her ear, never breaking my gaze from our reflection. "Look at us," I tell her, dipping a hand under the waistband of her leggings and panties. "After all these years, I finally have you the way I've always wanted. I can't tell you how many nights I've dreamed about being able to touch this pussy—to make it come all over me. And now that I can, I'm obsessed." She whimpers as I slide down further, brushing the tip of my middle finger along her wet slit, then dragging it back up to rub soft circles on her swollen bundle of nerves. "I've stroked myself to the thought of what you'd sound like as I worked you toward the edge, making you so needy that you'd beg for me to fuck you."

"Jackson. *Oh my God*." She exhales a shaky breath, her hips bucking against my palm. My cock is like steel under my sweatpants, soaking the inside of my boxers with precum, but I don't care. I literally have the girl of my dreams in the palm of my hand, and nothing else matters.

"Say my name again, baby," I demand. "Look me in my eyes and say my fucking name when I make you come." I'm desperate to hear it from her lips as I pick up speed, massaging her clit while it begins to spasm under my touch. I can't look away from her face in the mirror. She's more beautiful than ever, rocking into me until her mouth falls open and she sings my name, finding her release.

"Jackson." It's barely a whisper, but her pleading expression tells me everything I need to know. She wants me like I want her. Not just physically, but in every way I've longed for her since I was a teenager. I don't know how, but we're going to make this work. Me, Arden, and Hawk. I want to give her everything.

"That's a good girl, Princess," I praise, stroking my finger along her opening and gathering the wetness as she recovers. I pull her tightly to my body while her legs shake with aftershocks, and I can't stop myself from ghosting gentle kisses on her face and neck as she hums in satisfaction. The words I've been holding back are threatening to fight their way out, but I need more time. We only just confessed our feelings for one another yesterday, and I don't want to reveal too much, too soon—even though I've spent a lifetime keeping them inside.

She looks into the mirror, catching my gaze again as I pull my fingers from her panties and suck them into my mouth. My eyes roll back as the taste of her explodes on my tongue, and I'm suddenly hit with another pang of envy, because I'm sure Hawk has already licked the heaven between her legs, and now I want it, too.

"I can't wait to eat your pussy," I say quietly. "I can already tell I'll never want another meal for as long as I live." She turns her head, and I press my lips to hers, leisurely kissing her until there's a loud knock on the door. We both startle, and she stiffens in my arms, pulling away with a hand over her mouth.

"Just a minute!" I say, widening my eyes at Arden because I have no idea what to do. Even though I think our friends would be cool with us being together, I'm not sure getting busted after hooking up in the bathroom would be a great way to inform them.

"Blake?" Ace slurs, his voice muffled by the thick wood between us. "What are you doing in there?"

"Oh my God!" Arden whisper-shouts. "This is so embarrassing! He's going to know what we were doing!"

I chuckle quietly. "It's fine. He's hammered. He probably won't even notice, and if he does, he'll forget by the time he gets back to the kitchen. Act natural." She opens her mouth to protest, but I yank on the door, grabbing her by the hand and pulling her into the hallway while she attempts to hide her face like she's passing the goddamn paparazzi.

Ace's brows bunch in confusion. "Wait. Isn't that your—" he says, pointing at her. "I thought she was with—"

"Alright, buddy!" I cut him off, patting him on the shoulder. "Be careful in there. See you in the kitchen, you handsome devil." His perplexed expression fades, only to be replaced by a sheepish smile.

"Yeah, okay," he replies. "I'll see you in a minute." Stepping through the door, it closes behind him and Arden breathes a sigh of relief. But I'm not feeling it. In fact, it's the exact opposite now that we're back out in the open.

"What's wrong?" she asks.

I shrug. "I just hate having to keep our distance when people are around. I know everything is new, but I'm in this with you guys, and I don't want to feel like I'm not. The whole night, I've watched him subtly touch you, and it sucks not being able to do the same. Will it always have to be like this?"

She grabs the fabric of my shirt, pulling me close, her expression full of understanding. "Nobody said you couldn't touch me. The girls kind of already know what's going on, anyway. They could tell by the way you two were looking at me, and I didn't really deny it. Obviously, we have to be careful in public, but if you trust these guys not to out us before we're ready, I'm okay with it."

"I trust them," I say with complete certainty. "My teammates know how hard it is to keep our private lives private, and as much as we joke around and pull pranks, we always have each other's backs when it comes to the women we love.

"Alright, then." She pushes up to her toes, kissing me again as I wrap my arms around her waist and back her into the wall. Pressing into her body, I hungrily plunge my tongue into her mouth, tasting every part of her that I can. I should be able to control myself better than this, but with Arden, everything is different—more intense—and I just can't get enough. I'm not sure if I ever will. My hands glide down, palming her ass, and just as I swallow the quiet moan that works its way up her chest, Ace opens the door and enters the hall. Once again, he looks bewildered, catching us together for the second time in five minutes. This time, there's no hiding what we were doing.

"So," he says, pointing between us. "You're together."

"Yes," I blurt. Arden looks my way, but I don't acknowledge it—because, *yes*, we are.

His lips pull to one side, contemplating my answer before focusing back on her. "But you and Hawk…"

"Also together," I cut in. Maybe I shouldn't be speaking for them when I'm not entirely sure where they stand, but I know my best friend, and he's just as ready for wherever this thing leads us as I am. If there's only a handful of people we can do it freely around right now, why waste another second holding it back?

Realization hits him—at least as well as it can, considering he's three sheets to the goddamn wind— and a silly smile blooms across his face. But before it settles in, his eyebrows shoot up. "Oh, shit! Do you know what sounds really good right now? Hot dogs. I haven't had a hot dog in forever. Hey, Sweets!" he yells, blowing past us and heading toward the kitchen. "We should get hot dogs!" Arden and I exchange a befuddled look before she giggles quietly, making all the tension in my body melt away now that we talked.

"C'mon, Princess," I say, taking her by the hand and leading her back the way we came. Everyone is still deep in conversation when we arrive, barely even giving us a second look as we step up next to Hawk and he wraps a possessive arm around her waist. Keeping her hand in mine, I lean in and drop a chaste kiss to her lips, feeling the weight of the world fall off my shoulders as she smiles up at me adoringly. If any of our friends notice both gestures as they happen simultaneously, they don't let on, continuing to turn the shitty evening into an amazing one, just like they always do after a tough loss.

The rest of the night flies by, and we're exhausted by the time we pour ourselves into Hawk's bed at three in the morning. I consider sleeping in my own room, but the thought of not holding Arden as she drifts off, with him stroking her hair and gently scraping his teeth along the soft skin of her shoulders, just seems wrong tonight. She deserves all of this and more, so if that means not returning to my bed, so be it.

I spent too many nights wishing I had this, and waking up without the most important people in my life beside me is no longer an option I want to accept.

TWENTY-FOUR
ARDEN

"LEVINE, I need to see you in my office when you're done changing," Dahlia says, peeking into the locker room. We've been here most of the day—first watching tape from the joint practices we've had, so we can adjust things that aren't working, then hitting the court for the last two hours. I honestly just want to get home, eat, and get off my feet, but it looks like that'll have to wait.

"Be right there, Coach," I reply, pulling my crewneck over my head and tossing my dirty clothes into my bag. Zara shoots me a quizzical look, making me shrug in response. Dahlia has barely said two words to me all week, so I have no clue what this could be about. Trying to tamp down my nerves, I stand straight, checking my reflection in the mirror before heading toward where she waits for me behind her desk.

"Close the door," she orders firmly. I turn around, rolling my eyes at her snooty tone and carefully shutting us in alone. Giving her my best convincing smile, I walk toward the chair across from her, but she halts me before I can sit. "Don't bother. This won't take long." She focuses her attention on her computer, clicking the mouse a few times while I wait for her to speak.

"We're switching things up. From now on, I'll be calling the plays from the sidelines," she says, not even bothering to look at me while she does. She brings her fingers to the keyboard, tapping away as I stand there completely dumbfounded. I choke out an incredulous laugh, causing her to whip her head in my direction. I'm sure it's coming off as disrespectful, considering she's my coach, but *what the fuck*? "Is something funny?"

"Ummm, yes," I reply, blood boiling like hot lava in my veins as I struggle to keep from flying off the handle. "We've been working together for months, and it's taken me that long to learn what to look for in my hitters to know what plays to run. I've given you no indication that I'm incapable of calling the plays. You may not always agree with them, but everything I do is for a reason, and I always put my team first." She stares daggers at me as I stand awkwardly, feeling the need to fill the silence with more reasoning. "It isn't feasible to think you'd be able to see things from the bench. And even if you could, the chances of me being able to hear you and react quickly enough aren't good. We'd have to figure out a better system, and we have less than two weeks before our first match." I shake my head, exhaling a slow breath. "Respectfully, I think you're making a mistake, Coach." Emotion claws at my throat, but I do my best not to look affected because I know that's exactly what she wants right now.

She raises a brow, sitting straight and lifting her chin. "Are you attempting to undermine me? Maybe you've forgotten, but I run the Flare. I decide what's best for this team, not you. If you don't like it, feel free to leave. Just because those girls out there voted you captain doesn't mean they'd give a flying fuck if you were gone. The choice is yours, Arden. Either do the plays as I call them, or I can make sure every team in the league knows how combative and uncoachable you are."

I want to scream. This *has to* be personal. There's no way she'd be willing to risk a loss if there wasn't an underlying reason. But I honestly can't think of anything I've done—in college or now—that would make her treat me the way she has. And I really don't know if she has the power to end my career, so I need to be careful. I've worked too hard for this. The best I can do is go along with the change, and hope she sees that it isn't the right choice.

"Fine," I say, crossing my arms over my chest. I'm doing everything I can to stay calm, but rage and anxiety are battling one another inside me, and I just want to get out of here. If I don't, I'm either going to cry or launch myself over her desk and choke her the fuck out. I'm fully aware that neither of those are good options, but it's where I'm at.

"Good," she shoots back, looking at me like I'm a nuisance rather than a player who's gone above and beyond to show her that I belong here and am proud to be a member of this team, despite the way she's regarded me. "You can leave now."

I give her a tight nod before turning and exiting the room, not bothering to shut the door behind me. I'm still rattled when I pass by the girls lingering in the locker room, so I walk right out, making a beeline toward the parking lot. This is all very uncharacteristic of my commitment to showing up early and staying late, and shame washes over me that I've once again let Dahlia get in my head. Even though I'm not completely spiraling like I would've been two months ago, there's still a pit in my stomach and my body is wound tight all over. I hate the way it feels, and I need to get out of here.

By the time I'm walking into the condo, I've calmed down, but I'm still deflated at the thought of not being prepared for our first match. My teammates are going to turn to me for guidance when the change is announced at practice tomorrow, and I'm not sure how I'll be able to look them in the eyes and say that I think it's what's best. But I know I won't have a choice. It's my job to make sure everyone feels confident in the plan, even if I don't agree with it in the least.

I kick off my shoes, pushing them aside and dropping my bags to the floor. The hunger pains I felt before I got called into the coach's office have been replaced with a heavy knot, so I pass by the kitchen, relieved to find both guys on the couch with video game controllers in their hands. Racecars battle one another on the big screen, and I stop in the doorway to admire the scene. Jackson is on one end, elbows resting on his knees as he focuses intently on the TV. Hawk sits opposite him with both feet on the ottoman, his posture as relaxed as can be while his car comes up behind another before blowing right past.

"Did you just lap me, you piece of shit?" Jacks yells, quickly sliding his eyes to his best friend. Hawk smirks lazily, never breaking his easy concentration as he crosses the finish line. The opposing players funnel in behind him, a checkered flag waving across the screen before the standings appear on the screen.

"Dead last, again," Hawk says cockily. "With all the time you spend on this game, I feel like you should be better by now." The tension in my body melts away a little as I watch them, comforted by their playful banter and the feeling of always being at home when I'm in the midst of it.

Jackson scowls. "You're such a dick." He shoves a frustrated hand through his hair and reaches forward to set his controller down in front of him, catching me out of the corner of his eye as he does. "Hey, Princess. How was practice?" A hopeless cringe falls over my face before I move through the room, not stopping until I'm close enough to fall into his arms, which are already wide open and waiting for me. As soon as I curl up in his lap, his strong embrace enveloping me, I begin to melt. All the anxiety and worry that were plaguing my mind about what's going to happen tomorrow slowly fade away, and I sigh contentedly while he tightens around me.

"That good, huh?" he says, lowering his lips to the top of my head as I snuggle deeper into his body.

"Mhmm," I hum. "I don't want to talk about it. Right now, I just need to let it all go." My problems will be there tomorrow, and I'll deal with them then. That's one very valuable thing I've taken from my recent therapy sessions—to give myself some time to reset and reflect before looking at the situation from a new angle.

Another set of lips presses tenderly against my hair, and my heart does a flip in my chest because, while I love it when Hawk is rough with me, his gentle touches mean so much. "Hey there, Hellcat," he rasps in my ear. "I've got something that'll make you feel better. Stay here and take all the cuddles you need, then bring Jacks to my room. We're going to help you clear your head, okay?"

I turn, my eyes locking onto his. I hope he knows how grateful I am that he always seems to know what I need, even when I don't. "Yeah," I reply as he brings a large hand to my cheek, taking my mouth with his. The kiss is so soft, yet dominating, and I go dizzy with lust when his tongue just barely brushes mine. Tiny sparks of electricity begin to prickle on my skin, but before they can grow into the fire I know his touch is capable of igniting, he's gone, disappearing toward the staircase.

I whine quietly, and as if Jackson knew that I wasn't nearly finished with the kiss, he takes over, bringing my attention to his with a finger under my chin. His lips are fused to mine in an instant, leisurely licking and nipping while I sigh with satisfaction. This—having them both here to give me everything I could ever want —makes me feel like the luckiest girl in the world.

We take our time with one another, savoring the slow, sensual connection as wetness begins to soak the inside of my panties. I squeeze my legs together for relief, halfway annoyed at myself for getting worked up so fast, but this is the effect he has on me. One minute, we're kissing innocently. The next, my clit is throbbing, and my body is begging me to quell the ache.

He notices my dilemma, chuckling quietly against my lips as he stands with me in his arms. Unable to stop myself, I drop my head into the crook of his neck, dragging my tongue along his heated skin as goose-bumps rise in its wake. "Fuck, baby," he moans, care-fully taking the stairs one at a time until we're at the top of the landing and turning toward Hawk's room. "You're a needy little thing, aren't you?

"Mhmm," I hum, refusing to stop my teasing licks until he lowers me to my feet. I reluctantly let go of him just as Hawk steps toward me in nothing but a pair of black boxer briefs that hang low on his hips, show-casing every rock-hard muscle on his body. I vaguely hear the sound of Jacks removing his clothing through the fog in my brain, but I can't take my eyes off the tattooed god in front of me long enough to see for myself.

"You look like you had a rough day," Hawk says seductively as he pulls my shirt over my head, his eyes burning with desire when he sees that I never bothered with a bra after practice. He tosses it to the floor, moving closer until he's able to run his hands up and down my waist. "For the rest of the night, I want you to be a mindless, empty-headed doll for us. Just be here in this room, where you're allowed to free yourself from every one of life's stressors. The only thing that exists inside these walls is the pain and pleasure we're about to bring. Do you trust us to take care of you?"

Just then, another set of hands joins in, running up my thighs from behind and dipping under my waistband before slowly working my leggings and panties to the floor. Jackson kneels, pressing a soft, barely-there kiss to the sensitive skin of my ass as I step out of my clothes, leaning on the strong forearms in front of me to keep steady because I'm feeling like I could melt into a puddle at any moment. He moves them away, dragging his fingertips up as he stands, settling himself so close to my naked body, that I can feel the heat radiating from his.

"Yes," I whisper, almost forgetting that Hawk asked me a question. My brain is fuzzy already, and I let out a shaky exhale as he nods in approval.

"What's your safe word?" he asks, both of them going still as they await my answer. Blood pumps loudly between my ears at the thought of what they're going to do to me, and I give him what he wants, saying the word out loud.

"Muffins."

"Good girl, Princess," Jacks replies against my ear, making warmth bloom to life in my stomach before it snakes its way through my limbs. Even with the darkness that's washed over Hawk's expression in front of me, I've never felt safer and more cared for than I do right now, wedged between them. The thought makes my heart tighten inside my ribcage because, while I know without a doubt that I've been in love with one of them since I was barely even old enough to fully under-stand the emotion, it's becoming apparent that I'm developing something very real for the other. I don't know how or when it happened, but it's there—and it's getting stronger every day.

Hawk steps away, walking over to the dresser and digging through the same drawer he pulled the toys from last time. I watch with rapt attention to see what he returns with. He faces us again, but my eyes can't settle on one item long enough to make sense of anything—although none of that matters as he stops in front of me and speaks.

"Kneel."

TWENTY-FIVE
HAWK

AS SOON AS the rough demand is out of my mouth, Arden obeys, dropping down in front of me. Jackson steps around her, standing just behind me as I finally show her what I've got.

"This is bondage tape," I say, holding up the roll. She fixes her eyes on it, watching as I pull on the end and unravel a long piece. "It sticks to itself but won't hurt your skin. Feel it." Bringing a hand up, she skates her fingers along the shiny black strip. It's not sticky at all and has a stretchy, rubbery texture that's smooth to the touch. I opted for this, as opposed to rope, because it's quicker and easier for the type of binding I plan on doing. She won't be in it long—only until we move her to the bed. I just want to get her to give up control to us while she's on her knees. She needs this right now.

I could tell from the moment she walked into the living room that it was one of those practices that had her on edge. The way she made a beeline for Jacks solidified it, since he's her soft place to land. That's why

I gave them some time alone while I came up here to get ready, because she needed to feel loved and treasured before she'd be in the right headspace to handle what I have planned for her.

"Put your hands behind your back," I instruct. She does, and I round her small body, wrapping the tape in an X shape around her wrists several times so she can't escape. Shaky inhales expand her chest, and her nipples harden as I make sure everything is secure before standing to my full height behind her.

Lifting my chin at my best friend, I silently encourage him to get close, so that his already hardening cock is just inches from her face. I should discuss a non-verbal safe word with them, and if it were me in front of her, we would. But I know the last thing he would do right now is push her anywhere near her limits. I don't think he even has it in him.

I look down, watching as her tits continue to heave with every excited breath she takes. "Jackson is going to fuck your pretty mouth," I tell her. "Be an obedient little toy and make him feel good. Open." I land a light slap to her cheek, and she complies immediately, waiting as he slides his head past her plump lips. Just as I suspected, his thrusts are slow and languid, eliciting contended moans as she enjoys the feeling of his length gliding along her tongue. I allow it for several minutes, my erection growing harder while I watch them together.

"You're beautiful, Arden," he grits out quietly, rubbing gentle circles on her cheek with his thumb as he pumps in and out, picking up speed but still not letting loose. He may know what she needs when she's in his arms, seeking softness and comfort. But when it comes to emptying every haunting thought from her mind?

I'm her fucking salvation.

"You can take more, can't you, Hellcat?" I ask, my tone dripping with mischief as she does her best to nod in affirmation. I smirk, batting his loving touch away and replacing it with my own hands on each side of her head. As if she knows what's coming, she takes a sharp inhale through her nose, right before I shove her forward, not stopping until I hear her feet kicking the carpet between my open legs. Her torso thrashes slightly as she pulls at the tape, likely trying to push against his thighs. Jackson gasps, and I meet his nervous gaze with mine, telling him without words to hold still.

"There you go," I praise, feeling her body jolt, fighting the intrusion as her gag reflex kicks in. Garbled noises work their way up her throat, escaping around his shaft while I force her down. Waiting a couple more seconds before pulling her off, I watch as she sucks in large gulps of oxygen, strings of saliva hanging from her swollen lips. I give her a few seconds to recover before doing it again, this time controlling her movements and fucking her onto him while he struggles not to come early. I don't blame him. She looks like a dream, bound and dominated, choking on his cock. I'm not sure I could restrain myself the way he is if the roles were reversed.

Pulling her off of him, I tilt her head up to me,

focusing on how gorgeous she is after being used. Tears are streaming down her face, there's drool all over her chin, and her chest trembles as she continues to catch her breath. But the trust and submission I see when I look into her eyes is what makes her the most breathtaking being I've ever seen. She has no idea what we're going to do to her, yet there isn't an ounce of trepidation in her expression. She just wants to let go.

"Such a pretty fuckslut," I praise, hooking my thumb behind her bottom teeth and forcing her mouth wide before spitting onto her tongue. Her eyes roll back, and Jackson must see it, because the next thing I know, he's curling his pointer and middle fingers next to mine, leaning close, and adding his own saliva. Arden whimpers loudly, her attention bouncing back and forth between us as we tower over her. "Swallow." She doesn't hesitate, closing her lips and moaning as the mixture of us slides down her throat.

"Christ, Princess," he says, shaking his head in disbelief. It's like he's seeing her for the first time. In a way, he is. Because the sweet, innocent angel he's known since they were young is only a part of Arden. There are sides of her that he has yet to experience, and I hope he understands how lucky we are that she's willing to give every single one to us.

Crouching down behind her, I press a kiss to her cheek, carefully freeing her wrists from the tape. "Stand up," I order, helping her to her feet. He immediately takes her arms, checking them for signs of injury before ghosting his lips over the faint indentations from where she pulled at the restraint. Other than that, there are no visible marks.

"You're not done sucking his dick, Hellcat," I warn. "Both of you can get on the bed." I move back toward the dresser as they follow directions, grabbing the next item I have for her. Returning to them, I notice Jacks is on his back, and she's crawling between his knees, ready to take him into her mouth again. But before she gets a chance, I correct her with a firm slap to her ass. "Spin. Get that pussy on his face."

"Fuck, yes," he says on a relieved exhale, making me chuckle. I know he's dying to get his mouth on her right now, but I have ulterior motives for needing her in this position.

Without hesitation, she hops to his side, turning and slinging a leg over his head. A quiet whimper escapes his lips as she hovers above his face, and he pulls her down, wasting no time pressing his tongue against her swollen center. I can't tear my eyes away as he laps up the arousal that's coating her cunt, licking and sucking her clean while she grinds onto his mouth. Clearly, the bondage is something we need to explore more of, because she's absolutely soaked from it. Her breath hitches as she looks down, peeking between her legs and watching his tongue flick at her sensitive clit.

"Don't keep him waiting," I snap, regaining her attention. "Suck it." She leans forward, bobbing and moaning along his length as he continues to eat her like a starving man. I gather her hair in my hands, holding it back so I can see better. She swallows him even further, fueled either by me watching her like she's my favorite pornstar, or the way his hips buck up every time he hits the back of her throat. It doesn't matter which—she's got us both by the fucking balls, and I doubt she even knows it.

I enjoy the show until I can't take it anymore, moving back toward her ass and pulling her cheeks apart until her puckered bud comes into view. Jacks takes one long lick from the back of her pussy to her clit, and once he latches on, I lean in, flattening my tongue against her back entrance. She stiffens at first but relaxes quickly when I flick the sensitive skin, a deep moan working its way up her chest and struggling to find an escape around the cock that's filling her mouth.

"That's our good slut," I say, devouring her as I knead at the supple flesh in my hands. We both work her over, the tips of our tongues touching every now and then when we move to the spot between her holes. It's kind of unavoidable, and as much as I thought it might be weird for me, it really isn't. We have the same objective here, and that's to make Arden feel good. Being in this situation with her means getting comfortable with stuff like this. "How's her pussy taste?"

"Amazing. She's so fucking wet," he replies. "She's been gushing all over my face since you started eating her ass. I think she needs more."

"You think?" I ask, acting as if she's not even here. Other than her heavy breaths and needy whines, she's barely even moving, keeping his cock warm while we bring her closer to her release. But that means she's exactly where I want her for what's coming next. "Does our empty-headed doll need to be stretched out?"

"Fuck, yeah," he groans, and I'd bet every goddamn dollar I have that he's imagining the same shit I am right now. Eventually, we'll fill her up at the same time. But right now—she needs prep.

"Keep eating," I instruct, turning to the nightstand for the bottle of lube I keep in the drawer. I carefully and generously coat the item I pulled from the dresser earlier before returning to rub it along her tight hole. She arches in search of more, so I take that as the green light to push the silicone plug forward. Even though I know she wants it, I'm not surprised when she instinctively clenches, so I place a reassuring hand on her back to let her know I'm here.

"You're doing great, baby," I praise. "Focus on Jackson's tongue. Open up for us."

She sits up slightly to readjust, his cock falling from between her lips as she releases a shaky exhale. "Okay." She visibly relaxes after a few moments of consideration, leaning back down and resting her face against his thigh.

"Atta girl," he says softly, rubbing her hips as he latches back onto her clit, and gentle sucking sounds fill the otherwise quiet room. I wait until she's moaning in pleasure before adding a small amount of pressure to the plug, watching as her opening stretches before finally swallowing it whole.

"Look at that," I coo, admiring the small pink gem that's peeking out from between her cheeks. "So fucking sexy."

"Mmm," she hums loudly, clearly nearing the edge of her orgasm. I sit back, allowing her space to move freely as she grinds her hips against his face. His fingertips dig into the skin of her thick thighs, and she lifts her head, so I move in front of her, leisurely stroking my cock. Precum leaks from the head, and I smooth it along my piercing as I ghost over it with my fingers. The motion catches her attention, making her bite her lip in anticipation as she continues to ride him.

"Come on, baby," he demands against her pussy. "Come on my face so I can fuck you with that plug in your ass." His words do the trick, making her thrust into his mouth one last time before she explodes with a scream. Her legs shake, every defined muscle firing off under her creamy skin as he licks, punishing her sensitive clit until she's had too much and fights to squirm away. But he only tightens his grip, holding her in place and attempting to savor every last drop. She gives up, too drained to go on, whining in discomfort as he continues to lick and suck.

"Fuck," I say, pulling his hand from where it's practically melted into her thigh and helping her free. "One desperate slut is enough in this relationship. I don't need another." Reaching down, I lift her chin with my fingers, taking in her cum-drunk expression. Her lips are swollen, her cheeks are flushed, and there's exhaustion behind her sleepy eyes. "Poor girl," I mock. "I need you to focus for me, Arden. Because I don't give a fuck how tired you are right now. We need to come. So be a good little whore and get on all fours for us." She whimpers quietly, crawling off of Jackson, who immediately gets up and kneels behind her, clearly very ready for more.

I position myself so I'm on my knees in front of her, taking a fistful of chocolate hair and guiding her mouth to my aching erection. She parts her lips, and I slide inside, not nearly as gentle as he was. Her eyes water when I thrust all the way back, but I hold her to me so I can feel the muscles in her throat contract before finally letting go and allowing her to set the pace. She sucks me like she was made for it, running her tongue along my piercing while she bobs up and down.

"Holy fucking shit, look at this ass," Jackson says, unable to tear his gaze away from the plug as he scoots up behind her. "You ready to go airtight for us, Princess? Get each of these gorgeous holes filled until you can't even remember your own name?"

"Mhmm," she hums, the sound vibrating against my dick and making my eyes roll back. He spits into his hand and rubs it along his length before slowly pushing inside. Her jaw drops open as he bottoms out, and I land a tight slap to her cheek, bringing her attention upward.

"Did I tell you to stop sucking? Close those slutty fucking lips around my cock while your stepbrother fucks you into it." She whimpers loudly at my depraved words, and he drives forward, forcing me to the back of her throat as she gags.

"Goddamn it," he says through clenched teeth. "She tightens up when you talk to her like that." He pulls back before thrusting again, and I return the motion, setting a rough and punishing tempo as we fuck her back and forth like a ragdoll. We fall into a perfect rhythm, moving as if we were made to be one unit, just like this.

I look down, catching her watery gaze with mine and shooting her an arrogant wink. "That's because she's a filthy little whore. You always thought she was so sweet and innocent, but look at your princess now. Filled with both of our cocks like a fucking queen." My words make her whine loudly, her eyes slamming shut as she sucks my length further into her mouth. Her body shakes with the climax that's ready to pull her under while we continue to rock into her. She's still focused on me though, and I know it's because she's waiting for my permission to let it happen.

Good fucking girl.

Without a word, I give her a stiff nod, and she immediately goes off like a firework, tumbling into oblivion as she finally comes on a muffled cry.

"That's it, baby," Jackson grits out, using his thumb to put pressure on the plug. "Come on my cock just like that. You're so good to us." We slow down, letting the spasms inside her subside while her orgasm fades, finally ebbing away as she breathes deeply through her nose and resumes dragging her tongue languidly along my shaft. As much as I love to degrade Arden in the bedroom, Jacks is right—she really is so good to us. I'm sure she's exhausted, yet she's doing everything in her power to keep going so we can come.

I peer up at my best friend, silently telling him that we need to finish and get her to bed. He nods, looking back down to where they're joined and watching his dick as it disappears into her before shaking his head in disbelief. "This pussy is incredible. I'm gonna fill you up, Princess." A weak whimper reverberates against me and my balls draw up tight, my impending release speeding my way as he shoves her into me. She hollows her cheeks, and I erupt, grunting loudly as I fill her mouth with cum. She greedily takes every single drop, and before she can even fully swallow me down, Jackson detonates. His fingers dig deep divots into her luscious hips, and he trembles through his orgasm, her name falling from his tongue like it's the only fucking word he knows. We ride it out while Arden accepts everything we have to give, pulling off of me and collapsing forward onto my thigh as she struggles to regulate her breathing.

Jacks pulls out, his gaze glued to where I'm assuming the evidence of their pleasure drips from between her lips. He gently runs his fingers through it, eliciting a satisfied sigh against my heated skin as he pushes it back inside. "I'll never get sick of this," he says quietly. "Of us." Maybe he means him and her, but I can only hope that he means the three of us. Because I've been with my fair share of women—so has he—but I've never felt truly complete. Jackson has been a constant source of friendship and comfort in my life for years. But Arden? She's our center—the little piece of perfection we revolve around. I don't want to exist in a world without either of them. I hope I never have to.

I stroke her hair as he carefully removes the plug and tosses it to the side, wishing I had the words to tell them what's going on in my head. That I love them—

albeit in very different ways—and the feeling of fullness in my heart now that we stopped fighting the inevitable has given me a reason to wake up every day. But I've never been good at expressing my emotions, so I do the only other thing I know that'll show them I care.

He stands, wordlessly padding to the bathroom and returning moments later with a warm washcloth. She attempts to argue as he cleans between her legs, and I chuckle when she finally gives up, allowing him to carefully wipe the remnants of their releases away. When he's finished, he drops the cloth to the floor before leaning in and brushing his lips to her flushed cheek.

Reaching over, I pull on the corner of the comforter, peeling it down and helping Arden underneath. She settles against the pillow, a sleepy smile tugging at the corners of her mouth as I press a gentle kiss to her forehead. I make more room beside her, looking at him and patting the mattress in invitation. He hesitates for a moment, and I roll my eyes. "Get in. We sleep in the same bed now…don't make it a thing. Our girl needs aftercare from both of us."

His shoulders relax and he slides in beside her, his eyes brightening when he looks down to where she lies. As always, she's already drifted off, her plump lips parted as tiny snores fill the space around us. He chuckles quietly while he studies her features, ghosting the backs of his knuckles along her soft skin. Letting out a shaky exhale, his brows pull in, emotion blanketing his expression. "I've loved her for so long," he whispers, the words barely audible in the quiet room. "I thought I'd be forced to watch her build a life with someone else, never knowing what it felt like to hold her in my arms." He looks up at me, unshed tears glistening in the dim light as he swallows thickly. "Thank you." My chest twists at the admission. The fact that he's sharing it with me before actually saying the words to Arden almost feels like my reward for encouraging him to finally make the jump with her.

In reality, it should be me thanking him for bringing her into my orbit—and for selflessly stepping aside when he thought I'd want to keep her for myself, knowing it would hurt him more than anything. But, as always, the feelings are entirely too big for me to articulate in a way that would be worthy of everything he's given me. Those two words are simply just not enough.

I focus on the beauty next to me, admiring her flawless skin and long lashes as they fan against her face. Her chest rises and falls with steady, shallow breaths, and I can't help but be overcome with gratitude for all the ways she's healed pieces of me that have been hurting for so long. Inhaling deeply, I anchor myself to the monumental moment, knowing without a doubt that I feel the same way about her as he does.

"She's ours," I rasp, trying to fight the emotion that's clawing its way up my throat. I may not be able to outwardly express my love for her just yet, but *fuck. I feel it.*

He nods, slipping under the covers next to her as I mirror him on the other side. Reaching out, I band an arm around her waist, pulling her into my warm body and holding onto her like a lifeline. I can't stop myself from burying my nose into her hair, the unmistakable smell of both our colognes mixed together filling me with a sense of possession so strong it makes my head spin. She hums contentedly, turning so her back is to my front before instinctively extending her small hands toward Jacks. Immediately, he slides closer, pressing a ghost of a kiss to her lips as he settles onto her pillow.

We don't change positions for the rest of the night, holding Arden until the sun comes up—knowing that no matter where life brings us, nothing will ever top the feeling of having her in our arms.

TWENTY-SIX
ARDEN

"WHAT DOES THIS MEAN?" I say, dragging my fingertip along the dark, haunting tattoo inked on Hawk's right arm as Jackson sleeps peacefully behind me. Tracing the staircase that leads to a cluster of thick, black clouds, I stop and stare at the silhouette that ascends it.

He looks down, taking a slow breath before lifting his arm from where it's draped over me. "It's me. All my life, I've felt like I was climbing, but no matter how hard I tried, I could never reach the top. Even being drafted and getting called up to the Fury—I still felt like there were miles and miles to go before I'd ever be happy.

"When my dad took my brothers, I lost sleep wishing he'd have given enough of a shit to at least check in and let me know how they were. It sucked that he didn't want me, but I kind of understood because I was technically an adult. He wanted the family my mom wasn't able to give him, so he made it with his new wife while I stayed behind and ensured that she'd be safe after I left for the minors. I was barely legal, yet I was dealing with so much. Losing them sent me to a really dark place, and the only thing that kept me from drowning was the thought that someday, I'd have money and a big enough house to take them back. They'd each have their own rooms that they could decorate any way they wanted, and they'd never have to sleep on a dirty, stained floor ever again.

"The first couple of years were hard because not only did my dad cut off all contact, but I was also traveling nonstop most of the time. I was making money, but not enough to really get the things they'd need. It wasn't until I was called up that the bigger contract offer came, the one I knew would allow me to support them.

"I was so fucking excited. I got a financial advisor, and we worked on this big, elaborate plan to build a house on the beach where Hayden and Henry could come visit. Then, when they were old enough to choose, maybe they'd want to stay. But when I made the call to my dad to tell him that I was ready to have the boys in my life again, he threatened me with a restraining order. He said they were angry with me for choosing my mom —which I suspected was bullshit—and that as their guardian, he wouldn't allow me near them."

I bring my tear-filled gaze up to his, my brows pulled inward as my heart shatters for this amazing man. He gave up a proper childhood to raise his brothers, and they were ripped away like his feelings didn't matter. Under his broody exterior, Hawk Mason is one of the most beautiful human beings I've ever met, and it kills me that he lives every day without the one thing he wants most.

"Couldn't you get a lawyer and fight to see them? Don't the courts usually want to keep siblings together?" I ask.

He shakes his head. "Neither of the states we live in protects sibling rights. I've hired multiple attorneys and tried to get visitation, but as long as they're under eighteen, he's allowed to say no. I even suggested mediation with just him and me so I could show him that their best interest is always my main priority, but he refused. My only hope now is that once they're adults, they'll reach out. That's one good thing about being in the public eye—they'll always know where to find me."

Tears flow freely down my cheeks, and I reach up, wrapping a hand around the back of his neck so I can pull his mouth to mine. His tongue slides along my bottom lip, causing sparks of electricity to prick at my chest, and I open, allowing him to taste me. My heart flips and flutters as I breathe him in, feeling incredibly lucky that he's shown me parts of him that he keeps so close. Hawk has changed me in ways he'll never know, and I hope I can provide even half the comfort to him that he does to me.

I break the connection, pressing my forehead against his. "I'm sure they miss you so much. Someday, you'll get a chance to tell them everything. I'm sure of it." He nods weakly, taking my hand and stroking his thumb over my knuckles. The gesture is oddly intimate, but I love it when his touch is tender and full of emotion. I know he has trouble expressing himself—which isn't really a surprise since he wasn't shown much love growing up—but in these moments, I don't need words. I can feel it.

"And the other arm?" I ask, curious about the rest of his tattoos. The two couldn't be more different. Where the right is dark and chaotic, the left is bright and inviting. The only similarity is the faceless silhouette, leisurely wading in a shallow pond while airy trees hang overhead, running up the length of his bicep.

He rolls onto his back, lifting his arm and lying it over his stomach so I can study it more intently. "It's him," he says, lifting his head toward Jackson. I purse my lips, running my hand along the serene artwork, following the curl of the branches that wind above the man as he takes in his own reflection on the water's surface.

"By the time I was drafted, I was a shell of the old Hawk. I had a fresh wound from losing my brothers, and leaving the only place I'd ever known only made it worse. It wasn't that I really missed home because I never even knew what that word meant, but I wasn't exactly in the ideal headspace to meet and connect with new people. So, I didn't. I spent hours in my hotel room, avoiding any team events that weren't mandatory, and I was perfectly content falling into my anxiety and depression while everyone else got to know one another.

"On road trips, we had roommates, and I guess Jackson drew the short straw because he always ended up with me. He'd ask me to go out for drinks or to play video games, but I always said no. I didn't have it in me to fake being happy just to make him comfortable, so I figured if I turned him down enough times, he'd move on."

I giggle quietly, peering over my shoulder at Jacks as he sleeps soundly. His face is relaxed, and he looks truly happy, just like he always does. He's a ray of sunshine in this world, even when he isn't awake. "And he didn't," I say knowingly.

"Nope," he replies, chuckling. "He annoyed the fuck out of me until I finally agreed to a game of Fortnite. At first, we didn't talk at all. We wordlessly made our way around the map, learning enough about each other that we didn't even have to communicate out loud to win. I don't think he realizes it, but the friendship he offered without pushing me for more than I could give made things feel less hopeless. Like I could sort through my shit, and he'd still be there, ready and waiting with an extra controller in his hand. I'm not very easy to love, but you'd never know it with the way he does it so effortlessly. He battles my darkness with his light every day, and I'll never be able to thank him enough for that."

I smile tenderly, weaving our fingers together as I bring my eyes to his. "He knows. And for what it's worth," I say, swallowing the emotion in my throat, "you *are* easy to love." His expression softens, and he kisses me gently, telling me that he hears the words I'm not saying. I don't know if he's really ready for them to be spoken into the universe, but they're waiting on the tip of my tongue for the very moment he is. I love Hawk Mason with everything I have.

"Ask me about the tattoo on my back," he says against my lips. I smirk, because out of all the pieces on his body, that's the one I've gotten to examine the most. He's been comfortable walking around the house without a shirt since I got here, even before things became physical between us, and I always felt like I could really pore over every detail because when I was behind him, I knew he couldn't see me. I looked my fill many times, memorizing the scene that brings both sleeves together. On his right, the dark smoke flows over his shoulders, rolling toward the middle of his upper back before gradually dispersing. On his left, the intricate branch designs curl up and around, breaking through the black clouds and ending at the base of his neck. Below it all stands a beautiful woman with dark hair, looking up at the chaos as if she's completely unafraid. The first time I saw it, I nearly stopped breathing as I took in the bravery written across her expression, wishing I had that kind of dauntless strength within me.

"Tell me," I reply, wanting more than anything to hear the story behind it.

He exhales a slow, shaky breath, speaking quietly. "She came to me in a dream shortly after I was drafted. I shrugged it off at first because nothing about her made sense, but when she started showing up night after night, I couldn't help but wonder why. Every time, she walked toward me, stopping when she was close enough to touch. She'd reach out and take my hand in hers, and the strangest sense of calm would wash over me. It was unlike anything I'd ever felt before. At least until I met you." I freeze, my brows pulling tight in confusion, but before my mind has a chance to run away on its own, he continues.

"The first night you were here, when you brought me into your bathroom to check my face after you punched me—that was when everything started to connect. It was the most innocent, meaningless gesture for you, but it shook my world. At first, I tried to push it all away. I pretended that your fingers ghosting along my jaw didn't bring me that same feeling of warmth and safety I got in my dreams. I thought if I ignored it enough, I'd realize that your touch wasn't so unmistakably familiar. You were off-limits because, even though Jackson wasn't ready to admit how he felt, I knew you held his heart. I was afraid that if I let myself believe what was already so clear in my head—that she was you—I'd lose him.

"I know it sounds crazy," he says, shaking his head, "and maybe it is. But I have this feeling that, even before I knew you, you were my peace. We were meant to find each other—all of us—and now the two of you are inked on my body and soul permanently."

I lie there, completely speechless, blinking slowly as I process his words. I don't even realize I'm crying until he reaches out and smooths the tears running down my face away with the pads of his thumbs. My heart whooshes loudly between my ears, screaming at me to *say it*. To tell him what I'm feeling, regardless of the repercussions.

"Hawk, I—"

"I love you, Arden," he blurts, cutting me off. I suck in a quiet gasp, watching as an emotion I've never seen before passes over his face. It's soft, yet nervous, like he thinks there's even the smallest possibility that I wouldn't feel the same. But he's crazy if that's the case because there isn't a single part of me that isn't head-over-heels for him.

"I love you too," I whisper, and he exhales a relieved breath as a genuine smile tugs at the corners of his mouth. It's the first time I've seen him like this, and I'm shocked when two deep dimples sink into his tan cheeks. My jaw drops and I choke out a laugh, bringing my fingers up to run over them.

"Don't," he says, rolling his eyes in faux annoyance as he bats my hand away. My grumpy, broody boy is showing me another side of himself nobody else gets to see, and the fact that I'm the cause of it makes me feel like the luckiest girl in the world.

"Why?" I ask. "Afraid I'll tell the world Hawk Mason knows how to *smile*? Would that be the worst thing ever?"

"Yes, smart ass. It would." He darts his hand out, digging into my sides and tickling me while I squeal and try to escape the assault. My frantic movements shake the bed, and it isn't long before another strong set of arms is snaking around my waist and pulling me in. Jackson's warm face nuzzles into my neck as his lips press to my sensitive skin.

"You two are fucking annoying," he grunts sleepily. His voice is full of gravel, and I have to squeeze my legs together because, between that and the whole dimple situation in front of me, I'm on the verge of becoming a horny mess. As much as I'd love another round with them both, letting them use me until I see stars, now isn't the time.

"Oh, shut the fuck up," Hawk replies, sliding closer so I'm sandwiched tightly between them and dropping a chaste kiss to my lips. "It's the offseason. We can nap whenever we want."

I scoff. "Speak for yourselves. My season is just starting, and I need to get to the facility early so I can tell my team about the ridiculous changes our coach is making less than two weeks before our first match." I press my lips to Hawk's once more before turning my head and doing the same to Jacks'. They both groan as I reluctantly crawl down the mattress, my naked body still on full display while I saunter to the bathroom. I make sure to add a little extra swing in my hips, because if I have to be turned on, so do they. Warming up the shower, I listen as they playfully argue, unable to wipe the silly smile off my face at the memory of the moment Hawk and I just shared, and how it felt to wake up next to both of them after one of the best nights of my life.

I may have a long day ahead with the Flare, but this morning with my boys was everything I needed to feel like I can take on the world.

TWENTY-SEVEN
JACKSON

"I'M SO EXCITED!" Arden says, skipping as we make our way through the back entrance of the Daytona Aquarium. Hawk and I called earlier this week to set up a private tour so we could get out of the house without worrying about people seeing the way we are with her. The two of them can technically do whatever they want in public because speculation of a relationship wouldn't raise any red flags. But if I were to be seen holding her hand or kissing her, innocently or not, it could get back to our parents. We're adults, and what we do in our personal lives is our own decision, but I don't want my mom and Slade to find out from random paparazzi photos. They deserve a conversation where we sit them down and tell them how deep our feelings run, and how long they've existed. That's why it was so important for us to make sure the aquarium was closed to the public during our visit.

"Yeah?" I ask with a cocky grin. "It was all my idea,

in case you want to thank me by sitting on my dick later."

"A pity fuck," Hawk mumbles from her other side. "Nice." I flip him off, pulling on the door and moving aside to make room for them to walk through. As soon as we're inside, out of sight of any unwanted stares, I take Arden's hand in mine. She looks down, a soft smile pulling at her mouth as she blindly reaches out and grabs hold of Hawk. With our fingers weaved together, we make our way toward our group of friends as if it's the most natural thing in the world. Now that they know what's happening between us, we don't have to put on the same act as before.

"There you are!" Monroe squeals, waving wildly while Riggs keeps a firm hold on her waist. He leans in, nipping at her neck with his teeth and making her gasp before she slaps his arm. Those two have the strangest dynamic, but their love for one another is so intense that you can practically feel it in the air when they're around. I used to be so envious of what they had, but not anymore—because I finally have everything I've ever wanted.

"Hi!" Arden replies, letting us both go so she can greet her new friends properly, wrapping Monroe in a hug and then doing the same to Lark. She and Ace are taking a break from getting her old house ready to sell now that she's living with him in our building. I'm glad she is because it seems like the girls have hit it off really well.

We talk amongst ourselves, catching up on what's been going on since we saw each other last. It hasn't been long, so there isn't much to report, especially since the first few weeks of the offseason consist of catching up on all the relaxation we missed out on while we were traveling for weeks at a time. Pair that with Arden's riveting schedule of *volleyball, eat, sleep, repeat*, and we're pretty boring.

"Hello, everybody," a feminine voice carries across the room. We all turn to see a blonde woman, maybe in her late twenties, wearing a light blue collared shirt and khaki shorts walking our way. I'm assuming she's the manager I spoke with earlier when I called to ensure the non-disclosure agreements I sent over were signed, which she confirms when she introduces herself. "I'm Tara, and I'll be showing you around today." Reaching out, she shakes each of our hands, learning everyone's name before leading us through another set of doors. The long walkway is made completely of glass, arching overhead as hundreds of colorful fish swim in the water around us. Our heads are on a swivel, taking in the beautiful scene as Tara tells us all about it. Arden wraps her small hand around my bicep, leaning her head on me and making my heart swell with adoration. Hawk still has hold of her other hand, and we leisurely walk as a unit, going wherever she pulls us. Every now and then, he and I exchange a knowing glance, grateful that we were able to get her away from the stress in her life so she can actually enjoy herself.

"Oh my God," she says, dragging us toward the window, where a school of clownfish swims together before looking at me. "Remember that field trip to the zoo our senior year? Devon Pittman got lost inside the aquarium for like, two hours and everyone kept making *Finding Nemo* jokes for the rest of the day." She giggles, and my brows pull in as I try to recall the trip she's talking about.

"Oh, yeah," I reply, a grin tugging at the corner of my mouth as the memories wash over me. "You had on those denim shorts with the rips in them, and I had to keep standing behind you to stop all the guys from staring at your ass. It looked brotherly from the outside, but inwardly, I just hated the thought of them seeing what I wanted so badly to be mine. It took all my self-control not to wrap my arms around you every time I got close." Her jaw drops in shock, but it's quickly replaced with a soft smile as she realizes how long I've wished for moments like this one.

We follow our guide to the end of the long path, funneling into another room filled with various under-water exhibits. She explains them all, one by one, encouraging us to spend some time examining them. The other couples branch off, leaving the three of us alone in a dimly lit corner of our own.

As soon as their backs are turned, I yank Arden into my body, a quiet yelp of surprise squeaking out of her as I take her mouth with mine. The shock that had her going rigid just seconds ago melts away with the slide of my tongue against her lower lip, and she opens, allowing me to taste what I've been desperate for since we walked into the building. My arms tighten around her waist, and I feel the warmth of Hawk's body press against her back as he leaves a trail of kisses along her neck.

"What are you doing?" she says quietly. It's barely a whisper, but my cock swells with need as she sucks in a breath, releasing it on a shaky exhale. She's as turned on as we are, and all of a sudden, I start to realize that putting on clothes and leaving the house was the worst idea I've ever had.

"Just needed to be close to you," I reply, pulling away so I can look at her. Her lips are plump and swollen, and I wish we could just stay here and make out for the rest of the day. But just as I go to kiss her again, Tara's voice calls out to continue the tour. Hawk groans in annoyance, unlatching from her and turning to where Riggs, Monroe, Ace, and Lark are all waiting. We each take a hand in ours, leading her to the group so we can move on to the next room.

As soon as we pass through the heavy metal doorway, I'm on high alert. Where the others were completely empty—save for our group and guide—this one is not. A few employees move around behind a glass half-wall, where several penguins waddle and swim around the rocky exhibit. The girls squeal in excitement while the other guys smile and laugh at their reactions, but I'm too busy worrying about the new humans in the room to enjoy any of the animals. I make eye contact with one of the female workers, abruptly pulling my hand from where it's wrapped around Arden's like it's on fire. She looks down at the broken connection, bringing her eyes up to mine. Her brows pull in as though she's confused, but before I can come up with a way to tell her why I did it without sounding paranoid, Tara continues.

"Our aquarium has over a million gallons of water containing tens of thousands of fish and marine mammals," she begins, "but we also have several animals that frequent the land. Although these little guys spend almost seventy-five percent of their lives in the water, they make their way to dry land to breed and lay eggs." She leads us along the wall, pointing out different parts of the habitat and telling us fun penguin facts, but I don't hear a word she says. I have no idea if all these employees were given NDAs, and I'm worried they might tell people that they saw Hawk and I both being affectionate toward the same girl. A girl who—after a quick Google search—they'd find out is my stepsister.

I go into a silent panic, wondering if there were others hiding in the previous rooms that I didn't notice. She reaches for my hand again, but I shove it into my pocket, earning another perplexed glare. In an attempt to divert her attention, I point over her shoulder just as Tara opens part of the partition and releases a tiny penguin into the room. The others rush over to meet him, but Arden hesitates, finally relenting and walking toward the glass with Hawk by her side.

"This is Mickey," Tara says to the group. "He's one of our smallest African penguins, and as you can see, he put on his best tuxedo for the occasion." Everyone laughs at the corny joke, but not my girl. Instead, she offers a disconnected smile that doesn't reach her eyes. I feel bad, but I'm just looking out for all of us. Rumors spread fast and narratives can be spun out of control in the blink of an eye, so even though I did my best to ensure discretion today, I'm not willing to risk it. Not until we're fully ready to tell our parents, then the world. It has to be on our terms, or I'll lose them both.

It's not until the three of us are in the elevator of our building a few hours later that I realize I fucked up by not explaining things right away. I wanted to, but there were employees within earshot, then the driver of our car on the way home. I hoped we'd get a moment alone before now, but we didn't.

"Come here," I say quietly, reaching out to pull her from where she's cuddled into Hawk's embrace. Her demeanor has been quieter than normal since the penguin exhibit, and she hasn't said a single word to me at all.

"No, thanks," she replies, turning her head in the other direction. He gives me a look that says *You're a fucking idiot*, and I tip my head toward the ceiling, exhaling a slow breath, because *I know*.

Fuuuuuck.

TWENTY-EIGHT
ARDEN

I PUSH through the door of the condo, making my way toward the kitchen with Jackson hot on my heels. I don't know what his deal is, but the make-out session followed by nothing but coldness and rejection for the rest of the day really pissed me off, and the last thing I want is to be around him right now.

"Arden, talk to me," he pleads as I open the cupboard, take a glass, and step toward the sink. I turn on the tap, letting the cold water run before filling my cup halfway and taking a small sip. He slides in next to me and I roll my eyes, setting the drink down before angling my body toward him and crossing my arms over my chest defensively.

"About what?" I spit. "The way you were hot one minute, then acted like you didn't want to be near me the next? Is that what you mean?" I lift a brow, giving him the green light to speak, even though I'd much rather punch his stupid, handsome face.

"I'm sorry," he says with a resigned sigh, his

posture stooping as he leans his hip against the counter. "I got paranoid. When I spoke to Tara, she said the non-disclosure agreements had been emailed to my lawyer, but when I saw all the workers moving around on the other side of the glass, I worried that maybe their presence was an oversight. I didn't know if they had phones on them, so I backed away to avoid pictures or videos being taken of us."

I narrow my eyes, shifting from one foot to the other as I consider his words. I went the entire day, truly thinking he didn't want to hold my hand in public when all he had to do was explain why he was putting distance between us. It doesn't make it any easier of a pill to swallow, considering the fact that we're in a new and exciting stage of our relationship, and we can't even fully enjoy it. But at least my anxiety wouldn't have run away with the idea of him having second thoughts.

"Why didn't you just say that?" I ask. "It would've been easy enough to pull me aside and let me know instead of making me think you didn't want to hold my hand in front of our friends. Because even though they've already seen it and are completely supportive, that's exactly what it felt like."

He hangs his head, bringing his hand up to the back of his neck as he stares at the floor. "I didn't mean to hurt you. This isn't easy for me, either. I finally have the girl I've been in love with all my life, and I feel like I have to hide her. I hate it."

I freeze, my eyes going wide as I suck in a quiet

gasp. I've assumed for weeks that he felt the same way I do, but this is the first time he's said it out loud.

"What?" he questions, looking around the room before bringing his focus back to me for an answer. His brows are pulled tight, genuine confusion blanketing his expression as if he has no idea that he just uttered the most monumental words a person could ever say.

"You're in love with me?" I ask quietly, unable to stop tears from welling in my eyes. My breathing quickens and butterfly wings tickle the inside of my stomach as a soft smile blooms across his face. He steps forward, gliding his hand across the exposed skin above the waistband of my shorts.

"Of course, I am. I can't remember a time when I wasn't." He brings his free hand up, using the pad of his thumb to smooth away the wetness that's running along my cheek. "It started in the hallways of that elementary school and grew into something I tried to live without, but just...*couldn't*." He releases a slow exhale. "I love you more than anything in this world, Arden Levine. And I'm sorry I didn't tell you sooner."

"I love you too," I reply, smiling up at him with a sniffle. He laughs, dipping down and taking my lips in the sweetest kiss. My heart beats like a drum, feeling so full that it could burst at any moment, but I don't care. Jackson Blake—my rock and safe space—loves me, and I'm keeping him forever.

He tilts his head, and I open for him, his tongue immediately sliding against mine as I savor his familiar taste and smell. My arms instinctively wrap around his neck, and he lifts me off my feet, sitting me on the counter while he continues devouring me. He swallows every soft moan that works its way up my throat, showing me exactly how he feels without a single word at all. I can't believe I could've had this with him all along. We missed out on so much, but we have the rest of our lives to make up for it—because now that we're here, I refuse to go back to the way things were.

I pull away reluctantly, resting my forehead against his while we both catch our breath. His gaze finds mine and I'm filled with complete certainty because, as scary as it seemed before, the thought of what comes next has never been clearer. "It's time," I murmur. "We need to tell them. I'm sick of hiding."

He nods, rubbing reassuring circles on the smooth skin of my thighs. "You're right. I want to come clean about everything—Hawk included. They may not like it, but we both love you, and neither of us is willing to let you go. Whatever their reaction is, we'll deal with it together."

I swallow thickly, because I can't think of anything I want less than to have that conversation with my dad and Gina. But the longer we go without telling them, the longer it'll be before we can show the world how we feel about each other. Not to mention, it's only a matter of time before one of us slips and gets caught. This is such a delicate matter, and the worst possible outcome would be for our parents to find out from some shady gossip magazine or website. "Okay," I say. "I don't think we should do it over the phone. Let's invite them to come down here, and we'll tell them in person.

Maybe if they see that we're serious about each other, they won't hate the idea as much."

Using his thumb to free my bottom lip from where it's trapped between my teeth, he bends at the knees so he can look straight into my eyes. "It's going to be okay," he reassures me. "We're adults. If they don't like it, they'll have to get over it. We're not leaving you. Ever."

"They could lock you up in a tower, and I'll rip that fucker down brick by brick to get to you, Hellcat," Hawk adds, catching our attention as he moves toward us, stopping when he's close enough to reach out and touch my hand. I almost forgot he was here. He disappeared up the stairs as soon as we walked through the door. I assume it was because he wanted us to have time alone to sort shit out, but I'm not really surprised that he ended up back down here. This is how I always want it to be. The three of us, making our way through life's ups and downs together. "We're not going anywhere."

"That was a little dramatic," Jacks mumbles under his breath, making me giggle. I can always count on them to cut through a heavy moment with their banter. I'm not sure they'll ever know how happy they make me, but I'll certainly do everything I can to show them.

Hawk rolls his eyes. "I wouldn't expect you to understand. You've been in love with the same girl since childhood, and you blurted it out like you were reading a grocery list. At least I gave her a big, romantic story when I did it."

"Oh, yeah. That's you," Jackson throws back. "Mr.

Fucking Romance. Your first kiss was to snap her out of a panic attack." My eyes bounce between them as they verbally beat the shit out of each other, masking my amusement as they land one expert blow after the other, until finally, I can't hold it in any longer. I bark out a laugh, holding my hand over my mouth as they both slide their eyes my way. Freezing, I slowly pull my lips in to suppress the outburst, but it's too late.

"You think it's funny when we fight over you, Princess?" Jacks asks as I nod my head rapidly with guilt written all over my face, because *fuck yes, I do*. They exchange a knowing glance, and in an instant, I'm lifted from the counter and thrown over Hawk's wide shoulder. I squeal in surprise, squirming in a half-hearted attempt to break free when an open palm collides against my ass with a loud *crack.*

My jaw drops, and I suck in a harsh breath. "What was that for?" I yelp, flopping like a ragdoll against him as he climbs the staircase. Jackson, who's hot on our heels, reaches out, taking my cheeks gently between his thumb and fingers before lifting my head. A playful smirk tugs at his mouth and his emerald eyes sparkle with mirth, eliciting a dull ache between my legs.

"Bad girls get spanked, baby," he says. "And then, they get fucked."

Yes. Please.

TWENTY-NINE
HAWK

"DO I really have to wear this shit?" Jackson whines, glaring at the colorful outfit that hangs from his closet door. As soon as I saw Arden walk by with the couple's costume she picked out for tonight's annual Daytona Fury Halloween party, I rushed up the stairs behind her so I could enjoy his real-time reaction. As expected, it did *not* disappoint.

"Baaaaabe," she replies, batting her long, dark lashes. *Oof, she's laying it on extra thick with the pet names.* "It's nostalgic. Mario and Peach, back together again. Please wear it...*for me*?" Her bottom lip pushes out, and like clockwork, his body accepts defeat, slumping as he exhales slowly.

"Fine. But how come he doesn't have to wear one?" he asks, pointing to where I'm lying against his pillow with my arms propped behind my head, because this is *way better* than TV. I wink in his direction, and he flips me off.

"She looked, but they didn't have anything in my

size. Apparently, they only make them for dudes with small dicks." He looks at her with wide eyes like he's expecting her to say something, making me chuckle smugly under my breath. She shoots me a look, and I go silent, stopping while I'm ahead since I narrowly escaped what she so creatively called a *throuple's costume* when she placed the order.

"They were sold out of Luigi and Bowser because you both waited until the last minute to tell me about this thing." She puts a hand on her hip, her sassy fucking attitude making me want to put her over my knee and turn that tight little ass red.

Later, Hellcat. I have plans for you.

"That's because I didn't want to go," I quip under my breath at the same time Jackson shouts.

"Bowser? You gave him the option to be *Bowser*?" He shoves an exasperated hand through his hair, the other shooting in the air before dropping against his thigh with a *slap*. I hold in my laugh at his outburst, because I'm pretty sure he'll kill me with his bare hands if I don't. His ears are bright red, and his jaw opens and closes several times before he continues. "When I wanted that costume in the fourth grade, you told me no! And look what happened! All along, Bowser was in love with Peach! He even *wrote a song about it, Arden*!"

She steps into him, wrapping her small arms around his waist and pulling him in. He relaxes, hugging her back as he rests his cheek on top of her head. I love seeing them like this. Jackson has always been the guy who gives all of himself to others, easing their pain and anxiety without asking for a thing in return. Watching the way they connect, bringing each other peace and comfort, is something I feel lucky to be a part of. Even though the whole reason behind him losing his shit is fucking hilarious, this is them. And I love the way they love one another.

He pulls away slightly, looking down at where she has the cutest, most innocent expression plastered across her face. I know he's about to fold like a cheap lawn chair even before he does, because *fuck*, so would I. Arden has us both wrapped so tightly around her finger that we'd probably go to the party as slutty nurses if she asked us to.

"Okay," he says, smirking as a bright smile reaches her big brown eyes. "Mario and Peach are back together." She jumps up and down in celebration, pushing to her toes and planting a chaste kiss on his lips. He rolls his eyes playfully, cringing as he takes in the ridiculous costume one more time.

She pulls her phone from the pocket of her hoodie, gasping quietly as she checks the time. "I have to go. I'm meeting Monroe and Lark to get our hair done. I'll see you at the event center." Hurrying to where her outfit for the evening is draped across the corner chair, she quickly zips it into its bag before scooping it up. She gives Jacks one last kiss before leaning over the bed and doing the same to me. "Love you!" she yells, disappearing down the hall as we both return the sentiment in unison. We listen as she rushes down the stairs and pads through the entryway, opening and closing the door behind her.

He turns to me, an annoyed scowl creasing the skin

between his eyes. "What costume did you end up with? Something edgy and cool, I bet." He looks like a four-year-old who didn't get the candy he wanted in the checkout aisle, and to be honest, I'm really enjoying it.

I stand, smoothing the non-existent wrinkles from my clothes as I strut past him, smugness dripping from my demeanor. "You'll see."

THIRTY
JACKSON

FUCK. My. Life.

Not only am I standing—stone fucking sober—in the middle of a ballroom wearing an overstuffed pair of overalls, a fake mustache, and a stupid floppy hat, but Arden isn't even here yet. I showed up to the party on time, expecting the girls to be here, only to get a text shortly after saying they were running behind. It's been almost an hour, and there's still no sign of my Princess Peach.

"You good, bro?" Riggs says from beside me, a bottle of beer hanging haphazardly from his fingers. I can't even look at the jacked motherfucker in his gladiator costume without wanting to punch him. He looks fucking *awesome*.

"I'm fine. Where are they?" He pulls his phone from God knows where—since he's only wearing a pair of leather hoochie-daddy shorts and a red cape—and opens his text app. I lean back onto the bar, tapping my giant black shoe against the marble floor impatiently while he types out a message.

"Monroe said they'll be here in five," he replies just as Ace sidles up beside us in his cheetah print loincloth, every rippling muscle in his body on full display as I try not to roundhouse kick him directly in the nuts. "Maybe we should wait outside for them."

"Yeah, right," I scoff. "And risk someone taking a picture of me in this getup while you guys all look like Greek gods? Not a chance."

"Why'd you wear it if you hate it so much?" Ace asks.

A sly smile flashes across Riggs' face as he looks around to make sure nobody else is in earshot. "It's the power of the pussy," he says quietly, lifting his beer to his lips and taking a sip. "They can get us to do anything for them and they know it. Last week, Monroe spent thirty-five thousand dollars on a purse because it *spoke to her*."

My jaw drops. "What did you say about it?"

"Nothing," he replies, raising a brow. "She showed me her tits and all of a sudden, I wasn't mad anymore. That's how they get us."

Ace laughs, nodding his head in agreement. Not that I'd expect him to disagree. Lark could tell him to get on his knees and bark like a dog right here with hundreds of witnesses, and he'd do it without a second thought.

I roll my eyes. "I wore it because, unlike you guys, we can't be open about our relationship right now. Our parents are coming to visit next weekend, but we're laying low until we talk to them. So, if this is the only way I can make her feel like I'm loving her out loud"—I pat my hands on my stupid, giant stomach before giving it an exaggerated shake—"I'll do it."

"We get it," Riggs says, his eyes softening. "She's lucky to have you. Hawk, too." The sentiment makes warmth spread through me, because I realize how lucky we are to have friends that are supportive of our relationship with Arden. I know it's unconventional, but she makes us both really fucking happy, and knowing that they're behind us feels good. He looks around, surveying the room. "Where is he, anyway?"

I scan the crowd. We arrived in separate cars because he needed some extra time to get ready, and I haven't seen him yet. I'm honestly shocked he's dressing up at all. Last year, he showed up in black jeans and a matching hoodie, only staying for about thirty minutes before he disappeared. It was pretty on-brand for him—at least until Arden loosened him up a little bit. He's been a different person since she moved in, and I'm glad they both have someone that makes them feel seen and understood.

"No idea. Probably changing into the coolest, most badass costume we've ever seen." I grimace, using my fingertips to forcefully press the corners of my stupid mustache onto my skin. It's been coming unglued all night, and if it weren't for the fact that it's going to make my girl smile when she sees me, it would already be in the trash.

Just as I'm about to venture through the party in

search of my best friend, motion near the entrance catches my attention. Monroe struts through the open doors in a short white dress with a flowing cape and golden rope tied strategically around her torso. Metal arm cuffs match her shining gold leaf headpiece, and high stiletto sandals lace all the way up her thighs. Riggs chokes on his beer as he takes her in, frozen in place while she heads his way.

Behind her is Lark, wearing a bright yellow dress with a blue ribbon decorating the neck. Unlike Jane in the Tarzan movies, hers only hits her upper thighs, with a little white ruffle peeking out from underneath. Brown high heels adorn her feet, and I laugh to myself when I think about Ace in his loincloth. What a fucking oversight on his part, because I don't even have to look at the guy to know he's rocking a half-chub right now.

But none of that matters when Arden steps into the room, sucking every bit of oxygen right out of it. Everything around me stops when she starts walking my way, and I swallow thickly as I take her in. She's fucking stunning in a pink and white short-sleeved bodysuit that showcases every inch of the mouthwatering thighs I'd sell my soul to be trapped between right now. A big, floppy bow hangs from the low lace neckline, where her supple tits peek out just enough to have my heart stopping in my chest. White satin gloves climb up her arms, and a small gold crown sits on top of her head, her long, flowing brown hair falling in waves down her back. I have no idea how I'm going to get through this night without putting my hands on her. I knew her costume was a lot different from the cheaply made ankle-length one she wore when we were kids, but I certainly wasn't expecting her to look like a goddamn smoke show when I can't touch or kiss her.

"Fuck, Princess," I say quietly as she loops her arms around my neck. I wrap her up, trying my best to keep the hug as platonic-looking as possible when all I really want is to claim her in front of everyone here. I can't fucking wait until I can show the world she belongs to me. "You're the sexiest woman I've ever seen."

She pulls back, her eyes sliding up and down my body. "You're not so bad, yourself." She tucks her lips over her teeth in an attempt to hide her smile, and any frustration I was feeling earlier melts away because all I care about is making her happy. "I do need one thing, though."

I shake my head rapidly, taking a small step back. As much as I'd love to hold her for longer, there are some reporters here, and I don't want to take any chances. "Absolutely not."

"Jacks, you have to!" she whines, stomping her white stiletto against the floor as she pouts. Her arms cross over her chest, pushing her tits up even more as if she's fully aware of what that does to me.

"No," I protest, pointing a finger her way. "You're lucky you got me into this thing at all. I'm not doing it." She can beg all she wants. I will *not* embarrass myself any further.

She bats her lashes, pushing out her plump lower lip, and I feel my foundation start to crumble before the words even break through the air between us. "Please? *For me?*"

Son of a motherfucking fuck.

Our friends watch the exchange, eyes wide as if it's the most riveting thing they've ever seen. Sweat beads at the back of my neck, and I nervously shift from one foot to the other before clearing my throat and giving her what she wants.

"*It's-a-me, Mario,*" I mumble so quietly, the sound barely even filters through the goddamn caterpillar that's hanging over my mouth. I narrow my gaze, letting her know that she's in fucking trouble when we get home, but she doubles down, cupping a hand behind her ear and turning her head.

"What? I couldn't hear you." She folds her hands in front of her, swaying back and forth with a look of inno- cence plastered across her face. As much as I know I should stay strong, I fucking can't. The little brat owns me, and she knows it.

"It's-a-me! Mario!" I shout. Her eyes sparkle with amusement for several seconds before she finally breaks, and the sweet sound of her laughter swirls around us. I shove my tongue into my cheek, shaking my head in faux annoyance because there's no way I could ever really be mad at her. Especially not in *that* costume.

"What a fucking simp," Riggs quips, hiding a cocky grin behind his bottle as he takes another pull of beer. I slide my scowl in his direction, flipping him off before bringing my attention back to my girl.

"Anyway," I say, changing direction. "Have you heard from Hawk? I haven't seen him, and I don't know what he's wearing."

"No," she replies, looking around. "He said he'd be a little la—" She's cut off when two large, tattooed hands slip around her waist. He pulls her into him, hovering the mouth of his Ghostface mask over her ear.

"Hey there, Hellcat. What's your favorite scary movie?"

THIRTY-ONE
HAWK

"REALLY?" Jackson says, pulling his fake mustache off and slapping it onto the bar as we watch the girls on the dance floor. Arden looks hot as fuck in her costume, every single luscious curve on display as she moves her body to the music. As soon as I saw her, I wanted to throw her over my shoulder, grab my best friend by the collar, and drag them both home as fast as possible so we could get inside her—but I have something else to do first.

"What?" I ask, lifting my glass to my lips and taking a small sip.

"I was expecting something better than this," he says, waving a dismissive hand at my long black robe and the mask that's currently sitting on top of my head. "I mean, it's cool, I guess. But you made it sound like you had some big, epic plan for the night."

"Weird," I reply dryly, setting my drink down and standing up. "Come with me for a minute." Before he even answers, I walk toward the door, entering the hallway with him following closely behind. I turn toward the supply room, pushing the door open. Thankfully, it's still dark and empty, just like it was when I scoped it out earlier. Looking around to make sure we're going unnoticed, I step inside, motioning for him to do the same.

"Following the masked psychopath into a dark room is *asking for it*, bro. You better not kill me."

I huff a forced exhale, annoyed already. "Get the fuck in here." He narrows his eyes, studying me for a moment before he finally relents and shuffles past me. I close us in, turning the lock carefully before using the flashlight on my phone to locate the bag I stashed in the corner when I arrived tonight.

"What are you doing?" he whisper-shouts as the purr of a zipper fills the air. Reaching into my duffel, I pull out a costume that's identical to the one I have on before holding it up to him. His brows pull together, confusion marring his expression as he cautiously takes it. "What is this?"

I stand. "I know how hard it is for you to keep your distance from Arden in public. It sucks to watch because I'm fully aware that you'd give anything to be able to touch or dance with her out there. Now you can."

His eyes soften as realization and understanding wash over him. Looking down at the items in his hand, he swallows, nodding his head. I wish he could go out there as he is, showing the whole team how he feels about her—and he'll be able to soon—but for tonight, I wanted to do this for him—for them both. "Thanks, man." He looks at the ground, his shoulders drooping slightly as he blows out a shaky breath. "You have no idea how much this means to me."

"It's how it should be," I tell him. "Next year, we'll both be in whatever costumes she talks us into, loving her out in the open like she deserves." I'm sure people will have their opinions, but they'll get over it. If there's one thing I'm certain of, it's that Arden is the only person that matters in our world. As long as we have her, we can get through anything.

"What about you?" he asks, lifting his chin in my direction. "If they think I'm you, you can't go out there like that. And I don't want you to leave without us."

I peel off my robe, revealing a plain black hoodie and jeans. Reaching into my bag, I dig until I find the white hockey mask I packed, securing it over my face and pulling the hood up to hide any other features that may give me away. "I'll stay in the corner and watch. Nobody will recognize me." He works it out in his head for a moment, finally relenting and stripping out of his costume. He quickly changes into the new one, hiding himself behind it until there's no trace of Jackson Blake left to be found. The only way anyone would even notice it's him and not me is if they saw the lack of tattoos on his hands. But the sleeves on the robe are so long that he'd have to purposely pull them back for that to happen.

"You good?" I ask.

He looks down, smoothing the thick fabric with his hands and nodding in affirmation. "Yep. Let's go." Swinging the door open, he peeks into the hall before stepping out. I follow behind him by several feet, trying my best not to draw attention as we head back into the ballroom. He goes for the dance floor immediately while I nonchalantly walk to the far corner, finding an empty stool against the wall just as Jackson settles in behind Arden and puts his hands on her waist. She startles for a moment, relaxing as soon as she looks over her shoulder. Even from here, I can tell she thinks it's me by the devious grin on her face, which blooms into something much softer when he leans down and whispers in her ear. She scans the room, but I duck down, not wanting anyone to wonder who I am. They need this moment just as much as I need to give it to them.

I quietly observe them for the next hour as they dance and laugh, Arden slyly lifting the very bottom of Jackson's mask and pushing to her toes to kiss him every now and then as they blend into the crowd. She looks truly happy, and by the way his body is wrapped around her so comfortably, he is too.

When the party guests begin to slowly thin out, going home for the evening, I call for our car and sneak back out to the supply closet. Shoving his old costume into my bag, I zip it up and sling it over my shoulder, quickly shooting a text to our group chat before heading out the main doors with my mask still in place.

Arden Levine Fan Club Group Chat:

ME:

> I'm going to wait for you guys in the car. No rush. Just come out when you're done dry humping in front of our co-workers and making them think it's me.

IT TAKES a minute before a response comes through.

JACKSON:

Don't worry. I showed them my dick, and since it doesn't look like it got into a fight with a nail gun and lost, they figured it out.

ME:

> If you're jealous of my piercings, just say that. Your girlfriend certainly loves riding them every night.

ARDEN:

Do you two ever stop?

JACKSON:

No.

ME:

> No.

ARDEN:

😊 Be right out.

Ten minutes later, they're climbing into the back of the car, Arden settling between the two of us. I reach forward, pressing the button to raise the privacy divider as the driver starts toward our building. As soon as we're alone, Jacks and I remove our masks, inhaling deep breaths of the cool air that's flowing around us.

"You kids have fun?" I ask, catching her gaze and giving her a playful wink.

"Mhmm." She smiles, tilting her head toward her shoulder coyly and fluttering her long, dark lashes. *Fuck, this girl is a showstopper.* Unable to help myself, I lean in slowly until our mouths are just inches apart.

"Good." I close the rest of the space between us, running my tongue along the seam of her lips until she opens, granting me permission to taste her the way I've been dying to all night. As happy as I was to let Jackson have her full attention at the party, it was hard knowing I couldn't just walk up and steal a quick kiss. I get why it's so important to them to tell their parents what's going on between the three of us. The sooner they do, the sooner we can go public and stop having to worry about who sees.

Bringing my hand up, I gently collar her throat, satisfaction flooding through my entire body when a deep moan works its way up and vibrates against my fingers. I love how responsive she is to being domi- nated, and it just makes me hungrier to see how much further we can push her limits.

It's happening tonight.

"You going to let us fuck both of those pretty holes when we get home, baby?" Jackson whispers into her ear. I swear, it's as if we share a brain when it comes to her. He always knows what I'm thinking before I even say it, and it just further solidifies the fact that she belongs with us both.

Her eyes light up, and she pulls her lower lip between her teeth as she nods her head in affirmation. He drags his tongue along one side of her neck, while I dip down, nipping and sucking at the other. Her quiet whimpers fill the back of the car, and I place my palm over her mouth, muffling the needy sounds.

"Shhh," I say, my mouth hovering next to her ear. "You wouldn't want the driver to hear what a desperate slut you are, soaking your panties at the thought of two cocks being stuffed into your tiny body at once. I'm going to fucking wreck your tight little ass, Arden. And you're going to beg for more, aren't you?"

She releases a shaky exhale. "Yes."

"There's my sweet girl," Jackson praises. "I can't wait to pump my cum into your pussy, Princess. It's going to feel so good, huh?"

She stares up at me, leisurely nodding at his question. Her eyes are so glossed over with lust that I can already tell her head is emptying, just like it always does when we're like this with her. Where I'm rough and dominant, he's soft and encouraging. She doesn't know how to react to the contrasting demeanors, so she lets go, trusting us to take over and give her what she needs.

The car comes to a stop, and we usher her through the private entrance of our building, helping her to the elevator before ascending to our floor. As soon as we push through the door to our condo, it's game on, hands and mouths everywhere while we shed our clothing as fast as we can. The pleasantries Jacks and I normally take—undressing and worshipping Arden's body—don't exist as we wildly pull at our costumes, letting them fall in a trail from the entryway to the base of the stairs. She kisses me passionately, our lips and tongues devouring each other like it's our last meal as he drops to his knees behind her. He works her panties down her legs, and I can tell the moment he shoves his face between them, because it propels her right into my steel cock, creating enough pressure to make me see stars.

"Goddamn," he growls, a sound he only makes when he's particularly starved for her. "You're fucking delicious." She moans, breaking our connection to twist her upper body so she can see him.

Unable to resist having my mouth on her, I latch onto her neck, biting and sucking as my hands roam down her sides. I stop when I've got an ass cheek in each palm, squeezing and spreading them to give him better access to feast. It must expose her most sensitive parts even more, because this time, when he pushes against her, she yelps loudly before throwing her ass back into his face.

I reach up, gripping her chin and turning her head back toward me so I can whisper in her ear. "Greedy fucking girl," I chide, her needy breaths ricocheting off my cheek. "You just can't get enough, can you? Do you need two tongues again? One for each of those slutty holes so you can come like the depraved whore we know you are?"

"P-please," she stammers, her eyes squeezing shut as she attempts to regain her composure. "I want that."

"Aww," I mock with a patronizing pout. "Look at

you, begging to have your pussy and ass eaten." She moans loudly, and I hear the sound of her wetness around Jackson's finger as he pushes it inside.

I chuckle darkly. "You know why he's doing that, right?" I ask. "Because he loves the way your cunt responds to my degradation. Nothing makes you tighter than hearing how fucking pathetic you are, Arden." I press a rough kiss to her lips, sinking to the floor and throwing her thigh over my shoulder. She places a hand on each of our heads for support, which she's going to need in a second because I'm just getting started.

"Is she all snug and swollen, Jacks?" I ask. He mumbles his affirmation, still moving in and out of her as he swirls his tongue around her asshole. "Make room. I want to feel." Before he can even react, I work a finger into her pussy alongside his, filling her even more as I lean forward and latch onto her clit. A guttural cry tumbles from her lips, and she balls my hair in her fist, the bite of pain spurring me on to give her even more. Her leg that's lying along my back trembles, and I know she's seconds from falling into a boneless heap between us, but I don't give a fuck.

"You're taking our fingers so well, sweetheart," he praises, his soft tone a perfect contrast to the rough one I was using just moments ago. I stay quiet, working her over with my tongue while he continues. I want to make her head spin, and this shit works every time. "Such a precious girl, letting us make you feel good."

"Oh my God. Please. I need to come. Can I?" she begs. I laugh at how quickly she's become a moaning mess for us, the sound vibrating against her clit while she attempts to hold back. We pick up speed, hitting all her most sensitive spots and bringing her even closer to the edge as seconds tick by.

"Hawk...baby...*please.*" As soon as the term of endearment falls from her lips, I go *feral.* Nodding my head like a man possessed, I suck her aching bundle of nerves deeper into my mouth with the sudden over-whelming need to give her everything she's ever wanted. My head spins and euphoria washes over me in waves so intense that I feel like I might black out. I've never experienced anything like it in my entire life, but I refuse to lose myself to it before she explodes.

Pushing my finger further inside, I mindlessly curl it against her G-spot, finally pulling her orgasm to the surface. Every muscle in her body tightens as her pussy contracts, violently spasming and locking us inside her together so tight, we couldn't pull out even if we wanted to. We do our best to hold her up as she rides it out, but my head is still fuzzy from whatever the fuck just happened when she called me *baby*.

Eventually, it fades away and Jackson stands, supporting her full weight as I struggle for oxygen, still unable to rise from where I'm kneeling at Arden's feet. She reaches down, cupping my cheek in her soft hand, our hooded gazes burning into one another like nothing else exists outside this room. She's fucking beautiful, and I love her with every part of me.

"Can you hold yourself up?" he asks quietly, pressing his lips against her flushed cheek. "I need to go clean up quick."

Her brows pull tight in confusion as she slowly turns, her eyes roving over his body from top to bottom and freezing as she sucks in a sharp gasp. "Did you... come?" she chokes out, her eyes going wide with surprise.

He clears his throat, a cocky grin stretching across his face as he peers down at the mess that's splattered across his abs. "It's not mine."

She whips her head my way, and I look down, watching as cum continues to leak from my still throbbing erection. *Holy fucking shit.* Not only did I have a hands-free orgasm, but it was so mind-melting that I didn't even realize I went off like a firehose, inadvertently covering my best friend in my release. My heart rate speeds up, and I don't know whether to be mortified or not, but when I bring my eyes back up to hers, all I see is heat and mischief burning behind them.

She bites her lip, sinking to her knees between us as I stare, unblinking, to see what she does next. She wastes absolutely no time leaning into him and dragging her tongue through my cum, making sure to clean every drop while he throws his head back and lovingly caresses her hair.

"Fuck. That's hot," I whisper, my dick going rock hard again when she licks along his shaft, stopping to circle her tongue along the head before taking it between her plump lips. He exhales a slow, shaky breath as she slides down further, the muscles in his jaw clenching tight while she bobs up and down.

I stand slowly, making sure I'm steady on my feet before running my hand through her chocolate curls right beside Jackson's. She reaches back, finds my aching erection, and wraps her fingers around it, leisurely stroking while she sucks. A groan works its way up my chest as I take in the sight of her eagerly swallowing his cock, the sound of her small gags sending all of my senses into overdrive.

Pulling off of him and pressing a soft kiss to the tip, she releases me, rising to her feet between us. Her hands skate down our chests, stopping at the ridges of our abdomens before she walks forward, wordlessly making her way up the stairs like she didn't just have us dangerously close to blowing our loads mere seconds ago. We keep our eyes locked onto her full ass as it sways with every step, until she stops and turns back to us with a brow raised in question.

"Well? Are you guys going to fuck me, or what?"

THIRTY-TWO
ARDEN

"OH, FUCK YEAH," Jackson breathes on a forced exhale, rushing up the staircase behind me. I giggle when he lifts me into his arms, carrying me bridal style down the hall toward Hawk's room with him hot on our heels. We never really discussed the fact that we'd always sleep and have sex in here, but I guess it's a no-brainer, considering he has the biggest bed and a dresser full of fun toys. I love it, though—because when we're inside these walls, no matter what happens, I know I'm safe and loved.

"You ready, Princess?" Jackson says, tossing me onto the bed. I land with a bounce, nodding my head as he drops on top of me, immediately sealing his mouth to mine in a deep, demanding kiss. We make out, and I vaguely register the sound of Hawk digging through the drawers, no doubt getting everything we'll need for me to take them both at once. Jacks thrusts his hips, his long, veiny shaft grinding between my soaked lips as I whimper for more. I'm so wet that a slight tip of my pelvis would have him sliding right inside with ease.

So that's exactly what I do.

Lifting my lower half from the bed, I accept him as he pushes forward, his cock breaching my entrance as we both sigh in relief. I'm so ready, there's barely even a stretch when he bottoms out, dragging his heavy length back out before driving inside again.

"Yes," I moan. "Fuck me." But he keeps a slow and steady pace, refusing to give me what I'm begging for. I try to buck up into him, but he wraps a hand around my hip, pressing me into the mattress so I can't create the friction I need. A flustered, pitiful whine falls from my lips just as Hawk crawls up beside us.

"Is he being mean to you, baby?" he mocks. "Do you need more?"

I nod my head frantically, desperate for him to do something—anything—to cure the throbbing ache between my legs. "Mhmm."

He reaches out, nudging Jackson's shoulder as he lazily and deliberately thrusts into me. "Roll over. We need her on top of you." Before I can even register his request, a thick arm bands around my waist and we're switching positions so I'm straddling him. I seize the opportunity, immediately bouncing on his cock as my release blooms to life deep within me.

"That's it, Princess," he praises, bringing his hands to my tits and squeezing as I throw my head back in pleasure. "You look so beautiful right now. I love you."

"I love you too," I reply, barely able to form coherent words through the thick haze in my brain. Between everything that happened downstairs, the feel of him inside me, and the thought of what's to come, I'm ready to explode again at any second.

I whimper loudly, my clit beginning to pulse against his pelvis as I feel the mattress dip behind me. Hawk's minty breath ghosts along my cheek, and I savor the warmth of his body as he speaks much softer than I'm used to in these situations. "I'm going to get you ready. Keep riding and come whenever you want to. Use your safe word if you don't like something, okay?"

Turning my head, I meet his gaze with mine, conveying all the trust I have in him with a single look. "Yes," I reply, leaning back to kiss him one last time before lowering down so my chest is pressed tightly to Jackson's. I resume my movements, grinding my clit against him as his hands slide around and spread my ass cheeks apart. Sparks of electricity prick on my skin, and I feel something cool and wet drip onto my tight hole, followed by the pad of Hawk's finger gliding over it. I'm so close to coming that I barely even flinch as he presses forward, sinking all the way in and sending a bolt of pleasure right up my spine.

"Holy shit," Jacks grits out. "You're choking my cock. Let go for me, Arden. Fucking come." My body listens to his command, detonating around him as I fall over the edge. I cry out, chanting their names over and over while I shatter, consumed by the feeling of them working together to give me everything I need.

It goes on forever, until I finally begin to return to awareness, registering the slow slide of them moving in and out as I recover. Soft praises come from each side of my head, and I sigh contentedly as I resume moving my hips back and forth languidly.

"There you go, Hellcat," Hawk says, dripping more lube onto where we're joined before pushing another finger inside. It feels incredible, the stretch a welcome sensation as my pussy continues to pulse against Jackson's hard cock with aftershocks. "You're doing so good opening up. Bear down for me." I obey, and he gently works in a third finger, causing a deep, satisfied moan to rise up my chest before filling the air around us. I give him time to prep me completely as I become wetter and more desperate with every deliciously agonizing thrust. Just as I'm ready to beg for more, he pulls out, making me whimper in frustration.

"He's just lubing up," Jackson coos, his hands rubbing reassuring circles along my lower back as I continue riding him. His muscles are wound tight underneath me, and I'm sure he's hanging by a thread, considering he's the only one of us who hasn't had a release yet. I press my lips to his, both of us opening up to deepen the kiss just as the head of Hawk's cock presses to my asshole. I clench, but he curls himself over me, so close that all three of our faces are practically touching.

"We're here, sweetheart," he says into my ear. "Let us in." I keep still, exhaling a shaky breath as I relax my body, focusing on the way their skin feels against mine in this monumental moment. Opening my eyes, I lock onto the bright green ones in front of me, the softness in them giving me everything I need to feel safe and adored. Hawk pushes forward slowly, his head stretching me much wider than his fingers did before I feel the small metal barbell notch through the tight ring of muscle. He stops, but that's the last thing I want right now, because while there's a slight burn, the indescribable pleasure far outweighs the pain.

"More," I choke out. "I need more."

THIRTY-THREE
JACKSON

"FUCK, YOU'RE PERFECT," I sigh, gritting my teeth as Hawk drives further into Arden's ass, her satisfied moans ricocheting off my lips. He pauses when he's buried to the hilt, and I have to take several deep breaths, so I don't come early. Her pussy is tight as it is, but with him inside her too? I can't even think straight. "Are you okay?"

"Mhmm," she hums, her eyes rolling to the back of her head like she's completely lost to the sensation of being filled by us both at the same time.

"You're doing so good, baby," he says from behind her, lowering his heated gaze to where they're joined. "I'm going to move. Tell me if you need a break." He slowly retreats, thrusting forward again as a satisfied moan works its way up her chest. He repeats the motion, making me grunt loudly as I continue to fight the orgasm that's already starting to coil tightly inside me.

"Jesus Christ," I hiss, unable to stop the words from

coming out. "I can feel your fucking piercing. It's insane."

He grins over her shoulder, both of us moving opposite one another, sawing in and out as she mindlessly lets us use her. "Good. Maybe now you'll stop talking shit." I roll my eyes in response, but there's no fucking way I'll ever say another bad word about it, because it feels phenomenal through the thin wall that separates us.

"I love feeling you both inside me at once," she whimpers. "Please don't stop. I need to come so bad." The desperation in her pleading tone has me ready to blow at any moment, and by the look on Hawk's face as he picks up speed, he's right there, too. Normally, I think we'd both be able to last longer, but the entire experience, paired with how tight she is when she's stuffed with both of our cocks is making me feel like it's my first time all over again.

"Please, please, *please*." The chant sounds like a prayer as she begs us to push her over the edge, and the knowing glance my best friend tosses my way tells me exactly how this thing is about to end. The corner of my mouth tugs up in a coy grin before I get into character, ready to send her careening over the edge.

"That's my sweet girl," I say softly, lifting my hips from the mattress and thrusting into her warmth. "You're taking us so well. So beautiful. I can't wait to feel your cunt grip me when you fall apart. Do you want us to come inside you?" She nods her head rapidly, and I feel her inner walls flutter around me as they swell with her impending orgasm.

"Such a greedy cumslut," Hawk says darkly, his mouth hovering right next to her ear. "Ready to explode at the thought of us filling her up. You going to purr for us when we breed both of your pathetic little holes at once, Hellcat?"

"Oh my God, yes!" she cries out, convulsing wildly as his words finally hit their mark, making her shatter into a million perfect pieces between us. She pushes down, frantically grinding her clit over the muscles covering my pelvis before arching into Hawk's chest. A scream falls from her parted lips and her pussy closes in around me so tightly, there's nothing I can do to stop myself from being pulled under right behind her. Electricity moves through me and an unintelligible string of curses falls from my lips as I come, white light flashing behind my eyes as my balls contract and release repeatedly, pumping everything I have into her. It's intense—so much so, that I barely even register Hawk pushing in with one final thrust, his loud roar practically shaking the walls while his orgasm tears through him.

We ride it out together, moving as though we share a body until each of us is completely exhausted and unable to go on for another second. Arden collapses on top of me, her chest heaving against mine as she struggles to catch her breath. Her thighs shake, and my cock twitches with aftershocks, more thick ropes flowing into her as she greedily accepts every last drop. We lie there as we recover, both of us whispering gentle praises until she finally gives in to her exhaustion and falls asleep.

"I'm so fucking proud of you, baby," Hawk whispers, coasting tender kisses along her neck and shoulders. "We love you so much, I hope you know that." She hums in response, and my heart squeezes in my chest at the exchange, because it all feels so natural. I can barely even remember a time when it wasn't true. I've loved this girl for most of my life, even before I knew what the word truly meant—but him not being a part of what we have now seems unfathomable. Like, without him, we'd always have a missing piece.

He carefully pulls out, wincing as she unconsciously flinches. A small, pained whine falls from her lips, but she doesn't fully wake, nuzzling into me and finding a comfortable position before her breathing evens out once again. Wrapping my arms loosely around her, I ghost my fingertips up and down her back as he disappears into the en suite. I close my eyes, inhaling the scent of our cologne on her skin, filled with nothing but gratitude that she's right here where she belongs.

"Hey," Hawk says, placing a hand on my shoulder. I look up to find him wearing a pair of boxer briefs as the muffled sound of running water comes from behind him. "We have to get her into the bath. I've got it going now, and I already threw in some Epsom salts. You'll probably have to get in behind her since she's so tired. We'll let her rest for a bit, then wake her for food and water after."

"Okay," I reply, reluctantly rolling us over and immediately hating the broken connection as I stand from the bed and lift her into my arms. My legs feel like Jell-O, but I hold her close, following him to the bathroom and stepping over the side of the tub before lowering under the warm water. Settling her between my legs, I let my head fall back, lulled by the sound of her soft, steady snores. He goes to work, cleaning her from head to toe, finishing up, and leaving the room so we can continue to soak. There's no chance she won't be sore tomorrow, so hopefully, this helps.

The rest of the night floats by as we provide all the aftercare she needs to feel safe, happy, and adored. I can't help but recognize the way we've all changed since Arden moved in with us, and the bonds we've created while learning from each other, both inside the bedroom and out. Before I was forced to face my feelings for her, I never would've thought I'd be able to call her mine—let alone while sharing her with my best friend. But here we are, and I've never been happier in my whole life.

THIRTY-FOUR
ARDEN

"SHUT. UP," Stella says, her face filling the screen on my phone as her jaw practically slams against the floor. *"Both* of them? *At once?"*

"Oh my God," I reply, propping the device up against the vase of flowers on our kitchen counter so I can continue preparing my pre-practice meal. "I finally give you the full update on my life, and *that's* what you took from it?" I told her I was exploring relationships with both of the guys after Jackson finally came clean about his feelings, but with our busy schedules never matching up, I wasn't able to give her all the details. She's off work today and I have another hour before I have to leave for the facility, so this is as good a time as any to fill her in.

"Oh, I'm sorry," she shoots back. "My best friend just told me she had her very first double penetration experience. Pardon me for being interested in how *that* works. Also," she says, shoving an Oreo into her mouth, "how about you shut up and let me live vicariously through you? You're out here getting railed by your two hot, professional athlete boyfriends, and I can't even get a text back. Stop being so selfish, Arden. Let me have th—" Her brows pull in but quickly relax when she focuses on something in the background. I turn to see what's caught her attention just as Jackson comes up behind me, wearing only a pair of short athletic shorts. His chestnut hair sticks to his forehead, and a droplet of sweat drips down the side of his face, bringing my attention to his chiseled jaw as it ticks like it knows I'm getting hotter by the second. His bare chest glistens, and even though this isn't the time, my pussy clenches in response. *Fuck, my man is* sexy. He and Hawk went down to use the building's private gym a while ago, but I wasn't expecting them back for at least another thirty minutes, which is why I figured I had time to call my best friend.

"Hey, Princess," he says, darting his hand out and yanking me toward him. I squeal in protest, attempting to push him away, but he wraps his thick arms around me, smacking playful kisses all over my cheeks.

"Eww! You stink!" I shriek, laughing as I attempt to break free from where he's got me completely locked in. But he doesn't let up, continuing his assault until a large hand curls around his shoulder, pulling him away.

"Get off my girl, Blake," Hawk says, a cavalier smirk lifting one side of his mouth. He's less sweaty, wearing a pair of black basketball shorts and a white, formfitting t-shirt, the ends of his dark hair curling out from under a backward Fury hat. *This one was built for depravity—and he's all fucking mine.*

My heart rate increases as he steps closer, keeping his ocean-blue eyes locked onto mine. "I missed you." The words are a deep rasp, and he leans down slowly, his fingertips burning the skin of my hip through my shirt as his lips finally slide against mine. It's an innocent kiss, but the tension twisting inside me just from being near him has me whimpering quietly into his mouth as he steals my breath.

The heat of another warm body radiates along my back, and more wet kisses trail down the side of my neck. "*Our* girl," Jacks whispers into my ear, making me melt between them. My stomach flutters and I go lightheaded, losing myself to the feeling of being worshiped by them both. So much so, that I completely forget about the fact that Stella is watching the entire thing go down until her voice cuts through the air.

"What's it like to be God's favorite?" she sighs, and we all freeze, turning our heads to where she's still propped up on the counter. She's riveted, her chin resting in the palm of her hand as she enjoys the softcore porn she didn't ask for, but we almost gave.

"Hi, Stella," Jackson sing-songs. "How have you been?"

"Not bad," she replies. "Obviously not as good as the queen of double-dickings over here, but you know what they say. *Beggars can't be choosers.*"

I drop my head into my hands, groaning in embarrassment. *Of course*, she would immediately use her newfound knowledge to mortify me. It's who she is as a person, and I love her for it, even when her unfiltered thoughts are to my own detriment. Hawk chuckles, pressing a chaste kiss to my hair before they both move around the kitchen, taking over breakfast prep as I lift my phone in front of my face.

"Anyway," she continues, pushing out her bottom lip. "I'm so bummed to be missing your first match tomorrow. I was hoping I'd be able to come down with your dad and Gina this weekend, but I ended up getting a call from that travel nursing agency I applied to, and they offered me a job."

My eyes go wide, and my jaw drops. "Stell, that's so exciting! You've always wanted to do that, and you've worked so hard! Where do you go first? Somewhere exotic, I hope—with lots of hot, shirtless men for you to drool over when you're off the clock."

She scrunches her nose, shrugging. "Afraid not—at least, I don't think so. I'm going to Cleveland. They figured since it's not super far from home, it would be a good first experience for me. But seriously, what the *hell* is in Cleveland?"

"You're about to find out," I reply with a laugh. "It's better that you aren't coming to watch me play now, anyway. Maybe by the time you do, I'll have figured out my coach's motive for sabotaging the team. That way, we might not have to struggle to pull off a win for you."

With our home opener just over twenty-four hours away, I should be feeling all kinds of excitement and butterflies. But if I'm being completely honest, I'm kind of dreading it. The entire team was confused when I told them about the changes to our play-calling. I was hoping I could keep their spirits up, but the more we fell into Dahlia's new way of doing things, the more chaotic it became. Maybe after tomorrow, she'll realize that this is never going to work at the level we're playing at. I need to be able to read the court and make quick changes on the fly when I see something I don't like. If she doesn't trust me to do that, I may have to go over her head and speak to the team's general manager. As much as I was hoping to avoid it because I didn't want to make waves so early in my career, I'm also the team captain. Our success and failure will be on my shoulders, even if I'm not allowed to make any decisions.

"Mark my words," Stella replies. "That woman will be looking for a new job by summer. I don't even know her, and I can tell by the very minimal details you've given me that this is personal. She's probably jealous that she isn't good enough to be on the court with you."

"That's what I said," Jacks chimes in, setting a blue-berry muffin, mug of coffee, bottle of water, and my anxiety meds in front of me. I press up onto my toes, kissing his cheek before he walks away, grateful that the two of them support and care for me as they do.

"You're both wrong," I reply, picking up the mug and taking a cautious sip of the hot liquid. "She would definitely be good enough to play professionally, had she not quit her senior year of college. I was a freshman, and as much as I was looking forward to learning so I could take over her position after she graduated, she pretty much acted like I didn't exist. Then one day, she just cleaned out her locker and left. When we asked our coach why, he said it didn't matter and that we'd be moving forward without her."

She raises a suspicious brow. "Well, let her try fucking with you when I'm around. You may be a pushover, Arden Levine, but I will cut a bitch for making you sad."

"I like her," Hawk mumbles, putting a pan of dough in the oven. I saw it sitting in the refrigerator earlier, and I hoped he was making a loaf of my favorite bread for after the match. I have a funny feeling that—win or lose—I'll need the comfort of carbs tomorrow night.

"Alright, I have to eat and run," I tell her, noticing how much time I've wasted this morning. "I'll text you later. And I want every detail when you get to Cleveland, even if it's twenty degrees and everyone is wearing multiple shirts."

"You got it, babe. Love you." We blow each other a kiss, ending the call as I make quick work of scarfing down my breakfast. My coffee gets transferred into a to-go cup, which I grab on my way to the door, kissing my guys and heading out for my very last practice before the regular season begins. Luckily, it's also therapy day, which isn't a coincidence, since I have a feeling I'll need to talk through some stuff by the time I'm ready to leave the facility.

I keep reminding myself to focus on the things within my control and not put so much pressure on myself to change the things that I simply cannot. All I can do is go to practice, give one hundred percent effort, encourage my teammates, and do my job so we have the best chance at a winning season.

Let's just hope we can pull off a miracle, whether our coach wants us to or not.

THIRTY-FIVE
JACKSON

"HERE'S YOUR TEA, PRINCESS," I say, stepping into Arden's bathroom as she stands in front of the mirror in her fluffy pink robe. "And a muffin from Hawk. Fresh out of the oven, so be careful."

She sets down the brush in her hand, meeting my reflection with a grateful smile. "Why are you both so good to me?" she asks as I move in, wrapping my arms around her tightly from behind. Her first match was two days ago, and it was every bit of the disaster she thought it would be. It started off with them winning the first set, but as it went on, shit started going sideways, and it all went downhill from there. They lost the next three horribly, and I know Arden was putting a lot of it on herself. We've been doing our best to keep her mind off it when she's with us, but she's been on edge with our parents flying in this morning for their visit.

"Because we love you," I reply simply, pressing a kiss to the soft skin of her neck. I haven't been able to keep my hands or mouth off her for the last twenty-four hours, because I know once my mom and Slade arrive, we'll have to keep our distance until we talk to them about what's going on between us. To be honest, I'm nervous as hell. I've spent years putting space between myself and Arden to avoid anyone finding out the way I really felt about her. Now, not only am I preparing to tell them I've been in love with her since we were teenagers, but we're also coming clean about the fact that we're in a relationship—and that she's in a relationship with my best friend too, and I'm okay with it.

"How am I going to survive two days without touching you guys?" she asks, pouting at me in the mirror. "We've been sleeping in bed together every night, and now I'm just supposed to be all by myself, knowing the two of you are just down the hall? Maybe we should just tell them right away."

I chuckle, dragging my tongue from the base of her neck upward and nipping at the sensitive skin under her ear. She moans in response, bringing her hand up and curling it around the back of my neck to hold me there, as if I'd let her go right now. Until that doorbell rings and our parents are inside this condo, I'm staying right where I am.

"We have to wait," I tell her. "My mom has some business to discuss with you, and I don't want that conversation to be derailed if she freaks out about our news. Plus, I already told you...you're not sleeping alone. There's no reason you can't stay with Hawk in his bed. The guest rooms are far enough away from there, so you won't have to worry about them listening in. And who cares if they know you're together? They like him, and I doubt they'd be upset about it. Your dad may have the *If you hurt my daughter, I'll hurt you* talk with him, but that's going to happen anyway. May as well get it over with, right?"

Her eyes lock onto mine, dancing with amusement as she raises a brow. "Didn't *you* tell him the same thing already?"

I nod confidently. "Fuck yeah, I did. And I meant it. I love Hawk, but I love you more. When he told me how he felt, I wanted to ensure that he knew what he was risking if he fucked up. If I had to stand by and watch another man love you in ways that I couldn't, I was going to make sure he gave you everything you deserved."

She turns, both arms winding around my shoulders as mine tighten around her waist. "I couldn't imagine it not being the three of us. Tell me I'll never have to be without either of you, Jacks." She looks up, her deep brown pools brimming with unshed tears. They fall over as she blinks, but I swipe them away with my thumbs, shaking my head slowly.

"Never, Princess. We'll always be together. I promise." I know that's impossible to guarantee, but I don't give a fuck what our parents think. They love us. They'll warm up to the idea eventually.

When I look into the future, I see Arden as our wife —on paper or not—and the mother of our children. I imagine Hawk and I bringing them to watch her play volleyball all over the country until she's ready to retire, then we can go wherever life takes us. Maybe I'm crazy for envisioning forever so soon, but it's what I want, and I know he feels the same.

"Okay," she whispers, pushing up to her tiptoes and pressing her lips to mine in a sweet kiss. I tighten my hold, drawing her as close as possible so I can savor her fruity scent. Our tongues dance and tangle, and although I intended for this to be a soft, delicate caress, I'm becoming increasingly desperate for more. And when she moans into my mouth, I know she's just as needy as I am.

Without breaking our connection, I walk us through the doorway that leads to her bedroom, not stopping until the backs of her legs hit the mattress. I lower her down, continuing to swallow every delicious sound that escapes her as we kiss like we won't get to again for an eternity. My hands roam her body, and I put just enough space between us to unfasten the tie at the front of her robe, watching in awe as it falls away and exposes her flawless skin.

"Jacks," she gasps, her chest heaving as I skate my lips downward, claiming every inch of her neck and chest before swirling my tongue around her perfect, pink nipple. I cup the other breast in my hand, kneading gently and making her writhe beneath me.

"You're fucking perfect, baby," I rasp, my hot breath ricocheting off the hardened bud. "I can't believe you're mine."

"I'm yours," she whimpers, lifting her hips and pressing into me. My cock is like granite between us, and although I'd give anything to make love to her until we pass out from exhaustion, I know we can't. "Always."

"That's right, sweetheart. And I'm yours," I reply softly, continuing to leave a trail of wet kisses all over her gorgeous tits. Wherever my mouth moves, my hand does the opposite, ensuring that she's getting all the attention I'm capable of giving right now.

"I'm so in love with you," she whispers, the words hitting me like a bolt of electricity straight to my heart and making it beat wildly, only for her. I slowly work my way back up, pressing my lips to hers once more before smiling against them.

"What?" she says, quirking a brow at the gesture. I shake my head, pulling back and taking in her flushed complexion and messy hair that she'll probably kick my ass for when she sees it.

"You just make me really fucking happy," I reply with a playful shrug. Her smile mirrors mine, and her big brown eyes sparkle with emotion as she stares at me like I hung the moon just for her. I wish I could inject this moment right into my veins because I can't think of a better feeling than knowing I put that look on her face.

We're brought back to reality by a quiet knock on the door, followed by Hawk popping his head inside. His eyes go wide when he sees me lying on top of Arden, most of her body still on display, cringing with remorse when he realizes what he just walked in on.

"Sorry. I didn't know you guys were—" He pauses, probably because she's almost naked and I'm fully clothed, so it isn't really clear *what* we're doing. "The front desk just called. Your parents are on their way up. If you need more time, I can keep them occupied."

"No, that's okay," I say. "We shouldn't keep them waiting long." Arden pouts up at me, and I chuckle, pushing off the mattress before pulling her to her feet. She throws her head back dramatically, not helping in the slightest as I redo the tie at her waist and plant a small kiss on the tip of her nose. "Hawk will just have to finish what I started later." She looks over at him, and he winks, making her smile bloom back to life before she wordlessly saunters toward the bathroom to continue getting ready.

I'm glad I was able to ease the anxiety I know she's having about them being here, even though I'm currently feeling like I might shit my pants. I've been doing my best to stay calm for her, but inside, I know this could get rocky for a minute. She's extremely close with her father, and it would kill her if he didn't approve of us being together, or the fact that Hawk and I both love her. And my mom is her agent. Not only do they have a personal relationship, but a professional one, as well. I have to make sure none of that is put in jeopardy, so I'm hoping the right words will come to me when it's time to tell them everything. But for now, we just need to put on a show and not let the cat out of the bag too early.

THIRTY-SIX
ARDEN

"THERE'S MY GIRL," my dad says, opening his arms as I run his way. I feel like it's been years since I've seen him, even though I know it hasn't. But between my busy schedule and avoiding conversations because I'm afraid I'll blurt out every detail of my life, we haven't talked nearly as much as we usually do. Even when I was in Argentina, we had multiple phone calls each week. Since I've been in Daytona, we've checked in less, and I've missed him like crazy. "How's life?"

"It's good," I tell him. It's not a lie. Other than Dahlia making my work life harder than it has to be for no reason, I'm happy. Therapy is going well, the meds I'm on are working great, with very little side effects, and the boys are taking the best care of me. I still have bad days from time to time, but I'm also happier than I've ever been.

"So, Florida was the right move then," he says, not as much of a question as it is a statement. He's never doubted me, even when I doubted myself, and entering the PVF draft wouldn't have happened without his encouragement.

"It was," I reply, summoning the ear-to-ear grin I love so much. The same one he gave me after every match growing up—win or lose—that let me know he was proud of me. I can't lie, it makes me feel better in a way I didn't even realize I needed, and I'm so grateful that he's here right now.

"Hi, sweetheart," Gina says, stepping in for a hug. I pull her close, inhaling her signature perfume, which adds another layer of comfort to my racing thoughts. It's the same scent that enveloped me when I got my acceptance letter from Penn State—and when I came home from Argentina feeling like a failure. She never gave up on me, even when I was sure my career was over, and I'm so lucky to have her in my life.

"Hi," I reply, my heart swelling at the thought of all the most important people in my life being in the same room with me right now. It may be the calm before the storm, but it feels incredible to have a support system this strong.

"So," she says, loosening her hold on me. A bright smile blooms across her face, and she's practically vibrating with whatever she's holding in. "I was going to wait to tell you after dinner when we had more time to talk about the team, but I got an exciting phone call last week, and I might burst if I don't say it right now."

I furrow my brows in confusion because, other than Dahlia getting on a rocket ship and moving to another planet, I can't imagine anything she could have to say that would result in spontaneous combustion. Not that she really *knows* about Dahlia. At least, not yet. "What?"

"Rip-It Sports sent over an endorsement proposal. They're looking for new faces for their volleyball lineup, and they've offered a pretty nice contract. Between that and what you're getting from the Flare, you'll have no problem affording all your bills and getting into a place of your own. It's exclusive, so you'd have to wear their products on the court, but I've done my research, and I really think they might enhance your game. I have some samples in my suitcase that they sent for you to try out."

I stand there frozen, hearing only the blood pounding between my ears for what feels like minutes as I register her words. All I've ever wanted was to make a name for myself as an athlete—one that's respected and looked up to as a great player and team-mate. Not only am I playing the sport I love profession-ally, but this deal will show millions of little girls that if they work hard and don't give up, they can do anything.

"Are you okay, Princess?" Jackson asks, his voice cutting through the noise in my head and bringing me back to the present. I meet his gaze, my eyes filling with tears as I take in the sheer happiness written across his face. Without even thinking, I launch myself into his arms, laughing as he lifts me off my feet. Thankfully, he's got his head on straight, not lingering for longer than would be acceptable for two friends, before passing me to our parents to celebrate. Gina hugs me first, then ushers me into my dad's waiting embrace before she moves to the other side of the room to dig a few items out of her bag.

"Here you go," she says, handing me a box and beaming as I flip the lid back to reveal a pair of brand-new volleyball shoes. I lift one out, admiring the beautiful white and purple design. Studying each side as if it were a piece of priceless art, I try to keep my emotions under control. But when the back side comes into view, the dam breaks and I sob out loud. My free hand flies up over my mouth and tears fall freely because right there, in big, embroidered letters, are my initials and the number ten. It's the jersey number I've worn my entire life, and it'll be on the shoes of athletes around the world who have the same dreams and ambitions I once had.

"I-I can't believe it," I stammer. "My own signature shoe." I can barely choke out the words through the thickness in my throat. Every second that goes by seems more surreal as they stare back at me with pride written all over their faces.

"It's not just a *shoe*," she says, extending a t-shirt and athletic shorts my way, both with the same logo scrawled across them in vibrant text. "It's an entire *line*. Congratulations, Arden."

I stare at the garments, swiping more tears from my cheeks before they finally dissolve into an excited giggle. "Wow. This is crazy." After waiting a lifetime for a moment like this, I thought I'd have more to say, but truth be told…I'm speechless. It's a surreal thing when you achieve something you only thought existed in your imagination, and I need some time to process it all.

"Thank you," I murmur sincerely, hoping they understand how grateful I am—Hawk included—because, while he hasn't been here nearly as long as the others, his impact has been felt in such monumental ways. From providing the encouragement I needed to seek help for my mental health, to being a pillar of strength for me every day, he's just as much a part of my family as they are.

"I knew you could do it," my dad says, wrapping me in a warm hug. I breathe in his cologne and my heart overflows with appreciation because, while this is a huge accomplishment for me, it belongs to him, too. Nobody has sacrificed more to get me here than he has, and I love him so much for it. "This calls for a celebration!" he says excitedly before letting me go. "I know you're all elite athletes, but how about some pizza and beer to celebrate my baby girl being the next big thing?"

"Great idea," Jacks replies, ushering our parents toward the kitchen and trading a knowing look with Hawk. As soon as they're out of sight, my broody boy invades my space, placing both hands on my waist and pulling me into his hard body. I suck in a surprised gasp, melting into him as he drops his forehead to mine.

"I'm so fucking proud of you, Hellcat. This is just the beginning." He leans in, taking my lips in a kiss that starts innocent, but as always, becomes desperate and demanding before either of us can stop it. His fingers dig into the flesh of my hips, and I moan quietly into his mouth, but he greedily swallows it down, refusing to let it go to waste. "You're amazing. I love you so much." I consume his praises, each one lighting a fire inside me. I wish we could disappear for the rest of the night, but a muted laugh from the next room breaks us from our tryst and reminds us that we can't do that yet.

"Ugh," I groan, tilting my head up in frustration. But he just laughs, leaning in close so his mouth hovers over my ear.

"Tonight, baby. I'm going to take that tight little pussy rough, and you'll be such a quiet girl for me, won't you? They won't even know that their perfect angel is just down the hall getting fucked like a slut." He nips at my lobe, and I whimper in response, trying to stop the needy throb that's pulsing between my legs. I swear, this man has the filthiest corruption kink, and as much as I shouldn't like it, I fucking do. Everything he does turns me into a desperate, begging mess.

"Yes," I say on a shaky exhale, praying that my legs don't give out as he presses the softest kiss to my forehead—a stark contrast to the things I know he's imagining doing to me later. I know, because I'm imagining them too. The thought of him punishing me for making the smallest sound as he stretches my body to its absolute limit plays on repeat in my head as we join my family in the kitchen, ordering our food and falling into easy conversations while we wait for it to be delivered. I know Gina wants to talk about the team and ask why we're looking like hot garbage on the court. But I'm glad she's decided that the topic can wait because discussing Dahlia and her unnecessary disdain for me is sure to put a damper on the evening, no matter what kind of fun awaits me when everyone goes to bed.

We eat our food, Jacks and I stealing glances at each

other whenever we think we can get away with it. Hawk gives up on keeping his need to be near me whenever we're in the same room a secret, sitting close and rubbing soothing circles on my thigh with his thumb under the table. My dad doesn't seem to notice, but my stepmother passes me a few knowing smirks as we fill them in on life in Daytona. I have no doubt they'll give their blessing for us to date, but it feels like a giant lie even alluding to the idea that it's just the two of us in a relationship. I want so badly for Jackson to slide in on my other side, gently gripping my other leg like he always does. My skin practically begs for his touch from across the room, and by the look in his eyes as he longingly stares at me, I can tell he's feeling it too. When he can't take it any longer, he says his goodnights and retreats to his room for the first time in what feels like forever.

"Alright," my dad says, standing from the table and extending his arms above his head in a stretch. "We're going to head up to bed. It was a long day, and Gina isn't a spring chicken anymore." His wife's jaw drops, and she slaps his shoulder, making him bark a laugh. They really are adorable and still so in love. I just hope our confession at the end of the weekend doesn't mess that up. The last thing I want is to throw any wrenches in our family dynamic. But Jacks was right. We're adults, and if they're not on board with the idea of us being together, they'll have to get over it, because we aren't giving each other up.

"There are some extra blankets in the guest room

closet," Hawk says, shaking my dad's hand. "Help yourself to whatever you need."

"Thank you," he replies before turning to me. "Good night, honey. I'm so proud of you." He leans in, hugging me and pressing a kiss to the top of my head.

"Night, Dad. See you in the morning." With that, they head up the stairs, and I exhale a relieved sigh as soon as the door to their room closes. As happy as I am that they're here, I want to celebrate with my guy. I wish I could have them both, but I understand why Jacks is staying by himself. It's risky enough for me to stay in Hawk's room, but at this point, I'll take my chances. It's better than tossing and turning all night because I'm all alone.

"Let's go, baby," he says quietly, taking my hand and leading me up the steps, padding as lightly as we can toward his room. I feel like a teenager sneaking her boyfriend in while her parents are asleep, and excitement tumbles around in my stomach as we finally reach our destination. His eyes dance with mischief as soon as he turns the lock, safely separating us from everyone else in the house.

"Strip and get on the bed with your legs wide for me," he commands. "I'm fucking famished."

THIRTY-SEVEN
HAWK

"OH, GOD. HAWK. *PLEASE*," Arden moans quietly as I suck her clit into my mouth, fluttering my tongue before letting it go with a *pop*. I chuckle darkly when she growls in frustration, slapping the swollen bundle of nerves with my fingertips and making her entire body jolt off the mattress. We tore off our clothes the moment we entered the room, and I've had my face between her legs, making her ride the edge for far longer than she'd probably like, ever since.

"Aww," I mock. "So polite, but I'm having too much fun playing with this slutty cunt. Especially when Jacks isn't here to save you." Leaning forward again, I lick around her entrance, lapping up the wetness that's dripping from how desperate she is.

"H-he would never d-do this to me," she stammers. "I wish he was h-here."

I lift my head, quirking a dubious brow. "Is that so, *Princess?*" I spit his nickname for her, acting as though it's the most juvenile thing in the world. "Why don't you call him, then? Tell him I'm not letting you come."

"I w-will," she replies like a brat, trying her best to grind into my face. But I back away, refusing to let her have the friction she needs. She growls again, throwing her arm toward the nightstand and picking up her phone. I'll admit I'm a little shocked—I didn't think she'd actually do it. She wouldn't want to risk him coming in here and getting busted before they've had a chance to talk to their parents, and we all know Arden is extra loud when she's taking us both at the same time. I'm barely even keeping her quiet by myself right now.

I kiss and nip at the insides of her thighs as she dials, putting it on speakerphone and waiting for him to pick up. Several seconds later, his gravelly voice breaks through the air.

"Hey, baby. You okay?"

Jacks," she whimpers. "I miss you." I return to her center, wrapping my lips around her clit and adding just enough suction to elicit a breathy gasp. He clearly hears it, because the sound of rustling comes across the line, followed by his rushed demand.

"Turn the camera on, Arden."

Her eyes go wide and her panicked gaze locks onto mine, but I just laugh against her soaked skin, giving her a look that says *do it*. She bites her lip, and I shove my tongue into her tight pussy, making another hurried moan escape from her throat. I can hear Jackson's breath heaving as he waits for her to obey, but she's too lost in the feeling of me licking along her walls to take action.

"Arden. Turn the motherfucking camera on." His order is stern—unlike his usual way of speaking to her —and it gets her attention. She fumbles with the phone in her hand before finding the correct button and opening the camera so he can see. It must be front facing because she attempts to school her expression while I continue fucking her with my tongue.

"Hi," she murmurs, her voice quiet and shaking as she swallows. I use my hands to spread her thighs wide, flicking against her tender flesh as she does her best to hide the fact that I've got her dangerously close to the edge.

"Show me," he says, and if I didn't know without a shadow of a doubt that it was him, I'd be questioning it by the danger in his tone. At first, I'm worried that he's mad we're in here doing stuff without him, but we've each spent time with her individually over the past few weeks, so I'm leaning more toward him just being worked up and desperate to watch her get off. But I have an even better idea—one that'll make him feel like a part of this, even from the other end of the house.

I halt my motions, ripping the phone from her hand before she has a chance to protest. His face fills the screen, and I immediately notice the way his jaw is clenched tight, his green eyes impossibly dark as he glares at me like he's ready to tear the walls off this place to get to her. "What do you want to see?"

"Her fucking pussy," he says without hesitation. "I

want to see how wet she is." I flip the camera, focusing on the spot between her thighs before reaching forward and using my thumb and middle finger to spread her apart. I let him look for a few seconds before slowly sinking inside. The sound of her arousal adds to the effect, and he pulls his bottom lip between his teeth as I slowly slide in and out.

"What now?" I ask, waiting for his instruction. If he can't be in here bringing her pleasure, I'll do it for him…even if it means abandoning my normal tactics. Although, by the look on his face, I have a feeling we're about to see a much more sinister side of Jackson than we're used to.

"Rub her clit. Get her nice and worked up." I pull my soaked finger from her body, using her wetness to massage in tight circles over her swollen, aching bundle of nerves. Doing my best to keep her face in the shot, I smirk as she quickly heads toward the summit again. He has no idea that I've already been torturing her for a while, so this may end a lot sooner than he's hoping for. Or maybe he'll take a page out of my book and stop me before she falls over.

"Jacks," she moans, much louder than she should be saying his name right now. He knows it too, because his eyes go wide as he watches her writhe around against my hand. "Fuck, yes. So good." Every word crescendos into a louder one, but I keep going, stroking her in a steady rhythm just like he told me to.

"Gag her," he demands. At first, I think I heard him wrong, because he's always so gentle and gives her a hundred opportunities to listen before looking to me to correct her. But this time, I guess he's not taking any chances since the house isn't empty. And I'm certainly not going to argue.

I abandon where I'm touching her, making her whine quietly as I back off the bed and walk toward the dresser. Opening the top drawer, I make sure all the options are in perfect view so he can choose. "Pick one," I tell him.

"Which one will keep her quiet when she comes?" he asks, and I chuckle because he's completely out of his element. He's all about making her feel good and letting her get away with all kinds of shit. This is the first time he's ever suggested any type of bondage on his own.

"Well, if it were me, I'd use this," I say, picking up the roll of black gag tape. I've been dying to try it out with her, but in this situation, it doesn't feel right. "But I know you wouldn't want to hurt her, so how about a ball gag?" I reach down, plucking the pink silicone ball from where it lies and turning it so he can see. It's small enough that it won't cause a lot of strain on her jaw, but big enough to muffle any noises that might escape. The black leather strap is soft and pliable, making it the best choice for him.

"Okay," he agrees, nodding. Closing the drawer, I return to the bed, where Arden is steadily rubbing her thighs together to ease the ache between them. I flip the camera again, propping it up on the nightstand so we're both in the frame before wrapping my hand around the back of her head and lifting it from the pillow.

"Open up, Hellcat," I say. She does, and I place the ball between her teeth, smoothing my hands around and fastening the buckle. She whimpers, and I press a gentle kiss to her cheek, looking back to my best friend. "Now what?"

His eyes darken. "Make her come," he says. "And when she does, don't stop." I smirk, and he returns it as I slide down her body, settling my shoulders between her legs. Her pussy is glistening, and there's wetness smeared everywhere from the way she was grinding against herself. Her flesh is swollen, and I know if he were here, he'd be tripping over himself to give her relief.

Not wasting another second, I lean forward, swiping my warm tongue along her slit from bottom to top. She moans quietly, the sound halted by the ball in her mouth as I pull her clit between my lips and suck in quick pulses. Her hips immediately begin to lift from the bed, so I flatten a hand over her stomach to hold her down as I eat her like I'm dying of starvation and she's the only sustenance for miles.

"There you go, Princess," he says. "I wish I was in there tasting you right now instead of jerking off to the sight. You're so fucking beautiful."

"Mmm," she hums, her eyes fluttering closed and her muscles becoming more tense by the second. She's clearly nearing the edge of her orgasm, so I sink two fingers inside, filling her as deep as I can from this angle. Her inner walls grip onto me immediately as I curl them against her G-spot, flicking my tongue over her clit.

"Come for me, Arden," he orders, and that's all it takes for her to detonate. The first splash against my face catches me off-guard, but I only falter for a second before I realize what's happening. Pushing up to my knees, I fuck into her with my fingers as quickly as I can, watching as her back bows from the bed and involuntary convulsions rack her entire body.

"Oh, shit," Jackson groans. "Is she squirting?"

"Fuck yeah, she is. What a good slut," I purr, continuing my movements as she soaks everything around us. Her muffled sobs of pleasure are like music to my ears. "Look at that gorgeous cunt crying for us." I'm in awe of her beauty as euphoria overtakes her, giving everything I have while she rides out the most intense orgasm I've ever seen in my life. It's so mesmerizing that I don't even realize she's overstimulated until her feet start kicking against the mattress and she begins to squirm away.

I slowly pull my fingers from her, and she relaxes, her chest heaving as she attempts to catch her breath. She seems to be getting plenty of oxygen with every inhale, so I leave the gag where it is since I'm nowhere done with her, and she's only going to get louder. Jackson told me not to stop after she came, and since I'm a sadistic son of a bitch, I'm absolutely on board with that plan.

She's still completely inert as I crawl up her body, giving no warning before thrusting my hard, weeping cock into her soft pussy. Her eyes open wide, and she whines against the ball when I bottom out, clenching my teeth so I don't come early with how tight and wet she is.

"Be my special girl, baby," Jacks says, spitting into his hand before the sound of him stroking fills the air around us. "Give me one more."

"Oh, you'll get it," I grit out. "She's going to come so pretty for you." Pulling back, I drive forward, feeding her every inch over and over as she trembles beneath me. Her big brown eyes burn into mine, and even though I'm taking her so roughly, my heart squeezes in my chest at the love behind them. She never questions the things we do—she just trusts that we'll always take care of her and, even through pain, give her the most mind-bending pleasure.

"She's getting close," I tell him when her walls begin to close in around me, making black dance around the edges of my vision. "What do you want me to do?"

I continue pounding into her, the skin-on-skin friction of his fist passing over his cock getting louder and faster as the seconds tick by. Arden looks beautiful as she takes everything we're giving, drool slipping from the sides of her mouth and slowly crawling down her cheeks. My balls are so fucking tight with the need to release, but I refuse to go before they do, so I need his words. "Jacks," I bark, finally breaking the spell he's under.

"Rub her clit," he chokes out. "Make her fucking shatter for me." I follow his instruction, snaking a hand between us and using my thumb to work her over. The hardened bud pulses under my touch and her thighs clamp against my hips, shaking uncontrollably as I fuck her in long, rough strokes. She's so tight, her inner walls tug at the piercing under my head each time I retreat, and I honestly don't know how I've lasted this long with the way she's taking me like she was made just for this. *For us.*

"You can do it, Princess," he rasps. "Let go for me. I want us to come together."

She mumbles his name into the gag, her eyes rolling back as I hammer into her one last time, catapulting her into ecstasy. Her cunt pulses against my cock, and by some fucking miracle, I'm able to hold back as the waves wash over her, her sweet little body surrendering to the onslaught of pleasure before she finally floats back to reality. I vaguely hear the sound of Jackson groaning out his own orgasm, and I look up to see him slumping back against his pillow when he's completely spent. I slow my hips just enough to reach around and undo the buckle on the gag, pulling it away as she darts her pink tongue out to wet her lips.

"Such a good girl," I praise, lowering so my mouth is hovering over her ear. "But I still need to bust in this perfect pussy. And you're going to lie there and accept every single drop."

"Mhmm," she moans quietly as I continue, moving slowly as electricity begins to spark to life in my core, dancing throughout my body until I feel like I'm being zapped all over. Even though I usually get off from fucking her roughly, I want a deeper connection right now. Maybe it's the fact that Jacks is watching, trusting me to take care of her, and I don't want to let him down.

Or maybe it's hitting me that I'll go to any lengths necessary to make this thing work, even if it means stepping out of my own comfort zone to be what they need. Either way, I want them to see the ways they've changed me for the better. I'm no longer the closed-off, broken boy who couldn't offer more than his body for a short time before running away. He's gone, and in his place is a man who knows how to love and who's excited for whatever tomorrow holds.

"Fuck," I breathe, picking up speed as I pump in and out of her. "I'm going to fill this pretty pussy. So full, baby. *So. Fucking. Full.*" I punctuate each word with a deep stroke, finally exploding on the last one. Scorching hot satisfaction flows through my veins like lava, and I tremble uncontrollably while I unload. She moans, her mouth dropping open as short, sharp exhales leave her lungs in sync with the pulsing of my cock inside her. I can't stop myself from leaning down and fusing my lips to hers in a kiss so passionate; it says more than I ever could, even with all the breakthroughs I've made. I love this woman with everything I have, and the gift she gives Jacks and me, day after day, simply by waking up as ours, is something I'll never feel worthy of.

"I love you," I say, the rush of my orgasm fading slowly as I press my chest to hers, feeling our hearts pound against one another wildly. She hums content-edly, her rich, chocolate-colored eyes fluttering open until they lock onto mine.

"I love you," she whispers with a smile, turning to where Jackson is still propped up on the nightstand. I was so lost in Arden that I almost forgot he was here. "And I love you."

"I love you more than anything," he replies, a tired grin tugging at the corner of his mouth. "Always have." His gaze slides over to me. "I know you're a heathen and you'd leave her dripping all night, but she needs to be cleaned up."

"Or I could clean myself," she sasses. "The dick is good, but it's not so amazing that I can't properly function afterward."

"Ouch," I mumble. "Could've done without that, Hellcat." Jacks barks a laugh as I kiss the tip of her nose, pushing off the bed and heading to the bathroom for a warm washcloth. He's right. I *would* leave her dripping —at least for a little while—because I love the thought of knowing I've marked her in that way. But I'm the only one here to take care of her, so I'll do my best to give her everything she needs.

Returning to where she's curled up with the phone in front of her, I carefully wipe away the remnants of our releases, listening in as they talk.

"Are you ever going to tell me why you still wear that old ass chain?" she asks, nodding at the gold rope that rests against his bare collarbone. "It's not even the right number."

He smirks, wrapping his fist around the charm like I've seen him do a million times. "You never asked." He shrugs. "And *yes*, it is the right number."

"You were sixteen when I bought it a million years ago. Now you're twenty-six. You obviously had to change jersey numbers, so why not get a new chain?"

I chuckle, because he didn't *have to* do anything. His high school number was available when we were drafted. It was never an issue of being forced to pick a new one. He made that choice on his own.

"You're right. I was number sixteen. And you were number ten." I slide into bed beside her, looking over her shoulder at the screen while he waits for everything to click in her head. It takes a few beats, but she catches on, her bottom lip quivering slightly as she realizes the meaning behind his decision to not only wear the new number, but also why the necklace she gave him all those years ago has been with him through it all.

"You took me with you," she whispers softly. "Sixteen plus ten. It's us."

"Clever girl," he replies with a smile. "I had to put space between us because I was afraid of what would happen if I didn't. I'm sorry for that. But you were always with me, Princess. Right next to my heart the entire time."

She sniffles, batting at the tears that fall down her cheek. I do my best to comfort her, wrapping her in my arms tightly while they look at each other like this, right here, is the only thing that matters. Like, no matter what happens, or where life takes us, the love we feel in this moment will stay right at the top of those memories that made us who we are.

We stay awake a while longer, him murmuring gentle affirmations as I run my fingers through her hair. Eventually, her breathing evens out, and her adorable snores fill the quiet room, telling us that she's finally drifted off. I should hang up her phone, but it feels wrong to separate them, even if it's only until the sun comes up. So, I don't. I just close my eyes and fall asleep, hoping that whatever happens at the end of their parents' trip, they'll never have to spend another night hiding the way they feel from the world.

THIRTY-EIGHT
ARDEN

"GOOD MORNING, SWEETHEART," Gina says, pressing the button on the coffee maker as I pad into the kitchen. It's still pretty early, and I didn't sleep well without Jacks, so I decided to start the day, leaving Hawk out cold in bed. I'm sure it won't be long before he wakes up and realizes I'm gone, but this is a good opportunity to talk about the things she wanted to discuss yesterday. With all the excitement of my Rip-It endorsement, I'm glad we didn't dig into the Flare drama. It certainly would've put a damper on things.

"Morning," I reply, opening the cupboard and filling a glass with water before moving to where my anxiety meds are sitting on the counter. I pluck one from the bottle before placing it onto my tongue and taking a sip. I'm supposed to take it with food, and normally, it would already be next to whatever breakfast was waiting for me when I came down the stairs. But since I'm the first one up, and I don't know if we will be sticking to our normal routine, I may as well just get it out of the way now. "Did you sleep okay?"

"Yeah," she replies. "Your dad can't sleep without the white noise machine these days. A commercial airliner could've flown through here, and I wouldn't have heard it."

Well, fuck. If I had known that, I wouldn't have stayed away from her son all night. It's funny how, after such a short time of sleeping with the two of them, I can't seem to fully rest if I don't have one of my boys on each side. Maybe I'll be able to sneak Jackson into bed tonight so we don't have to go through that all over again. It's still a risk, but it beats tossing and turning all night.

"Anyway," she says, carefully walking over to the table with her steaming mug and taking a seat. I make a cup for myself before sitting down across from her because, if I have to tell her all about how Dahlia is running our team into the ground, I'd like to be caffeinated while I do it. "I looked at your stats the other day. Unfortunately, the match broadcasts were blacked out at our house, so I wasn't able to watch. I saw some of the plays on the team website, but you didn't look like yourself. Is something going on?"

I sigh, slouching a little because she's right. I looked like shit, and it translated onto paper. My assists were almost half of what they were in Argentina, and I have better chemistry with my hitters here. If I was in charge of what we were running on the court, things would be so much different. "I mean, it's fine. My teammates are great. It took me a little while to learn what they like, but we figured it out. Coach has insisted that she be in charge of calling the plays, though, so it's been a rough transition."

Her brows furrow in confusion. "Wait. She *what*?" She blinks rapidly, turning her head slightly as though she didn't hear me right the first time.

I shrug. "Dahlia calls our plays from the sideline. And before you ask, I really don't know why. About two weeks ago, I made a few dumps she didn't like, but other than that, I can't think of any reason she wouldn't trust me to make the right choices." I decide to leave out all the details about the way she's spoken to me, and how it's affected my mental health. Having the boys' support and working with my therapist has really helped me cope with the pressure I'm under, and I don't want to bring Gina into that side of things. It's only a matter of time before Dahlia realizes that her decision is hurting the team, then we'll be back to normal. There's no way she'll risk her job by letting us lose match after match just to prove a point. At least, I hope not.

She takes a sip of her drink, thinking for a moment, still clearly befuddled by what I'm telling her.

Me too, girl.

"I don't think I've ever heard of a coach doing that outside of high school. Do you want me to say something to her? As your agent, I can't let her run your career into the ground. So, if you feel like that's a possibility, I think we should nip it in the bud before it becomes a real problem."

I shake my head, worry washing over me. "Not yet. Let's give her another match or two to figure out that it's not going to work. With any luck, she'll change things back to the way they were, and it won't affect our chances at making playoffs. It'll be easier on everyone if she thinks it was all her own idea."

She gives me a skeptical look but eventually backs off. "Fine. We'll see where things are at in a couple weeks. By the way, I'll need you to sign the paperwork for your endorsement. I know they want to roll out the merchandise as soon as possible, to strike while the iron is hot with the league kicking off their first season. Let me go grab that from upstairs so we can get it out of the way and enjoy the rest of our visit."

"Sounds good," I say, just as Jackson enters the room. He looks delicious in a pair of low-hanging gray sweatpants, with his mouth-watering chest and abs on full display. His hair is messy, just like it is every day when he wakes up, and it takes all my self-control not to walk over and drag my fingers through it. He's always so warm and cozy in the morning, and I can almost smell him from here. I'd give anything to have his strong arms wrapped around me right now.

"Hey, honey," she says, rising from her seat. "I was thinking we could go for a drive along the coast later. I need it to get through another Pennsylvania winter."

He laughs. "You got it, Mom. Maybe we'll even steal you a bucket of sand to bury your feet in on the really cold days."

Her jaw drops, and she throws a hand over her heart in faux shock. "Jackson Matthew, that's illegal. I thought I raised you better." She pauses, pushing her bottom lip out thoughtfully. "If we get caught, I'm telling them it was your idea." He rolls his eyes, an adorable smile breaking through his poor attempt at an annoyed expression. "We'll go this afternoon. I just want to get Arden's contract signed so I can send it over to Rip-It Sports as soon as possible. Be right back."

She exits the kitchen, and as soon as her footsteps fade up the stairs, I'm being yanked to my feet. He wastes no time placing a hand on each of my cheeks and lowering his mouth to mine in a desperate kiss. I suppress the moan that works its way up my throat, opening as soon as his tongue presses between my lips. It's sloppy and hurried, but a much-needed connection after our night apart.

"Fucking missed you," he whispers on a quiet exhale before plunging back inside. It's like he's trying to get his fill, tasting me like he doesn't know when he'll get to do it again. He's not wrong. We agreed to wait until right before our parents leave to tell them that we're together, so at the very least, we still can't be affectionate out in the open for another day.

My hands slide up his arms, clutching onto his warm biceps as he claims me, while his move down my body, gripping onto my ass firmly. I fight my instinct to throw a leg over his hip, but the need to feel him grind into me is almost overwhelming.

We lose ourselves in the kiss, only breaking apart when we hear a familiar voice cutting through the air behind us. "What the fuck is going on?" Gina says loudly, letting go of the papers in her hand as they flutter to the floor at her feet. We step away from each other abruptly, but the damage is already done. She saw everything, and now she's staring in horror as she awaits an answer.

"Mom," Jackson says, putting both hands up in caution. "Let me explain." My heart beats a deafening cadence in my chest, and suddenly, I feel like I can barely breathe. The plan was to tell her all along. But we definitely didn't want her to find out like this.

"Explain *what?*" she yells angrily, bouncing her gaze my way. "I saw how you and Hawk were touching each other yesterday. I thought you were with him." Her brows are pulled tight, and she glances around as if the otherwise empty room will validate her assumption. I swallow thickly, attempting to gather saliva with my tongue, because I feel like I have a hundred cotton balls in my mouth, making it impossible to speak.

"I—" I croak, clearing my throat. "I am…with Hawk."

"Does he know you're down here kissing Jackson right now?" Apparently, Jacks doesn't like the accusing tone behind her question, because he steps closer to me, wrapping his fingers tightly around mine in a silent show of solidarity.

"He knows everything. We love her, and we both want to be with her." He says the words with so much confidence, my heart flips in my chest, but anxiety creeps its way back to the forefront as she scoffs in disagreement.

"No," she snaps in my direction, the kind, loving woman I've known since I was a child nowhere to be found. "Absolutely not. This will *ruin* your image. If you go public with the fact that you not only have *two boyfriends*, but one is your stepbrother, you'll get torn apart in the media. If it gets bad enough, Rip-It will revoke your deal. Not to mention, if the league doesn't like the negative press, they could say you violated the morality clause in your contract. That would void everything."

Jackson whips his head my way, and his grip loosens around mine before he severs the connection I so desperately need. I look down at my empty hand as panic begins to flow through my veins like poison. My stomach churns, and my insides twist uncomfortably while they both stare at me, waiting for a response. But I don't have one to give. It's been my dream to play volleyball at a professional level since I first stepped foot onto the court. I can't remember ever wanting anything more—at least not until he and Hawk made me theirs. Now, they're the best part of my day. My peace in the storm. Without them, I don't even want to think about how incomplete I'd be.

I can live without volleyball. I've already felt the sting of that loss once. But could I truly survive loving and losing my boys?

The thought hits me like a speeding train, and I feel the panic as it snakes throughout my limbs, wrapping tightly around my throat and stealing the breath from my lungs. Every muscle in my body tenses to the point of pain, and without even thinking, my feet carry me backward, creating even more space between myself and the one person in the world who's calmed me since we were kids.

"Arden, wait!" he says as I bolt toward the stairs,

taking them two at a time as fast as my trembling legs will carry me. I vaguely hear him running after me, but I blow through the entrance to my room, closing and locking the door just as he hits the top.

"Arden!" he shouts, pounding on the thick wood with heavy, closed fists. "Open up and talk to me!"

"Go away, Jackson. Give me a minute, please," I reply weakly, my feet feeling like two cinder blocks as I trudge toward the bathroom, closing and locking myself in before lowering to the floor. Sucking in gulps of air that never seem to fully fill my lungs, I focus on not falling into the darkness. I don't want to be there…I want to be here. I'm just not ready to have whatever conversation awaits me outside these walls.

I know Jacks better than anyone, and I could practically hear his thoughts in the kitchen. Gina's words put doubt in his mind, and now he's second-guessing whether or not we should be together. If that's the case, and he wants out, I'll do whatever I can to stop him. But if he ultimately chooses to walk away, he'll take a big piece of me with him—and I just want to keep it for a little while longer.

The muffled knocks stop for a while, and I let my tears flow freely, feeling more and more numb with every second that ticks by. I allow my head to fall onto my knees when I can no longer support it on my own, and I wrap my arms around my legs, doing my best to hold myself together. My entire body aches as it trembles, and I jolt up as more thundering blows beat against the bedroom door. I vaguely hear Hawk's booming voice, but I ignore it, knowing I'm too weak to answer loud enough for him to hear me anyway.

Remembering what I've worked on in therapy, I look around the room in an attempt to ground myself, starting with five things I can see.

Shower. Towel. Bathrobe. Lotion. Fluffy rug.

I inhale deeply, leaning to the side and running my hand along the plush fibers. The deep, velvety texture is soft against my palm, and I feel myself relax a little as I pass back and forth over it. Getting lost in the sensation for several minutes, I'm startled as a loud *crack* brings me back to reality. Heavy footsteps approach the bathroom door, followed by the sound of Hawk's concerned voice.

"Baby, it's me. Can you let me in?" His tone is full of gravel, yet breathless, which means someone likely woke him after I ran in here.

"I just need a few minutes," I reply. "I'm okay." It's not a lie—at least, I don't *think* it is. A few months ago, this panic attack would've sent me somewhere else. But right now, I'm coping by using the techniques I've learned. Do I want him in here, holding me and telling me it's going to be alright? Yes. But I'd rather not face anyone until I'm ready.

"I'm right here," he says. "You can stay in there as long as you want, but I'll be sitting on the other side of this door. You aren't alone." My eyes fill with tears again, grateful that he understands what I need. It's just too much all at once, and if I don't take the time to find my center, I'll spiral before we can even get to the bottom of things.

I try not to get swept away in the what-ifs as I think about what may come next for us. Jacks has always been the type to put others' happiness and well-being before his own, and knowing that my career could be in jeopardy isn't something he'll be able to ignore. My hope is that he'll talk to me, and we'll figure out a way to get through this together.

I take more time for myself, listening to the calming softness of Hawk's even breathing through the wood that separates us. As soon as I stand from the cold floor, I'm hit with my own reflection in the mirror. My eyes are red and swollen from crying, and my skin is covered in blotches. But *I'm here.* And no matter what happens in the coming days, I'll get through it, hope-fully with Hawk and Jackson by my side.

Turning on the sink, I splash a few handfuls of cold water on my burning face, carefully blotting it with a towel. I take another deep, soothing breath, filling my lungs with oxygen before reaching forward and pulling on the doorknob. Hawk looks up from where he sits with his back against the wall, hurrying to his feet and yanking me into his comforting arms. Doing my best to stop more tears from falling because I don't want to spiral all over again, I inhale his scent, focusing on the deep connection his embrace provides. I need it right now, and I'm grateful that he gets me the way he does.

"It's going to be okay," he whispers, pressing his lips to the crown of my head. "He went for a drive, and your parents took off to give us some time. Your dad was consoling Gina because she was pretty rattled, so I promised him I'd take care of you. He's going to call to check on you later. We'll let the dust settle, and then you and Jacks can talk about everything." He pulls back just enough so that I can see his face when he tilts my chin up toward him. "Whatever you need from me, it's yours. I'm not going anywhere." The sincerity in his eyes is like a tranquilizer straight to my heart, and I lean into him, allowing him to bear the heavy weight of my body.

"I need *him*," I say weakly, my voice shaking with emotion.

"I know." He leads me to the bed, sitting against the pillow before pulling me into his lap. I curl up, focusing on the warmth of his chest against my ear as we sit in silence for what seems like hours. But as soon as I hear the faint sounds of someone moving around downstairs, my pulse speeds up. I go rigid, looking at Hawk with fear written all over my face as footsteps come closer and the bedroom door—which now has a broken lock from his entrance earlier—pushes open.

"Hey," Jackson croaks as I take in his dismal appearance. He looks about as rough as I do, his slumped posture and sullen expression telling me that he's been going through it, too. "Can we talk?"

THIRTY-NINE
JACKSON

"I'LL BE RIGHT DOWNSTAIRS," Hawk says to Arden as he rises from the bed, kissing her gently before he heads in my direction. I'm expecting him to look at me. Talk to me—*anything* to give me some indication of what he's thinking—but he doesn't. He just keeps his eyes on the floor, stepping past me as he exits the room. Maybe he's pissed that I left when she needed me, but I had to get out of here for a while. Between Arden being so upset, and my mom attempting to reason with me after I told her I needed space to think, I couldn't take it. I knew Hawk would take care of her, so I got the fuck out before I did something stupid, like break up with her without weighing every single pro and con.

I drove along the coast for almost an hour, thinking about what would happen if we went public with our relationship. Would people rip her apart? Would they say terrible, hateful things about the woman I love, tearing her down every day because she's made room in her heart for two men? Would it cost her the endorse-ment she deserves more than anything in the world? Would she lose her job?

Even if there's the slightest possibility of that, I have to do everything I can to prevent it. I can't be the reason she doesn't get to live her dream.

Walking toward her slowly, I lower to the mattress, sitting next to where she's got her back against the headboard and her knees hugged tightly to her chest. It's a protective position, and it fucking kills me that it won't be able to shield her from what I'm about to do. I hate myself already, and I haven't even forced out the words.

"Before I say anything, I want you to know that I love you with all my heart," I tell her. "I'll always be yours, just like I have been since the day we met." Tears prick at the backs of my eyes, and my already broken heart threatens to shatter in my chest as she brings her pleading gaze to mine. I want to hold her—to tell her it's going to be okay—but the truth is, I don't know. And I refuse to put her future at risk. So, I swallow the lump in my throat, continuing the speech I rehearsed all the way home.

"My mom is right. The three of us being together could cost you your career. You've worked too fucking hard to get here, and I can't let you throw it all away. We have to end this," I barely choke out the final sentence, my chest tightening to the point of pain as it fights its way past my lips.

She shakes her head rapidly in disagreement, shooting to her knees and darting her hands out to clutch the fabric of my t-shirt. "No, Jacks—I don't *care* about any of that," she argues, the words rushing from her mouth in a panic. Her eyes well with tears, and I want to take it all back, so she doesn't have to feel the pain I know is surging through her body right now. I know, because I fucking feel it, too.

"Yes, you do," I reply, doing my best to reassure her with a hand on her soft cheek. "And I wouldn't be able to live with myself if you woke up one day and resented me for being the reason you lost it all. Just be with Hawk and love each other out loud. That's what you deserve, Arden—you shouldn't have to be anyone's secret. Least of all, mine."

"I don't want this," she says, tears spilling over as her eyes squeeze shut. "I want both of you. I want us to fight for each other. Fuck anyone who thinks our love is wrong."

I exhale a shaky breath, unable to hold back my emotions any longer. Moisture streams down my cheeks, and I smile weakly, because it's all I have to give her. "This is me, fighting for us, Princess. And it'll be the hardest thing I've ever done—knowing how it feels to have you, but letting you go anyway."

"You're making a mistake, Jackson," she whispers, small tremors shaking her hands as they continue gripping onto my shirt. "We don't even know if I'll lose my deal or my spot on the team because of this. And if it makes you that nervous, we'll just continue doing what we're doing. Nobody has to know what goes on in the privacy of our own home."

I peel her fingers from the fabric, encasing them in

mine before bringing her knuckles to my lips. I linger for just a moment, wishing I could rewind the last few hours and make this easier for her. But this was inevitable, and I was stupid to think there wouldn't be some kind of consequence for us when I first told her how I felt.

If it were just me and Hawk in the public eye, maybe we could make it work. Riggs has done a good job of protecting Monroe from the media after her shitbag father was put in prison earlier this year. And even with their ten-year age gap, Ace and Lark have managed to tune out the noise from internet trolls who talk negatively about them on social media. But we're different. Arden is a professional athlete as well, and women are held to a much higher standard when it comes to their personal lives, as unfair and fucked up as that is. It isn't just a matter of whether or not the public would call her names for being with two people at the same time—it's much bigger than that, and the risk isn't one I'm willing to let her take. If that means leaving without giving her a choice in the matter, so be it. I can only pray that she doesn't end up hating me when all is said and done. Hopefully, one day, she'll understand that I'm doing this because I love her more than anything in the world.

"I love you, Arden," I say quietly, taking one last look at her flawless face before standing up and heading to the door. She sobs loudly, crying out my name as she falls forward onto the mattress, and I fight every instinct in me that's telling me to turn around and beg for her forgiveness. But I know I can't. I have to give her the life she deserves, even if it means watching from afar as my best friend holds her hand through it all. Part of me expects her to follow me as I hurry down the stairs, but I'm grateful when she doesn't, because it'll only make this harder.

"What's going on?" Hawk says, standing from the couch and stepping toward me as Arden's muffled, broken cries fill the air around us. "What the *fuck* did you do?"

I shake my head, my chest heaving as every single part of me continues to shatter into a million jagged pieces. Not only am I losing the woman I love today, but I'm not sure if my decision will end up taking my best friend, as well. My eyes and chest burn as I look up at him, voice cracking as I force out my final request. "Love her hard, Hawk. Love her in all the ways I wish I could."

His brows pull tight. "Dude, *don't*," he warns. "Don't do this. We'll figure it out."

I scoff, wiping the tears from my cheeks. "There's nothing to figure out. The longer we act like this isn't going to eventually ruin her life, the worse it'll be. Just let me do the right thing."

He takes a step back, a mask of disgust falling over his expression. "You're a fucking bitch, Blake. You're going to regret this."

"I already do," I mumble, turning and heading toward the door. He doesn't waste another second before rushing up the stairs and into Arden's room. I stand there frozen, listening as he attempts to comfort her, but her cries only get louder as the pain from what I've done intensifies. It's not until I hear his promise to her that I'm snapped back to the harsh reality I'm about to live.

"You and me, baby," he says. "Always."

And with that, I walk out of the condo, leaving what's left of me behind with the two people who own it all.

FORTY
HAWK

JACKSON:

How is she?

JACKSON:

I know you're getting my texts. Your read receipts are on.

JACKSON:

Hawk, please. Just tell me how she's doing.

JACKSON:

I'm staying at Ace's until I can figure something else out. I know she has practice at eleven, so I'll come by then to grab some stuff.

JACKSON:

I'm sorry. I'm just trying to protect her.

I SET my phone on the counter, ignoring the last string of texts from Jacks this morning. He's been sending them non-stop since he left yesterday, and to be honest, I'm too fucking pissed to reply. I don't know if my anger is toward him or just the situation in general, but holding her as she cried herself to sleep last night was the hardest thing I've had to do in a long time. It had me ready to spiral myself, but I refused to break in front of her. So, I held it in. I still am—at least until she leaves in a couple of hours. For now, I'm distracting myself by baking as quiet music plays in the background because the silence around me without him here is deafening.

I still don't know everything that went down in the kitchen yesterday, but I was able to put enough of the pieces together to understand his reason for leaving. That doesn't mean I think it was the right choice—because I think we could've talked it out and come up with a plan—but from his point of view, I see why he thought there wasn't a better option in the heat of the moment.

Jackson is a protector. He may not be scrappy or short-tempered like I am, but he acts on instinct when it comes to the people he loves—no one more so than Arden. That's why he's been such a huge source of comfort for her all these years. Because she knows that if something bad happens, he'll shoulder the burden and help her through it. This time, that was the exact thing that took him from her.

And from me.

It's only been twenty-four hours, but I'm feeling his absence more than I ever could've imagined. I know our friendship isn't over, and that his love for me and Arden is still just as strong as it was before he walked out the door, but it feels like everything has changed. He's always been the sunshine on my darker days, pulling me back to reality when I wanted to give up, and not having him here to keep me grounded while I'm trying to ease her pain is hard. I feel like I'm walking on a tightrope, telling her it's going to be okay while attempting to fend off my own anxiety about the future. Will he come back? Will he move out completely? Will they be able to be around each other, or will it cause them too much heartbreak?

I know this is all stuff I need to discuss with him, but for now, I'm only worried about my broken, beautiful girl. She was ready to risk everything to be with us both, and it isn't lost on me how huge that is. She's worked her whole life to get to where she is, but her love for me and Jacks is so strong, that she was prepared to choose us if it came down to it. That's why I'm here—because I want to show her what that means to me. I just hope I can be enough.

The timer beeps, and I slip an oven mitt over my hand before pulling the muffin tin out of the heat. I set it on the rack to cool, hoping I can at least get Arden to eat before practice. She refused yesterday, and I didn't push the issue because I didn't want to upset her any further. But she needs to take her meds, and I don't want her leaving without some carbs in her system. She has another match in two days, and I know she needs all the energy she can get to prepare.

Just as I'm getting a glass for her water, quiet footsteps pad along the floor and into the room. I turn, pasting on the most reassuring smile I can muster as my eyes settle on her tired face. She's fresh from a night of interrupted sleep, wearing one of Jackson's old t-shirts and a pair of panties. Her hair is wild and knotted from tossing and turning, and her skin is still blotchy from crying. It's raw and real, and even with everything that's going on, I feel like the luckiest motherfucker in the world. She's mine. She chose me—and that's something I haven't gotten to experience many times in my twenty-five years. I'll spend every day for the rest of my life showing her how grateful I am that she's trusting me with her heart.

"Morning, beautiful," I say, stepping in and pulling her into a hug. "Pumpkin muffins are ready. I even threw together some cream cheese frosting, just for you." Her sad eyes light up as she raises her head, and for the first time since yesterday, a small smile tugs at the corners of her mouth. My heart squeezes in my chest at the sight, because part of me was afraid I wouldn't be able to console her with the same softness he does. And I certainly can't fuck this kind of pain away—at least not right now. She needs easy and gentle…and she needs it from me.

"Where is it?" she asks, lowering her long lashes as she runs her hands over my shirtless chest and abs, stopping at the waistband of my black basketball shorts. I'm happy she's even entertaining the thought of food right now; I was worried about her going another day without eating. It's exactly why I went all out, using the unhealthiest, most sugar-filled recipe I have. If it makes her feel even a fraction better, I'll hook her up with all the junk food she wants.

I raise a playful brow. "Gimme a kiss, and I'll tell you." Her smile grows even bigger as she pushes to her tiptoes and brushes her warm, plump lips against mine. Electricity zaps across my skin, and my stomach flips as she wraps her arms around my waist and melts into my body. Pressing my cheek to the top of her head, I breathe her in, and at this moment, I know that, even if we have to do it on our own, we'll make it to the other side of this shitstorm. I hope Jackson gets it together and realizes that his place is right here with us, but if not, Arden and I will be okay.

She gasps as I secure my hands on her hips, lifting her to sit on the counter before turning to the refrigerator. I reach in, pulling out the bowl I've had chilling for the last thirty minutes, then return to my girl. She tilts her head shyly, and I take a chance, dragging my finger through the sweet mixture and raising it to her mouth. Just like the first night we touched each other, she parts her lips, wrapping them around me and gently sucking it from my skin. It isn't filled with tension and desire like it was then. This time, it's something different. The trust and appreciation in her deep gaze tell me everything I need to know right now. That she's in this with me for good, and I'll never have to feel the sharp sting of being left alone again.

"I love you, Hellcat. We're going to figure this out, okay?" I whisper, dropping my forehead to hers. Her brown eyes flutter closed, and a wave of sadness tightens her expression before she exhales a shaky breath.

"I love you too," she replies quietly. "Thank you, Hawk—for staying here with me. I know this affects you too, and I'm going to look into getting a place of my own as soon as I can. I don't want Jacks to be uncomfortable, and I don't think I'll be able to handle being here if he comes back and acts like we're nothing." The despair in her tone makes me want to walk to the other side of this building, rip my best friend out of Ace's guest bed, and haul him back here to see the consequences of taking matters into his own hands. I'm sure he's confused and hurting too, but that's even more of a reason to consider the pros and cons of his relationship with Arden instead of just ending it like this.

I take her hands in mine, rubbing my thumbs along her knuckles. "Let's not make any rash decisions so soon, baby. He's fine where he is at the moment. My main priority right now is making sure you're alright, and I'm positive he wouldn't want you leaving, either. Let's just get through today, then we'll worry about tomorrow. Okay?"

She nods, smiling weakly. "Yeah."

The word makes the tightness in my chest dissipate slightly, and I'm grateful she's not acting on impulse the way Jacks is. With her new endorsement and contract from the Flare, she could definitely afford to move into a place of her own, but I'm determined to keep her here with me—and eventually, with him.

I have no idea how I'm going to do it, but I have to find a way to get my family back together.

FORTY-ONE
JACKSON

"YOU GOOD, MAN?" Ace asks, shoving his keys into the pocket of his jeans. "I'll be gone for a few hours, but Lark will be in and out of her office. Just let her know if you need anything."

I look up from where I'm lying on the couch. Even though it's only been a few days, I feel like a freeloader. I go from the guest bed to the couch, too fucking weak and dejected to do anything else. I've considered going to a hotel or something, but the thought of being even further away from Arden than I am already makes me sick to my stomach. I know this is my fault, and I could walk right back through our door and beg her to forgive me for leaving, but I'm still convinced that I need to do this for her.

"I'm fine," I say. "I'm going to get up and go for a run soon, anyway. I'm hoping the exercise will help me sleep tonight."

He gives me a look that says *yeah, right*—which I don't acknowledge because we both know I'm not going anywhere—before turning and leaving for his monthly trip to visit the kids at his old therapist's clinic. I sigh, returning my attention to the TV, where a random rom-com is playing. It's one I haven't seen before, but it has all the makings of something Arden would be into if she were here.

I close my eyes, trying to imagine her body in front of mine, my arms wrapped tightly around her as she giggled at the guy's dumb jokes. I'd give her a hard time, telling her how cliché it all was, and she'd argue, telling me that I just didn't know enough about romance to appreciate the cheesy storyline. I'd prove her wrong by pulling her even closer and coasting my lips along her soft skin as I told her how much I loved her. Then she'd whisper it back, reminding me that I'm the luckiest guy in the world for having the privilege of calling her mine.

I miss her so much, it hurts. It's been a struggle not to just say *fuck it* and go back home, but I'm trying to remember what's at stake if I don't stay away and the public decides to drag her through the mud. The delusional side of me thinks maybe it wouldn't happen, and that everyone would be cool with her being with me and Hawk, but that's not realistic. Both Fury and Flare fans would have opinions, and no amount of showing them how strong our love is would stop them from making small-minded comments—ones that could obliterate her career.

"You look like a lost puppy," Lark says as she enters the room, pulling me from my thoughts.

I huff a laugh, sitting up and dragging my hands

down my face with a groan. "Sorry. It's been a weird few days. I *feel* lost." She rounds the couch, plopping down on the opposite end, and relief floods over me as her sympathetic eyes meet mine. Lark and I have had this unexplained kinship from the moment we met, and I know if there's anyone I can open up to without the fear of judgment, it's her. Maybe talking it out with an objective third party is what I need to move forward— because right now, I feel like I'm stuck between a rock and a hard place.

"Talk to me, Jacks," she coaxes. "Why are you rotting on my couch when you have two people who love you more than anything on the other side of this building?"

Wiping my sweaty hands on the front of my sweatpants, I slump back into the cushions, releasing a shaky breath. "A few days ago, my mom and Arden's dad were visiting from Pennsylvania. We agreed that at the end of their trip, we'd come clean about everything. We planned on telling them that Hawk and I were in love with her and that no matter what they thought, we were going to be with her. We figured they'd maybe be against it at first, especially with the two of us being stepsiblings, but we didn't care. We knew they'd eventually get over it. But when my mom walked in on us kissing, she kind of freaked out—and brought up a whole other issue we hadn't really even considered."

Her eyebrows squish together, and she pulls her feet up onto the couch, hugging a throw pillow to her chest as she tries to get comfortable. "What issue?"

I slowly shake my head, my eyes fixed on my hand

as it rests on my thigh. "Arden was just offered her dream deal with a really popular and well-respected brand. My mom went into agent mode when she put all the pieces of our situation together, warning us of the risks we'd be taking with Arden's career if we went public. It's obviously not illegal to be in two relationships at once, but it's also not something that's widely accepted in society. The way her contracts are set up leaves room for them to be voided if she does anything that could be deemed immoral. She could lose everything just by being with both of us, which she was fully prepared to do—so I made the choice for her, and I left."

"Wait," she says, blinking rapidly. "You left because there's a chance that *maybe* she could lose her job? And she was willing to put that on the line because she loves you, but you decided to walk away without even hearing her out? Don't you think that was kind of a dick move to dismiss her feelings the way you did?"

I wince because it sounds pretty bad when she says it like that. My intention was never to make Arden feel as though her wishes weren't important to me. I just knew she'd choose us, and I wanted to shield her from all the bad things that could've come with that choice. Did I handle it well? Probably not. But I'm human, and there just isn't a clear answer for this. No matter what, we're all losing in some way or another.

"Yeah," I mutter.

"And are you planning on going home at some point? Or are you just going to run forever?"

I lean my head back, looking up at the ceiling as I

take a slow, deep breath. Leave it to Lark to call me out like this. I know it's something I need to think about, but the thought of living there and having to watch them do things as a couple makes me want to vomit. Not because I don't want them together—I definitely do. I just can't imagine going back to the way things were before we talked about the future and pretending like I'm fine with it being *them* and not *us*.

"I stopped by yesterday to grab some clean clothes and stuff while Arden was at practice. Hawk barely even looked at me, and when I asked him how she was doing, he said—and I quote—to *stop being a selfish piece of shit and ask her myself*. I understand why he's pissed at me, and I'm glad he's trying to protect her, but *fuck*. It's hard not being able to talk to my best friend when I need his support the most." I meet her sympathetic gaze. "I know I can't run forever. And truthfully, I *want* to go home. But will I be able to stay away when I know they want me in their bed? Will it be hard not to kiss her every morning when we pass each other in the kitchen? I don't think I can trust myself not to fuck everything up."

She scoots over so she's right beside me, placing a gentle hand on my forearm. "I'm going to ask you one more question, and then I promise I'll leave it alone. But you have to give me an honest answer. Can you do that?"

"Yeah," I reply, swallowing the lump in my throat.

She looks up, her expression full of compassion as she speaks softly. "If the roles were reversed, and you were forced to choose either a happy life with Arden and Hawk right now, or playing baseball for the Fury, what would you do?"

My face twists with emotion and tears prick at my eyes before spilling down my cheeks. I don't have to say the answer out loud, because we both already know it. I'd choose them—every day for the rest of my life. I'd hang up my cleats without hesitation if it meant waking up each morning to her lying between us.

She pats my bicep, pushing to her feet. "A really smart lady once told me that some risks are worth taking. I don't have the right answer for you, Jacks, because I know there's a lot on the line. But please don't shut them out because you think it's the right thing to do. At least consider that you're not the only one in this situation who's willing to give up one dream for a much bigger one."

And with that, she walks away, leaving me even more confused about what to do next.

FORTY-TWO
ARDEN

"THANKS FOR THE RIDE," Zara says, lifting her luggage from my back seat. "I'll see you at practice on Monday. We'll get to work on those new plays."

"Sounds good," I reply as she waves, shutting the door before turning toward her building. It's almost midnight and we just got home from an away trip to Nashville. We managed to pull out a win, but that's only because Dahlia finally loosened the reins enough to let me have some control on the court. After losing two in a row at home, I know the team owner was putting some pressure on her. Unfortunately, there are still some plays I'm forbidden from running, and she wants to work on some new set combinations, because obviously, I'm still not trusted to decide on my own what's best for my team. It's annoying, but it's a step in the right direction, so I'll take it.

The flight back to Daytona was only about two hours long, but it may as well have been fifteen minutes with the anxiety I was feeling about going home. Hawk texted earlier and said Jackson had returned to the condo yesterday from Ace's, where he stayed for nearly a week. Apparently, he's done clearing his head after everything that went down when my dad and Gina were here—although I don't know what that means for us. Will we go back to having miles of space between us like before? Or will he actually let me tell him what I want? Because the last conversation we had ended before I even got the opportunity.

I'm grateful my time has been occupied with work because it's given me less of a chance to dwell on the fact that he hasn't been around. I knew he'd come back at some point since he literally owns the place, but now that it's here, I'm beyond nervous to see what it's going to look like. From the moment I arrived in Florida, I felt the same pull I always have to him. Even with all the distance we were trying to close after years of being apart, I craved the familiarity and comfort he provided. But now, I feel like I'm about to walk into a home I'm sharing with a stranger.

Maybe I'm overreacting and it won't be the way I've conjured it up in my head. Maybe the week we spent apart made him realize us being together is worth the risk, and he'll tell me he wants to work it out. I haven't lost hope that I can still have a future with both him and Hawk, even though not entertaining the possibility would surely shield me from more pain. As delusional as it all sounds to still see Jacks and I together in the end, it's the only thing that's preventing me from spiraling completely. And with the way he left so abruptly, with so many unanswered questions, I just can't bring myself to let go of the small shred of optimism that remains in my heart.

I mindlessly make my way home, pulling into the underground garage and parking my car between both of theirs. My stomach flips with nerves at the thought of the three of us being in the same place again, and I wonder if they've talked at all while I've been gone. Hawk said things were definitely tense between them the day Jackson came by to get his clothes, but now that they've had time to reflect, have they started mending their broken fences? The last thing I want is to be the reason their friendship is strained, so even if the three of us can't work through this whole thing, they absolutely *have to*. I'd be devastated if they didn't.

Pulling my bags from the trunk, I sling them over my shoulder. I nervously move toward the elevator, stepping inside and shakily pressing the button for our floor. The entire building seems desolate because of the late hour, which means the ride upward is a straight shot, not stopping until I'm mere steps away from what used to be my favorite place in the world. I would rush home from practice to be with my guys, anticipating what awaited me when I walked through that door. Now, it all feels different, my feet mindlessly propelling me forward as anxiety creeps up my throat until it feels like I'm choking. I pause when I'm there, staring at the lock pad with indecision for far too long before finally reaching out and pressing my finger against it. As soon as it beeps, I push the lever and hold my breath as I enter the dark, quiet space. I didn't text Hawk to tell him I had landed, so I knew there'd be a possibility that he'd be asleep when I arrived. But by the silence that continues to surround me when I step further inside, it looks like he's not the only one.

"Thank God," I whisper, dropping my bags and breathing a sigh of relief. I know I'll see Jacks eventually, but after a long trip and a flight that left much later than we had anticipated, I need time to rest and prepare for whatever tomorrow brings. All I want is to crawl into bed with Hawk and feel his strong arms around me, reminding me that even though my entire world has been flipped on its side, he's got me. But first, I need to shower.

I ascend the stairs, deciding that it'll be best to use my own en suite. It's late, and I don't want to wake him with the running water, so I quietly pad into my room, not bothering to turn on the light as I make my way through. My vision adjusts to the darkness, and I'm startled when movement on the bed catches my eye. Sucking in a hurried gasp, I back up, slamming into the dresser in a panic. Pain radiates throughout my back, and before I can even react, the lamp on my nightstand clicks on and a set of familiar hands darts out to keep me upright.

"Shit," he says, his voice cutting through me like a thousand knives. "Arden, I'm sorry. I didn't mean to scare you. Are you okay?"

I lift my head, trying to focus through the lightheadedness that's washing over me. Whether it's from the throbbing discomfort in my body, or because he's here, I don't know. "Jackson?" I rasp. "Why are you in my room?"

"I—" he pauses, "I'm not sure. I couldn't sleep. I was going to take a walk along the beach but ended up here instead. I fucking miss you so much." The last sentence comes out more like a choked whisper as he drops his hands from where they rest on my arms.

"Then *don't*," I reply, my eyes filling with tears. "You don't have to miss me, Jacks. I'm right here. I don't give a fuck what anyone thinks, or what it costs to be with you and Hawk. If Rip-It or the PVF thinks our love is wrong, I'll find another job. As long as I have you, that's all that matters."

He reaches for my cheek, but stops mid-action, curling his fingers into a fist and pulling back. My heart twists and cracks, because although we're standing right next to each other, I've never felt further away from him, and I hate it. "You say that now, but what happens in five years when we're still playing while you're wishing your dream wasn't stolen from you? You can't deny that women are treated differently when it comes to dating and sex. The Fury wouldn't bat an eyelash at our situation, but the Flare might. I've gone back and forth over this for a week, Arden—but every time, I end up staring at a future where you're full of resentment toward me, and I just…*can't*."

I scoff, putting more space between us. My cheeks heat as sadness and anger flow through me. "You're a coward, Jackson Blake. You're so afraid of how all this is going to affect you, that you're not even listening to what I want." I lift my chin, mustering up all the courage I can find as his stare falls to the floor. He looks broken and dejected, but I don't give a fuck—because so am I. "One day, you'll be forced to watch me marry him. And while you're standing there next to us as a witness, I need you to remember one thing." His gaze finds mine, his eyes filling with tears as I deliver the final blow. "He'll never have all of me. And that'll be *your fault*."

I don't give him a chance to answer. If he wants to break us, he's going to have to do it on his own. Placing a hand on my lower back to ease the ache, I push past him and into the bathroom, mindlessly going through the motions of undressing as his words play over and over in my head.

*I just...*can't.

As soon as I step under the warm spray of the multiple shower heads, I break down—crying for the boy I'm losing, and the future we could've had.

FORTY-THREE
HAWK

"WE'RE HEADING OVER," I say, peeking my head into Jackson's room as he stands in front of the full-length mirror, buttoning his dress shirt. He's been home from Ace's for almost a week, and things have grown tense between all of us. Arden told me about their run-in when she came home from Nashville, and as much as I wanted to beat his ass for, once again, shutting her down before she could really tell him how she felt, I'm trying to let him figure it out on his own. He's convinced himself that he's doing the right thing by staying away from her, and telling him otherwise is like talking to a wall.

"Go ahead. I'll be there in a bit," he answers quietly, not even bothering to look at me. Their relationship isn't the only one that's taken a hit since their parents' visit. He and I are hardly speaking, which fucking sucks. I'm doing my best to be there for him because I know he's hurting, but whenever I try to talk to him, he tells me to focus on Arden. He barely spends time in the main areas of the house, even when she's not here. It's like he's punishing himself for tearing us apart with solitude, only leaving his room to go to the gym or grab something to eat. He's a shell of the happy-go-lucky guy he used to be, and I can't seem to get through to him, no matter how many times I try.

"Okay," I grunt, making my way down the stairs to where my girl awaits. Today is Friendsgiving at Riggs and Monroe's place, and they've invited us over for dinner. His best friend and brother-in-law, Tanner Lake, is the quarterback for the Boston Blizzard, and since they have a game on Thanksgiving, they decided to celebrate a few days early. Arden had a home match yesterday, and she's off for the next two, so it's perfect timing. She can relax and have a few glasses of wine with her friends, not having to worry about being hungover at practice. She deserves to let go a little after all the shit she's been through lately.

As soon as I round the corner, I'm stopped in my tracks. She looks gorgeous in a formfitting red dress, with her long, brown hair falling in waves over her sun-kissed shoulders. My eyes trail down her toned legs, stopping where her freshly pedicured toes peek out from her strappy stilettos. She's a wet dream standing in the middle of our living room, and I can't wait to get her home tonight and unwrap her like the gift she is.

"Wow," I say, exhaling slowly as she raises a coy brow, spinning in a circle so I can see the full outfit. My cock thickens behind the zipper of my dress pants, and I briefly consider tossing her over my shoulder and bringing her to my room, but I can't do that yet.

We've barely been intimate since the night Jacks left, but I understand why. Arden has been battling her demons while working through everything, and I'm sure sex is the furthest thing from her mind as she fights to hold her head above water. She's been doing amazing, keeping up with therapy and leaning on me when she needs it. I was afraid maybe she'd retreat into herself again, but she's stayed strong, even though I know it's been killing her.

"Do you like it?" she asks, tilting her head as I stalk toward her, unable to stop myself from reaching out and yanking her body into mine. I've done my best to treat her as delicately as possible because I want her to feel safe and comforted, but I can't lie—I miss being us.

"*Like* isn't the word, Hellcat," I growl, dropping my mouth to the soft skin of her neck and latching on, eliciting a quiet moan from her open lips. Her arms wind around my neck, holding me tightly and giving me the connection I've been craving. I go feral, my fingers digging into her hips as my growing erection throbs between us. It feels like a lifetime since we've touched this way, and fire burns in my core as lust flows through me.

"Hawk." My name is nothing more than a hushed breath, but it makes me swell with so many different emotions that I can't pick the most dominant one. I'm proud of us for working out our shit, separately and together, and getting to a point where we've opened up to each other in ways I never thought we'd be capable of. Prior to Arden moving here, I was perfectly content only letting Jackson in, never giving anyone else an opportunity to really know me. But she showed me that, even though my past isn't pretty, I deserve better from this life and have so much more to offer than I could've ever imagined. I'm so fucking in love with this woman, and although the road we're currently on is full of uncertainty, I know we'll make it. It may not be easy, and the outcome might be missing the one piece we so desperately long for, but no matter what the future holds, we'll always have each other.

Dropping my mouth to hers in a passionate kiss, I savor the way she tastes, sliding my tongue along hers and swallowing every soft whimper that comes from her gorgeous body. I vaguely hear footsteps behind me, but I'm too wrapped up in my girl to register what's happening until the door to the condo slams shut. I'm snapped back to reality as I whip my head up, realizing I hadn't even noticed Jackson blowing past us until he was already gone. Part of me feels bad that we were making out in the open like that, but the other part of me is glad he witnessed us attempting to move on together. Arden tried her hardest to be clear with her wishes, but he refused to hear it, still convinced that this was what's best for all of us. As much as I don't want her to lose her endorsement or spot on the Flare, I trust her to make the right decision for her own happiness, and I'm willing to stand by her side while she fights for what she deserves. I just wish he would, too.

She clears her throat, sadness melting back over her expression as she brings her eyes to mine. "We should go." I hate that she's on this roller coaster ride, and I've gone back and forth with the idea of suggesting that we get a place of our own, away from Jacks, but it just feels wrong. For years, he was my only lifeline—and even though he isn't saying it out loud, I know he needs me to be the same for him right now. He finally had everything he'd ever wanted for a split second, just to let it go, and I know he's broken. He may not think he's worthy of my love and support right now, but I'm here anyway. And I'll continue to be, until my last breath.

"Yeah," I reply, pressing one last soft kiss to her lips before wrapping my fingers around hers and leading her into the hallway. It's a short walk across the building to Riggs and Monroe's, and as soon as we step inside, I'm hit by the unmistakable sense of belonging I always get when I'm with my teammates. Although my life is kind of fucked up right now, I'm blessed to have this—because I'm all too familiar with the feeling of celebrating holidays by myself. As much as I miss Hayden and Henry this time of year, it certainly softens the blow to look around and see that I'm not alone. I have my Fury brothers, and now I have an incredible woman who loves me and all my battered pieces, even if I had to fight tooth and nail to feel like I deserved any of them.

"What's up, bro?" Riggs says, reaching out to shake my hand as Arden moves toward where the girls are congregated in the kitchen. I don't answer, watching as Monroe greets her, immediately pouring a glass of red wine and sliding it across the counter. She smiles, lifting it to her lips and falling into their conversation as I stare like an obsessed stalker. *Fuck, she's the most beautiful thing I've ever seen, and she doesn't even have to try.*

He clears his throat, catching my attention. I look down to see that I'm still clasping his hand in mine, moving them up and down mindlessly like I have been for God knows how long. He laughs as I let go, dropping my arm to my side.

"Shut the fuck up, Valentine," I grunt before he has a chance to roast me the way I did to him when he and Monroe first got together. I never thought I'd be a lovesick fool like him and Ace—and even Jackson, when he isn't being an idiotic piece of shit—but I guess none of us are immune to it. Because I'd not only walk across hot coals for Arden, but I'd do it while holding her bright pink purse in one hand and her fancy Starbucks drink in the other like the desperate little pet she's turned me into.

I want to throw her over my knee and turn her ass red for all of that, to be honest.

He puts two cautious hands up between us. "I wasn't going to say anything. Come on in. I want you to meet Tanner." He leads me to the living room, where all the guys stand as highlights from this year's NFL season play across the TV screen. Jackson looks up from the couch, anger radiating from him and thickening the air between us as we lock eyes briefly. For a moment, I feel bad that he saw me practically dry-humping Arden before we left, but *fuck that*. He better get used to it, because I'm not going to stop showing her affection just to spare him when she practically begged him to stay.

"Hawk, this is my brother-in-law, Tanner Lake. Tan, this is my third baseman, Hawk Mason." I reach out, shaking his hand in greeting, although it seems weird because the dude is pretty much a legend. He led the Blizzard to back-to-back Super Bowls and holds more records than any quarterback his age ever has. Not to mention, he's known for being an amazing teammate, which is something I really respect.

"Nice to meet you, Hawk," he says, taking a sip of his beer. "I've seen you play in person a few times, including at this year's All-Star game. You're a hell of a ball player, man."

I give him a tight nod. "Thank you. That means a lot." Although I've opened up a bit when it comes to my teammates, I'll admit I still get nervous around new people—especially reigning MVPs, apparently. But I'm growing, and that's all that matters.

"My wife, Grace, is a big fan," he continues. "They always like the mysterious ones, don't they?" My brows shoot up and I chuckle as he tips his bottle toward the kitchen. "Is that your girl over there talking to her?"

I turn, watching as a pretty blonde throws her head back in laughter right before Arden joins in. The sight of her enjoying herself after the weeks of pain and frustration she's endured makes me swell with pride at her strength. "Yeah. She's all mine." No sooner are the words out of my mouth than I hear a bitter scoff from across the room. I whip my head over just in time to see Jackson stand, weaving his way through the group of unassuming guys and hurrying toward the door. Following him, I wrap my fingers around his shoulder as he reaches for the knob, abruptly spinning him toward me.

"What the fuck is your problem?" I ask, trying to

keep my voice down so we don't attract any more attention than I'm sure we already have. But between the daggers he shot at me when I arrived, and now this, we need to sort things out before the entire evening gets ruined. His chest heaves and his green eyes, which are normally full of so much kindness, burn holes right through me as I await his answer.

"I need to get out of here," he growls. "I can't sit around and watch you two be happy like this while I'm fucking *dying inside*. The whole situation is bullshit, and you're flaunting the fact that you get to be with her right in front of me."

My blood boils and I take a step into him, getting in his face. "You did this," I grit through clenched teeth. "She told you she wanted us both, and that we were more important to her than anything. But you thought you knew best, so you completely dismissed her, and you left *me* to pick up the pieces. So, excuse me for doing exactly what I'm supposed to—comforting *my* girl and showing her that she's worth fighting for while you're busy acting like a martyr to save something she doesn't even give a fuck about." I shove my finger into his chest. "You're a selfish, scared piece of shit, Jacks. And you don't deserve her."

Before I can even react, his fist connects with my jaw, sending waves of pain throughout my entire face and head. On instinct, I tackle him to the ground, fighting for dominance as we roll around, bumping into furniture and knocking decorations to the floor. Glass shatters around us and people rush our way, gasps and screams cutting through the air as we're finally pulled away from one another.

"Jesus Christ!" Riggs shouts, his arms wrapping around my body as he yanks me backward. Tanner does the same to Jackson, separating us and pulling him up the stairs before disappearing into a vacant room as he roars in protest. I'm speechless, trying to replay everything that just happened as Arden runs up and cradles my cheeks, concern evident in her expression.

"Oh my God, are you okay? What happened?" she says as my teammate loosens his grip and takes a few steps away. Everyone is staring at us in shock, but I'm only focused on her as she ghosts her fingertips along the already swollen skin under my eye.

"I'm good, Hellcat," I reassure her, placing my hands over hers and squeezing. "Really." She lets out a relieved breath, stepping in and enveloping me in a comforting embrace.

I lift my head, looking to where Riggs stands with a protective arm extended to his side as Monroe peeks out from behind him. Suddenly, I feel awful for what just went down, and the fact that I literally fucked up their entire dinner by approaching Jacks when I knew he was already pissed.

"I'm sorry," I say quietly, swallowing the thick lump in my throat as they all stare at me silently. "I'll pay for all of this." I wave my hand at the damage, even more embarrassed when I see how bad it is. The leg of the entry table is broken off, and the glass vase that had been sitting on top is in a million shattered pieces at our feet. Red roses are scattered across the floor, with a large puddle of water surrounding the wreckage.

"It's fine, Hawk," Monroe replies, a mask of sympathy slipping over her shocked expression. I'm not sure how much she knows, but I can tell it's enough to understand that this fight was more than just a heated disagreement.

"We're going to go home," Arden says, stepping forward and wrapping Monroe in a tight hug, then doing the same to Riggs before glancing up the stairs. Her eyes well with tears, and I know she's conflicted, because so am I. None of this feels natural. "Will you please make sure he's okay?"

He gives her a soft smile. "If there's anyone Jackson needs to hear from right now, it's Tanner. I promise he's in good hands."

She nods, turning my way and taking me by the hand. We quietly step into the hallway, neither of us saying a word as we make our way home, unsure of how to move forward when so much devastation continues to fall on our path.

FORTY-FOUR
JACKSON

"FUCK," I say, pacing the guest room as Tanner sits on the bed. I just met the guy thirty minutes ago, and now he's saddled with calming me down after whatever the hell that shitshow was. I don't even know what the fuck I was thinking, hauling off and punching Hawk like I did. Every word that came out of his mouth was the truth, even if it sucked to hear.

"Want to talk about it?" he asks. I pause, a dull ache throbbing in my chest at the thought of reliving it all. As if he can sense my unease, he softens his tone. "It might help to get it out. It certainly can't hurt to have a completely unbiased opinion."

I sigh, my shoulders slumping in defeat as I plop down in the accent chair across the room from where he's perched on the edge of the mattress. He's right— I'm obviously not doing well with trying to work through this alone, and since my best friend is so ingrained in the situation, I haven't been able to talk to him like I normally would.

"I've been in love with Arden since high school. It took me a while to figure it all out because I was young and dumb, but by the time I came around, she went from being my best friend to my stepsister. When our parents got married, I backed off, and I thought I was over her—until she got drafted to a pro volleyball team here in Florida and ended up living with me and Hawk.

"I knew pretty early on that they'd be good together, but it wasn't until I actually saw it with my own eyes that I realized I'd never stop wanting her for myself." He listens, leaning back onto his palms quietly with not even a hint of judgment in his expression as I continue.

"One night, I walked in on them while they were having sex, and I just...couldn't tear myself away. I was mortified, but instead of telling me to leave, they invited me in. As weird as it should've been, the two of us sharing her just felt so natural—so we agreed to keep doing it.

"We had planned to tell our parents about it a couple weeks ago, but when my mom—who's also Arden's agent—found out, she made us aware of how negatively this could affect her career. My head immediately went to the worst-case scenario, thinking about how she could lose her job simply because she was in a relationship with two men. I fucking panicked, breaking it off with her even though she sat there begging me to work through it with them. I thought I was protecting her, but at this point, I don't know what's right anymore."

He stays silent for a moment, leaning forward with

his elbows on his knees as he spins his wedding ring around his finger. His eyes are fixed on the gold band, and he looks like he's being transported to another place entirely. Just as I'm getting ready to fill the deafening silence, he takes a long, slow breath—and then speaks.

"When I was in college, I made the worst decision of my life. A girl that I had no business falling for gave me her heart, and all she wanted was mine in return. Little did she know, she already had it, but I was too stupid and stubborn to say the words out loud. Instead, I told her she meant nothing to me, and I left her to live the dream I knew she had always wanted." He looks up at me, his eyes shining with emotion. I can almost feel his past heartbreak as he goes on, telling me more of the story.

"I spent five years beating myself up for leaving the way I did. I don't know what made me decide it was time to face her again, but when I finally did, nothing could've prepared me for it." His brows pull tight, and he swallows, pain washing over his expression. "Seeing her with another man's ring on her finger—was like someone took a branding iron right to my heart. I knew I fucked up before then, but I never actually felt like it might kill me until that moment. Are you truly ready to experience that? Because I can tell you that no matter how much you think you are, nothing compares to the reality of knowing you lost her. I'm telling you firsthand that you don't want to do this, Jackson. It's not worth the agony you'll both feel in the end."

I know he's right. The longer I go without touching her, and the more space I put between us, the less my reasons for doing so make sense. First, it was Lark calling me out about what I'd do if the roles were reversed. Then, it was Arden's words when she told me I'd always have a piece of her heart, and that she'd never be able to give herself fully to Hawk. But now that I'm seeing the vulnerability and hopelessness in Tanner's eyes as he relives his past, it's so fucking real —and it's clearer than ever that the road I'm headed down isn't one I can bear to be on forever.

"What did you do?" I choke out, desperate for his advice.

He huffs an amused laugh, shaking his head in what almost looks to be disbelief. "I crawled, man. I got on my knees, begged for her forgiveness, and I fucking *crawled*." He pauses, a satisfied grin curling the corner of his mouth. "Then I married the girl before she realized she was entirely too good for me."

My eyes go wide, and I blink rapidly trying to process everything he just said. The girl he was talking about is Riggs' sister, Grace. He lost her for five years before making things right, and by the sound of it, it brought nothing but anguish for them both. I don't want that for Arden, Hawk, and myself.

"I have to go," I say, shooting up to my feet. "Thank you, Tanner."

He stands, extending a hand between us for me to shake. I take it, then pull him in for a hug, grateful that this man, who I barely know, just brought me so much clarity through his vulnerable admissions. "Go get her," he replies with a sly smile. "Good luck with the groveling."

And with that, I'm gone—running as fast as my feet will take me back to our condo so I can do whatever it takes to right my wrongs.

FORTY-FIVE
ARDEN

"BABY, I'M FINE," Hawk says, leaning against the counter in his en suite bathroom as I press a cool washcloth to his cheek. There's a small spot where the skin is broken, and shades of red and purple are beginning to bloom to life as it continues to swell. Just looking at it has me fuming with rage.

"I can't believe he hit you," I say, ignoring his attempt to placate me. "What the fuck was he thinking?" Picking up the bottle of peroxide that sits next to the sink, I pour some onto the terrycloth before pressing it to the wound. He flinches at the contact, and I soften my touch, looking at him with sympathetic eyes. "I'm sorry about all of this."

He reaches out, taking my chin between his thumb and forefinger before tilting my head to meet his gaze. "What do you have to be sorry about? None of this is your fault." His expression is full of sincerity, and I honestly can't believe this is the same emotionally distant man I desperately wanted to know when I moved here. His walls were so high, I never thought he'd let me in, but here we are, holding one another up through one of the most emotional experiences I've ever endured.

I sigh, my chin quivering as my shoulders curl inward. I'm so full of shame over this entire situation, and the fight at Riggs and Monroe's really put things into perspective for me. "You can say it's not, but we both know you and Jacks wouldn't be here if it wasn't for me coming in and fucking things up. You had the most genuine, beautiful friendship, and now you're beating the shit out of each other because I came between you. You should be mad at *me* right now, not him." Tears fill my eyes, and I fidget with the cloth in my lap. But he keeps his hold firm, refusing to let me look away.

"Arden, listen to me," he demands. "You did *nothing* wrong. He was in love with you long before I ever met him. I knew that, and no matter how hard I tried, I couldn't stop myself from falling for you too. The only reason I'm pissed at him is because he made a decision that affected all of us without actually listening. I know his heart is in the right place, but watching him dismiss you over and over the way he did because he felt like it was his job to fall on the sword—I just couldn't continue letting him do it."

A single tear escapes, sliding down my cheek, but he wipes it away with the pad of his thumb before leaning in for a soft kiss. It's like a balm to my broken heart, which is still somehow so full of love that it feels like it could burst as his full lips slide along mine. I whimper quietly into his mouth, and he holds me close, enveloping me with the warmth that's become my home over the last two weeks.

"Let's go to bed," he whispers. "I need you naked and pressed against me." I fist the fabric of his t-shirt as heat gathers between my legs for the first time in forever. Even though it's been an emotional evening, I want this connection with him more than anything.

"Okay," I reply, pulling my dress over my head so I'm only covered by my red lace bra and panties. Mischief falls over his expression as he attempts to reach for me again, but I back away abruptly. "Hold that thought. I need a drink, first. I'll be quick." Pushing up to my toes, I steal one last peck before heading out of the room and down the stairs. Just as I turn toward the kitchen, the door flies open so quickly that it bounces off the wall behind it, and Jackson steps through, looking utterly panicked until his gaze lands on me. I stop in my tracks, watching as his expression softens, showing me a part of himself I haven't seen in what feels like a lifetime, even though it hasn't been.

"Princess," he chokes out, and my breath hitches as he drops to his knees, looking at me with tear-filled eyes for a moment before falling onto his hands and crawling toward me. My heart pounds behind my ribcage as he slowly eats up the space between us, stopping when he's right in front of me and sitting back on his heels. All the air is sucked from the room, making me go dizzy as I look down at him.

"There's no excuse for the way I treated you, so I won't give you one," he begins. "I was stupid and selfish, and I couldn't see past my own fears about what kind of future you'd be faced with if we were together. You were trying to tell me what you wanted, and I fucked up by refusing to hear it. You deserve better than that, and if you let me, I'll spend the rest of my life showing you how fucking sorry I am. Whatever comes our way, I want to face it together—you, me, and Hawk. Please forgive me, Arden. Let me fix us." He places his hands gently on the outsides of my thighs before dropping his forehead to my stomach. His shoulders shake as small sobs rack his body, and I reach out, sinking my fingers into his hair while tears of relief begin to fall from my eyes. We stay there, crying together for several minutes before he raises his head, his red-rimmed eyes locking onto mine. "Please, baby," he begs. "I *need* to fix us."

Maybe I'm dumb for being so open to forgiveness when he made the last two weeks a living hell for all of us, but truth be told, I don't care. The empty space in my heart that's only ever belonged to him is aching to be full again. He may not have gone about any of this the right way, but sometimes you have to go through a hard loss to see the error of your own mistakes—and judging by the fact that he's here right now, in such a vulnerable position, he has.

I lower to my knees, tilting his head so we're face to face. "Look at me," I say, sniffling. He obeys, and I release a shaky exhale, smiling softly. "From now on, we're in this together. No more taking things into your own hands because you think it's your job to shield me from all the ugliness in the world. I know what I'm walking into with you and Hawk, and if it costs me deals, jobs, or relationships with small-minded people, so be it. As long as we have each other, I'll have no regrets. Got it?"

He nods rapidly, all the pain in his expression melting into gratefulness at my words. "I love you so much, baby. I know I don't deserve any of this, but I promise you won't regret it."

I lean forward, pressing my lips to his passionately. His fingertips burn into the skin of my waist, and I throw my arms around his neck, pulling him closer. Just having him back like this sends my entire existence into orbit, until I feel like the only thing that's stopping me from floating into outer space is the way he's holding onto me like I'm his reason for living. I begin to go lightheaded, but *fuck it*—I'll happily suffocate if it means trading oxygen for the mind-melting feeling of his mouth being sealed over mine.

"Jackson," I breathe into the kiss as it starts to grow frantic, like we've spent years away from each other instead of weeks. My entire body aches with the need to be closer, though with the way we're fused together, it's almost impossible.

"I'm right here," he replies, banding an arm around my midsection and yanking me so his rock-hard erection is trapped between us. The feel of it sends my hormones into overdrive, wanting him to prove just how sorry he is for leaving me hungry and desperate for the kind of touch only he can provide. "Tell me what you need."

Entirely too turned on to form words, I grip the hem

of his shirt, peeling it over his head as fast as I can. It's barely even hit the floor before I've moved on to the button of his dress pants, lowering the zipper and shoving my hand inside. A rushed exhale pushes past his lips as my fingers wrap around the velvet skin of his cock, slowly jerking up and down as he involuntarily thrusts forward. The eagerness in his movements has my nipples growing painfully hard, and I can't help the thirsty moan that tumbles out of me as they graze against the rough lace of my bra. He somehow manages to work the remaining garments off his legs until he's completely naked, kneeling in front of me.

"Wow," a dark voice rasps, and I break away to see Hawk watching over us from the top of the stairs. "I expected more from you, Hellcat. All the shit he put you through, and you're letting him off the hook this easily?" He sucks his teeth, slowly shaking his head in disappointment, but I don't miss the subtle tilt of his lips as he attempts to hold back a grin.

I shrug, sliding my eyes back to Jacks. "I mean, he *did* crawl. And he begged so pretty. It's a shame you missed it."

"Is that so?" he replies. "Well, why don't you bring him upstairs? I'd love to see what a sweet, obedient boy he can be for you." Jackson's pupils blow wide as I bite my lip in faux contemplation, finally rising to my feet and towering over him. So what if he apologized and I forgave him? It's not a crime to enjoy a little bit of groveling—and if it is, *lock me up*.

"You heard him." Desire drips from my tone as I raise a daring brow. He attempts to stand, but I use two fingers to keep him on his knees, bending down to his level. I grip his chin firmly between my thumb and fingers, licking my lips as my gaze burns into his. "Bad boy," I scold. "I didn't tell you to get up. You can follow me, but you'll crawl the entire way. Understood?"

"Anything you say, Princess," he chokes out. I move toward the stairs, tossing a look over my shoulder to make sure he's coming, and growing even wetter at the sight of him on all fours behind me. I have no aspirations to be dominant in my everyday sexual experiences with either of them because I truly enjoy submitting, but I can't say I don't feel powerful after everything I endured during the time he was gone. As much as he deserves every bit of this, so do I.

We climb the staircase, heading down the hall to Hawk's room, where he awaits right inside the doorway. I pause, and he gives me a soft smile, dropping his lips to mine in a tease of a kiss. "I love you," he whispers so quietly I can barely even hear him, and I return the sentiment, mouthing the words back just as Jackson stops behind me. Hawk winks, silently telling me that we're all good, but I don't miss the playful devilry in his expression. With a hand on the small of my back, he ushers me inside the dimly lit space, stepping in front of Jacks before he can fully enter. I watch as he kneels down, just now noticing the items that are hanging from his clenched fist.

"I bought these for us to use on Arden," he says to his best friend, holding up the black leather collar and leash between them. "But I think they'd look much better on you, *pup*."

FORTY-SIX
HAWK

AS SOON AS I heard the door close, followed by muffled voices downstairs, I quietly snuck down the hall to see what was going on. Part of me was on high alert, ready to jump into action if he hurt her again, but the other part of me—the one that knows every corner of Jackson Blake's heart—just wanted to witness him coming to his goddamn senses. I'm glad he's back, but he needs to do a little more apologizing to our girl—because as quick as she was to forgive, I plan on making him work for it. I don't give a fuck if he's my best friend and realizes what he did was wrong. I'll go to the ends of the earth for her—and making sure he's properly punished will prove that to both of them.

He looks up at me, a mixture of humiliation and unease swirling behind his eyes as I reach out and fasten the collar around his neck. I show no trace of emotion, staying completely stoic while I wordlessly hook the leash to the D-ring and stand to my full height.

"You're so sexy, baby," I say to Arden, making her bite her lip at the praise. "Why don't you take your bra and panties off? Show Jackson what he's been missing out on." She obeys, both of us staring at her as she undresses, revealing the most flawless body. As soon as she's completely nude, I step forward, pulling on the leash in my hand while Jacks trails behind me. Stopping in front of her, I press a gentle kiss to her shoulder before reaching down, feeding the leather loop between her spread thighs, and grabbing it with my free hand behind her. I turn so we're both facing him as he stares up at her from all fours.

"Are you sure his sorry was good enough, Hellcat?" I goad. "Because I think he owes you a much better apology."

"I guess he could've done a little more," she replies, the sultry lilt to her tone making my cock thicken inside my boxer briefs. "I definitely like the way he looks on his knees for me." I love this playful side of her—it's one I wasn't sure I'd ever see again after he left. I want to keep her here, and at the same time, give her the reparation she deserves.

"I agree, baby. What if I just—" Yanking on the leash, I pull him forward, forcing his face into her bare pussy. She yelps in surprise, but a satisfied moan slips from her lips as soon as he gets to work, sucking her aching, swollen clit into his mouth. She widens her stance, allowing him easier access as he slides his tongue back, devouring her like he's starving for it. I imagine he probably is, because it's been almost as long for me, and just the smell of her arousal as it permeates the air around us is making me salivate.

"Tell him he's a good boy," I whisper in her ear. "Desperate animals like him love to be praised."

She takes a large gulp of air, letting it out in a shaky exhale as her fingers grip the hair at the crown of his head. "G-good boy," she stammers, barely able to speak with how turned on she is.

He growls against her skin, reaching up to lift her thigh over his shoulder. The change in position catches her off-guard, but I'm right there to catch her before she falters. I drop the leash so I can bear her weight—not that either of them notices with the way he's buried himself so deep between her legs.

Sliding my hands upward, I squeeze her heavy tits in my palms. The added pleasure causes her to whine even louder as she rides his face, searching for the exact spot that'll make her detonate. But I already know what's missing. She needs both of us to get over the edge, and I can't wait to watch her fall.

"What a fucking whore you are," I mock, scraping my teeth along her neck. She reaches back, finding my erection and making me almost blow in my pants from how worked up I've gotten watching them. "That needy little fuckhole is just dying for our cocks, isn't it?"

"Y-yes," she breathes, her eyes fluttering closed as Jacks continues to roll his tongue over her sensitive pussy.

"Good," I reply. "Because tonight, we're filling it all

the way up. But not before you come all over him. Baptize him with your forgiveness, Arden. Make him pay for what he did to you. Then, he can watch me stretch that sweet cunt nice and wide, so it'll swallow us both."

She cries out, her release hitting in a rush as every muscle in her body shakes uncontrollably. He works her through it, tasting and slurping her juices while I hold her up. The sounds they're making are utterly porno-graphic, and I have no idea how I'll ever last long enough to prep her with how fucking hot she is. Just seeing her take this pleasure while he gives her every-thing she deserves has me teetering on the precipice already, and I've barely even been touched.

Her flushed body begins to relax, the sweeping euphoria ebbing away as her orgasm fades. Jackson laves the swollen skin around her pussy with teasing licks, not letting a single drop of the gift she gave him go to waste. He presses soft kisses on the insides of her thighs, moving to her stomach and tits, then finally rises to his full height before cupping her warm cheeks in his hands.

"You're so perfect, Princess," he whispers, brushing his lips against hers in a gentle, but claiming caress. "I'll never hurt you again. I promise." He wraps his arms around her, and I undo the collar, letting it drop to the floor beside them. We had our fun—but I'm going to need his help for this next part.

Backing away, I give them a moment together as I retrieve the bottle of lube from the nightstand, shed my boxer briefs, and sit at the edge of the bed. He looks over her shoulder at me, remorse blanketing his expression, but I don't need words to tell him how I feel about everything that went down tonight.

We're square. If she's happy, I'm happy.

He breathes a sigh of relief, planting another chaste kiss to the top of her head before leading her over to me. She watches with rapt attention as I squirt some of the clear liquid into my palm, coating my almost painfully hard erection before summoning her with a lift of my chin.

"Turn around and have a seat, Hellcat," I say with a smirk. She obeys, spinning so her back is to my front before lowering onto my length and enveloping me with her warm, wet heat. I groan at the feeling of her wrapped around me, taking several slow breaths to collect myself. When I'm sure I'm good, I hook my hands under her knees, pulling up so her feet are flat on the mattress, right outside my thighs. She's spread wide as Jacks drags the chair from the corner of the room and sits down, close enough to see, but far enough so she's out of his reach.

"I'm going to prep you slowly," I tell her. "If it hurts, or you just want to stop, use your safe word."

"Okay," she replies, squirming as I cover my pointer and middle fingers in lube. At first, I just use them to rub her clit, but when I feel her walls loosen enough to accept more, I push, adding a single digit along with my throbbing cock. It's a tight fit, but before long, I'm able to sink all the way in, giving her control to move freely as she slides up and down.

"Atta girl, baby," Jacks praises, his gaze glued to where she's taking me. He stands, reaching for the bottle and assisting by dripping more of the slippery liquid over us before settling back against the plush cushion. "There you go. Your body is amazing."

I thrust up gently, moving until her tight whimpers turn into satisfied moans. Taking it slow, I enter her with another finger, relieved when my name falls from her plump lips in a breathy song.

"Hawk. I'm so full. It's so, so good. I want more." She throws her head back as I pump in and out, shocked when she greedily accepts my ring finger alongside everything else that's stuffed inside her. She's stretching like a dream, and I can't wait to see her take us both at once.

"I knew this slutty hole could do it," I rasp, and I feel her tighten around me. I'll never get over how reactive Arden is to my degradation and Jackson's praise. She truly was made to be ours. She relaxes slightly as I work her open more, all while he ghosts his palm over his weeping cock in anticipation. And when I feel like I've done all I can do, I decide it's time to give it a shot. "Should we show Jacks how well you gape for us before we let him join? I bet he'd love to see it."

"Mhmm," she hums, barely even able to hold her head up as I scissor my fingers, reaching under her ass with my free hand and lifting her off my cock. Her pussy stays open wide, and his eyes glaze over with lust as he stares, making me chuckle.

"You gonna drool over it, or are we going to fuck it full of our cum?" I quip, scooting back onto the pillow with her in my lap. He doesn't say a word. He just crawls onto the mattress, waiting for more direction. I take a moment to think, because I've never done this before either, finally deciding on a plan of action. I want it to be pleasurable for Arden, so using my piercing to rub her clit while we fuck her is the best way to ensure that she's able to get off.

"Turn toward me, baby," I tell her, and she flips around, straddling my hips. I smooth more lube over my shaft, tossing the bottle to Jackson before helping her sink down slowly. Stars explode behind my eyes as I bury myself, and I take a few moments to enjoy the feeling because there's no way I'll be able to get this deep when he's in here next to me. She grinds against the barbell, moaning in pleasure as he appears behind her, trailing sloppy, open-mouth kisses across her neck and shoulder.

I run my hands up and down her creamy thighs, allowing her to take all the time she needs. "Whenever you're ready, lean onto my chest," I instruct. She grazes her swollen bundle of nerves over the warm metal a few more times before falling forward, her supple tits pressing against my pecs as she settles.

I peer over her shoulder, where Jacks is giving me his undivided attention. He looks nervous, so I do my best to speak softly, using the most reassuring tone I can muster. "Squirt more lube onto us, then on yourself. As much as you can, or this won't work." He nods his head, and I feel the cold liquid as it coats our skin, followed by the mattress dipping as he finds the right position. The last time we were both inside her at the same time, I was in back and had all the control. This time, it'll be up to him to do the work.

"Ready, Princess?" he asks, earning a slow, yet confident nod in response. I retreat several inches, so just the head of my cock is inside her as he presses against me, working himself in. She whimpers quietly but doesn't use her safe word, so we continue filling her up until there isn't a modicum of space for her to take any more.

"Jesus Christ," I grit through clenched teeth. "So fucking tight. Are you okay, Arden?"

"Yeah," she replies, the sound barely audible, even with her mouth right next to my ear. "Can you move a little?"

My gaze connects with Jackson's, and I nod, giving him the green light to start thrusting. He does, and we all moan in unison at the hot friction building between us. She's so warm and wet and perfect that I'm barely controlling the intense instinct to buck my hips, which would definitely push her beyond her limit. Pair that with the slide of his cock against mine, and I'm doing everything I can not to empty my load so deep, she'll taste me for days.

We fall into a rhythm as he fucks her, her clit rubbing along my pubic piercing and bringing her closer and closer to the edge with every pass. I've never felt more connected to anyone than I do with these two right now, and warmth travels through me, squeezing in my chest because I'm just so fucking complete. I know Arden and I would've made it if Jacks hadn't come back, but *fuck*, we'd have felt the hole he left behind. I'm grateful we're here, and that we'll never experience that kind of agonizing emptiness again.

"I'm gonna come," Arden says on a gasp, her warm

breath ricocheting off the skin of my neck. "Please. Please don't stop."

"I'm not stopping, baby," he says, drawing back before driving forward again. "Come on our cocks. Let us feel it." A few more short strokes and she's clamping down, so tight I almost pass out as she cries her release into the air. Within seconds, he follows her, throwing his head back and shooting hot ropes of cum into her spasming pussy. The sensation of them both climaxing at the same time makes my head spin, and like a rubber band, everything pulls whipcord tight before launching me into oblivion. An unbridled growl tumbles past my lips, and I fill her up, my body convulsing as currents of pleasure run through me like electricity. I give her every drop I have to offer, until the mixture of the three of us has nowhere else to go and she overflows as we ride out what's left of our orgasms. We're a mix of whimpers, moans, and heavy breaths, returning to awareness together after what was easily the most intense experience of my entire life. Usually, it's Arden who goes empty-headed when we fuck, but right now, I don't think we have a coherent thought between the three of us.

Jackson stops moving, lowering his head between her shoulder blades as he recovers. We focus on our girl, skating gentle kisses along her skin and reveling in the soft hums of contentment that vibrate against us. He slowly pulls back, making her wince, and I feel the mixture of our cum gush out as soon as he's gone. She obviously feels it too, because her eyes flutter open, her nose scrunching up as she shifts above me.

"Something wrong, beautiful?" I ask, chuckling. She pulls off my almost completely soft cock, freezing as it falls from her body.

"Holy shit," Jacks chokes on a laugh, staring at her pussy as it leaks all over. "That's one hell of a mess. But it's hot as fuck."

She groans. "Glad you think so. You guys are going to need to carry me to the shower after that—and probably hold me up, because I don't think I can walk right now."

"We've got you," I say, cradling her cheeks in my palms and pressing my lips to hers. "You did so good. How do you feel?"

She takes a deep, soothing inhale, slowly releasing as she contemplates her answer. "A little sore, but also indescribably happy. I love you both so much."

Jackson curls over her back, peppering playful kisses all over her face while she giggles and squirms in an attempt to get away. "We love you too, Princess. Thank you for being ours."

And as always, it's like he knew what I was thinking —because I couldn't have said it any better myself.

GINA:

I just got off the highway. I'll be there in about ten.

ME:

OK. Dahlia just went into the owner's office. I'm nervous. What is this about?

GINA:

There's nothing to be nervous about. I promise. Just trust me.

I SHOVE my phone into my purse, looking around the sterile waiting room as my leg bounces about a hundred miles per hour. When Gina called yesterday in a tizzy, telling me she was catching the first flight to Florida so we could meet with the Flare's owner, I had a million questions. She was pretty vague, saying she was still trying to fill in some of the blanks, and promised to tell me everything she knew when she arrived. Unfortunately, her plane was delayed, so it looks like I'll be finding out what's so important at the same time everyone else does.

On top of the anticipation of what's about to happen, I'm also nervous to see her for the first time since she and my dad visited. They left abruptly, which I don't really blame them for, since they were pretty thrown off when they learned about Jackson, Hawk, and me. Other than business and surface-level conversation, we haven't talked much. My dad checks in every couple of days via text, but I honestly think he's waiting for me to break the ice.

It's been a few days since Jacks came home, and I know we'll need to sit down with our parents and tell them we're together for good—consequences be damned—but I'm certainly not looking forward to it. If Gina's reaction before was anything to go off of, we have our work cut out for us in making them understand that we're not breaking up. We make each other happy, and we aren't willing to give up on what we have.

"Sorry I'm late," she says, busting through the door. Her hair is wild and windblown, she's wearing yoga pants and a t-shirt that she clearly tried to dress up with a formfitting black blazer, and she looks like she just did the most hardcore cardio workout. "Did they come out yet?"

I shake my head. "No. Dahlia went in with the owner and general manager about twenty minutes ago, but other than that, nobody's been here. Can you tell me what's going on?"

She plops down in the chair next to me, setting her tote bag on the floor at our feet before leaning close, making sure that if anyone comes into the room, they won't be able to eavesdrop. "When you told me what was going on with your coach, it really bugged me. You're an exceptional decision-maker, especially under pressure, so the fact that she wasn't trusting you to be in control raised some red flags. I figured I'd just keep an eye on it, but when I saw how badly it was affecting your stats, I couldn't stand by and let her continue to drive your career into the ground. So, I did some digging and was able to get ahold of your old college coach. He told m—"

She's cut off when the door opens, and the Flare's general manager, Justin Ramos, pokes his head out. "Ladies, we're ready for you." I swallow the thick lump in my throat, standing and smoothing the wrinkles from my dress before following her into the office. It's bright, the warm Florida sun filtering through the wall of windows. The team's owner, Marcus Chambers, sits behind a luxurious mahogany desk, a stern look on his face as he greets us.

"Miss and Mrs. Levine," he says with a nod, motioning to take the two empty seats across from him. I've only met him twice, but both times, he terrified me with his reserved, surly demeanor. You think I'd be used to it by now, considering one of my boyfriends is very similar, but it still makes me want to vomit every time I see him around the facility.

I turn toward my chair, catching Dahlia out of the corner of my eye. Her usual hardened expression is nowhere to be found, and it's clear that she isn't having the best day so far. She looks like they've already put her through the wringer—I'd have given anything to have been a fly on the wall for whatever went down before we were called in.

"Thank you for reaching out to us about your concerns," Justin says to Gina. "Seeing as how the Flare hasn't gotten off to a great start, we certainly want to know if something is going on that might affect the team. We were expecting better than a two-and-six record a month into the season, and on paper, we believe our players are capable of much more than that. So, hearing that there may be some discrepancies with our staff is something we want to address before it gets worse."

Gina sits up straight, confidence radiating from her petite body as she addresses the group. "As Arden's agent, it's my job to make sure the organization is setting her up for success. When I found out that Ms. Owens was insisting on calling the plays from the sideline, it immediately raised some red flags. My client has played her position for years and has always shown how capable she is of making sound decisions. She works hard to learn her teammates' likes and dislikes, and prior to their first match, had succeeded in creating an amazing dynamic with them on the court. So, I knew there had to be another reason for the mistrust, and excuse my frankness"—she looks over at Dahlia—"blatant sabotage."

"That's ridiculous," she retorts with a scoff. But I don't miss the way her wide gaze darts to me before focusing back on Gina.

Marcus sits forward, clasping his hands together on the desk in front of him. "That's a pretty serious accusation, Mrs. Levine. Why would Coach Owens want her own team to fail?"

"Well," she continues, "at first, I couldn't figure that out either. But when I talked to Buddy Taylor, who coached both women at Penn State, it all started to come together.

"When Arden was a freshman, she was in line to become Dahlia's successor. She worked hard every day, just as she has with the Flare, hoping to become the starter her sophomore year. But Coach Taylor started to notice how Dahlia's attitude changed, and how whenever Arden wanted to put in extra work with her, she refused. So, he decided to change things up. It was a risk, but he planned on benching his senior and letting Arden start a few games. When he called Dahlia into his office to tell her, she threw a tantrum. He told her it was just until she proved that she could be a good leader, but instead of graciously accepting his decision, she quit on the spot. He never told his players what happened because he didn't want it to cause a distraction, but he definitely didn't hold back when pro teams were calling for recommendations. I believe Coach Owens has been using her own personal vendetta against Arden to ruin her career because she's upset that hers ended the day she was benched. The Flare's inaugural season record is just collateral damage."

Both men turn to Dahlia as she sits with guilt written all over her beet-red face. She shifts uncomfortably, refusing to make eye contact with any of us as my jaw practically hits the floor. Was she really ready to let our whole team suffer because she didn't want one player to win? And how could she hate me so much when all I did was try to learn from her? I wasn't even aware of her reason for quitting until just now, nor did I know about Coach Taylor's plan to start me over her, so why is she faulting me for any of it?

"Is that true?" Justin asks, eyes boring into her as her skin goes paper white. She fidgets with the ring on her finger for several moments, her attention bouncing around the room nervously before she finally speaks.

"She's not good enough to be here," she replies quietly, her words cutting like a knife to my heart as she fixes her gaze on me. "I tried to tell Taylor back then, and you both at the draft, but nobody wanted to hear me. She skated her way through college on the back of the team that *I built*, then got drafted to a pro team with some of the best hitters in the league—ones who would've made her look far better than she actually is if I hadn't stepped in. The Flare deserves better than some below-average setter who's been handed everything she has on a silver platter. They deserve greatness."

Marcus' expression goes tight, his chin jutting up as he regards her. "Ms. Owens," he says firmly, "with all due respect, that was never your decision to make. We hired you to coach this team, not to run it into the ground because you couldn't handle losing your spot to a better player nearly a decade ago. I've spoken to several of my athletes recently, all of which had nothing but kind words to say about Miss Levine as a teammate and captain. I'm appalled by your behavior, and I won't stand for it. Your past may have slipped by your previous employers, but that ends here. Effective immediately, you're relieved from your duties with the Flare. Assistant Coach Slater will act as interim head coach until we can find someone who embodies this organization's morals and values. Now, please leave the premises before I have you removed."

She freezes for several moments, her nostrils flaring with every sharp inhale until she stands abruptly and points an accusing finger between the two men. "You'll be sorry," she spits. "You've all been fooled, and I can't wait to watch you fail without me."

Justin smirks, giving her a patronizing nod. "Enjoy doing it from your couch."

And with that, she turns, glaring at me and Gina as she exits the room. I'm still reeling from what just went down when Marcus turns my way, softening his expression. "Arden, please don't let any of what that wretched woman said get into your head. We were very deliberate with our draft picks, and you weren't chosen on a whim. We saw your exceptional talent and leadership abilities—and we're sorry you had to endure such treatment during your first season here. Going forward, please come to us if you need anything."

"Thank you, sir. I won't let you down," I reply, earning an affirming nod before he turns to Gina.

"Thank you again for bringing this to our attention. I'm sure you've got your hands full with your current job, but if you'd ever like to give coaching a shot, let me know. I've seen your highlight reels, and I think our ladies could learn a lot from you." My eyes go wide, and a bright smile stretches across my face as I take in her shocked expression. She was an amazing player in college. Had she not been injured, I know she would've been a shoo-in for our Olympic team. Not everyone has the raw talent Gina does, and I have no doubt she'd be a phenomenal coach.

She clears her throat, her cheeks turning pink with embarrassment. "Thank you, Mr. Chambers. Good luck with the remainder of your season."

That wasn't necessarily a no, was it?

We say our goodbyes before heading out of the building, quietly walking side-by-side through the parking lot. I have a million things to say, but for some reason, only one sits at the tip of my tongue as we stop at the hood of my car.

"About me and Jacks," I say, looking down at my feet nervously. "I just wanted t—"

"I knew it would come, eventually," she cuts me off. My eyes shoot up, brows practically disappearing into my hairline as she continues. "You two were meant for each other. That was clear to me the first time I saw you together. I even mentioned it to your father before we started dating, but we couldn't stop ourselves from falling any more than you and Jackson could. My reaction to it was all wrong, and I should've been more of a mother and less of an agent in that moment. I'm really sorry about that, Arden. You both deserved better from me. And as far as your relationship—it'll take a little getting used to, especially with Hawk in the mix, but we'll be okay. As long as you're ready for the possible backlash when the public adds their two cents—which they will—I'll be there to fight for you every step of the way."

My eyes shine with emotion, and I reach out, pulling her into a tight embrace. Her comforting arms wrap around me, warming me from the inside out just like they always do as I inhale her signature perfume. Going so long without having her to confide in about everything has been extremely hard, and it made me realize how big of an impact she's had on my life—both on the court and off. She's always treated me as her own, and I'm beyond grateful for her love and support as we navigate what I'm sure will be a trying time for us all.

I pull back, batting at the tears that run down my cheeks. "Now we just have to get Dad on board," I joke.

She huffs a laugh. "He came with me. He got a ride to your place, where I'm sure he's having quite the talk with both of your boys as we speak."

Oh, shit.

JACKSON

I clear my throat, uncomfortable silence hanging thick in the air as Slade stares, looking like he might strangle us with his bare hands at any moment. I've known this man for most of my life and have seen him in many situations, but I've never been more terrified of him than I am right now as Hawk and I wait for him to speak.

"So," he begins, "I understand you're both in a relationship with my daughter."

Fucking awkward.

"Yes, sir," Hawk pipes up, doing his best to sound confident when I know damn well that he's shitting his pants too. "We love her very much."

Slade narrows his eyes, looking between us. It's giving off *I'm plotting your murder* vibes, and I've never wanted a conversation to be over as badly as I do this one right now. But stepdad or not, he's the father of the woman I love, so I'll be respectful and let him say his piece. "I have some questions before I give you my blessing. First of all, are you planning on marrying her? Having babies? How will all of that work?"

Fuck. As much as I know Arden is our endgame, we haven't really discussed all of that in depth. It's a complicated situation, and I have no idea how it'll look for us. I open my mouth to tell him that, but Hawk interrupts with an answer.

"As far as marriage goes, it'll be completely up to her. If she wants to marry one of us, that's fine. If she wants to do a commitment ceremony where we all say our vows, but there's no paperwork, we'll be good with that. She's the boss. And we'll leave the babies up to fate. Whether Jackson or I end up being the biological father won't matter, because we'll always be a family, and we have plenty of love to give."

I turn my head, several emotions swirling around in my chest as I look at him. It's hard to believe this is the same guy who pushed everyone away, falling into darkness all alone night after night, until I came along and forced my way into his life. He's worked so hard on himself, and I'm filled with pride as I watch him talk about the future like it's the most natural thing ever.

"Okay," Slade says, relaxing back into the plush couch cushions and pulling his foot up onto his knee. "And what happens when the public comes after the three of you for being together? You boys will get off easy, but I have a feeling they won't extend the same kindness to Arden for dating two of Daytona's most popular athletes at the same time. Are you willing to do whatever it takes to shield her from that?"

I swallow, glancing at Hawk to tell him I've got this one. As much as this particular issue scared me—and was a factor in my decision to leave—the answer to his question is crystal clear. "You're right," I begin, my expression softening as I speak. "People will talk. They're going to call her names and question her character. But the thing I realized over the weeks we were apart is that the love we have for each other is stronger than anything some shitty keyboard warrior can throw at us. Hawk and I are prepared to show the world how we feel about Arden, and that having her heart makes us both better men. We'll stand by her side, no matter what, and she'll fall asleep every night knowing that she's exactly where she belongs."

Seemingly satisfied with my words, he nods his head, a ghost of a grin tugging at one corner of his mouth. "Alright, fine," he relents. "But if either of you hurt her, you'll be dealing with me."

"Dad," Arden says, rolling her eyes in annoyance as she enters the room. "Leave them alone."

His face lights up with pure happiness as he stands, welcoming his daughter with open arms. She melts into the embrace, smiling softly against his chest. I've always loved their bond, and one day, I hope I'm half the selfless father he is. "I'm just giving them the rundown, honey," he replies. "Gotta make sure they're taking care of my baby girl."

"They're perfect gentlemen." She winks in our direction, almost making me bark out a laugh because we're far from gentlemen when it comes to her. Just last night, Hawk told her what a pathetic slut she was while I overstimulated her with my tongue for hours. That'll be our little secret, though.

We spend the rest of the evening hanging out with my mom and Slade, eating dinner and talking about what happened at the Flare facility earlier. I knew Dahlia targeting Arden had to be personal on some level, but I certainly wasn't expecting it to go back so many years. Either way, I'm glad they took care of the situation so the world can continue to watch my girl shine.

We head to bed early since she has a match

tomorrow and needs a solid night of sleep. It's a little weird going into Hawk's room instead of my own as our parents head toward the other end of the hall, but I'm relieved that we no longer have to hide from them. Do I plan on fucking her into oblivion while they're under the same roof as us? No. But it feels good to know I can hold her while we sleep and not be worried about getting caught. Now that we have their approval, I have a plan to show the rest of the world just how happy Arden makes us, and how we're never letting her go.

FORTY-EIGHT
HAWK

"DID I mention I *hate* this idea?" I say to Jacks as we enter the arena. We're here to watch Arden play, and although we've been here before, I have a feeling today's appearance will draw a lot more attention. And while I'm proud of my girl and the life we're building, I'd much rather do it without a million cameras pointed at us all the time.

"Once or twice," he replies, a self-assured smile plastered across his face as we make our way toward our seats. We're right up front, so hopefully our message will be heard loud and clear, so we can move forward out in the open.

Slade slaps a hand against my shoulder. "Girls go nuts for grand declarations of love. That's how I got this one." He tosses a thumb over his shoulder to where Gina walks beside him, earning an eye roll.

"I'd hardly call you sending jealousy flowers to my place of employment a grand love declaration," she deadpans.

His jaw drops as if he's offended. "Those were not *jealousy flowers*."

She rolls her eyes again. This time, they go so far back, I'm afraid they might actually get stuck before she looks toward us. "My boss' name was Frankie, and I was spending a lot of late nights at the office. He could've just shown up to pee on my leg and given the same message."

He whips his head her way, brows pulled tight as his face heats with embarrassment. "How was I supposed to know Frankie was a sixty-five-year-old woman? I just wanted to make sure any potential suitors knew you were taken." I chuckle quietly at their exchange as we shuffle down the first row, Jackson lifting his stupid sign above his head so it doesn't get bent. He went off the rails with his hair-brained scheme for today, but I have no doubt Arden will love it, so I couldn't say no. If I end up looking like an idiot in order to make her smile, so be it.

The arena goes dark, loud music playing through the speakers as multicolored spotlights and smoke dance across the floor. "And now," the announcer says as the whole place fills with cheers and whistles, "your Florida Flare!" The team explodes from the tunnel, led by the most beautiful girl I've ever seen. I don't think it'll ever get old watching her command the court, and I couldn't be prouder of her strength and resilience. Her first season has already been a tough one, but I just know the rest of her career will be legendary. I'm one lucky motherfucker for being able to call her mine.

They begin warmups, jumping at the net with their

arms up before rotating around the court and settling into their positions. Arden takes her spot right in the middle, clapping and hyping up her teammates as the coaching staff tosses balls out to be passed. As soon as they come her way, she sets them up, every one perfectly placed for her hitters.

We watch them go through drills, and when they're done, Jackson sends a knowing grin my way. "It's time," he sing-songs, and I can't help but huff an annoyed breath before throwing caution to the wind and doing exactly what we practiced—or what *he* practiced in front of me twenty times this morning while I pretended to ignore him. He sets the sign at his feet and we both stand, pulling our hoodies over our heads to reveal matching Flare jerseys. Arden's last name and number are stretched across our backs as fans around us start to zone in on the two pro baseball players in the stands. But it's not until he lifts the sign that our message is sent—loud and clear—to the hundreds of thousands of people watching here and in their homes. Because in big, bold letters above us are the words *We love #10* with two arrows pointing down. The crowd cheers, several phones being lifted to record as the player next to our girl taps her shoulder and motions for her to turn around. As soon as she does, her cheeks pinken, and a sheepish smile blooms across her beautiful face. She leans over, saying something to her coach and getting a quick nod in response before jogging our way.

"Nice sign," she says, her big brown eyes bouncing between us in adoration.

"I made it," Jackson offers. "He didn't help." *Such a fucking brown-noser.* I inhale a soothing breath so I don't throat punch him in front of all these people, bending over the railing so she can hear me.

"Get out there and kill it, Hellcat. Head in the game —visualize the win."

She lifts her chin, confidence radiating from her expression as she pushes to her tiptoes and puckers her lips. I smirk, not expecting things to go in this direction, but *fuck it.* I'm certainly not turning down the chance to kiss this woman, so I lean down further, pressing my mouth to hers. It's quick, with a definite PG rating for any younger viewers, but speaks volumes—especially when she turns her head, beckoning the same treatment from Jackson. He immediately obliges, kissing her as though it's the most natural thing in the world...*because it is.*

"Go get 'em, Princess," he says, and she nods, turning and running back over to join her team as they prepare to take the court. Playful whistles and cheers erupt from the bench, and I even notice some of the coaching staff clapping as she cradles her bright pink cheeks in her hands. I hear a few whispers behind us, likely in reaction to the fact that we just publicly proclaimed our love for the same girl, but I don't give a fuck. Whatever happens from here on out—we face it together. And nothing will tear us apart.

I watch in awe as Arden leads her team like a true captain, moving together like a well-oiled machine as they rack up point after point against their opponents. Everything about her game is on today, from the serving to the setting—to even getting a few great solo blocks. And when they win the match in three games, we celebrate, cheering as loudly as we can like the devoted boyfriends we are.

Our journey wasn't easy, and I'm sure we'll be faced with all kinds of adversity as we move forward, but one thing will always remain true. Jackson and Arden are my people—two perfect souls I managed to find in this great big world, and whose love and friendship helped me become the best version of myself—a man they can be proud of, who will stand strong beside them through everything life throws our way.

This is us, scars and all, showing the world how true love can always conquer the darkness.

EPILOGUE

ARDEN - 5 YEARS LATER

"COME FOR ME, PRINCESS," Jackson whispers as he eases in and out of me from behind, hitting my G-spot perfectly with the head of his thick cock. "They're gonna be here any second. You need to hurry."

"Right there," I breathe as heat begins to coil tightly in my core. "Fuck…don't stop. Please." He doesn't let up, reaching around and using the pad of his middle finger to flick my clit so expertly, every muscle in my body begins to wind tight, craving that moment of release. And when he picks up speed, fucking me at the perfect pace, I'm swept away, losing myself to the rush of ecstasy as it crashes into me. I cry out, slapping my hand over my mouth in a seemingly unsuccessful attempt to muffle the sound—because I'm pulled back to reality entirely too soon as a heavy fist bangs against the pantry door.

"Are you two fucking *kidding me*?" Hawk whisper-yells through the thick wood. "You can't go five seconds on our daughter's first birthday without acting like horny teenagers? The Valentines are here."

My eyes go wide as Jackson chuckles, finding his release and emptying inside me with a quiet groan. He curls his chest over my back, burying his nose into my hair until we've both caught our breath. Pulling out, he covers my center with the panties he'd pushed aside, and I stand from where I'm bent over the counter before shooting him a dirty look. "It's not funny. You lured me in here by asking for help carrying out the snacks, and now there's a strong possibility Riggs and Monroe just heard me have an orgasm."

He spins me around, and I don't miss the cocky grin that tugs at his mouth as he pulls me in for a passionate kiss. I immediately melt as his tongue slides against mine in a soft, deliberate caress. Sparks explode around us, and even though I just came, my body is already begging for more of him—not that it ever stops.

He breaks the connection, his eyes sparkling with adoration as he looks down at me. "It's going to be a long day with everyone here, and I needed my fix before it got crazy. I wouldn't have had to resort to lying and cheating if you'd just slow down for a second. You work too hard, baby."

I sigh, smiling softly. "I just want Wyatt's first birthday to be perfect."

He takes my face in his hands, pressing his lips to mine once more. "It will be. And even if it isn't, you're still the best mom in the world." I snuggle into him, grateful that he and Hawk always know how to keep me calm when my mind and body are going a million miles a minute. "Now let's go before he loses his shit."

I giggle as we open the door, immediately feeling judged by the way both Hawk and our daughter stare wordlessly as we exit the dark room. My expression goes serious, and I try to hide my amusement at their matching party hats. "Sorry," I say, reaching out and taking her from his arms. Her toothy grin makes my heart do flips in my chest as a thick line of drool runs down her chubby little face.

"Yeah, right," he replies playfully. "I bet."

"You started this," Jacks says to his best friend. "I'll fuck our wife in there every chance I get, and you'll only have yourself to blame."

"Language!" I yell, attempting to shield Wyatt's ears, but I can't deny the butterflies I get every time one of them calls me that.

Although we aren't legally married, we said our vows to one another in an intimate ceremony on the beach two years ago. It was everything I'd always dreamed of for my wedding, with more love and support than we could've hoped for—even from the public.

When we first announced our relationship dynamic, I expected the worst. And while we got our fair share of hateful comments from online trolls, it wasn't nearly as bad as we had anticipated. After discussions with the Fury and the Flare, where we were assured that both teams would stand behind us, we were able to take on the world. And that's how it's been ever since.

"Give me my baby," Monroe says, waddling into the

kitchen with her giant bump leading the way. I swear, she's been pregnant forever—but she and Riggs have two beautiful sons and one on the way, so I bet she'd tell you it was worth every single minute. I drop a quick kiss to Wyatt's cheek, handing her over to her crazy aunt and leaving them to greet our other guests, but I'm stopped as a set of thick, muscular arms wraps around my waist.

"Hey there, Hellcat," Hawk drawls, his mouth hovering next to my ear and sending warmth throughout my entire body. "After we're done here, I'm taking you on a date—just us. Then, I'm going to bring you home, tape you up, and fuck you until you beg me to stop. Sound good?"

"So good," I whisper, clenching my thighs together to calm the throb between them. Spinning in his arms, I look at him like a fool in love as he dips down and brushes his lips over mine in a sweet, but claiming kiss. It's feather-light, yet somehow it still sucks all the air from my lungs just like it always does. He never fails to make me see stars, even after five years together—and as much as I'd love to disappear with him right now, I know I can't. We have a party to host.

He shoots me a devious wink, patting me on the ass just as my dad and Gina approach. "There you are!" she says as I break away from Hawk and lean in for a hug, shuffling aside and stepping into my dad's arms as he pulls me into his chest. They recently moved to Daytona, and it's been nice having them close. Although I wish I could say she took Marcus up on his offer to coach, it didn't happen. I'm grateful she's still my agent, but the real pleasure has been watching her bond with our daughter as the most doting Mimi I've ever seen. We don't know which one of the guys is Wyatt's biological father—nor do we care—but it doesn't matter because our family and friends would love her the same either way. "Is there anything I can help with?"

I quickly scan the room, making sure nothing is left undone. "I don't think so," I reply. "The food is all set up in the kitchen, Lark and Ace are picking up the balloons, and the rest of the guests are on their way. Why don't you two sit down and relax?" Ushering them to the couch, I'm startled by a loud ruckus as a very tan, wide body pushes through the door.

"Party's here! Where's my niece?" Hayden yells through cupped hands, looking like he just stepped out of an ad for whatever board shorts fuckboys are wearing these days. He's also new to the Daytona Beach lifestyle after moving here last year, and he's been soaking up everything the city has to offer. I know Two-for-One Drink Night hates to see him coming, that's for sure.

It wasn't two weeks after his eighteenth birthday that Hawk got a message on social media from his middle brother. Apparently, his relationship with their father had become strained as he got older, and he began to see the manipulation for what it was rather than believing his brother would ever willingly give him up. Henry is still coming around, but that's okay. I have faith that my husband will eventually get back all the things he lost.

"In the kitchen," I say with a laugh. "Good luck prying her out of Monroe's arms."

He clicks his tongue, strutting past me and heading toward the kitchen. "Roe loves me. I'm just waiting for her to leave that zero and get with the hero." His cocky smile is annoyingly adorable as Riggs pipes up from where he and Tanner are talking on the couch.

"You couldn't handle her, Hayden. And you *definitely* couldn't afford her." I laugh, watching as the most important people in our lives gather to celebrate our little girl, my heart overflowing with love for each and every one of them.

If you'd have told me when I moved here to play for the Flare that I'd end up with two adoring husbands, a beautiful baby, two PVF championships—and hopefully more to come—along with so many amazing memories, I wouldn't have believed you. It sounds crazy on every level—but here we are. And now that it's all mine, I wouldn't change a single bit of it for the world.

ACKNOWLEDGMENTS

My husband - You never fail to support me in the most monumental ways, and I'm beyond grateful to have such an amazing man in my corner. Life would suck without you. I love you infinity.

My kids - You are my pride and joy, and I couldn't be more blessed to call you mine. I love you both to the moon and back.

My mom - If you read this, no you didn't. (Also, I love you.)

Breanne - I'll never get over the fact that we're out here creating entire worlds together. I couldn't do any of this without you, personally or professionally, and I'm so glad I don't have to. Your talent is unmatched, and I'm so thankful you use it to help me make my books the best they can be.

Hannah Gray - My bestie...my sounding board...my partner in crime. Your love and encouragement keep me going and remind me that I belong here. I'll never be able to thank you enough for holding my hand through all the scary stuff this life throws our way.

Lexi James - From the wild, unfiltered voice messages to talking me through plot issues on a weekly basis, I'm beyond grateful to have you on this journey with me. I can't wait to see how you continue to shine!

Jaime Rayyan - Nobody knows how to handle me like you do, and I don't think I have the words to tell you how much that means to me. I'm so thankful the book world brought us together, and that seven books later, we're still going strong. #nootherbitches

Clair Truitt - Your encouragement and support were monumental in the making of this book. The hours you put into reading and helping me perfect everything are beyond appreciated, and I can't wait to do it all over again with the next one!!

Maggie Marrero - You make my life easier in ways I can't even begin to explain. I'm truly blessed to have you as a PA...but even more so as a friend. You always know how to lift me up and dust me off when doubt settles in. There will never be enough thank-yous. I love you.

Chelsey Bodkin - Where do I start? You see me at my best and my worst, and you're always ready with the exact words I need to get me through it all. I'm so grateful to have you as a social media guru, and most importantly, as a friend.

Kristina Andrews - I swear you have a direct line to my brain, always knowing what I need without me even saying a word. Thank you for always being there when I need you,and for being a listening ear when life gets crazy.

Lorelei and Maggie Caraballo - I can't thank you enough for taking the time out of your busy schedules to be sensitivity readers for this one. Having your love and support on this journey makes me feel like the luckiest girl in the world.

Ashley Boyle - Your feedback is so valuable to me, and I'm grateful to have you with me on this crazy ride. I hope I made you proud.

Autumn and the Wordsmith Publicity team - Thank you for doing all the heavy lifting for these releases. I'm so thankful to be part of such an amazing group of authors and professionals.

My content team - You did it again!! You kept me motivated and made me feel more love than I ever thought possible through what was, arguably, my biggest challenge as a writer so far. I'm in awe of the way you selflessly promote my books, and I'll never be able to express my gratitude for everything you do.

My readers - Your love and support keep me going on my darkest days. You continue to make it possible for me to live my dream of creating these stories, and I'm forever grateful for your unwavering support.

ABOUT THE AUTHOR

C.L. Rose is a wife and mother of two. She lives in Northeast Ohio with her husband, son, and daughter. When she isn't writing, you can find her reading in front of a space heater, wrapped in a thick blanket, probably complaining that she's cold.

authorclrose.com

MORE FROM C.L. ROSE

Boston Blizzard Series

Hot Route
The Stunt: A Boston Blizzard Novella
Run Game
QB Keeper
The Throwback: A Boston Blizzard Novella

Daytona Fury Series

Wild Pitch
Scoring Position
Double Play

Rock City Renegades Series

Mr. Irrelevant - Coming Summer 2025

Printed in Great Britain
by Amazon

61809748R00241